G.S. DENNING

WARLOCK HOLMES

The Hell-hound of the Baskervilles

TITAN BOOKS

Warlock Holmes: The Hell-hound of the Baskervilles
Print edition ISBN: 9781783299737
E-book edition ISBN: 9781783299744

Published by Titan Books
A division of Titan Publishing Group Ltd
144 Southwark Street, London SE1 0UP

First edition: May 2017
10 9 8 7 6 5 4 3 2 1

Names, places and incidents are either products of the author's imagination or used fictitiously. Any resemblance to actual persons, living or dead (except for satirical purposes), is entirely coincidental.

A CIP catalogue record for this title is available from the British Library.

Printed in the USA.

WARLOCK HOLMES

The Hell-hound of the Baskervilles

To Baba Yaga, my own feeble but beloved hound.

To my in-laws, George and Stephanie, whose ridiculously low estimation of what they should charge me in rent financed this book.

To the readers and fans who supported book 1. Thank you. I'll keep churning out adventures if you keep reading 'em.

CONTENTS

The Adventure of the Blackened Beryls 9

Silver Blaze: Murder Horse 55

The Reigateway to Another World 91

The Adventure of the Solitary Tricyclist 125

The Hell-hound of the Baskervilles 177

THE ADVENTURE OF THE BLACKENED BERYLS

"MADAM, SURRENDER YOUR POSIES!"

I raised my voice and brandished my cane as I said it, as if to proclaim, "I am John Watson! A doctor! A man of worth and station! Would you dare to refuse me my desire? *Would you?*"

My flower-girl opponent was unimpressed. She raised an eyebrow, stuck out a hip and laughed. "I'll surrender more than that, guv'na."

"No. I don't want more than that. I thought I made it especially clear. I want your flowers."

"Yeah... me *flowers*..."

"No! Well... yes... but from your tone I can tell that we are still discussing two very different transactions. Honestly, I want the actual flowers. Those blooms. Those posies. Those colorful things you are holding in your left hand that grew on the tops of plants. That is what I want. How can I be more clear?"

"What, these?" she asked, pointing at the battered bouquet.

"Yes! Thank God, yes."

"But… you just gave me two shillings."

"I know."

"Nobody pays two shillings for a handful of dead posies."

"I did! Or anyway, I am certainly trying to."

"No. Didn't you realize what we was talking about?" she asked, pointing at her lap.

"I never was! This conversation has always regarded actual, real, in no way double-entendre-fied flowers! Now hand them over, if you please."

"No!"

"Why the hell not?" I howled. A few heads turned. I drew forth my handkerchief, wiped some of the frustration sweat from my brow and tried again. "I apologize for my language, madam. But… why not?"

"Constables will run me off, if they sees me with no flowers! How can I be a flower girl if I ain't holdin' flowers?"

"How can you be a flower girl if you *refuse to sell flowers?*"

For an instant, it looked as if I were to have a particularly saucy answer to that, but her eye caught a flash of blue and she hissed, "Aww, bollocks! It's the coppers."

By the time the constable had reached us, every trace of annoyance was gone from her tone, replaced by sappy-sweet coquettishness. She gave a clumsy curtsey and cooed, "Ooh… Hallo, Tony."

"Wot's all this, then?" Constable Tony wanted to know.

"Constable, I am trying to purchase flowers from this young lady, here."

"Gaw! And you just up and admit it, to an officer of the law? I shall have to ask both of you to accompany me to the station, forthwith!"

"No. Please. I am not propositioning any indecent services. I wish to purchase those flowers, right there. How could that be illegal?"

A look of consternation crossed Constable Tony's face and he turned to ask my flower girl, "Wot's he talking about, Molly?"

"I dunno," she shrugged. "He says he wants the actual flowers."

"What, those?"

"Yes!" I cried.

"But Molly's a prostitute, don't you see?"

"Yes! But I don't care! Those! Those flowers! That is what I want! That is what I paid for! Give them to me!"

Constable Tony recoiled from me. He scanned me from the top of my head to the tips of my shoes and back again, searching for any clue that would allow him to understand my peculiar fancies. Finally he grunted, "Well, you're a right sick one, ain't ya?"

Thank heaven for small mercies: there was a florist on the way home from the police station. I think it must have taken me almost an hour to make my case that trying to buy flowers from a flower girl was not yet a crime. At last, the sergeant on duty was forced to admit that I had broken no written law and that he was therefore compelled to release me, but that he personally found my lifestyle disgusting and that I really ought to look to my eternal soul.

By the time I reached the florist, my hands were shaking such that I could hardly count out my coins. Despite my recent return to poverty, I bought as many flowers as I could carry. Funny, less than half a year before, I had been watching my funds dwindle and feared I would be unable to purchase food to sustain me. Now, though procuring edibles would soon become problematic, my chiefest worry was obtaining flowers.

What a horrible risk it was turning out to be. I'd given the police a false name and escaped before it was put to paper, but… simply trying to get flowers from a flower girl had brought my affairs before the law. If they'd had reason to examine my doings—or worse, my home—I'd have still been in custody, bound for the gallows.

I put my head down and headed back to 221B Baker Street. I was just mounting the stairs to my rooms, when a tiny, pink-clad whippet of a woman lunged forth and blocked my path.

"Aaugh! Mrs. Hudson!"

"Where is Holmes?"

"I've told you: he's vacationing in the south of France."

"Why's he gone so long? He's late with me rent."

"He has assured me that the rent is on its way. Patience, Mrs. Hudson."

I began pushing my armload of flowers up against her. If only I could drive her back with them, I could slip past her, up to my door.

"Yes, but where is Holmes, eh?" she protested, working her way around my floral shield, maneuvering to stay between myself and my flat.

"We've just been over that, Mrs. Hudson."

"Well… What's the idea with all these flowers, then? How many you got up there anyways? You been bringin' armloads of 'em home for weeks. Me whole house stinks like rotting delphiniums!"

"Yes, so sorry, Mrs. Hudson. I am engaged in a botany experiment. Very important. Detective work, you know. Lives may hinge on its outcome. Though they may seem humble, these flowers are for science. Science!"

She stared up at me. Her hate was unguarded and unbounded.

"Er… except these…" I mumbled, selecting a little yellow nosegay, "these are for you."

Her gaze wavered for just an instant, before she slapped the proffered pansies from my grasp. They careened to the floor and exploded into a sad little could of petals, stems and misplaced expectations.

"Yes… Well… Good day, Mrs. Hudson."

With a final lunge, I flew clear of her and through the safety of my own door, which I flung shut against her.

"I want me rent!" cried her muffled voice from without.

"Yes. I know. Holmes though, don't you see? South of France, and all that."

I stood there, gasping for breath with my ear against the door. I tried to control my breathing, listening for Mrs. Hudson's step upon the stairs. At last, she shuffled off. I pressed my face amongst my hard-won flora and… wept? I could hardly tell. I was certainly shaking. Just as certainly despairing. I was lost once again. In the longer view, I had no idea what to do with my life, or even how to sustain it. At least, in the short view, I knew exactly what I must do.

I went into the smaller bedroom and began packing flowers around the rotting corpse of Warlock Holmes.

I was wakened by a long, rattling gasp.

"Stop it," I said.

I nearly slid from my book pile. It was a sort of throne I had built myself in Holmes's room as I realized just how much time I was spending in there. I had a few blankets on it and a handy side-table constructed of ancient tomes of unspeakable evil, upon which I often balanced a cup of tea.

I looked about, blearily. I could not tell the hour, but it must have been deep within the night. I could see out through Holmes's door to the window in my own room. Outside, London was all but silent. The promise of dawn was some hours off, but by the sputtering light of the gas lamps, I could see an unseasonably late snow was falling. The lamp below my window cast ghostly shadows upon my ceiling as the flakes fell past.

I knew what was coming next. I did not relish it, but I leaned in to wait nonetheless. What if it didn't come, you see? If it did not come then I was free. My guilt would be by no means assuaged and my future still uncertain, but I would be relieved of the terrible burden Holmes had become. I got my stethoscope and placed it to his chest.

"Lub."

And then, some twelve or fifteen seconds later, "Dub."

The breath he had drawn fell back out, escaping betwixt his dried and shrunken lips.

"Stop it, I say! I have told you this before, Holmes: the dead do not breathe! Nor are they possessed of beating hearts! You're doing it all *wrong*!"

Holmes had no rebuttal.

"I do not mean to be a complaining sort of fellow and I do not mean to harp upon your faults, but… *can't you do anything right?* Even expire? Can't you do that?"

Holmes remained pensively quiet, as had become his habit—one he'd formed shortly after I poisoned him, kicked fire in his face and shot him twice through the chest. Which had been partly his fault, if I'm honest. I mean, he'd been possessed by the spirit of Professor James Moriarty and had just claimed ownership of me. What was I supposed to have done?

"Look here, Holmes, I'm sorry for what I did. You know I am. But you mustn't do this to me. Either you are dead, or you are not. Now, you haven't moved in almost a month. Your front half is all dry and crackly. Your back half, down amongst the flowers, seems to have gone to juice and rot. I am positive that mattress is ruined. Ruined! You are *clearly* dead! So stop all this breathing nonsense, won't you?"

Since castigation made no difference, I turned to cajoling.

"Just stop. As soon as that breath is gone, as soon as that heart is still, I can chop you up and sneak you out of here.

Won't that be nice? I can bury you, then. Or burn you. Or throw you—chunk by chunk—into the Thames. Whatever you prefer. But our current position is untenable, Holmes. I need you to make up your mind, don't you see?"

He didn't see. His eyes were open, but they were shrunk back inside his head like tiny, month-old poached eggs.

We had reached our nightly impasse. I pulled the blankets up around my chin and settled back onto my throne. Out of the corner of my eye, I could see my own bed. I missed it, in a way. But I never slept there anymore.

At a quarter past eight in the morning I was woken again. A positive flurry of blows erupted upon my front door, along with a man's deep voice calling, "Holmes! Holmes! For God's sake, Warlock Holmes! Answer your door!"

I jerked into wakefulness, fell off my book-throne and blearily stammered, "Augh! Help! South of France!"

Gathering my wits somewhat, I stumbled towards the front room, calling, "I am sorry, sir. Warlock Holmes is unavailable at the moment. He is… indisposed."

"Let me in, I say! I need him!"

"Unfortunately, Mr. Holmes is taking his holiday in the south of France and cannot be reached. So you see—"

"But he must help me!"

"He cannot help you. Warlock Holmes cannot help anybody right now!"

This did not dissuade my visitor, who began throwing

his whole weight against our door repeatedly, crying, "Please! Please! He must steal the Beryl Coronet from me! He's the only man who can!"

"Yes, but as I've been telling you, he can't. Now stop causing a scene, sir, and be on your way."

"Don't you see?" the man howled. "I have in my possession a powerful magical artifact. He has to steal it!"

"Well, he can't."

"He must steal my resurrection crown!"

"Your what?"

"*Resurrection crown!*"

"..."

"..."

"Won't you come in?"

The gentleman's name was Alexander Holder, which, he explained, was more than only a name. It was his family's job, since antiquity. Once I had introduced myself as Warlock Holmes's assistant (and the only help he was likely to get) he threw up his hands, violated sworn secrecy and told me all.

"My home is built over an ancient catacomb," he said. "It is a magical place, deeply enchanted. Few can see it. Fewer can open it. As such, it has not been... overly subject to the rigors of the law. It's safer than any bank. Moreover, it is good for storing things no reputable bank would touch. Mysterious things. *Evil* things. For centuries my family has been paid to guard this repository of secrets. Most people cannot even see the vault door. If it is closed, their gaze will slide away from it like water off wax. Even if it could be found, it cannot be opened except by one who is Holder by blood and also by law. If a family member is stripped of his name or forsworn, he cannot open the vault. Oh, if only I had forsworn my son! If only!"

"Your own son? Why do you say so?" I asked.

"Because he stole from me!" Holder flung a battered black case onto my table and opened the catches. Within lay a circular depression lined with flesh-colored velvet. In this lay a broken gold fixture holding three black crystalline rocks. It was clearly a fragment of a larger whole. He took it out and set it on the table before me.

"Behold: the Beryl Coronet," Holder announced, with a flourish.

"Well... clearly not," I said.

"Yes, of course. Not *all* of it."

"It occurs to me, Mr. Holder, that beryls are an amber-brown or green stone. These are black. Obsidian or jet, I should think."

"Yes, yes. *Normally* beryls are green or amber—"

"So when you say, 'Behold: the Beryl Coronet,' what I think you mean is, 'Behold: a broken bit of jewelry that contains no beryls.'"

"Look here, I'm getting to all of that," he harrumphed. "But the important thing is: you have heard of the Beryl Coronet, I trust?"

Of course I had. It was not one of the official crown jewels, but it was the next best thing. Its sudden disappearance some two hundred and thirty years earlier was still the stuff of national interest.

"It's King Arthur's crown, they say."

"So I have heard," Holder replied, with a shrug. "He had it from the fairies, if you believe that sort of thing. All the beryls were green, then. When he died at the Battle of Badon Hill, his knights bore him to the edge of a sacred lake. There came a boat crewed by maidens in black hoods which took him away, into the mists. But, as Sir Bedivere chronicles, the ferry returned some moments later. The chief of these ladies told the knights that Arthur was no longer dead, but would return to lead them some day. She gave Bedivere this crown. One of the thirty-nine beryls had gone black."

"So... the color of the gems has something to do with resurrection?"

"It is thought that each gem holds a powerful, life-giving spell," said Holder. "When the spell is cast, the magic is exhausted and one beryl burns itself black. But it's a difficult thing to get it to work, you see. Despite repeated efforts, only seven of the beryls have ever been used—and that includes King Arthur's. Until last night, this crown was whole and contained thirty-two green beryls and seven black. The current owner has had the most success with the thing, having blackened three beryls himself."

"And this current owner is...?"

"Professor James Moriarty."

My eyes darted involuntarily towards Warlock's room and I think I began to perspire. There was every possibility that the individual Holder spoke of was lying dead, not twenty feet away from him. I'd formed the habit of speaking to the body as if it were Holmes. But was it? Who was it that lay, not quite dead, in that room?

"Moriarty?" I croaked.

"That's why I need Holmes," said Holder. "I need to find someone capable of stealing from me who wishes to hurt Moriarty's criminal empire. And somebody close! By God, I have only until tomorrow to find help. The Chinese Triad does not operate here—not in force. The Yakuza would never cross Moriarty. The Pinkertons' rivalry with Moriarty is well known, but how could I possibly get one of his agents here, all the way from America?"

"Well you may have some luck there," I told him. "Allan Pinkerton has hundreds of agents in his employ. I am sure there must be one or two in London."

Holder waved this away. "No, no. I do not mean one of the mundane men in Pinkerton's employ. I mean one of his *true agents*. There are only nine."

"Nine?"

"Nine riders, clad in black. Woe to you, if you should ever meet one, Dr. Watson. But the nine have not been seen to walk abroad for many a year. They sleep, it is said. They await their master's summons, lying dormant in some faraway land—a land of gray skies and shattered hopes, where no man ever smiles. Philadelphia, I seem to recall."

Mr. Holder fell silent for a time, staring away into the middle distance. Then he shook his head and muttered, "It matters not. Holmes is the prize. He's been the positive bane to Moriarty's gang—they've never had such a rival.

If it appeared he had come to rob me of the coronet, it would be believed, don't you see?"

"Yes, but might that not be a bit ruinous to your family trade?"

"I don't care!" Holder cried. "Worse is at stake! My son stole the rest of the coronet! He broke it! Thirty-six stones are missing. Those that remain have all gone dark—they are useless! On Monday morning—*tomorrow* morning—one of Moriarty's most trusted men is to come and reclaim the coronet from my keeping. I have every reason to believe that Adler, Moran or McCloe will be at my door tomorrow, demanding a treasure I cannot deliver! I cannot produce even one useful stone."

"And you wish Holmes to take the blame, rather than your son?"

"Yes. I will pay you, of course. Holmes must come to my home and lay magical siege to it. The damage must be extensive and there must be no doubt that Holmes is the source."

I shook my head. "I fear I can be of no use to you, Mr. Holder. I was in earnest when I said Holmes is unreachable and unable to help. Perhaps it would be wiser to try and find your son and reclaim the coronet from him."

"Oh, I have my son. He didn't even make it out of the corridor by the vault. Amongst my home's defenses is one of the original Aethereal Guardians. Though it broke my heart, I summoned the guardian to bind my son. He stands within the corridor still, waiting for Moriarty's man to come and mete out punishment to us all."

My brow furrowed. "He didn't leave the corridor?"

"No."

"Yet you did not retrieve the rest of the coronet from him?"

"Er... no."

"Why not?"

Holder gave a shrug. "He didn't have it."

"How is that possible?"

"I have no idea! I caught him in the corridor with this fragment still in his hands. I confronted him, but he would not admit the theft or say where the rest of the Beryl Coronet lay. I told him Moriarty's man would have the answer out of him through worse methods than I dared speak of! He was unmoved! In my fury, I summoned the guardian and bound him. Now he cannot make an answer, even if he would. But oh, the more I think of what they will do to him—or to me if I try to shelter him—maybe to both of us... I cannot bear the thought." He leaned in close to me and spoke in a whisper. "They punish you, you know. If the job they wish you to perform for Moriarty is of high importance, they punish you before they hire you. Then they pay you for your pain—a lavish amount! This way, before you come to deal with them, you know the agony they can bring and also the rewards. They know that any who think to betray them will dwell on how much they preferred the one to the other. I cannot let them do that to me again! I cannot let them do it to my son!"

In retrospect, it seems foolish of me to have brought comfort to a man who was part of an evil magical empire.

Yet, in that moment I saw no villain, only a father grieving for a son yet living. I asked him, "Your son: is he a very powerful magic-user?"

"What? No. Not at all."

"Er... he's not?"

"No. He's always had a disdain for such things. No respect for the family trade. He's never bothered to attempt so much as a parlor-trick illusion."

"Then, your story makes no sense. Your son did not take the coronet."

Holder paused. First hope, then confusion lit his face. "What?"

"He did not take it. Think: your son had no time to stash away part of the coronet—you caught him nearly in the act. Even if he had possessed sufficient time, why would he employ it in the way you describe? Successful thieves are not in the habit of making off with an item, smashing it, hiding half and then returning to the scene of the crime to stand around holding the other half. Do you follow my reasoning, sir?"

"Well... yes."

"Now, I do not know exactly *how* a sorcerer could make part of a coronet spirit itself away from your house, but I don't doubt he *could*. Yet, you say your son has no magical abilities. If there is no mundane explanation as to how he could have stolen it and no magical one either, then we must conclude that he did not take it. Not by himself, at least. No, something else occurred last night."

"What?"

"How should I know?" I shrugged. "I propose we go to your house and see."

Mr. Holder was most amenable to the idea. However, if I thought his would be the next home to face examination, I was mistaken. I spent a few moments procuring suitable clothing, so I didn't notice as Holder began to sniff the air and make faces. My brief absence was enough for him to follow his nose to Holmes's door and push it slightly ajar. "Good Lord! Dr. Watson, what have you done?" he cried. "You can't keep *corpses* in a London lodging house! Honestly! You shall be caught. What you want is a country estate or an underground tunnel, like mine. I don't mean to be rude, but you have much to learn about keeping secrets."

We spoke little on our journey, not wishing the cab driver to overhear us. I was somewhat surprised by the perfectly average appearance of Holder's Streatham home. It sat in the middle of a line of houses, every bit as quiet and respectable as its neighbors. One would never guess at the secrets it held below.

Holder dismissed the servants who gathered to take our coats and offer refreshments. We made our way down a narrow hallway towards the back of the house, then turned onto another which ran to the scullery on our left and the kitchen and pantry on our right.

"My son: Arthur Holder," Mr. Holder said. "Oh, and the Aether Guardian."

There in the middle of the corridor stood one of the strangest sights I have ever seen. I do not think that statues have ghosts, but if they do that is what I beheld. It looked like the marble figure of an armored knight except that it was made of nothing more than translucent white threads of luminescent fiber. One of its hands was resting on the shoulder of a young man, who must have dressed hastily, for he wore nothing but trousers and a shirt, both only half fastened up. His face bore an expression of shock but aside from that, most signs of life were gone.

"Is it safe to touch him?" I asked.

Holder gave a nod and I bent in to examine his son. Arthur Holder's heart rate and breathing had slowed until they were similar to Holmes's current state. As I felt his wrist to time his pulse, I made a discovery.

"Hello! This is a boxer's fracture."

"A what?" asked Mr. Holder.

"Do you see the swelling in his right hand and the way his little finger sags towards his palm?"

"What does that mean?"

"It means he has recently hit something or someone— hard, but not well, for he has broken his hand."

"But what is the significance of it?" Holder asked.

"I don't know," I replied. "I think I'd like to take a look at the vault, if I may."

"If you can," Holder scoffed. "Can you see what is on that portion of the wall, right there?"

I beheld it. Or attempted to. Mr. Holder was right: every time I tried to look at the section of wall, my gaze swerved and my mind wandered. Either I found myself looking towards my right, wondering if there were any unguarded biscuits in the pantry, or to my left, fondly remembering the pretty scullery maid who had smiled at me on my way in. I was still struggling to see the catacomb's entrance, when a voice from behind me asked, "Who is this, Father?"

I looked around to behold a mousy young lady in her mid-twenties. Her features were drawn; I guessed she'd had no sleep the night before.

"This is Dr. Watson. He's here to see if something can be done to help Arthur," Holder said. "Dr. Watson, this is Mary, my niece."

"Then why did she call you 'Father'?" I asked.

This seemed to irritate Holder, who said, "Yes, why did you, Mary? I have asked you not to, I think."

"Oh! I am sorry," she replied. "Habit, you know. I have been used to calling you that for so many years, it still slips out sometimes."

"And why has she been calling you that?"

Holder sighed. "By birth, she is my niece. When my brother died, I adopted her as my daughter. Thus, she became accustomed to calling me Father."

"And why must she cease?"

Mr. Holder reddened somewhat and Mary stepped in, saying, "Mr. Holder has several times expressed a wish that Arthur and I should wed."

"Oh, I see," I said. "And even in evil magical circles, it is considered improprietous for siblings to marry? I learn something new every day."

Mary suppressed a giggle and flashed me a grateful smile. A fool could see she found the prospect of engagement to her brother worrisome, to say the least. Mr. Holder gave a great sigh and insisted, "Arthur needs you, Mary. Can you not see that? He is wayward, Dr. Watson. He spends all his time at that club of his, in the company of his disreputable friends. He plays at cards with that American cad, George Burnwell."

"There is nothing wrong with Mr. Burnwell!" Mary cried. I found the sudden heat with which she rose to his defense... telling. So did Mary, it seems, for she demurred and added, "Nor is there harm in Arthur keeping the society of other men his age, is there?"

"He loses money. Did you know that, Mary? He came to me only last night, asking for two hundred pounds. It was the third time this year! I told him no! He would not have a further ha'penny from me. And then, not five hours later: this! I find him stealing an artifact of incalculable value, no doubt to cover some paltry gambling debt. The fool has exposed us all to Moriarty's ire! And for what? If only I had forsworn him!"

I pursed my lips and said, "I am still unconvinced Arthur is the thief. Look at him—he has no shoes or stockings on. It snowed last night, if you recall. Does he look like he is dressed to flee? No, I think we must begin looking at other possibilities. I must know the name of everybody in the household and hear what they were doing last night."

"I think most of them were abed," said Holder.

"Not all of them," Mary interjected. "When I heard Father… er… *Mr. Holder* cry out, I was just doing my final check to see if all the doors and windows were locked. Just a few moments before, I had to chase Lucy away from the kitchen window. She was speaking with somebody."

Holder snorted. "Probably that Francis Prosper again. Lucy's a pretty girl, Dr. Watson. She has no shortage of admirers."

A sudden thought struck me: the snow.

"I need to go outside," I said.

I returned not twenty minutes later, beaming from ear to ear. Mr. Holder met me at the door with an eager look on his face. "I am no tracker," I told him, "but with a freshly fallen blanket of snow, even an amateur like myself can be of use. It seems, sir, that you had two men lurking about your windows last night."

"Or the same man, twice," Holder reasoned.

"Not unless part of his plan was to leave, amputate one of his legs, replace it with a wooden peg, and return to finish his crime."

"Ah," said Holder. "Well, I can tell you the identity of one of them. Francis Prosper has a wooden leg."

"Then he stood outside the kitchen window, probably flirting with Lucy," I said. "But there was another gentleman who came to the scullery window—very close to your vault."

"And broke in through there?"

I shrugged. "Perhaps. I cannot see any telltale scrapings upon the sill, nor did I note any sign of mud or melted snow inside."

"So, you have no idea whom it might have been?"

"I have some. I've already seen how Mary feels about the prospect of marriage to Arthur, but tell me—honestly now—does he share the same reluctance?"

"Oh God no," Holder grunted. "Why, he's perfectly smitten with her. Follows her like a puppy, trying to be noble, do good deeds and impress her with his character. It's not working."

"Indeed. And what of that fellow you mentioned earlier? The one Arthur plays cards with?"

"George Burnwell?"

"Yes, that's the fellow. An American, you said?"

"Disgustingly so. He's always hanging about, telling Arthur and Mary tales from the age of the gunslingers. Oh, they're both quite wrapped around his finger. It's a damned shame, I tell you! The man is nothing but a layabout and a cad!"

"Whom Arthur met at a gentleman's club?"

"Yes."

"Which one?"

"The Bachelor's Club, down on Piccadilly. But you can't suspect Burnwell," Holder said. "Remember that the vault is heavily warded. Even if he could perceive it, he could not open it."

"And yet, Mr. Holder, I feel I have most everything I need, with only one exception. I am sorry to say, but if you wish to see the main body of the coronet, you must leave the fragment in my possession."

He frowned at that, but eventually assented. After all, how much more murder could Moriarty work over the loss of the last, useless piece?

On my way out, I said, "Fear not, Mr. Holder; I have every hope of bringing this adventure to a satisfactory conclusion."

"You must hurry! Tomorrow is Monday and Moriarty's man will come with the dawn!"

"Then I suppose neither of us will sleep much tonight."

I went around to Piccadilly, first thing, and knocked on the door of The Bachelor's Club. It opened to reveal an impeccably dressed butler.

"May I help you?" he asked.

"I hope so. I was looking for George Burnwell; is he here?"

"I am sorry, sir. Mr. Burnwell has not come today. I believe he is bound for America."

I had thought as much.

"I wonder if you might have his address?" I asked.

The butler harrumphed and said, "It is not the policy of this club to disclose the private information of its members."

"Well, that is admirable, but I owe him quite a bit of money. I rather thought he might like to have it before he left on his trip."

"Ah... well... if it lies on that footing, then I suppose..."

* * *

The address wasn't too far from Baker Street, just on the other side of Regent's Park. Thus, after a quick stop at 221B for some essentials, I made my way to George Burnwell's abode and rang the bell.

"Who is it?" asked a voice behind the door.

"The man who has the other piece of the Beryl Coronet."

The door opened to reveal a fit fellow in his early thirties. He was rakish and handsome, or would have been if one of his eyes was not swollen almost shut.

"Looks like Arthur Holder hit you pretty hard, eh?"

"Lucky shot," Burnwell said. "Maybe you'd better come inside, where we can talk."

"Thank you, Mr. Burnwell, but I prefer to remain on the street. Here in the public eye, it is less likely that you and I will begin shooting at one another in a misguided attempt to determine who owns the coronet."

"Oh," he said. "So that's why you've got that hand in your pocket."

"Just as you have one in yours," I pointed out.

"You're a pretty cautious fellow," he noted.

"Yes, and you are a Pinkerton."

The flicker of shock across his features showed I had guessed the whole thing right. He took a breath and asked, "Why would you think that?"

"Mr. Holder could name only four parties with the wherewithal to rob him. Two were oriental, one was my friend, Warlock Holmes, and the other was the Pinkerton

Detective Agency. The Pinkertons are American, just like you."

He gave me a grudging nod and said, "You must be John Watson, huh? We've got a file on you."

I'll admit I was shaken, but I persisted. "Mr. Burnwell, I must ask you to lend me your part of the coronet."

"Now why would I do a dumb thing like that?"

"Because, if you do, I can use it to procure the rest of the coronet, and I will bring it to you."

"All right, then. Let me rephrase the question: why would *you* do a dumb thing like that?"

"I want it gone," I told him. "I want it safe from Moriarty. From what I understand, Allan Pinkerton and his nine friends are some of the only folk who can keep a thing from Moriarty."

"Yeah," said Burnwell, visibly disturbed by the depth of my knowledge. "Most of the time they can, I guess."

"And they must do it this time," I insisted. "But it must be the *whole coronet*. If you do not aid me, the missing fragment will be reclaimed by Moriarty tomorrow morning."

"So? I got most of it," he said defensively.

I put on my best lord-how-hard-it-is-for-us-Britons-to-tolerate-you-foolish-Colonials voice and demanded, "If he had sent you out for milk, would you have brought him half a cow? Sorcerous devices are generally unlike farm animals, but here is one trait they share: either they are whole and they function, or they *are* not and they *do* not. Now, which is it?"

He gave me the sort of look toddlers give Brussels

sprouts, hesitated a few moments, then mumbled, "How long would you need it?"

"I would think… three or four hours."

He shifted uncomfortably, then said, "I have security, you know. If you tried to make off with the coronet, Mary Holder would suffer."

"You cad!"

"Yes… well… most spies are."

Damn. If it were true he could hurt Mary—and I had every reason to assume he could—then this whole affair was on a very different footing. Common sense might suggest that I should just bow out. Let Pinkerton take the coronet, with its thirty-two remaining stones. Let Moriarty's henchmen get their three used beryls and vent their rage. Let Holder reap the fruits of his own incompetence.

Then again, if I could get both parts of that coronet in my hands for a few hours, I could…

What?

Resurrect Holmes?

Probably not. I didn't know how to use the coronet, after all. But I could try. Moreover, I could *claim* I tried. Then I could cut him up. I could say, "Look here, Holmes, I used conventional medicine. When that failed, I went and got you King Arthur's resurrection crown. If this is not enough to please you, I really don't know what else I can do. I am going to chop you up, now. I don't care if you're still breathing. I'm going to cut you up and dump the pieces and just be done with this whole affair."

"You have my word," I told Burnwell. "The coronet

must leave these shores. Lend me your piece and I will bring you the whole."

"I am leaving by carriage at two this morning," he said. "If the entire coronet is not in my possession, first Mary Holder and then you will suffer for it. Is that clear?"

I nodded.

"Wait here," he said.

Fifteen minutes later, I was ravaging 221B. I didn't know precisely what I was looking for. Some form of solder, I supposed. Tin? I set the two pieces of the coronet on my evil-tome-side-table and set about ransacking Holmes's miniature alchemical laboratory. I didn't know how to fix jewelry. Much less: crown jewels. Much less: King Arthur's crown.

By God, if I was coming to believe these far-fetched, fairytale notions Holmes and all his clients kept saying to me, then I was all but forced to accept the fact that this was *Bloody King Bloody Arthur's Bloody Crown*! The idea was insane. But also invigorating. I had the sudden urge to try it on, to behold myself in the looking glass wearing the very badge of Arthur's majesty.

No. Inadvisable. Allowing myself to toy with powerful magics was as wise as letting a five-year-old play with a loaded pistol. I resumed my quest to find something to bond the broken pieces together.

Ah-ha! From the back of one of Holmes's drawers, I withdrew a small cube of gold.

Hmmm…

That might have helped with the rent. Perhaps I should have ransacked his room sooner. In any case, I had what I needed. Now I just had to find a way to melt it…

An hour later, I held the Beryl Coronet. The clumsiness of my welds proclaimed my lack of skill as a jeweler, but still, it was whole. Well… whole*ish*. I turned to Holmes's corpse and said, "This is it, Warlock. This is your last chance."

I placed the coronet upon his brow.

Nothing.

"Um… Yes… Go crown!"

Still nothing.

"By the right of Arthur and the will of the fey, I command you to imbue this body with life!"

Yet more nothing.

"Er… abracadabra?"

Silence. I slouched in my book-throne and looked out the window in my room across the hall. Darkness was gathering. I supposed I must bring the coronet to Burnwell and figure out a way to save Holder. I'd done my best. I'd tried.

Suddenly, there was a flash of light and the sensation of a terrible force. It almost knocked me over, but it disturbed none of the papers scattered about the room. With an audible crackle, all thirty-two green beryls singed themselves black. Lazy tendrils of acrid smoke drifted up from the blackened stones. I leapt to my feet and hovered over Holmes, waiting to see a change.

Nothing.

I just didn't understand. But what more could I do? I sighed, placed the still-smoking coronet back in my bag and prepared to leave. A sudden idea struck me and I threw in a few medical supplies, hoping they might help me save the Holders from Moriarty's gang.

George Burnwell was not well pleased by the state of the coronet he'd stolen.

"What the hell's wrong with it? Why are the stones all black?"

"Because the coronet was broken, then rejoined, I think," I told him. I had no intention of informing him I'd tried to use it.

"But… this strange color change… what does it mean?"

If he didn't know, I was in no mood to tell him. "I am not a magic-user," I said. "You may need to ask your boss. Ahem… I shouldn't let him know it was you who broke the coronet, by the way."

The night was well along by the time I returned to Alexander Holder's house. I found him on the threshold, pacing back and forth.

"Have you done it?" he cried. "Have you found the Beryl Coronet?"

"Yes, but I do not have it. Nor would it help you, if I did.

The magic is spent. All thirty-nine gems are gone black."

His face went ashen.

"Never fear, Mr. Holder; I think I can save you and your family. Let's go in, shall we, and find a quiet place to talk."

The servants were all abed, which was good. I settled Holder in his own kitchen and began making tea, while I told him, "First, you should know: your son is innocent. In fact, you owe him a great debt. He was injured in an attempt to recover the Beryl Coronet. He struck the thief in the face, breaking his own hand in the process. I suspect that it was Arthur struggling to wrest the coronet from the thief's grasp that broke it in the first place."

"But, who was the thief?"

"George Burnwell, just as I suspected."

"How could it be? He could not open the vault! He could not even see the thing! If he talked Arthur into doing it, then why did they come to blows? It makes no sense!"

"His accomplice was never Arthur, don't you see?" I said. "It was Mary."

"But how? Why?"

"How?" I laughed. "She is your brother's daughter. Once you adopted her, there was no ward to protect the vault from her. She was of Holder blood and a legal member of your immediate family. As to why, it is the simplest of reasons. She is in love with George Burnwell. Think: an unmarried girl, in her mid-twenties, facing a life of lonely domesticity or marriage to the man she considers her brother—it's a rather hopeless situation. Then, along comes a handsome American who tells her wild tales of gunslingers and adventure. Within five minutes of meeting Mary, I'd seen her shy away from engagement to Arthur and jump to defend Burnwell; her preference was plain. How happy it must have made her when he told her he'd take her away with him, if only she'd do this one thing: if only she'd open her father's vault and hand him the Beryl Coronet, out the scullery window. It would have worked, too, if Arthur hadn't caught him at it."

"Fiend!" Holder cried.

"Hmm, yes, but you see: a *well-informed* fiend. I suspect I would not have thought of a rival organization trying to steal your treasures, if you had not spoken of it when first we met. Yet, the more I puzzled over it, the more I realized that such must be the cause of your troubles. Whoever the thief was, they were attempting entry into a vault they could not perceive, nor had any hope of opening. Yet they seemed to know you were in possession of their target and how to go about getting it. Two of the organizations you mentioned were oriental and famously close-knit, but the Pinkertons… an American… that was not such a stretch."

"Burnwell is a Pinkerton?" Holder gasped.

"I had it from his own lips," I said.

"And he has the coronet? King Arthur's crown is bound for America?"

"I'm afraid so, Mr. Holder."

"Then I am doomed!" he cried. "I shall have nothing to deliver to Moriarty's man when he comes in the morning. I've only a few hours!"

"Hope yet remains," I said. "I think I may save you and your family, though not without cost. When we spoke, earlier, you seemed to think you would be held blameless if it were apparent Holmes had taken the treasure."

"Yes, I think so."

"What if it were clear that the Pinkertons had done the same?"

"Moriarty's men would be furious, but more with Pinkerton than myself."

"And your family would be saved? Your own life, your son Arthur's, Mary's as well?"

"That is my hope."

"And what would you give, to keep that hope alive?"

"Anything!" Holder exclaimed. "I'd give my right arm and think the price light."

"Well, there's no need for such drastic measures," I said, then looked down into my tea and sighed. "I would think I could do it for the price of your left hand."

He stared at me, aghast.

"I'm sorry, but that is the only remedy I can foresee. I think I can make it clear to Moran, or whoever else should come, that you have been besieged and victimized by the Pinkertons. But I fear I cannot do it without removing one of your hands."

I fell silent. He stared at me for a few minutes. I could see a flood of thoughts battling in his mind. Finally he said, "Yes. Yes, what must I do?"

"Just drink your tea. You've hardly touched it."

"What? You dosed my tea?"

"I did," I said, with a shrug. "I'm afraid it's becoming a bit of a habit."

"So, if I drink this…"

"You will wake in the late morning or early afternoon. Your hand will be gone. Moriarty's man will have come and left, having found your house cracked by the Pinkertons. I suspect they will find no further need of your services."

Hoarse and wide-eyed, he choked, "All right," and raised his teacup.

"Wait!" I cried. "Now that all is known, it might serve my policy if you would come with me, before you drink that. I'll need you to open your vault, and leave it so."

Five minutes later, we sat in the kitchen. In the corridor behind us was an open vault. Before us were two empty cups. Ten minutes after that, Alexander Holder was face down on his table, snoring.

I sighed.

I reached into my medical bag and withdrew my bone saw. Well, there was nothing for it… Besides, it might be good practice for chopping up Holmes.

As I was about to make the first incision, I paused. Did I really expect Pinkerton raiders to remove a limb with surgical precision?

With a silent apology to Alexander Holder, I searched his kitchen until I found a meat cleaver. This, I thrust into the hearth until the embers heated the blade to a dull orange glow. Knowing its heat should be sufficient to cauterize any wound, I withdrew it and—with one determined blow—struck away his left hand.

Well… *two* determined blows.

Two and a half.

There was this bit of skin, holding the thing to the… anyway…

I carried my grisly trophy to the fireside and reheated the cleaver a few times, using the hot edge of its blade to scorch my message into Holder's palm.

In the morning, Moriarty's man would arrive to find Holder's back door had been forced. Holder would be drugged and maimed. His son, immobilized by a spectral guardian. His vault, open. The Beryl Coronet, gone. On the floor they would find a disembodied hand—one of the only hands capable of opening the vault in question. Burned into the palm of that hand they would find the image of an all-seeing eye, over the promise "We never sleep"—the logo of the Pinkerton Detective Agency.

I hoped that would be sufficient to save Mr. Holder. Or, what was left of him…

I didn't know which of Moriarty's lieutenants would be the one to make the discovery—and indeed I had only encountered one of the names Holder gave, Moran—but I filed the others away for future use.

Moran. McCloe. Adler.

By the time I reached 221B Baker Street so much of the night had gone I didn't know if there was any point sleeping or not. But I was damn well going to try. I hung my hat and coat and made for my room, for my own warm bed.

"With one determined blow…"

Yet, guilt assailed me.

I had no intention of cutting Holmes up that night. I'd had a full enough day, as it was. Tomorrow night would be soon enough.

So, perhaps one last night's vigil by his bedside, before I bid him farewell? Yes. I headed for his open door.

I was on the threshold when a voice behind me said, "Watson? Is that you? I feel terrible."

In Holmes's favorite chair by the hearth sat...

Holmes.

To say he looked a bit out of sorts would not be unfair. When I say I have seen corpses that look better, I am not exaggerating. Recently deceased individuals look much like still-living ones, with the exception of bullet holes, or other trauma. Long-dead corpses are only bone or mummified—dry and devoid of odor. Thus, there is only a certain window where corpses are even *capable* of looking as bad as Holmes did in that moment. Yet there he sat, awaiting an answer.

Which is something I found myself utterly incapable of delivering. I just gaped at him.

After a time, he spoke again. "Can I have some soup?"

I nodded and went to the pantry, where I must have dropped the pot six or seven times before I finally managed to get it filled and set above the fire.

"Am I sick?"

"Well... no, Holmes. The truth is: you've been poisoned."

"Oh..." he said, then, "You know, that's funny, Watson.

I don't remember mixing myself anything."

"Well, you wouldn't. I poisoned you, Holmes, I must confess."

"I see. That must be why my chest hurts so badly."

"Ah… no. I may also have shot you. Twice."

"Oh." He nodded, then stared at the remains of our fire for a few minutes before asking, "Did I say something wrong? Or betray our friendship?"

"Holmes! No! By God, no. Nothing like that. Do you not remember?"

I told him all. Of our disastrous misadventure with Charles Augustus Milverton. Of the woman who interrupted our encounter with the blackmailer and how she murdered him. Of the tiny, burning name that flew free of Holmes when she did. Of my horrified realization that the personality within Holmes's body was not his own. Of the revelation that Moriarty had taken control of Holmes's physical form and how he had threatened me with a fireball.

At this point, Holmes interrupted me to scoff, "Bah! This was surely an illusion. Moriarty was never one to expend power so readily. His art was in using very small amounts of magic to great effect. I cannot imagine him—"

"Holmes, touch your face."

"Why? Hmmm… What is this hard thing? What am I feeling?"

"Your cheekbone. That fire was quite real, I fear. You see, I'd already poisoned you, before Moriarty revealed himself."

"Why?"

"Because I knew something was wrong. I'd also taken the precaution of slipping my pistol into my coat pocket. When he pulled out the fireball and proclaimed ownership of me, I panicked. I kicked the fireball into his face—your face—and shot him twice in the chest."

"I say! Well done, Watson! Bravo!"

"How can you say that? I shot you! I… Holmes, I'm not sure how to tell you this, but… I think I sort of *killed* you."

"And well done, too. Right through the heart! Look how close these bullet holes are. That takes marksmanship!"

"It's really not the sort of thing a doctor is supposed to do."

"But you did. That's what matters."

"Holmes… aren't you angry?"

He leaned in and smiled. Well, I suppose with his charred lips in the shape they were, he'd been smiling the whole time. I still shudder when I recall that familiar, friendly gaze in his rotting eyes.

"Watson, you must believe me when I say: death is a far preferable fate to being trapped in my own body, watching Moriarty run around in it. Ye gods, when I think of the damage he could have done… You did the right thing, Watson. You saw your friend and your world in danger and you acted. I applaud your initiative. But for now, there are other matters I must attend. Oh, that soup! It smells heavenly, Watson! How long has it been?"

However long, it appeared it would be a little longer still before Holmes got the fix he was craving. As I watched in horror, Holmes fed himself that first, much-anticipated spoonful of soup. It dribbled right through his half-detached lower lip, down his shirtfront and onto our table.

"Ah…" he said. "Yes… this might take a little work, I suppose. Look here, Watson, why don't you leave me to it and have a rest, eh? You look a bit worn out, if it's not too crude to speak so plainly."

Without making any comment as to how he himself might look at the moment, I rose and walked into my chamber. There was my bed, long-foresworn but looking every bit as tempting as it ever had. I suppose some folk might find it impossible to sleep, knowing that the half-mummified remains of a beloved friend sat not twenty feet from their bed, giving itself a clumsy soup-bath.

I had no such difficulty.

When I arose, I rather fancied I would find the events of the previous evening to be a pleasant dream—a phantasm concocted by my guilty mind to assuage itself for a time. But no. There at our table—which now looked nearly as terrible as the man himself—sat Warlock Holmes. He'd clearly had a devil of a time with his soup, which now speckled every surface. His lower lip had come almost all the way off and he'd also found two significant leaks through his right cheek and neck, which seemed to have made the successful delivery of food to his waiting stomach something of a trial. Half-chewed toast lay amidst puddles of soup, interspersed with the odd desiccated flower or little bit of Holmes that had given up and fallen off.

"We're out of bread," he told me. "I wanted to go to the market, but... I don't suppose you'd go for me?"

"I think that might be best."

So strange to say, but my joy at having Holmes returned to me was such that I hardly minded the state of him. Indeed, if I were not looking directly at him it was easy to imagine him sitting in his chair, looking as he ought, wearing the same friendly, slightly confused expression he always did. The only thing that betrayed his current state was the muffled quality of his speech, due to the sad condition of his lower lip and other vocally important bits.

Oh, and the smell.

We sat together for a time, catching up on all that had passed. When I told him of my agonies over when to cut him into pieces, his look became tortured. I suppose my voice must have cracked a few times, too. As I spoke, I realized I had no way of apologizing for my behavior or the callous disregard I had shown for his mortal remains. Even as I was beginning to craft a suitable contrition, he beat me to it.

"Oh, Watson," he sighed, near tears, "I am sorry. It must have been so sad for you. So very sad."

"For me? What about you?"

"Oh, I didn't mind. How could I? I was dead. Let me tell you, until I got that delicious blast of life-force, I had no mortal cares."

I had told him of the Beryl Coronet already, but now confessed, "I have no idea how I even got it to work, Holmes."

"Well... don't take this the wrong way, Watson, but you probably didn't. I'm a bit of a sponge for magic. Place any powerful quantity of it near my body and I will drink it right up, whether I wish to or not. Anyway, I'm sorry to hear you had such a bother while I was gone, especially over a trivial concern like money. Did it not occur to you to look in your ear?"

"What are you speaking of?" I began to ask, but was interrupted. Holmes reached a hand towards my left ear and performed that most familiar of carnival-conjurer's tricks. As a boy, I'd been amazed to see tuppence emerge from my ear, seemingly by magic. As an adult, I was even more amazed, for three reasons.

First, because this time it was not a trick.

Second, because I could hear it. Have you ever had someone crinkle paper, near your ear? Well, this was *in my ear*. It was deafening.

Third, because I could feel it. There was a terrible, dry scraping as a banknote unfolded from deep within my aural canal.

There stood Holmes with a look of satisfaction on his face and a crumpled, bloodstained ten-pound note in his hand.

"Ow! Holmes! What have you...? How...?" I slapped a hand protectively over the ear. "Quite the trick, Holmes, but let us remember that you are the conjurer, not I. I have no power to simply reach into my ear and pull forth money, whenever I lack funds."

"Of course you do," smiled Holmes. "Try it. Use the

left ear. The right won't do. Get a good grip on the money. Don't want to rip the corner off, eh?"

I stared at him, silently challenging his ridiculous joke, yet he seemed in earnest. Slowly, incredulously, I reached my finger as deep as I could within my ear. I couldn't believe how deep that was. I felt something: dry, flat and crinkly. Pinching it betwixt thumb and forefinger, I drew it out.

"A hundred! Well done, Watson! You've bested me entirely," Warlock cheered.

"How...? How has this happened?"

"Don't worry yourself over such things," Warlock said. "Oh, and don't overdo it. That ear is bound to have a finite amount of cash in it, you know. But when you're in a pinch, just a moment digging about in your ear is bound to solve your problem, I would think."

He smiled at me, but his smile drifted to the dirtied stack of soup pots and became a sigh. I shook myself. I was staring at the bloody ruins of one hundred and ten English pounds. Well, at least now I had something to use at the grocer's, I supposed. Perhaps even to make amends with other parties I had wronged...

A few hours later, I stood before the door to Mrs. Hudson's downstairs rooms and knocked.

"What?" barked a shrill little voice, from within.

"It is John Watson," I said. "Holmes has forwarded some funds, from the south of France, to cover the rent. I therefore—"

I didn't get to finish. The door skreeked open and a tiny, withered hand shot forth to snatch the notes I held. As soon as they disappeared, the door swung shut again. Or, it would have, if I had not thrust my foot into the crack, just in time.

"Wait!"

"What d'you want?"

I blinked away a few tears, related—one may easily understand—to the unnecessary force Mrs. Hudson employed when closing hinged devices.

"I wanted to apologize. I got you something."

"What?"

"You have heard of William Shakespeare's *The Two Gentlemen of Verona*, I trust?"

"Don't care for it."

"Nor did I expect you to, Mrs. Hudson. Yet, in a proof that small words can have great importance, I am holding a copy of *The Two Gentlemen* in *Verona*. By this author's interpretation, Verona is a down-on-her-luck servant girl who finds herself sandwiched—quite literally—between the affections of a country squire and a poor groo—"

"Already got it," Mrs. Hudson said and remounted her efforts to force her door shut, even though—I am certain—she had not forgotten my foot was still inside it.

"Again, I am not surprised. But this volume I am holding— Ow! This one is special! Ouch! Augh! Please stop!"

Mrs. Hudson had now abandoned all veneer of propriety and was venting her frustration at the rent's delay against the digits of my lower extremity. Her tiny arms whipped the door open and shut again, over and over, with the terrible strength and regularity of a steam piston. I realized I must come to my point quickly, if I wished any chance of preserving my bipedalism.

"It's *illustrated*!"

The door stopped. In the shadows behind, I could see Mrs. Hudson's beady little eyes, gleaming up at me. There was hatred in them, of course, but no small amount of hopefulness, too. She reached one tentative paw out of her slovenly den. It probed the brown-paper parcel I held forth, experimentally at first, then clutched it and dragged it inside. Her expression wavered, for a moment. Rather than let me see her fury falter, she directed her gaze downwards, at my foot.

Which, I quickly withdrew.

The door slammed shut. From within came the sound of ripping paper, followed by a squeal of bestial glee.

I gave myself a congratulatory nod. It had been the right thing to do.

Yes. Stiff upper lip, John.

I turned and limped back towards the stairs to 221B.

SILVER BLAZE: MURDER HORSE

ON TUESDAY, I SURPRISED A VAMPIRE.

That first day of Holmes's return—Monday—was spent situating my newly re-alive friend and making sure that 221B was a fit haven for his recovery. The next day, I found myself more at liberty and decided to spend my time in the most satisfactory pursuit I could devise: petty revenge. You see, immediately following Holmes's "demise" Lestrade had taken special care to make sure he and Grogsson disappeared from my life. This wasn't easy as Grogsson is not the type to turn away a friend in need.

But no, Lestrade had said, Holmes was dead and beyond helping. I was a human and—no, more to the point—I was an *idiot* who refused to dispose of Holmes's body. This would soon be discovered and Grogsson would get to see me exactly one more time: as my face purpled at the end of a hangman's noose.

It was therefore with utmost satisfaction that I marched up to Lestrade's miserable little desk in his dark corner at Scotland Yard to say, "Holmes wishes to see you."

Oh, how rewarding the look on his face was. If you've

never surprised a vampire, allow me to recommend it wholeheartedly.

"Holmes," Lestrade said.

"Yes."

"*Holmes?*"

"Yes, of course," I said. "Bring Grogsson too, if it's convenient."

It was not convenient, but it was also not the kind of occasion one skips. When we reached 221B Baker Street I showed the two inspectors in myself, not wishing Mrs. Hudson to see the state of Holmes. I'd managed to hide the fact of his return from her and intended to keep it so, for as long as I could. Why ruin a triumphant day by being cast out onto the street by a terrified, septuagenarian porn-addict? I gave a soft knock on my own door and announced, "Holmes? I have brought a couple of old friends to see you."

"Have you, Watson? Who is it?"

"Grogsson and Lestrade."

"How nice. Do come in."

I swung the door wide to reveal Holmes, clad in his oriental silk dressing gown, sitting in his favorite chair by the fire. His expression was pleasant, but unmoving— understandable seeing as his face was still basically mummified. Lestrade gaped, trying to discern if this were truly a living Holmes, or if I had finally snapped, dressed the corpse, propped him in a chair, learned ventriloquism and devised an off-color joke.

Grogsson displayed no such reluctance. Springing across the threshold, he cried, "Yah! Yah! Torg knew!

Torg said: 'Warlock can never be killed!'" He then landed a celebratory punch in the center of Holmes's chest that very nearly disproved his words. Holmes's chair tumbled backwards, spilling my friend onto the floor. Coughing and fumbling, Holmes regained his feet and nodded his thanks. I nearly laughed out loud; not at Holmes, but at Lestrade's expression. If anybody were able to feel at ease while watching a dead man rise to his feet, I would have thought a vampire to be the most likely candidate. But no, if Lestrade were ever coerced into laying an egg into an upturned top hat, while the House of Lords watched and judged his performance, I think he would look equally uncomfortable as he did on that *wonderful* Tuesday.

Realizing it was his turn to address Holmes, Lestrade lurched forward and announced, "Yes. Yes, of course. We are all so pleased to see you, Warlock. So glad to have you back, at last. Er… Oh! Here! I got you this, my friend—to commemorate your return to us."

After a quick rummage of his pockets, Lestrade drew forth a crumpled piece of paper and presented it to Holmes. It was a twenty-pound bet on a horse named Silver Blaze, to win the Wessex Cup. My eyebrows went up. Twenty pounds was a princely sum, even when it wasn't coming from a glum penny-pincher. I suspected there must be some reason the paper was valueless and that Lestrade knew it.

My cynicism was not shared by Holmes. One hand went to his heart and it looked as if his rotted eyes might run with tears. His voice caught in his throat as he said, "You did? But this… this is wonderful, Vladislav! You know, there's nothing like being dead for a month to make one examine his life. I've been taking stock of myself all morning. And do you know what I found? I am an unremarkable fellow. I've squandered my advantages. I had just decided to bring myself up a bit—to become the gentleman I should have been—and now here you stand with this wonderful gift. What could possibly be more gentlemanly than a gambling problem?"

Grogsson shrugged and suggested, "Monocle?"

"Oh! Good point! Watson, remind me to pick up a monocle, won't you? Why, with the right eyepiece and a cultivated gambling habit, I am sure a title must follow. But, enough of such things! I must have missed so much. Sit! Sit and tell me all."

There was nothing of importance. Following a short catch-up and tea, our Scotland Yard friends took their leave. Grogsson's spirits were high; he left a few dents in my coffee table so that we might remember this joyous day. Lestrade remained just as shaken when he left as he was when he arrived. After they had departed, Holmes turned to me and mused, "How lucky am I, to have friends such as these. And what a princely gift! I don't deserve it, Watson."

"I think you may be overestimating Lestrade," I said, eyeing the battered race-slip.

"One can never overestimate the value of a true friend, Watson."

"Be that as it may, I am sure that bet must be worthless. Come now, would Lestrade ever give up twenty pounds?"

"Well... loathe as I am to admit flaws in the character of my closest comrades... it does seem a tad unlikely. But, let us provide him with the benefit of the doubt. Yes! I have decided! Lestrade believes this ticket to be valid. What's more, he is hopeful that I will win and that this first taste of victory will plant within me the seed that shall flourish into a gambling addiction, worthy of any duke!"

I rolled my eyes at Holmes and reached over to the pile of newspapers I'd allowed to accumulate, unread, during Holmes's ordeal. I snagged the top one off the stack and flipped to the sport pages. The very first article answered my every question.

"Well, Holmes, it seems I have underestimated Vladislav Lestrade in only one aspect: the Wessex Cup has not already been run…"

"There! You see, Watson?"

"But the gate drops in less than twenty minutes and the overwhelming favorite, Silver Blaze, is still missing following the murder of his trainer, John Straker."

"By the gods! Get your coat, Watson!"

"What? You don't mean that you intend to—"

"To solve the mystery, Watson! Quick! We've little time to lose!"

"Holmes! I absolutely forbid it!"

"No, but, don't you see Lestrade's true gift? I am now certain that he was presenting me with a case—something to stimulate me back into action!"

"Holmes, I think it is much more likely that he was relieving himself of some wastepaper. Even if he were not, the Wessex Cup is run in Dorset and this newspaper notes that Colonel Ross—Silver Blaze's owner—keeps his stables at King's Pyland on Dartmoor! Do you propose that we might make it to either location in only fifteen minutes? Let us recall, Holmes, you remain unable to bend either knee and every time you move faster than a waddle, little bits of you fall off. No, I am sorry to say: it is impossible to solve this case in the time we have."

"Bah, Watson! Nothing is impossible."

"Actually, a great many things—"

"Not for me!" cried Holmes and the terrible green fire lit in his eye-sockets.

"Holmes! No magic!"

"Ha! Magic? I can solve it with a simple parlay." At this, he curled his left hand into a claw and shouted into it, "Parlay! Parlay! All you who creep or crawl on Dartmoor, hear me! Those with force but no vision, I abjure thee! You with sight but no strength, heed my call! Come to me now and sit in parliament!"

"Holmes! Are you… are you calling demons?"

He snorted. "None that you need fear. As I've told you before, there are powerful outside forces that wish to live within our world, but are held out."

"Yes, I recall as much and would rather not have them in my sitting room, thank you."

"Yet there are also those demons who love our world so well that they have given up all their power, just to dwell near us. They can clearly see our world. They can fool themselves into thinking they exist within it. They can observe the changing of our seasons and the business of man and beast, yet they have no power to act."

"So they are like…"

"Football fans," Holmes sneered. "Like those fellows who hang upon every shot and every block of their favorite team—who curse and shout from the sidelines—loving the game and the players, forever banned from participating themselves."

"It's a bit sad," I said.

"No," Holmes corrected me. "It is *pathetic in the extreme*. But hush! They are coming."

And suddenly, the air around me was thick with murmurs. The shadows in our room began to convulse and solidify. In the pantry, one of the cupboard doors creaked open and a little man made all of willow bark fell out. He gave a queer sort of curse, then asked Holmes, "Who are you, Sorcerer? What do you wish of me?"

"Knowledge," Holmes said. "That is why I call this parliament. Just… er… just take a place over there on the sofa, won't you?"

From every corner and cranny, more of the little creatures came. One was made all of smoke. One, a ball of moss with a disgruntled sneer. A man of twisted brambles crossed his thorny little arms and stared up at Holmes. There was a splatter of mud and a walking slick of thick, oily tar (whom I made sit upon newspapers, to preserve the upholstery). One was a crow—or no, let me say: it looked as if someone who had never seen a crow but had heard one described had attempted to carve one out of roast beef. These and many others crowded and jostled around our settee, until each had his place.

"Is this all?" Holmes demanded.

"We are met," they answered all together. "What would you have of us?"

"I seek Silver Blaze!" said Holmes. Smoke-Puff tilted his head quizzically to one side. The parliament of demons stared at Holmes, uncomprehending, blinking.

"It's a horse. Silver Blaze is the name of a horse," I volunteered.

"Ohhhhhh," said Meat-Crow. "That makes sense. What about him?"

"Wait!" shouted Willow-Bark, jumping to his feet and spreading his dry little hands. "Why should we speak? What will this man pay?"

Holmes smiled and replied, "I will give you that which you most crave. If you help me find Silver Blaze, show me the truth of his abduction and of Straker's murder and return him to his owner in time to race, I will give you a home. You will have a piece of this world to call your own—with walls of stone and cool, deep shadows."

The mish-mash of tiny demons shouted and cheered. Meat-Crow flapped his horrid little beef-wings so violently that he blew Smoke-Puff completely apart. It took the poor fellow almost five minutes to piece himself back together.

"Holmes," I hissed, "are you sure about this? Think of what you are saying. Demons from other planes seeping through to live here—that is exactly the phenomenon you are always trying to prevent!"

Holmes turned to me and declared, "This is important!"

"But… it isn't."

"No! Lestrade is a true friend! This race-slip is a princely gift! Mischief has been done upon an honest horse!"

"What about the murder of his trai—"

"And I am going to have a crushing gambling problem! This affront shall not go uncorrected."

"But…"

"Tut, Watson! Tut!" He turned from me to gesture at his gathered demons, proclaiming, "These are the seers of hidden deeds, the knowers of secrets. What other way have we to gain information on this case?"

"Well… there's the newspaper, which we have yet to read."

"Ha! A useless trinket!"

"You think so, do you?" I swept up the paper and settled into my accustomed role: the defender of human normalcy. We would just see which might prove more useful: a gaggle of lesser demons or a good old London daily.

"Now," said Holmes, "what do we suppose is the most likely thing to happen to this horse?"

"Had four legs!" one of the demons offered.

"Ate oats!"

"Pooped!"

If nothing else, they were eager to please, desperate for their promised fee.

I raised one eyebrow and opined, "I should think the most likely explanation would be that a rival horse-owner, or someone who stood to lose a great deal of money if Silver Blaze won, might have absconded with the beast and murdered him."

"Yes! Excellent!" said Holmes, clapping his hands together. "Minions, bring me the fallen! I need every horse that has died upon the moor since… When was the disappearance, Watson?"

"Tuesday last."

"Tuesday last! Now go! Fly forth and do my bidding!"

Six of the little demonettes blinked out, one by one. It was as if they were soap bubbles, gently popping— once present in splendid, iridescent strangeness, gone the next instant.

"So, Holmes, I am unclear on this point," I said. "What exactly did you mean when you asked them to—"

But I did not finish, for Ball-Moss and Slop-Tar reappeared in the middle of my sentence and dropped a dead horse onto my coffee table, crushing it utterly. I was about to protest, when an even worse delivery came in. The second horse must have died in one of the many Dartmoor bogs, for its carcass was bloated and covered in thick, sticky peat. This second corpse was deposited right atop the first and quickly followed by a third, which must already have been sold off for scrap, since it arrived in several large chunks—midway through the process of being chopped up for dog meat. Only its head had any skin left on it, and in its cadaverous eyes I thought I detected something akin to surprise at being invited into a London sitting room.

"Is that all?" Holmes asked, staring at the pile of ex-horses with some measure of disappointment.

"Only these, Master," confirmed Thorny-Jim.

"Hmm," Warlock mused. "Which one is Silver Blaze, do you think?"

"According to this article, Silver Blaze is a chestnut-colored stallion, named for the distinctive silver marking that runs from his forehead, down towards the tip of his nose," I said, adding, "Wonderful thing, the daily newspaper. Any who want one can have it for tuppence, without any need of consorting with demons or betraying the race of man."

"So then, Silver Blaze is…"

"None of these, Holmes."

"But…"

"Well, that's good news, isn't it?" I reasoned. "That means he's likely to be still alive."

"Likely? It means he must be, doesn't it?"

"No. You asked for every horse that died *on the moor*. What if he was removed from the moor and then slain?"

"Oh! Curses!" Holmes roared, then turned to the demons and said, "Bring me—"

"Holmes, don't you dare! There is not space in this sitting room for every horse that's died since Tuesday, anywhere in the world!"

Holmes wilted a bit and whined, "Well, what else am I supposed to do?"

"There may be other approaches," I said. "It occurs to me there are several inconsistencies in the official account of Straker's death."

"Such as?"

I scanned the article, gathering salient points. "Well,

Scotland Yard has arrested a man named Fitzroy Simpson for the murder. The man is a notorious rogue in racing circles. It seems he was caught snooping around the stables earlier looking—he claims—for useful tips."

"Somewhat suspicious," Holmes noted.

"They set a dog on him and he ran off, it says. Now—this bit is important—he claims to have dropped his cravat as he ran."

Holmes's face contorted as he wondered, "Yes, but… how does one drop something that is tied around one's neck?"

"Exactly, Holmes!" I said. "Simpson is clearly lying. And it is that lie that cemented his guilt, in the eyes of the police. You see, that cravat was found in the dead man's hand. Straker's body was found on an abandoned stretch of moor, with the back of his head bashed in, a cut on his leg, Simpson's cravat in one hand and a cataract knife in the other. Based on that, Inspector Gregory concluded that Simpson returned later that evening and stole Silver Blaze, but was seen by Straker, who grabbed a cataract knife and gave chase. Inspector Gregory goes on to infer that Straker caught up to Simpson out on the moor. The two of them fought, Straker received a wound in the thigh from his own knife, then was finally brought down by a single blow to the back of the head from a heavy 'Penang lawyer'-style walking stick, which Simpson had in his possession."

"It's looking pretty poor for Simpson, eh?"

"So far, but listen to this: Straker's coat was found hung on a hawthorn bush, not far from his body."

"Minions! Get me that coat!" Holmes ordered. Mud-Splat disappeared for a quick instant, then returned bowing and proffering a battered workman's jacket. It was well used and much worn, but basically unremarkable. In the pockets, I found a tallow candle, matches and a bill for twenty-two guineas for a lady's dress, which had been sold to one "Mr. Derbyshire".

"That's an odd assortment," I said.

"What does it mean?" Holmes asked.

"No idea. But the important thing is this: the coat was hung on a nearby bush."

"Er... But I don't..." Holmes was not the only confused party; several of the demons were looking perturbed as well.

"Well, it is one of five points that makes Inspector Gregory's theory just ludicrous! First: Straker sees a thief, so he reaches for the nearest weapon—so far, so good—but he finds a cataract knife? That is a surgical tool, as the name implies. What would a cataract knife be doing in a stable? It has a small, narrow, flexible blade—ideal for surgery but something close to useless as a weapon. And I don't think I've ever been to a stable that didn't have shovels, shoeing hammers, hook knives and all manner of tools, both blunt and sharp, that would have served better."

"Hmm... I hadn't thought of that," said Holmes.

"Nor has Inspector Gregory, it seems. Second point: Straker took no horse. If you saw a thief escaping on foot, having just stolen the *fastest horse in England*, would you simply run after him? Might you not fear the thief would simply mount up and gallop away, the instant he saw you? Straker was a horse trainer, surrounded by horses, yet he went on foot? Preposterous!"

"Ooooooooh!" Even the demons seemed impressed by that one. I got a smattering of muddish, barkish, meat-wingish applause.

"Third point," I continued, "the positioning of the clothes. The cravat was in Straker's hand. I don't care how hard you pull, you don't yank off a cravat that is tied around somebody's throat. He'd have strangled Simpson before then, or broken his neck. And what of the coat? Do we presume Straker chased his man down, offered battle, but begged a moment before they began to carefully hang his coat upon a tree? And fourth point: no alarm was raised. No noise was reported, not so much as the dog barking. Let us keep in mind that the same dog had been set on Simpson earlier that evening; are you telling me he wouldn't bark if he saw his earlier quarry returning in the dead of night? And why did Straker not seek help? His own wife and three stable lads were sleeping within earshot. Why did he not cry out as he set out after Simpson?"

"And what of the final point?" asked Holmes. I will admit, I relished those times when my deductions caught him up.

"Fifth," I announced, "the wound is to the back of Straker's head. If two men are involved in a physical altercation, wouldn't they be facing each other? Why would one of them turn around long enough to allow the other fellow to land such a haymaker? Can you imagine the strength necessary to crush a skull with a walking stick? I don't know why, but it seems to be a uniquely British failing to view a walking stick as a deadly instrument. We do it all the time."

"Inspired! Genius!" Holmes proclaimed, then leaned towards me and asked, "So, what *did* happen?"

"Oh… er… well, I hadn't gotten that far," I admitted. "It's hard to guess, without seeing the clues or examining the body, but…"

And then I realized what I'd said. I lunged towards Holmes crying, "Wait!"

Yet in that moment between realization and action, Holmes declared, "Bring me the body of John Straker!"

"Damn it, Holmes!" I cried as a pair of gleeful demonettes dropped Straker's days-old corpse on top of the three unfortunate horses. "Oh, very nice! What a fantastic pile of carnage you've constructed, and where I take my tea, too!"

But Holmes ignored me. He had drawn himself up into an impressive stance with both hands raised. "To my left hand, I summon the walking stick of Fitzroy Simpson, thought to have claimed a life!"

With a crack and a whoosh, the walking stick materialized in mid-air, six feet or so from Holmes, speeding towards his hand. He caught it and continued, "To my right, I call the knife of John Straker, which is thought to— Ow! Agh! By the gods!"

"That was nobody's fault but yours, Holmes."

"Yes. Yes, I know. Remind me, Watson, if I ever

summon a bladed instrument again, to call for it to arrive *handle first*."

"Please don't do it again," I said. "I'm quite concerned about the amount of magic you're using today and all this congress with demons…"

"Well anyway, Watson, you've got your clues. Now, what do you make of them?"

"Well to start with, let's have a look at this…" I pulled the cataract knife from where it had lodged through Holmes's right palm.

"Aaaaaarh! Damn!"

"As I guessed, this is an instrument of surgery, not a weapon. And see, if I hold it next to Straker's right hand, the blade points right at the cut on the outside of his thigh? This is just where the blade would be if his arm were hanging naturally. Yes, I think the wound was self-inflicted and accidental."

"And this?" Holmes asked, handing me the walking stick.

"Hmm… Let's see if we can get Straker turned over."

Up to that point, it had not occurred to me that the parliament of demons might follow my command, but I learned that it was indeed possible when three of the little blighters gleefully flipped Straker face down on the pile of horse chunks.

"Yes… ahem… thank you," I mumbled.

It took me only an instant to realize what had happened. "Look here!" I said. "See how the impact site is larger than the weighted orb on the end of this stick? Far larger! And furthermore, though the base is rounded, just here, the sides are flat. What fools we've been, Holmes! And that Inspector Gregory fellow even more so. He laid the murder on Simpson because he thought there were only two individuals present at the scene. He overlooked an obvious third party and it is that forgotten third who did the deed."

"Eh? Who?" asked Holmes.

"Silver Blaze. That is a horseshoe mark."

The tiny demons chittered and cheered.

Holmes, with a scandalized look, shouted, "Oh, bad horse! Murderer! Why, I'm almost ashamed to be holding a betting slip in his name."

"I'm not sure how much blame we can assign to the horse, Holmes."

"But, Watson, don't you see? He must have lured Straker out onto the moor to do him in!"

"And why would a horse do that?"

Holmes shrugged. "Hatred? Personal vendetta? Oh! What if Silver Blaze had placed a large bet on another horse—"

"Horses do not bet on horse races, Holmes."

"Why not? They're the ones who have to run them. And who better to tell the fitness of a particular horse, than another horse?"

"Nevertheless, it is not the custom."

"But *why* not?"

"We just don't allow it, all right?" I huffed, adding, "Horses don't tend to pack a lot of cash around with them, anyway."

"Fine, then. Fine," Holmes retorted. "If you think my theory is so ridiculous, what did happen then? Eh?"

I squinted at the newspaper article, then at the pile of human and equine wreckage that lay atop the remains of my coffee table. So many clues, so many strange occurrences and questions, yet I could devise no narrative which tied them all together.

"I don't know," I said. "There's still so much that remains hidden… For instance, what the devil was Straker doing with that cataract knife?"

"Oh!" Willow-Bark shouted. "I knows! I knows!"

He gestured eagerly to two of the other sprites. The three of them popped out of existence for a moment, only to return the next instant and deposit three perfectly normal-looking sheep in my sitting room. If I was a bit surprised by this, my own alarm was nothing compared to that of the sheep, who stared about wild-eyed and bleated their protest. Two of them did, anyway. The third was elderly and must have seen one or two strange things before, as the change in scenery seemed to upset her very little. She limped over to the Afghan rug, sniffed it, then turned up her nose in disdain at the rather poor grazing options on offer.

She *limped*.

"Wait…" I mumbled. A strange idea had just begun to intrude itself upon me. I jumped at the other two sheep and shouted, "Ha!" The two of them recoiled in alarm and limped away as fast as they could. "All three lame," I said. "All three. This is beginning to come together, Holmes.

Ah! The candle! Oh! Ah! The dressmaker's bill!"

I leapt to the coat and again emptied Straker's pockets. After unfolding and checking the bill, I told Holmes, "Luck is with us. This is a London address; I shall take a cab around and speak to the man. If my guess is correct, he holds the final clue."

"If he does," Holmes replied, "then there is no time for cab rides."

There was a flash and loud cracking noise and suddenly a confused dressmaker stood in front of me. He had the most magnificent bush of graying sideburns and an expression of deepest befuddlement.

I turned to my friend and shouted, "Holmes! Magic!" But he just gave me a little shrug and smiled.

The dressmaker was staring about, left and right, sputtering his confusion. I approached him, showed him the bill and said, "You are Mr. Alfred Hill?"

"Why, yes I am."

"I wonder if you could help me identify this man."

I gestured back to Straker's earthly remains, which were instantly seized by three or four tiny demons and flipped face up with just as much zest as they'd flipped him down.

"Good Lord!" the dressmaker cried. "Whatever have you done to Mr. Derbyshire? And, are those... horse corpses? What are all these little creatures?"

"Disregard them," I suggested and, realizing it was time to do some damage control, asked, "But do tell me, Mr. Hill, is there any chance you might be sleeping right now? Might this all be a disturbing dream?"

"No, sir, it is the middle of my working day. I was speaking with Mrs. Handswaddle a moment before, I am sure of it…"

"Did you perhaps have a drink or two, at lunch?" I asked.

"I would never!"

"Hmm… Are you taking any medications right now?"

Alfred Hill touched the side of his face and admitted, "A bit of laudanum, for this toothache."

"Ah-ha! I am, of course, a figment of your imagination," I told him, "but I am also a certified medical doctor and I can state with confidence that laudanum is more than capable of causing just such a hallucination. I would urge you to be judicious in its application in future."

"Oh… er… thank you," Mr. Hill stammered.

I turned to Holmes and suggested through clenched teeth and with raised eyebrows, "I think he can *go now*."

There was a second flash and crack. Mr. Alfred Hill was gone.

"And do we still feel we aren't overusing magic today, Holmes?"

"No!" he cried, and his voice was deep and rumbling. "I will have the truth! Truth! Triumph! Gambling addiction!"

"Easy, Holmes, easy! I think I've almost got it solved. I still don't know where Silver Blaze is, but I'm sure he can't have gone far. He must still be on Dartmoor."

"Very well," Holmes rumbled. "To my side, I summon—"

"Don't you do it! There's no room here for every horse on Dartmoor, not even all the race horses."

Holmes nodded in concession, but not the one I was hoping for. He waved one hand and two walls of our sitting room tore away. Beyond them lay an open expanse of gray, blasted dust. The sky above was an infinity of swirling black clouds, intermingled with tendrils of red mist—a sky of vaporized obsidian.

"Oh, very good, Holmes. Very nice. Well done, indeed."

"Now there is room. To my side, I summon all the race horses who dwell on Dartmoor."

From the swirling mists, they emerged, frightened hooves stirring up puffs of ash. White ones, gray ones, black, chestnut, dappled and paint—there must have been more than three dozen.

"Which of you is Silver Blaze?" Holmes demanded in his otherworldly baritone.

A note to horse trainers: your average steed does not respond well to demonic threat-questions, especially if they've just been teleported out of their comfy stalls to an unfamiliar hellscape. They whickered their fear and ran about. One stumbled, two reared and one flicked his ears forwards.

"Which of you is Silver Blaze?" Holmes repeated, even more threateningly.

"Holmes, come now, you're scaring them," I said.

"But I need to know—"

"It's that one."

"Eh?" said Holmes, his expression doubtful. "But that

one doesn't have a silver blaze on his nose."

"You'll notice, though, that he does have boot-black smeared all over his face and some wonderfully unconvincing spots of the same, painted on his rump. I suspect someone has tried to mask his identity. Yet, there are some traits that are harder to hide than others."

"Such as?"

"He pricked up his ears when you called his name."

"Then he must answer for his crimes," Holmes growled and began closing on the unfortunate equine.

"No, Holmes, I think I've figured it out. The fault does not rest with Silver Blaze—he is the victim. Or, let me say, the *intended* victim. No, your true criminal is there."

Holmes followed my outstretched finger to the gristly pile the demons had constructed, then asked, "One of the other horses?"

"No. The man. Straker. It's all his fault."

"Come now, Watson, are you suggesting he bashed the back of his own head in with a horseshoe? Queer method of suicide, don't you think? Full marks for originality, I admit, but—"

"No, it's… Listen, the bill in his pocket was in the name of Mr. Derbyshire, correct?"

"It was."

"And the dressmaker knew him by that name as well. So, we will start there. Why does a Dartmoor horse trainer have a secret identity for buying dresses in London?"

"He doesn't want anybody to know he wears dresses?"

"Holmes, that is…" I paused and admitted, "…

actually possible. Still, I think it more likely that he has a mistress—one with expensive tastes. Twenty-two guineas on a trainer's salary? That's a bit steep, don't you think? Let us suppose that Straker was in a little over his head, over-keeping his kept woman. He'd be desperate to make money. Enter Fitzroy Simpson—a gambler, a bookie and a fixer with a nose for mischief and an idea. Silver Blaze is the far-and-away favorite for the Wessex Cup; therefore, if he were to fail to win, whatever horse did would pay back at stellar odds. Simpson could make a fortune if only he had leverage on somebody with access to Silver Blaze."

"Straker?" Holmes wondered.

"Yes! Simpson is a familiar villain to everyone on the racing scene—always snooping for an advantage. Suppose he heard of Straker's money troubles. Suppose Simpson approached Straker and taught him how to subtly hobble an animal with a cataract knife, and promised to share his winnings."

"Oh! And that's why we find a surgical tool in a horse stable," Holmes realized. "But how would Straker hide what he'd done?"

"Ha! There's a fine point. Though it is possible to weaken a tendon without leaving an easily visible wound, it takes a practiced hand. So, he did."

"Er… did what?"

"Practiced," I laughed. "Do you see those sheep? They all drag their left hind leg! It would be too much to be coincidence even if your little demon hadn't told us they'd all felt the touch of that blade. Straker practiced on them, learning to lame an animal without externally maiming it."

"Cad!" cried Holmes and he gave the body of John Straker an angry kick. Then he paused to consider for a moment. "You know though, Watson, your theory still does not cover the cravat, the coat or the dog who didn't bark."

"Well I haven't gotten that far," I said, "but let us further suppose Simpson has his doubts about Straker. He comes by to check on his reluctant accomplice before the race, just to be sure Straker was really going to do it."

"And they fought and Straker pulled his cravat off?" Holmes offered.

"No. They talked and Straker told him he had nothing soft, yet strong enough to hobble Silver Blaze's front legs, so he wouldn't run off when Straker cut the back one. Simpson *loaned* him the cravat. Rope would leave a mark on Blaze's front legs if he struggled. But a silk cravat…"

"Then why did Straker set the dog on him?"

"Maybe they were caught speaking together," I shrugged. "Let us recall that Simpson is a well-known rogue in racing circles. I'm sure he would prefer being run off by a dog to having his plans come to light."

"And why did the dog not bark when Simpson came back?"

"Because he *didn't*. Why would he? Once he was sure of Straker and the tools were in place, all that remained was for Straker to lead Silver Blaze far enough onto the moor that he would not be heard if he screamed out at the cut. Remember that there were no witnesses placing

Simpson at the scene of Straker's death. It was only the presence of Simpson's cravat that suggested his guilt."

Holmes nodded his approval.

"The contents of Straker's pockets paint the scene," I continued. "He brought the candle to light his work, the cravat to secure the horse from bolting, and the knife to make his cut. But he must have done something wrong; he must have spooked the horse. Instead of getting rich, he got his brains kicked in."

"Wait! So Silver Blaze did kick him to death?" said Holmes, recoiling.

"Well… yes."

"Then he must answer for his crimes!" Holmes tottered cadaverously towards the terrified stallion, pointed an accusing finger in the poor horse's face, and demanded, "Well, Murder Horse? How do you explain yourself?"

"Holmes, horses cannot—"

I was a fool not to see it coming. Holmes was utterly without governance that day, and would not shy from any expenditure of magic, no matter how pointless. Silver Blaze tossed his mane, thrust forward his massive jaw and said, "Explain it? Why should I be called upon to explain the operation of hearts and hooves that have felt the gentle touch of love and—so close thereupon—venomous and intimate betrayal? They are forces of nature, sir! If their ways are foreign to you, you would be better served to seek their secrets by gazing upon the delicate intricacies of the new-formed leaf than asking a simple sufferer, such as I."

"Oh," I noted. "That's a fairly eloquent… horse."

"Did you kill that man?" Holmes demanded, indicating Straker's body.

"If I did, the transgression was slight compared to the one he offered me! Do you know what he meant to do? A cut on the leg—no great thing, it would seem. Yet to me, it was the destruction of my very identity—a way to rob me of that gift which makes me special. I gave him my heart, my body and my soul and see how he repaid it?"

My eyebrows went up. "So, you and Straker were…"

"We were together," Silver Blaze confirmed. "True, for us there was no legal course towards matrimony—"

"Yes, and I shouldn't hold my breath for one, I think…"

"But the heart will always know its home and I had found mine. Or so I thought. I knew not what secret delight he intended when he led me out upon the moor that night, but I flushed with exhilaration to discover it. I rather hoped he might wear his special dress."

"Wait! Straker *did* purchase that dress for himself?" I cried.

Silver Blaze snorted. "He purchased it for my benefit, sir. A grand gesture, to impress himself upon my notice. And let me tell you: it worked. Oh, you should have seen him in it!"

"Sad," said Holmes. "How very sad. Watson thinks Straker may have tried to lame you to secure funds to pay for that very dress."

Silver Blaze recoiled. His mouth dropped open and for a moment he stood as dumb as… well… as I think horses ought to, if I'm honest. Then his great head drooped towards the floor and he muttered, "What a world."

Holmes went to him and laid a comforting hand on his shoulder. Blaze gave a great, equine sigh, sniffed back a tear and said, "It would almost have been worth it. Such an exquisitely crafted thing... By God, it made him look just like Catherine the Great."

"No! All right! That's enough!" I cried. "Enough of horses talking! Holmes, turn the magic off!"

"But, Watson—"

"No! Off!"

"As you say, Watson," said Holmes. Silver Blaze looked as if he wished to lodge a protest, but even as he began it the unseeable light of arcane possibility faded from the room and whatever words the wise horse had chosen emerged as a simple snort. Holmes stood staring into the depths of Silver Blaze's dark, liquid eyes for a few moments. I could tell he was deeply moved, yet seemed to be struggling with an ethical dilemma. Finally, he spoke. "Very well, I shall forgive you. But it's a very bad thing for a horse to do. Do you understand that? No murder! Bad horse! If you make a habit of it, I shall be cross with you. However, in view of the extenuating circumstances, you shall still be allowed to run in the Wessex Cup."

"Actually, Holmes—"

"And I shall keep this wager in your name—"

"Holmes, there's no—"

"Which I'm sure shall be the start of a life of magnificent fiscal irresponsibility—"

"*Holmes!*"

"No murder! Bad horse!"

"What do you want, Watson? I was talking to this horse."

"It's too late."

"Eh?"

I pointed at the clock. "Too late. The gate has dropped. If the Wessex Cup is not over, it shall be in only a few seconds."

"No!" Holmes cried out. The fire lit in his eyes again and swirls of the ashen dust rose and danced around him. "Unfair! We worked so hard!"

"But... well... at least we solved the mystery," I stammered.

"Insufficient! Silver Blaze will run the Wessex Cup!"

"But, it's too late! He didn't!"

"*He did!*" Holmes roared. "Rhett Khan! Rhett Khan, mighty one, hear my call!"

"What? Who is Rhett Khan? Holmes, what are you—"

"A fact has occurred which displeases me!" Holmes intoned. "Undo it, Rhett Khan, and replace it with a better one!"

Holmes walked up to Silver Blaze and gave him a ceremonial bump on the snout, as if he were knighting him. Silver Blaze recoiled back in surprise and then...

Well...

...became a silver blaze. It was as if the flesh, muscle and bone dissolved from him. He became a being of living ether, of airy strands and silver mist. I could see all the way through him—see the ghostly muscles pulling phantom bones as the great, translucent heart thudded and strained. Then, he was gone.

"Holmes! What did you do?"

"Oh, I've got a demon friend who's in charge of reality," Holmes said. "I had him send Silver Blaze to the race. I look forward to news of his victory. I have confidence in him, Watson. He's a good horse, notwithstanding that one murder."

Holmes sagged. The exhaustion came over him suddenly, but with such totality that I almost feared he would fall down dead all over again. I ran to steady him. Our guests showed far less concern for Holmes than they did for his promises. Willow-Bark ran up before Holmes and challenged him. "Sorcerer! We have fulfilled our oath! Where is our payment? Where is our home?"

"Middlesbrough," Holmes answered. "Go. You will find it. You should be drawn strongly thence, it being the only place on this earth you can exist, uninvited. Your contract is fulfilled."

The tiny roars of triumph echoed off into the vastness of the obsidian skies for a moment, then silence took it all. The minor demons of Holmes's impromptu parliament were gone. I couldn't say I missed them, though I had rather hoped each of them might pick up a dead horse or a live sheep and take it with them.

"Holmes, this must be put to right."

"Eh?"

"We can't very well live in a surreal plane of ash with a pile of carcasses on our coffee table."

"Why not? We've got three sheep, now, and all these horses."

"Holmes…"

"Oh, very well, Watson," he sighed. "It won't be easy, you know. It tends to take more magic to undo a thing than it took to do it in the first place."

This claim appeared to be true for, as he slowly cleared the bodies and restored our walls, he grunted and strained. He'd wave a hand at a thing that displeased him and it would instantly disappear, but he was left paler and shakier with each correction he made. When our rooms were at last restored, he was too weak even to speak to me. He gave me a look as if to say, "There," then turned and staggered back to his bedroom and collapsed on his disgusting mattress.

He stayed there, unmoving, for a day and a half. I would have feared him dead, were it not for his ragged, panting breaths. It wasn't until Thursday that I brought the paper into his room and told him, "You won."

"Eh?"

"Or rather, Silver Blaze won."

"Oh? Well, I must say, that's glad tidings."

"Sort of," I said. "He was the overwhelming favorite, let us recall, and propriety fairly demands that you return the original bet to Lestrade."

"Which would leave me?"

"A little less than four pounds."

"Four? That's hardly worth it."

"What sum would you have preferred, Holmes? Need I remind you of your customary disregard for the value of money?"

"Ye gods! That's right! I don't care about money!

Well… how am I to maintain a gambling addiction if I don't care for the spoils?"

"I couldn't say."

"This is dashed inconvenient, Watson," Holmes huffed. "Ah well, perhaps I'll try the monocle."

"I don't see why not," I said. "Yet, there is more to the matter, I'm afraid. Your victory was not without cost."

Not only did Silver Blaze win the Wessex Cup, he has won every single horse race held in Great Britain since. As soon as the gate drops, one of the animals will buckle and vomit, collapsing in its gate as the spectral form of Silver Blaze erupts out of its body, bearing its surprised jockey on a nightmare ride to victory. He's getting faster and faster, but ever less real.

The sensationalism of such events has, of course, rocked Britain and the world. It's also somewhat spoiled the traditional betting custom, since the outcome of every race is now guaranteed. The only interesting things left to bet on are who will come second and which horse will be unfortunate enough to spawn the ghost of Silver Blaze.

With so much national attention focused on the case, it wasn't long until the truth came to light. We gave my information to Lestrade, who wasted no time verifying most of it and solving the few details I had not accounted for. I was pleased to have guessed most of it correctly. Well… at least as far as the humans were concerned. Holmes was quick to point out my shortcomings. "You shall never truly be the greatest detective so long as the tender intricacies of the equine heart remain a mystery to you," he said.

"Well then, Holmes, I wish *never* to be the greatest detective."

As to the few details I'd missed, here is how they played out: Simpson, though unhappy to be caught in his attempted fraud, was nevertheless pleased to see his murder charges dropped.

The boot-black that had been applied to hide Silver Blaze's identity proved to be the fault of Silas Brown, neighbor and bitter rival of Silver Blaze's owner, Colonel Ross. Inspector Gregory eventually concluded that, after the botched hobbling, Blaze had roamed the moor until— scenting one of Brown's mares in heat—he wandered into the stables. If he'd taken the time to get to know Silver Blaze as Holmes and I did, he'd have known this was a ridiculous supposition. Nevertheless, Silas Brown wasn't long in realizing his windfall. The one horse who stood to beat his own contender had just wandered, unattended, into his hands. As soon as it became clear that nobody knew Blaze's whereabouts, the temptation was such that Brown could not resist disguising the horse and deciding that maybe the best time to return him would be *after* the Wessex Cup.

We fooled him, I suppose.

Yet, we'd done a great deal more than that. For the first time, I'd seen Holmes do real and permanent damage to the fabric of reality. Magic was now, irretrievably, in the public consciousness. The first sign that our world was unwell could be seen by anybody who cared to purchase a race ticket, anywhere in Britain. Holmes took this as a personal defeat. Often I would catch him reading the racing report with a pained expression on his face. "Help me remember, Watson," he would say, "Rhett Khan-ing a thing always causes more problems than it solves."

And there was more. The Williamson family crypt sits in a disused and disregarded cemetery in the country west of Middlesbrough. Once, the Williamson crypt was the pride of that humble place of rest—the only granite building in a field of modest limestone markers. Once, it was a repository of disused flesh, a home for dry bones. Now it is constantly alive with chirps and chitters and squeals.

Now, it is the house of parliament.

THE REIGATEWAY TO
ANOTHER WORLD

AS I LAY IN SLUMBER ONE NIGHT IN EARLY SPRING, I WAS awakened by a muted clamor. I listened in case I was being summoned by Holmes, who often called me to help button his shirts and such—his mummified fingers had their limitations. But no, the only thing I could hear was an early spring storm just outside my window. The wind rattled the panes, and as it curled over the rooftops and around London's irregular forest of chimneys, the wind took on that familiar, hollow muttering. It sounded like an old woman chiding herself or, on the occasion of a particularly potent gust, as if it were calling out, "Holmmmmmmmmmes."

I laughed at my fancy; night-time imagination can be a macabre thing. Yet the safety of a good bed is one of life's greatest comforts and this benefit is increased, not diminished, by the sound of a storm whose winds cannot penetrate one's sanctum. I pulled the blankets up around my shoulders, settled in and smiled.

For about six seconds.

Because, yes: the wind was absolutely, unequivocally calling Holmes's name.

"*Holmes... Holmes?*" came a hollow, reedy voice, quickly followed by the whoosh-and-thump of the street door being blown open and crashing against the wall.

"*Holmes?*" called the wind.

And I had the sudden realization that I wished to speak to the exact same person. "Hoooooooolmes!" I leapt from my bed and into Holmes's chamber. "Holmes, the wind is asking for you!"

"Well, what does it want?" he asked, and tutted at the intrusion.

"Er... I don't know. I haven't inquired."

"But won't you, Watson? I am somewhat indisposed."

This was true. Holmes remained in feeble shape. He spent his days and nights propped up in his bed, begging for toast and soup, slowly recomposing.

"No, Holmes, you don't understand: it is not normal for the wind to speak."

"I am surprised at you, Watson. Afraid of a little wind..."

"Also, it seems to have opened the front door."

This, at last, seemed to pique his interest. "Hmm... So it seems unlikely to be *just* the wind, then."

As if in answer, there came a heavy *tunk, tunk, tunk*-ing up the stairs, like someone thumping the steps with a heavy oaken staff. The sound drew ever closer to our own door, accompanied by a scraping, like a handful of sticks being drawn across a wall.

"Best get out of bed, then," Holmes grumbled. "Dashed impertinence... All hours... Honestly..."

"*Holmes? Holmes, I need your help,*" the voice moaned,

from just outside our door. I believed it for not one second. Though it still sounded like wind being drawn through some unseen crevice, its tone was wheedling, mocking— exactly the way a lion would taunt a wildebeest, "Oh no, please don't hurt me, Mr. Harmless Herbivore!"

"Get the door, Watson," Holmes suggested.

"*What?*"

"Well, it's just such a long way over there, you know. I'm really not at my best. I'll just stand here in the hall and speak to… whatever that is."

"*Help meeeeeeeee.*" *Tunk, tunk, tunk. Scrrrrrrrrrrrreck, click, click.*

"Um… Holmes, are you sure that's wise?"

"You are perfectly safe, Watson, I assure you."

Despite my companion's history of frequently, incorrectly assuring my safety, I crept closer to the door. Now there came a rattling knock and, "*Holmes? I need your help.*"

I looked back at him and let my eyes ask, "Are you sure?"

"Yes, yes," replied his twice-flapping hand.

I sucked in breath. I gritted my teeth. I opened the door.

There was nothing there.

Then the scarecrow leaned in from his hiding place beside the door and grabbed me by the throat. He smelled musty and wet. His clothes hung dank and weathered across his fence-pole frame. His fingers were dried scratchy sticks, his face a grinning pumpkin stuck atop a rough-hewn pole. In its rictus smile there was something that closely resembled triumph. I cannot answer to its effectiveness at frightening crows, but it worked pretty well on me.

"Aaaaaigh!" I cried.

"*Aaaaaigh!*" it agreed, but in a high-pitched, mocking whine that left no doubt as to its low opinion of my character. I froze, forgetting to struggle for a moment, stunned by the impertinence of the beast. If someone must be strangled, why then, someone must be strangled, yet I see no reason or excuse to do it so *disrespectfully*.

I paused, unsure whether to fight for my life, or reproach the thing for its churlishness. As I dithered, the air around me exploded with purple light. Three bolts of violet flame howled past me in irregular arcs and slammed into my scarecrow assailant. The first struck him dead center and cracked his wooden backbone in two. The second smote away one of his arms and sent it clattering down the stairs. The third passed so close to my cheek that I feared it had singed my whiskers away (and I proved to be half right, for though the morning would reveal that cheek to be hairless, the stubble had not burned, it had rotted). This final blast caught the scarecrow right in the middle of his brow. His head exploded into purple-flaming wads of pumpkin-glop, which spattered themselves all across the opposite wall and the front of my nightshirt. The wrecked scarecrow collapsed backwards into a corner and moved no more. With a gasp, I set about the task of stomping out the little spatters of flame, lest they find purchase and burn down our home.

"There," said Holmes, with an air of exhausted finality, his outstretched fingers still smoking. "That's all settled. Back to bed."

He turned back towards his room, but was interrupted

by my observation: "Whhuaaaaaaaauah! Aiigh!"

"Watson! Hush! Do you want to wake Mrs. Hudson?" His tone turned piteous. "Please, *please* do not wake Mrs. Hudson. Oh, I don't know how I could tolerate her at the moment."

"But... what was that thing?"

"Oh, you know, just one of those... pumpkin... scarecrow... monster... thingies. They're quite common; you read about them in the paper all the time."

"No you don't!"

"Well, of course you do. I think one of them... oh, I don't know... robbed a bank last week or something."

He was edging back towards his room, eager to end this conversation. Yet I was unwilling to let him go.

"Well known, is it? In all the papers? What are they called, then, if everybody is so familiar with them?"

"Oh. You know... pumpkin... scarething... with crows... Pumpcrow! That was it: merely a pumpcrow, Watson."

"Pumpcrow?" I howled at him. "*Pumpcrow?*"

But it was too late; Holmes fell down upon his mattress and there he lay, insensible to the world. Shaking with anger and no small amount of residual fear, I turned and stomped off to my own room.

When I awoke... Well, no... that is a lie. When I decided it was time to stop fearfully huddling under my blankets, I found Holmes still sprawled out upon his bed. Feeling that

I needed some air, I hurriedly dressed and stepped out.

There, just outside our door, amidst the wreckage of our pumpcrow assailant, stood Mrs. Hudson. She did not look well pleased by the morning's discovery. Lacking an explanation, I realized my only hope lay in taking the offensive. Even as she opened her mouth to begin her vicious harangue, I tutted, "*Mrs. Hudson*, I realize that this is your home and that decorating choices outside my rented chambers are not mine to make. Nevertheless, madam, Holmes and I do business here and I think we would be most appreciative if, in the future, you could maintain an entryway decor that is more welcoming to our visitors!"

I harrumphed past her, down the stairs and out onto Baker Street. Once there, I let my feet carry me where they would. I had no destination, only troubled thoughts.

Holmes could not stay in London; that much was clear. He had too many enemies and too many friends. Moriarty's men and the occasional pumpcrow seemed to have no difficulty determining his whereabouts and I could think of no better time to strike at Holmes than now. If word got out that he was enfeebled, the previous evening's assault might prove to be only the opening act of a greater tragedy. What would stop Grogsson and Lestrade coming round as soon as they got a case that stumped them, to quite interrupt Holmes's recovery? And clients: was there any reason to suppose that they would cease their pleas, just because Holmes was mending? Oh, and it was nothing short of miraculous that Mrs. Hudson had yet to discover that Holmes had returned to her care. Likely, it was only her extreme indifference that kept her from asking after him. If she discovered his current state, what would she do? Panic? Evict us? Call an exorcist? The more I thought it over, the more I realized: if a moment's peace were on the cards for Warlock Holmes, it would not be found on Baker Street.

Here, let me pause to mention one of Holmes's most infuriating traits: his remarkable good fortune. Let us suppose Holmes were in the mood to read the newspaper, but had none. He might go to the window to catch a breeze and while there, he might stretch his hand out to check for rain. As soon as he did, a cart-driver on the street below would suffer a sudden heart attack. His cart—loaded with innumerable panes of window-glass—would veer astray, plunging through man and horse and flower-girl alike, tipping glass left and right and generally shredding half the people on the street until it at last collided with a newsstand, slicing the proprietor into several dozen meat strips and propelling hundreds of newspapers high into the air. One of which would land, neat as you like, in Holmes's extended palm.

My own luck was identical, except that instead of a newspaper landing in my outstretched hand, it would be a disembodied loop of the newspaperman's abdominal viscera. This would surely be followed by all the surviving people on the street crying out, "Tragedy! Catastrophe! Oh please, is there a doctor present who wouldn't mind patching up our several dozen wounded for no financial compensation?"

In those early days, I still supposed this to be blind luck. I had yet to realize that it was in fact demons, doing subtle, unbidden favors for Holmes. I should have known better sooner, as is evidenced by what happened next. The exact second I decided that Holmes must leave London, I caught my walking stick between two cobblestones, slipped sideways and tipped bodily into the fellow to my right. I hardly managed to stop the two of us from tumbling into the gutter. I was beginning to formulate an apology, when I caught a glimpse of who it was I had upset and immediately snapped to salute. I would not have thought I served long enough for such things to become habit, but there I was: spine straight, fingers to my brow, shouting, "Sir! Colonel Hayter, sir!"

The old gentleman blinked twice, squinted at me a moment, then said, "Oh... hullo... that's Watson, isn't it?"

"Sir!"

"At ease, Watson. No need for such formalities. I'm retired, you know. Would have thought you would be too, after that gunshot wound."

"I am, sir. Only... I suppose you surprised me. Dreadfully sorry. Where are you bound, Colonel?"

"Oh! I thought I'd take a walk in the park, only I can't find the damned thing. It has to be around here somewhere."

"Just around the corner, sir. Shall I see you to it?"

"That would be capital, Watson, capital!"

So I led my former commander back past my rooms, towards Regent's Park. Though it had been only a few years since I'd seen him last, he appeared notably more gray, more bent. It made me sad to see him so; I'd always liked the man.

"How is it that you find yourself in London, sir?"

"Oh, I don't know." He shrugged. "I just wandered here, I think."

"I thought you had that country place down in Surrey, near... Where was it?"

"Reigate! Reigate is its name! God damn the place! God damn!" He shouted this with such sudden passion that half the street turned to stare at him. "The devil made that place, Watson, which I would not have minded, if he had not then deeded it to me!"

"But I had always thought the idea of retiring to be a country squire was rather... nice."

"Did you know, Watson, did you know that the snow stayed unseasonably late this year? And yet, *and yet*, the lilac buds came two days earlier? Did you know that? I did! Why? Because it's the most exciting thing that's happened to me in two whole years! Hellish place!"

"Oh. Well, perhaps invite some visitors?" I suggested.

"I tried to. I tried. 'Come down to the country,' I said. That's what Londoners do, isn't it? They get sick and go to the country to recuperate. Set up the whole south wing as an infirmary. Know what I got? My milksop, fart-wit nephew came down because he had the flu. Moped around for a week or so, before he realized just how boring Surrey is, then off he ran. Then my niece got 'the vapors' after reading a saucy French novel. She only lasted two days and I can't say I miss her. Oh, I want a real patient, Watson!"

A man with stories to tell! With scars! With some horrid tropical disease that's slowly dissolving him, you know?"

I stopped, stunned, in the middle of the street. "So, what you want most in the world is to provide an out-of-London getaway to an odd, interesting person who has horrible physical afflictions?"

"In a perfect world: yes. But you know, we don't always get what we want, do we, Watson?"

"You might, sir. I really think you *might*."

I smuggled Holmes out by night, with a blanket over his head, into a waiting carriage with the curtains drawn. To be caught with a corpse in one's possession is one thing; to be caught with a corpse that walks around and asks for soup is quite another. Colonel Hayter met us at the door of his home, as we had agreed, and helped me spirit Holmes out of the sight of the driver and into the infirmary. When I was sure we were unobserved, I handed Hayter the corner of the blanket and allowed him to open Holmes up like a Christmas present.

"Good God! He's marvelous!"

"Thank you, good sir," said Holmes, with a cadaverous bow. "You seem to be a most impressive gentleman, yourself."

From that instant, the two of them were fast friends. Their chief entertainment was in declaring boredom—a practice at which they sometimes tried to best one another, or else they served as a sympathetic ear to the other's travails.

"Do you see that laurel branch out there? Do you see

it?" Colonel Hayter asked, on the third morning after our arrival. He was spending far too much time with Holmes, if indeed this trip were for rest and recovery's sake. Yet his presence so delighted my friend that, even as a doctor, I felt it was not an unwelcome thing.

"I think I see the one you mean," said Holmes.

"Well, it's awful! Look at it! The way it droops! No good will come of a branch like that, and no ill either! Nothing will, because nothing ever happens to it. Look: nothing is happening! Watch!"

"Why, it's not doing a thing! Just hanging off that tree," Holmes agreed.

"Indeed, sir!" thundered Hayter. "Not contributing, not pulling its weight… What purpose does it serve? I tell you, Mr. Holmes, nothing ever happens in Surrey! Nothing!"

After the briefest pause, he added, "Well… apart from the burglary, I mean."

I sat forward in my chair and gave my former commander a hard look. Before coming, I had made him agree that no news that might disturb Holmes should be mentioned in his presence. The very last thing I wanted was for my recovering friend to be presented with a case to solve. Realizing his misstep, Hayter stammered, "Nothing to interest you fellows, I am sure. Somebody broke into old Acton's house—into his library—and stole a few things. Nothing of value, just some old grimoire…"

"What?" I cried, flinging my newspaper to the ground. "Not only have I forbidden this very topic, but… well… it strains credulity! Why would an aging country squire just happen to have an ancient book of magic lying around?"

Hayter gave a guilty shrug. "There's not much else to do."

Fortunately, though it seemed the perfect lure for Holmes's interest, he failed to take the bait. "Ugh," he moaned. "Dreadful. Dull. Let me tell you: most grimoires are filled with utter drivel. Just tedious sorcerers, droning on and on about their favorite subject: themselves."

"Yes… yes I suppose so," Hayter said. "Acton lost nothing but that and an old druidic dagger. He says it was originally used for human sacrifice, but came to serve as his letter opener."

"Ha!" Holmes scoffed. "He's lying. Don't you see? Probably keeps it around in case he ever needs to do himself in—too bored to keep on living, I suspect."

"Just so, just so," said Hayter with visible relief at Holmes's indifference. "Those were the only items taken. And some string."

"String?"

"Yes."

"What kind of string?"

"Oh, I don't know. The usual kind: very small rope."

"But why should a burglar want string?" Holmes wondered. He was sitting up in bed now, looking perplexed. "And why should he want *another man's* string, enough that he breaks into a house to get it?"

"Holmes, this is no business of ours," I insisted, with a warning tone.

"But, Watson, I can't think of any reason he'd need this

man Acton's string in particular," Holmes mused, "unless he were using it to bind something of Acton's. Or to mark off an area he wished to use or possess, which belonged to Acton... I don't suppose this Acton fellow is involved in any property disputes, is he?"

"Er... well... he is," admitted Hayter, shrinking from my withering gaze. "The other magnates of these parts—Mr. Cunningham and his son, Alec—are constantly bickering over this disused old windmill that they say belongs to them instead of Acton. It is a baseless claim. Honestly, I think they only pursue it so they'll have something to stave off the boredom."

"Ha! I shouldn't wonder! Dullest place I've ever been. So quiet... stagnant, even."

I was relieved to see my friend settle back down into bed. Hayter's disclaimer might have been enough to quash Holmes's budding interest if one of the neighbors had not chosen that very moment to come running across the front lawn crying, "Help! Colonel Hayter! Come quickly! Murder! Murder! Oh, it's the best thing ever!"

In a flash, that customary British military briskness reinfused itself into Hayter's aging spine. His eyes gleamed. His back straightened. He practically kicked the French window open, leveled the stem of his pipe at the approaching man and demanded, "Is this true? Has something happened in Surrey?"

"I know! It's quite unaccountable, but no mistake..." the man began, but he did not finish, for his gaze fell upon Holmes. He stopped, mouth still open, blinked.

"Eyes on me, lad, eyes on me!" Hayter insisted. "Now, who is it you think's been murdered, eh?"

"Oh! Bill Kirwan, sir."

"Young William? The Cunninghams' coachman?"

"Yes, sir, that's the one. Everyone's in a right stir. We all… Pardon me, Colonel, but what's the matter with that gentleman?"

He pointed at Holmes, but Hayter blustered, "Never you mind, Randal, never you mind. You just go round the front and wait for me there. I'll fetch my boots and we'll see if someone's really been murdered or what!"

Hayter plopped his still-smoking pipe on the dish beside my chair and shuffled out of the room. To my dismay, Holmes began pulling himself out of bed.

"Holmes! No! You mustn't!" But he tottered to his feet. "I forbid it, Holmes!"

He glanced back at me and just a flicker of a smile crossed his lips. The smoke from Colonel Hayter's pipe, which had been drifting in lazy loops, wrapped itself around my chest. With sudden force, it yanked me backwards into my chair and began winding itself about me like strands of ghostly rope.

"Holmes!"

Without looking back at me, he gave me a little "what can I do about it" shrug and reached for his jacket. The smoke began twining upwards towards my mouth and I realized he meant to gag me with it, so I might raise no protest.

"No, damn it! If you're going, I'm going with you!"

The smoke tendril hesitated, hovering just beside my

right ear. Holmes paused too and wondered aloud, "You won't try to stop me?"

"I promise."

"Then I shall be most happy to have your company, Watson."

And just like that, the smoke released me. To some, it might seem nothing but a trick of the imagination. To me, it was a clear warning: I had no hope of stopping Holmes. The best I could do was go along and try to minimize the damage.

The neighbor, Randal, was waiting upon the front step. Colonel Hayter commanded him to lead us to the scene of the murder, which he dutifully did, though not without stealing several sideways glances at Holmes, who staggered up the hill like the recently-reanimated corpse he was. Despite Holmes's slow pace, we eventually reached the Cunninghams' home. A low stone wall with a wooden gate separated it from the road. On the other side of the lane stood the aforementioned, property-disputed, battered old windmill. It was in such a state of disrepair that it could not possibly be functional, yet its mere proximity to the estate did provide some reason for the Cunninghams to covet it, I supposed.

Around the wooden gate stood a knot of locals, hemming and hawing and muttering to themselves as a bedraggled constable shuffled about, trying to remember how to investigate a crime. As we neared, Colonel Hayter imperiously bellowed, "Make way! Make way, I say! I have brought Inspector Warlock Holmes from London to investigate the matter." His statement at once promoted Holmes to a police rank he did not possess and implied that Colonel Hayter—having heard of the morning's difficulty—had just run all the way to London, secured help and returned. Yet the worst part of the ridiculous statement was that it included a direct invitation to look at Holmes. The skin had yet to grow back over the scorched portion of his face, so his cheekbone was clearly visible. His lips had somewhat un-mummified, but his eyes were still shrunken, milky orbs. The crowd stood and gaped. There was nothing I could do but offer the best explanation I could think of.

"Er... he's not well."

I got a few scattered nods of acceptance, but most of the locals continued to stare.

"Constable Forrester, what has happened here?" Hayter demanded.

"Well, sir... don't really know. Granny Nora saw the body this morning, as she's walkin' down the lane. She come straight round and raised me. I've been here ever since. Word must have got about, though, because..." the beleaguered constable trailed off and gestured meekly at the crowd around him, then added, "It's Bill Kirwan, sure enough. Left him just as I found him."

Perhaps, but he'd also let the gawkers crowd around the body and poke at it. Their feet had churned the ground to a muddy morass and ruined any chance of getting useful footprints. When I commented on my displeasure, Colonel Hayter shouted, "All right, you've seen him. Now, off with you. Only Constable Forrester, Inspector Holmes, Dr.

Watson and myself are to have access to the crime scene. Be about your business."

"But Colonel Hayter, sir," one of the men protested, "this is the only thing that's ever… *happened*."

"All right then," Hayter conceded. "Off to the tavern to have a drink and talk about it."

This was viewed as fine advice. As the happy crowd dispersed, Hayter noted, "Looks like just about everybody came out to see."

"Not everybody," I said, gazing up at the house. "I wonder that Cunningham and his son Alec did not appear. The body is practically in their garden, after all."

"Oh, no," said Forrester. "They was here. They come out, expressed sympathy for Bill and his mum, said it was a shocking event that'd rock the community, gave a bit of good news and headed back inside."

"Good news?"

"They're hiring a new coachman! I mean, we're all very sorry about Bill, but employment vacancies is rare, in these parts."

I pushed past him to examine the body. It didn't take me long to determine a cause of death.

"Holmes, his heart has been torn right out of his chest!"

"That doesn't prove it's murder," said Hayter, who was still unwilling to believe that something had actually happened in Surrey. "Look how sharp these gate posts are. He could have fallen on one and torn his heart out. I imagine we'll find it around here somewhere…"

Since the scene was already disturbed, I allowed

Hayter and Forrester to look around for the "misplaced" heart, while Holmes and I examined the body.

"What do we think, Watson? Redcap? Chupacabra?"

"Not unless they were armed," I said. "Though part of the wound is ragged, the top and right side are clean. Whoever did this used a blade."

"Remarkable."

"That's not the only thing that's odd. There are no bruises, no other cuts, no damage to his clothing—his hair's still combed, for God's sake. If someone were after you with a knife, trying to cut your heart out, don't you think you'd struggle? And look at his face: what would you call that expression?"

"Contentment?" Holmes ventured. "Relief?"

"Hardly what I would have expected. Perhaps he was drugged. Oh! Hello! What's this?"

Clutched in Bill Kirwan's rigid right hand was a piece of paper—a scrap of a handwritten note, torn from a larger whole. Though it had not profited by the morning's mud-bath, it was still legible:

...D AT QUARTER TO TWELVE
...ST, WHICH SHOULD
...WE SHALL
...U ARE RID

"Written in blood," Holmes noted.

"No. *Half* written in blood. Look here, two different people have contributed to this note, alternating words.

The words in blood are written in a strong, confident hand. But these are writ in normal ink and see how shaky the letters are? It is as if the writer were scared. Or else infirm. Why would anybody choose to make a note in this extraordinary fashion?"

To my surprise, Holmes had a ready answer. "Blame. Two men have entered into a confederation to perpetrate dark deeds. One is certain in his conviction. One is not. The strong man wished the other fellow to put his hand to it also—to prove his mettle and take some of the blame upon himself, if ever this should come to light."

It was one of those occasions when I found it hard to guess whether his information came from previous experience or some far-off demon feeding him the answer. Whatever the source, I had to admit the idea made a great deal of sense. I rose and walked over to Constable Forrester.

"Did the victim have anything in either of his hands?" I asked.

Forrester scratched his head. "Er... not that I saw."

Since the entire note would have been more noticeable, that left only two possibilities and one certainty. Possibility one: Granny Nora had taken the rest of the note when she found the body—a remote chance, I thought. Possibility two: the murderer or murderers had ripped the note from Kirwan's hand, failing to notice that a portion of it remained in the dead man's grip. This I thought more likely and it meant that if we could find the other half of the note, its bearer would be our chief suspect.

The certainty: Forrester was an idiot.

I returned to Holmes's side and whispered, "I think Kirwan knew the killers and agreed to come. The words 'at quarter to twelve' suggest an appointment."

"Just before midnight," Holmes noted. "Perfect time to tear a heart out."

"But what did they want with it and where were they going? A disembodied human heart is not the sort of thing you can put in your pocket and go to the shops."

I looked around for answers. The road led off in both directions, so the killers could have made quick progress either way. If they had stayed in the vicinity, there were only two options: the Cunninghams' house or the disused windmill. I pointed to the latter and asked, "Constable Forrester, did you search that old mill?"

"It was locked," he said with a shrug.

"And you let that deter you?"

"Of course I did," he said, defensively. "Every trooper knows: if the door's locked, move on to the next one."

Yes. An idiot.

"We'll get the key from Acton later," I decided. "For now, let us go talk to the Cunninghams."

As the four of us walked to the door, I whispered to Holmes, "Nobody knows about the note but you and me. If anyone should mention it, they may well be the killer. The man in possession of the other half of this note is almost certainly guilty."

Holmes nodded. Hayter knocked. The door swung open to reveal an aging butler with a face like a droopy old hound's. He stared at us blandly.

"Colonel Hayter, Constable Forrester and two London investigators, here to speak to the Cunninghams, father and son," I said.

He gave a curt little bow and retreated, returning swiftly to announce, "The masters will see you in the drawing room. This way."

The instant he led us in, I saw that things were amiss. The whole place stank of brimstone and blood. The room was in disarray; books and papers lay strewn about. Alec Cunningham stood, wearing an expression of frantic fury. His father leaned on the mantel, dewy-eyed and complacent.

"Ah. Hello, chaps," Alec Cunningham said, absolutely failing to appear friendly. "Any luck with the investigation?" His weight was on the balls of his feet, as if he might lunge out to strike us at any moment. His father just looked happy to have company. Cunningham Senior was one of those pleasant, doddering old country gentlemen that England manufactures in extraordinary quantity. His limbs had contracted somewhat with the advancement of age and, as I noted the palsied shaking of his hands, I surmised that I might be looking at one of the authors of our mysterious message.

"Quite a bit of luck," said Holmes, brightly. "It turns out the murderer left part of a no—"

I elbowed him in the stomach. I only meant to stop him speaking, but in my surprise I think I jabbed him harder than I meant to. Holmes reeled to one side, bent double and vomited forth a horrible stream of congealed blood, complete with a few writhing worms. Probably this was some of his own bodily fluid, trapped in his abdomen during his month-long deathbed stint. It made for an awkward social introduction, but—from a medical point of view—I was rather glad to have it out of him.

If he noticed one of his guests had just regurgitated a pile of scabby blood onto his carpet, Cunningham Senior seemed to take no special care of it. Instead, he waved a friendly finger at us and said, "Now, now. I am not certain it can be called murder if the slain party came willingly and allowed—"

It was Alec's turn to elbow his father. My force had been accidental, but Alec undertook the exercise with purposeful brutality, whereupon the old man proved himself the equal of Holmes by turning to one side and counter-vomiting all down the mantelpiece. The two stricken gentlemen both reached out for something to steady themselves. Fortunately for our investigation, Holmes picked an unstable pedestal beside a lounging chair. No sooner had he placed his weight to it than it tipped forwards, sending both Holmes and the fruit basket that rested atop it plunging to the floor. The basket tipped over, sending three apples, two pears, a sacrificial dagger and a disembodied human heart bouncing across the carpet.

I raised an eyebrow. "The murder weapon, I presume?"

"Ah-ha! So that's where I put it!" Cunningham crowed, ignoring the dribble of vomit that still clung to his cheek. "Now… why should I have left it in a fruit basket? Dear me… Must have been hungry, I suppose."

The discovery of guilt seemed to remove none of the

joviality from the elder Cunningham, but his son was another matter entirely. Alec's hand darted for the pocket of his jacket and yanked forth a small revolver. With wild eyes, he swung it towards us and fired three quick shots. As Forrester, Hayter and I went diving for cover, Alec Cunningham scooped up the heart and jumped out of the window. He made no effort to open it, just put his shoulder into it and let the wooden frame come apart as he plunged through. He rolled out onto the lawn, gained his footing and made a beeline for the old windmill.

"Oh, I say!" said old Cunningham. "He's going to open the demon portal. He said I could watch."

Holmes gave me a look of dread severity. I turned to Cunningham and demanded, "Why on earth would you want to do that?"

He sniffed defensively and said, "I have lived in Surrey all my life, young man. When I was nine, a boy in town accidentally broke a window and cut his arm."

"So?"

"It is the only happening in Reigate's history. The laceration of thirty-four, folks call it. Those who are not old enough to have been there curse their youth that they missed it."

"And you feel that is sufficient reason to release a demonic invasion upon your unsuspecting peers?"

"Might be a nice change of pace," he said, airily.

"How bad is the situation, Holmes?" I asked.

He gave me the kind of shrug to say that I was his friend and he still respected me and valued my company, but that I did, from time to time, come up with astoundingly stupid questions.

"Damn!" I cried. "Forrester, arrest this man for the murder of William Kirwan. Hayter, stay here with them. Holmes, you and I had better go see what we can do."

He nodded and we set off. Eschewing the door, we elected to follow Alec's route. As we opened the broken window to climb out, Forrester began clumsily arresting Cunningham Senior. The old man was visibly delighted.

"Wonderful! Wonderful! I've never been under arrest, you know. Fascinating process. I say, would anybody care for a cup of tea while you detain me?" Cunningham rang a small silver bell and, when the dog-faced butler arrived, said, "Houndsworth! I'm being arrested!"

"Indeed, sir?"

"Yes! Dashed exciting business! And I think it calls for tea."

"Very good, sir."

As Holmes and I picked our way down the sloping lawn, I reminded him, "Alec Cunningham is armed, Holmes. We are not."

"I don't care, Watson."

"Yes, well… bear it in mind, won't you?"

He nodded.

"Holmes… what are we to do?"

"That depends on how good the grimoire was," he said. "I was in earnest, earlier, when I said most of them are rubbish. I should hardly be worried at all, if Alec hadn't stolen the string."

"The string, Holmes?"

"He is in a place owned by Acton. If he were to mark off an area of summoning, it would be better if it were delineated by something that, likewise, belonged to Acton. The fact that he knew this indicates that either Alec or the book he's following contains some considerable level of arcane expertise. Guard yourself, Watson." He strode up to the windmill's door, laid a hand upon the planks and said, "Alec Cunningham! Betrayer to the race of man! By what right do you bar us? This place does not belong to you!"

The wood gave a tortured creak and began to writhe and bend. The boards contorted like seaweed in a strong current, while the iron nails that bound them together pulled free one by one. In an instant the way was open.

The windmill was nonfunctional, as I had guessed. Its heavy millstone had been removed from its trundle and leaned up against the far wall. Upon the flat face of this stone were scribed hundreds of arcane characters. On the floor, a circle described in string and marked by candles laid a stage before the foot of the millstone. There stood Alec, with the heart of William Kirwan in his left hand. As we watched, he rubbed the heart against the millstone, leaving an arc of gore across its surface. Even so, it was not Alec's left hand but his right that concerned me, for that one clutched the pistol.

"Get back!" he cried. I considered that to be fine advice, especially when he sent a bullet whistling between Holmes and me. I ducked back to one side of the doorway and pressed my back to the stone wall of the windmill.

Holmes did the same on the other side. His teeth were gritted and his eyes shone with unalloyed fury.

"Wretch! Betrayer!" he shouted. "Why would you do this? Why would you treat so cruelly with the world that spawned you?"

"It's that old fool Acton's fault! He was going to tear down the windmill! What would become of the millstone? Of the voices within the stone? They have spoken to me since I was a child, playing here alone. I had to protect them, don't you see? And they helped me! They told me of the book, of the passage wove of string and blood! Now, at last, I shall greet them! Finally, I shall meet my friends!"

"Fool?" Holmes growled. "You think *Acton* was the fool? Can you not feel what is on the other side of that stone? Do not let them in here!"

"Ha! You cannot stop me!" Alec shouted and sent another shot at us. The bullet chipped the stone beside my face and ricocheted into the field.

"Oh, I rather think I can," said Holmes. There was a crack like thunder, a swirl of black smoke and Holmes was gone. Then just as suddenly he reappeared, standing in the circle, face to face with Alec Cunningham. Cunningham gasped and raised his pistol to fire, but he was too late. With his left hand, Holmes grasped Alec's wrist. With his right, he seized Cunningham's collar.

"You wish to see another world? You wish to know what lies without? I will show you! Then, if you still wish to set your friends loose upon this world, you need only tell me so and I will allow it."

"Er... you'll what?" I asked. "Holmes, perhaps we ought not make any hasty promises."

"Mantoroth! Admit him!" Holmes cried, then he thrust Cunningham backwards with great force. I thought he meant to dash the young man's brains out against the stone, but Cunningham's head went right through the rock's face, as if it were the surface of a pond. To compound this image, Cunningham's arms began to thrash about like a drowning man's. He pulled his wrist free of Holmes's grasp and flailed wildly, smashing Holmes's exposed cheekbone with the barrel of his pistol. Holmes ignored the blow and resolutely held Cunningham down. Cunningham was in the stone up to his shoulders now, and Holmes was up to his wrist. Soon Cunningham's strength began to fail. His movements lessened until they were naught but feeble twitches. Finally, Holmes drew him back out of the stone and dropped him. Cunningham fell, first to his knees, then against the millstone, his cheek resting against the now-solid stone. His hair had gone stark white. A strange steam clung to his mouth and nose, curling up in sickly strands. His eyes rolled back and forth in terror. He tried to give a scream but, though his chest heaved with all its might, the sound that echoed forth was weak and distant—hardly even a whisper.

"There," said Holmes. "Now you have met your 'friends'. You have beheld a thing that has been seen by probably no more than five or six living men. Perhaps only by you and me. Do you love them still? Shall I let them come? Only ask and I will do it."

"You wish to see another world?"

Alec Cunningham answered, but his voice made no sense to me. At first, I supposed it to be only random noise: cheeps and chitters. Yet soon, by the careful diction of these sounds and by the repeated pattern of certain syllables, I recognized it as a language. What language it might be, I could not say; it was as foreign to my understanding as English had suddenly become to Alec Cunningham.

"I'm going to suppose that to mean 'please don't'," said Holmes. "Come along, Watson. We're safe now. Tomorrow we'll send men with sledges to break that stone to powder. We'll see that Alec here is the last fellow it ruins."

But had it ruined him? Certainly not without a little help from Holmes. And yes, Alec Cunningham was a killer. Yes, he'd been armed. Yes, engaged in an attempt to doom our world. But to see him… to behold the look of horror in his eyes… had there been no gentler path to victory?

"Er… can we help him?" I asked.

Holmes harrumphed. "No man can, I should think."

He meant it to sound disdainful—and it did—but I knew him well enough to hear the ring of terrible guilt beneath his words. Why did he act so rashly, if he knew he'd regret it? I could not fathom why Holmes—who drew all his powers from demonic sources—should be so angered to see the same act perpetrated by another. Why did he hold himself harmless, yet lash out so violently against his lesser peers? Then suddenly, I realized:

He didn't.

True hate can be focused outwards, but that is not its natural direction. It is an inward-facing malady. True, young Cunningham had nearly caused a catastrophe, yet his was a single act. How much more damage had Holmes himself done over his many years of magical practice? How much more intimately had he woven the brimstone thread into our world through trivial but oft-repeated acts of magic? I knew Holmes was not ignorant of that balance. And yes, some superficial elements of his anger might be directed at Cunningham and the other dabblers he met, but the love he bore for the world of man must perforce demand that Holmes reserve the core of his hatred for the man he knew to be the worst of all their ilk:

Warlock Holmes.

Wretch.

Betrayer.

Holmes turned and stalked back towards the Cunninghams' house, eyes downcast.

That is about all there is of the matter, except to relate a few closing points.

The second half of the murder note was found in Alec Cunningham's jacket pocket. When joined with the scrap Holmes and I had recovered, it read:

If you will only come round at quarter to twelve we will tear the heart from your chest, which should kill you fairly quickly. Better still, we shall use it to open a demon gate. Thus, you are rid of the terrible boredom we are heirs to and

THROUGH YOUR DEATH, THE MOST INTERESTING EVENT
EVER TO GRACE REIGATE SHALL OCCUR. CONSIDER IT.

In light of this evidence, the local magistrate had difficulty classifying Kirwan's death as murder. He was quite stymied by the case. As a compromise, Cunningham Senior agreed to remain under house arrest and be warden to Alec (which indeed, was exactly the state in which he had spent his life up to that point).

The events caused quite a stir and all Reigate residents went, with frequency, to visit the old man and behold his ruined son. Rare was the day when Cunningham had no gawkers to keep him company. Colonel Hayter was bitterly jealous.

Alec Cunningham never again reclaimed his tongue or his senses. Though his father had a devil of a time getting him to take food, Alec would feverishly devour any hair he could lay his hands on. He plucked himself bald in the matter of a few days, much to the delight of the crowds who came to view him.

Holmes and I fled. No town so small can contain a secret so large and Reigate, I knew, would soon become a bit hot for us. I hired another carriage to secrete us back to London that very day. Warlock's mood was black and distant as the journey commenced but eventually he mumbled, "I didn't mean to slight you, Watson."

"Eh? Slight me? How?"

"When I said that only Cunningham and myself had seen such horrors—in the heat of the moment, I forgot your own ordeals. I did not mean to make light of the things you've suffered."

"Bah. I've had nothing *that* terrible ever happen to me. Worst I've ever been is shot."

"No, I seem to remember that you once had the entirety of time and space thrust through your chest."

"By Jove! I had forgotten!" I laughed.

Holmes shuddered. "Can't have been pleasant…"

"Oh, no. No. I certainly don't care to repeat the procedure."

He smiled. I smiled back. Still, I could not help but wonder aloud, "Are you sorry for what happened? To Cunningham, I mean?"

"Not really, Watson. He got what was coming to him and the next fellow to endanger our world so callously deserves the same."

He sighed, peeped absentmindedly through the crack in the window curtains and added, "Even if it's me."

THE ADVENTURE OF THE SOLITARY TRICYCLIST

AS RECUPERATIVE TRIPS TO THE COUNTRY GO, I CANNOT
say that Holmes's and my visit to Surrey was an unqualified
success. Trouble, it seemed, would find Holmes wherever
he chanced to go, so I saw no benefit to denying him the
pleasures of his own hearth. The main bar to domestic
peace was no supernatural assailant, but—just as always—
Mrs. Hudson. I could conceive of no realistic plan to
prevent her from discovering Holmes's ghastly condition.
My best option, I concluded, was to take the fight to the
enemy. In other words: to force the revelation upon her,
but on my own terms.

I prepared a deception.

The day of our return, I intercepted her in the hall and
said, "Holmes is back."

"So?"

"I have prescribed a course of recuperation for him,
following his excursion to the south of France."

"No care of mine, so long as the rent is reg'lar."

"Yes. Yes quite. But you know, Mrs. Hudson, I wished
to speak with you and ask you not to stare…"

"Stare? At what?"

"I fear Holmes's vacation included a dalliance with a chorus girl…"

"*No!*"

"And that he has contracted—in my medical opinion—a case of Indo-Brazilian super-gonorrhea. So please, if you could refrain from gawking—"

This request was instantly disregarded. Mrs. Hudson bludgeoned me aside with her wrinkled forearm and charged into our rooms to see if Holmes's affliction was an equal for the horrific exaggerations of carnal illness she'd read of in her collection of illegal novels.

I think she was not disappointed.

In fact, Holmes was a bit of a hero to her for a time. 221B Baker Street became a healing haven and we passed our days in comfortable torpor. I deflected every client I could, trusting much to Grogsson and Lestrade. Day by day, Holmes mended, the skin over his scorched cheekbone slowly closing as his withered eyeballs re-inflated. After a time, he could wander down Baker Street, knowing he would draw only surreptitious glances of pity, rather than the outright screams of horror he'd first engendered. He was rather proud of himself on that score and took frequent strolls in Regent's Park. The spring and summer passed easily until, just as August waned, adventure found us once more.

One day our door swung open to reveal Lestrade, looking sullen. By his side stood a young lady, and by her side stood Mrs. Hudson, examining her with some vigor. She pulled at the woman's sleeve and poked her in the hip appraisingly, eyeing her up and down like a racing fan scrutinizing a thoroughbred. I think Mrs. Hudson was at once repelled by the strangeness of our guest and enraptured by the beauty that strangeness failed to mask. I'll confess, I felt the same. Though, in my defense, I wasn't agonizing over whether our visitor was fit to be the heroine of an illicit novella, which—I suspect—was the trap that had caught my landlady.

The woman was tall—taller than me and nearly the equal of Holmes. Her eyes were steady and betrayed no hint of fear, yet they did demonstrate a certain social ignorance as they peered at us from behind brass-and-leather cycling goggles, which she had failed to remove despite being indoors. Her limbs were long, and she held herself with a strange, athletic stiffness. She wore trousers and seemed to show no awareness that this was shocking, perhaps even more so than her goggles. Strangest of all was her hair. Neither styled like a gentlewoman's nor drawn into a working woman's bun, it hung straight and loose, down her back in the fashion of... well, of an eight-year-old, I suppose. It bespoke utter social ignorance, yet it was also rather—I don't know—long and silky and strangely fascinating to gaze at. My low estimation of her social aptitude was vindicated the moment she opened her mouth. She gazed at Holmes, pointed a finger at his chest and said, "You look scary."

"Yes, I know," said Holmes, "but I'm really quite nice."

"There's something wrong with that one, too," said our guest, swinging her finger over at Lestrade.

"Absolutely," Holmes agreed. "Hideously wrong. Well spotted."

Finally, the finger came my way and its owner muttered, "That one looks normal though."

"*Vexingly* normal, most days," said Holmes.

"Except that moustache," she added.

"Wait! My what?"

Lestrade cleared his throat pointedly and announced, "Gentlemen, I have a case I think may interest you. This is Miss Violet Smith. She gained some notoriety last year, when she won a newspaper contest for a Starley's Ariel bicycle."

"Oh yes," I said. "I think I recall it." She'd been London's darling, for a while. *The Daily Telegraph* had not thought to post "men only" in the contest rules, for it simply hadn't occurred to them that any lady might enter. Not only had Miss Smith entered, she had dominated. Every day, the contestants gathered to ride the cycle they hoped to win through another ridiculous challenge course. Every day, Violet swept the field. Her victory was made all the more popular by her extreme poverty—the recent, untimely death of her father had left her and her mother in such dire straits that it would be hard to construct a more perfect underdog.

"Lestrade, Miss Smith, won't you step inside?" said Holmes. "Mrs. Hudson, won't you bugger off?"

"Holmes!"

"What? We all want her to."

"Immaterial!"

Nevertheless, I was rather pleased to see Mrs. Hudson

do as Holmes suggested. As I settled Lestrade and Miss Smith into their seats and set the kettle on to boil, I said, "I have heard nothing of you, since the contest. I hope the victory improved your fortunes?"

In a monotone staccato that a Gatling gun might envy, Miss Smith replied, "No. It was only a bicycle, not a lot of money. And we were still poor. And then a letter came from South Africa. And we thought it might be from Uncle Ralph. And perhaps he got rich in the diamond mines, like he promised. But it wasn't him. Just his friend, Robert Carruthers. And when he got here, he told us Uncle Ralph had died. So that's no good. And we still didn't have any money. So that's no good. But Mr. Carruthers is really nice. And he gave me a job. So that's good. And he said I should come live in his house and teach his daughter Sylvia to play music. And she's ten. And she's nice. And he said he'd give me a hundred pounds a year. And I said, 'Wowie! A hundred!' And he said I could ride my bike down to the train on Saturdays and go see Mother until Mondays. And it's six miles to the station. And it's a good ride. So that's good. And I live at his house now."

"Where you teach his daughter music?" I asked.

"I can play all the notes, really fast."

"Do you know, I believe you can," I reflected. "So, you live with Mr. Carruthers, in his house in…?"

"He has rented Chiltern Grange, near Farnham," Lestrade interjected. "Indeed, that six-mile ride to Farnham station shall prove to be of importance. Miss Smith, why don't you tell Holmes about Mr. Jack Woodley."

"Oh? Who is that?" asked Holmes.

"I don't like him," said Violet, with a distasteful grimace. "He's big. And he's mean. And he has a huge red moustache. And he says he came back from South Africa, too. And he's a friend of Mr. Carruthers. And Mr. Carruthers says so, too. But they don't look like friends. They look like they always want to fight. And once they did—over *me*! Mr. Woodley came over to visit, all silly like he'd been drinking. But he didn't smell like drink. And he said he was almost ready to claim me for himself. But Mr. Carruthers said I was a person, not a parakeet, and I didn't belong to anybody, except myself. And maybe Cyril. And Mr. Woodley said he didn't care. And he grabbed my wrist. And Mr. Carruthers hit him. And Woodley didn't mind, because he's so strong. And then he hit Mr. Carruthers back. And we thought he'd killed him for a minute. Because part of the top of his head came off. But they sewed it back on. So that's good."

My mind reeled beneath Violet Smith's barrage of facts. Which were important? What had caused her to seek police aid? For that matter, what had caused the police to seek *our* aid? Thus Holmes—who cared for people, not for details—bested me.

"Who," he asked, "is Cyril?"

"Um…"

For the first time since being invited to speak, Violet Smith seemed to have no words. She colored from the tips of her fingers to the roots of her hair.

"His last name's Morton but I just call him Cyril.

And I've known him since we were little. And now he's a mechanical engineer, almost! And he doesn't mind if I'm big. Or if I say what I'm thinking. And when I won a bicycle he bought a bicycle. And he's not a very good rider. But I like to ride with him, anyway. And he falls down, sometimes. But I pick him up. And he said he wants to marry me. And I said I really, really want him to. And Mother said she always thought as much. So that's good. That's... really good."

Holmes turned to me and fixed me with a knowing grin. "Do you see?" his smile said. "She's wonderful."

It was the very best quality of my friend, Warlock Holmes. Yes, I was always one to be burdened by the particulars of a case—swamped in the minutiae, looking for that one, elusive clue that would turn the whole tale. Holmes never cared for such things. He'd simply find the person he liked best—then he'd do anything for them.

I nodded. Yes. Here was our client. We would not fail her. I mean... once we found out what her problem was.

"And so... what brought you to the police, Miss Smith?" I asked.

"Well after the hitting and the other hitting, Mr. Woodley had to go away. So that's good. But then, I was riding to the station to go see Mother. And I saw this man with a big black beard. And he follows me. Every Saturday and Monday, he's there. And he speeds up when I speed up. And he slows down when I slow down. And last week I tried to trick him. I went around the corner, past Charlington Hall, and I stopped. And I hid. And I waited for him to come around the corner. So I could ask who he was."

I might have boggled at the bravery of it, if it had been anybody else. But no, five minutes in the company of Violet Smith had taught me this was exactly the sort of behavior that might be expected of her.

"But he never came around the corner. I looked for him. But the lane was empty."

"Was this strange pursuer on a bicycle, too?" I asked. "Or on foot?"

"No. He's got a tricycle."

Lestrade gave a pained smile and said, "It seems Farnham is currently experiencing a sort of mania for them."

Violet nodded vigorously and agreed, "Lord Charlington lives at Charlington Hall. And he says bicycles are old-fashioned. He says tricycles are the new thing. And the better thing. And he's got about forty of them. And the second day I was at Chiltern Grange, he said he'd show me the wave of the future. And he made me get my bike. And he got his tricycle. And he made me race him. And it wasn't very good for his heart. Because he couldn't keep up. But he also wouldn't give up. So we went round and round for hours. And he fell over. And we thought he was going to die. But the doctor said he'd be all right. But he had to go recuperate in the country. And I said we were already in the country. And they said he had to go to a different part of the country, far away from me. So he's been gone ever since. And now someone's got his house and all his tricycles. And someone was following me on one of them. So, the next time I was in town, I went and told the police."

"Yes," said Lestrade, flipping through his notebook with feigned nonchalance. "It seems she reported the happenings to one Inspector... Torg Grogsson."

I gave a tortured groan and put my head in my hands. To my surprise, Holmes did the same. But then, why not? Did it not all make perfect sense? She was pretty. She possessed an odd sort of charm—anybody in a room with Violet Smith would have difficulty paying attention to anything else. She certainly had no care for convention and, as a special bonus, she was tall enough that she might not look out of place on the arm of a hulking behemoth of a detective inspector who'd been feeling rather lonely of late.

"I only just found out about the situation," Lestrade said. "When I did, I was forced to wonder if Miss Smith's visit might possibly correspond with the last time I'd seen my fellow inspector. Can either of you gentlemen recall seeing Grogsson in the last two weeks?"

"And now—and this is odd—" said Violet Smith, "there are *two* men with black beards following me on tricycles! And one of them is really, really big!"

Knowing that Miss Smith would return to Farnham station on the Monday morning 9:50, Holmes and I took the 9:13. No sooner had we arrived in Farnham, than one of the mysteries solved itself.

Or perhaps it deepened.

"Big, black bee-ahds!" cried a barker, from behind his stand of artificial facial hair. "Get yer big, black bee-ahds, hee-ah! Sandy side-burns! Red moustaches that challenge credulity! Get 'em all for the anonymity dance! Facial hair of all sorts, to hide your identities from the lovelies! Don't let 'em know who they're marryin' until it's too late—that's the wise man's way! Bee-ahds, hee-ah!"

"You… you have an *anonymity* dance?" I said.

"Why else come to Farnham?" the barker asked. "It's the only thing that sets us off, i'nt it? Big beards for small men and a chance to dance before they know what you've done!"

"Oh, Watson!" Holmes enthused. "It sounds perfect for you!"

"What? No it doesn't! What are you talking about? I'm a perfectly respectable—"

"We can't let an opportunity like this pass us by! It may be your last."

"But… I'm a highly eligible—"

"He'll take one false red moustache, please."

"No I will not, Holmes! No! Thank you, sir, but no. Come on, Holmes, we've got business to attend to. Miss Smith's train arrives in half an hour. We've got to get out on the road to Chiltern Grange and lay in wait for our client and her pursuers."

"But, Watson… consider… a life of solitude…"

"Look here, Holmes, the only thing I wanted from that barker, I have got! Information! It seems the only description we have of our suspect is moot. With Farnham in the grip of a false-beard epidemic, the man Miss Smith describes might be anybody. Now, come on! All your blithering about toast this morning cost us the early train. We must hurry. Recall that all our quarry will be mounted, while we must go on foot."

"No we don't," said Holmes, pointing at the next barker down the line.

"Tricycles! Get-cha tricycles hee-ah!"

"No."

"But, Watson, look at them: they're beautiful!"

Holmes led me towards the line of gleaming machines and spread his arms, as if he wished to hug the whole lot of them. The barker—no fool—took this as an invitation to do business. Probably his first business of the week. Lord Charlington's enthusiasm for three-wheeled, pedal-powered conveyances did not seem to have spread to his social inferiors. The sign above the stall conveyed not only his patronage, but the fact that he had originally valued the rental of a tricycle at two shillings per hour. Via a series of cross-outs and pencil-ins, this price had been reduced to tuppence a day and yet still a line of tricycles sat waiting.

"I see you've come to invest in the wave of the future, friend!" the barker barked. "Ain't they gorgeous? Transportation of tomorrow, and that's a fact!"

"Nope," I said. "Holmes, come on! We have to go! Miss Smith will be here soon and she is a formidable bicyclist; we must get the start on her."

"Bicycle? *Bicycle?*" the barker cried out, raising his hands to his head in professional horror. He ran to the side of his stall and fetched out the demonstration bicycle he kept for just such occasions. He trotted it out, then let go of the handlebars. It crashed to the ground.

"Oh no!" he cried. "Wouldya look at that?" He raised it up, but let go again, sending it earthwards for a second time. "What a dangerous design!" the barker decided. "Why, it can't even stay up at a standstill! Can you imagine what she's like at speed? I think I've just saved your life, friend! Hey… you know what…? Rent a tricycle!"

"No," I told him. "Come on, Holmes, we've got to go."

I grabbed my friend by the arm and dragged him towards Charlington Lane.

"But, Watson, even if it's not as fast as a bicycle, surely it's better than going on foot! Why not?"

"Because I am a grown man, Holmes, and I still possess a shred of dignity."

By the time we reached the top of Crooksbury Hill, I possessed no shred of dignity. My shirt was soaked through with sweat and my every breath sounded as if it must have been issued by an asthmatic goat. Holmes had little trouble keeping up with me. This, I ascribed to his preternaturally long legs. Or perhaps he had called upon demonic aid. The idea that he was simply fitter than me, despite the month he had spent dead, was not an acceptable theory. It came as a wondrous relief when Holmes glanced behind us and exclaimed, "Look! There she is!"

As I turned to look, my foot caught a divot in the lane and I plunged face first into the dirt. I lay, panting. If only the road had been muddy, at least I might have had a drink, but luck was ever my enemy.

Through the clouds of face-induced dust, I could just make out the solitary figure of Violet Smith, beginning her laborious ascent. Yet, as the dust began to settle, I could see she was not solitary at all. From the heat haze behind her, a figure materialized. Then a second. Then a third. Then a fourth.

Twice as many as we'd been promised.

All four of her pursuers were male. All tricycle-mounted and all bent to their task with earnest vigor. The closest figure was the smallest and also the least formidable. One could see the ride had taxed him—and why not—even Lord Charlington's tricycle-of-tomorrow seemed to lack adequate pedal-to-handlebar clearance for the adult knee. This first fellow huffed and puffed piteously, through his bushy black beard.

The second displayed no such troubles. He must have started a ways behind the first gent, for though he was still behind he made up the pace with every thrust of his pedal. The man moved with a liquid grace and such strength that, after watching him for a few moments, one could not help but wonder if maybe a tricycle *was* a reasonable form of transport. He wore a grand red moustache that cleared his face by an inch or two at either side.

The third was... *clearly*... Grogsson. His size and his ill-aptitude for subtlety proclaimed him, even at great distance. I'm tempted to say he looked like the proverbial circus-bear-on-a-tricycle but, since there was never a bear as large or powerful as Torg Grogsson, the description beggars itself. In a sad attempt to conceal his identity— or perhaps *two* sad attempts—he had purchased both a big black beard and a big red moustache from the local facial-hair vendor. This mismatched array waggled back and forth with terrible force as Grogsson's unequaled leg muscles powered him up the hill. I might have thought him the clear favorite in this unexpected race, but a moment's observation told a different tale.

He was struggling. Firstly there was nowhere near enough room for Torg's massive legs between the pedals and handlebar of his beleaguered vehicle. In order to make himself fit, he'd been forced to hang his buttocks well behind the tricycle seat, propping himself upright with main strength, against the handlebar. Of course, this meant that as he pedaled, he yanked the bar this way and that, ensuring that each powerful thrust either forced him well off course to starboard, or equally so, to port. Then there was the fact that a simple tricycle tire cannot convey the amount of force Torg was expressing onto a dusty lane without sliding. At every pump the front tire skittered and slid. Yes, Torg may have the advantage of strength over his competitors, but what could it avail him, if not to dig a one-wheel-wide, zigzagging trench down the center of Charlington Lane? To compound it all, the tricycle had surely not been designed to withstand even a tenth of the mechanical force it was undergoing. At every third or fourth pedal, some piece of it would break free and bounce away.

The fourth rider was so far back, so piteously slow,

that I could discern little of him. Oh, except his large, false black beard.

"Watson?" said Holmes, staring down the hill at the oncoming assemblage. "What in the *nine hells* am I looking at?"

"No idea, really."

"What should we do?"

"Still no idea."

It was too late, anyway. Violet Smith crested the hill and rattled past us.

Holmes glanced downwards at me, granting me one final chance to offer a strategy. I had none. Left to his own devices, Holmes elected to step into the road, wave his arms and bellow, "Hey! Hey! Who are you fellows?"

The first tricyclist looked up in horror. It seems he must have feared detection, or at least identification. Quickly—before he neared enough for us to discern his features—he turned around and raced back down the hill.

The second tricyclist seemed to fear detection not only by us, but also by the first tricyclist. He wrenched his wheel to the left, propelling his vehicle off the lane and onto the neighboring pasture. As he was by far the finest cyclist of the lot, this presented little problem for him. With supernatural affinity, he pumped off over the field, his red moustache waving a jaunty farewell.

The third cyclist seemed to fear any kind of discovery whatsoever. He was—after all—a detective inspector, engaged in a stunning piece of covert police work. He wrenched his handlebars to the right, which was the final straw for his overtaxed machine. The front wheel separated from the rest and bounced free. An instant later, the front fork augured into the dirt lane and Torg's magnificent bulk came crashing down on what remained of his tricycle, crushing it to a puddle of mechanical scrap. Before he'd even come to a halt, Torg bounded up from the dirt and took to his heels.

The fourth rider fell from his saddle, lay gasping in the road for a few moments, then remounted and trundled back towards Farnham.

"Really, Watson," said Holmes, watching them all go, "what do you think we're looking at?"

"Something... very odd," I said.

As I deemed it unlikely that our mysterious tricyclists would pursue Violet Smith on a day when she was not present, it seemed safe to assume we had until Saturday morning to plan our second attempt. This is not to say the week passed uneventfully.

On Tuesday, I attempted to confront Torg Grogsson. I had no luck. He was neither at his home, nor at Scotland Yard. The sergeant on duty informed me that he had reappeared earlier in the week, filed for a leave of absence for "police technologies development" and disappeared again with a gas-welder, a cart-load of steel tubes and one of the Yard's more easily frightened engineers.

On Wednesday night we had a telegram from Violet Smith:

TO WARLOCK HOLMES AND THAT OTHER FELLOW,

MR. CARRUTHERS HAS PROPOSED MARRIAGE. THAT'S NOT RIGHT IS IT? AND I ALREADY TOLD HIM I'M MARRYING CYRIL. AND I'M PRETTY SURE I'M ONLY ALLOWED TO MARRY ONE PERSON. AND THAT'S ALL I WANT ANYWAY. AND HE SAYS HE LOVES ME. AND I SAID HE'S TOO LATE. AND HE'S TOO OLD. AND I FEEL A LITTLE STRANGE TEACHING HIS DAUGHTER PIANO. BECAUSE HE'S GOT HER CALLING ME MUMMY NOW. AND I'M NOT HER MUMMY. BUT I THINK HE GIVES HER A SHILLING EVERY TIME SHE DOES IT. SO SHE WON'T STOP. AND THERE'S THIS MAN WITH A BLACK BEARD WHO KEEPS PEEPING IN THE WINDOWS. AND HE'S REALLY, REALLY HUGE. BUT HE RUNS AWAY WHENEVER I TRY TO ASK WHAT HE'S DOING. AND I DON'T LIKE IT HERE ANYMORE. AND I WANT TO GO HOME. SO WHAT SHOULD I DO?

·   It's a good thing she had a hundred a year, or she could never have afforded such telegrams.

I cabled back that she must try to avoid trouble until Saturday—that if only she could maintain the façade of normalcy, Holmes and I would have another chance to discover the identity and motives of her multiple pursuers. I promised I would redouble my efforts.

Which I did. On Thursday, Holmes and I went back to Farnham. I had a devil of a time dragging him past the beard and tricycle vendors, yet I knew I must stay focused on my task. Violet Smith had said her original pursuer had vanished from the lane near Charlington Hall. With Lord Charlington gone, who was in residence? This was the sort of gossip most of the locals would know and all of them would be willing to discuss at the local tavern. Once I had Holmes settled with some toast and soup, I walked to the bar and asked the landlord, "I don't suppose Charlington Hall is available to rent, is it?"

He gave a gruff snort and said, "There's plenty round these parts who wish it was. But no, that crazy clergyman has it. Horton Williamson, that's 'is name."

"Ain't a clergyman no more," one of the locals said. "He's defrocked."

"Aye's right," the landlord remembered. "'Cause he wouldn't shut up about crucifixion and angels."

Holmes looked up from his soup, tilted his head doubtfully to one side and said, "Er… but isn't that what clergymen are for? Talking about crucifixion? And angels? If memory serves, they're fairly large parts of that whole… thing… aren't they?"

"Well yes," the local conceded, "but Horton Williamson's extra keen on it. Says he can uplift the mortal man to be more like an angel."

"So much that your average Jack would be able to survive crucifixion," the landlord laughed.

"Right," said the local. "And if that's what lifted Jesus to divinity, it can't be all that bad for his followers, either."

"Thinks we all oughta try it," the landlord said. "Not

all that eager to go first, though, is he?"

"But… that is inane!" I said.

"Insane," the local agreed.

"Admirable," decided Holmes. We all turned to stare at him. "Well I mean, there's something noble about the man who holds to his convictions, isn't there? Even if he knows they can never become the mainstream practice?"

"Well, let's hope they don't," I said. "Come along, Holmes; I think it's time we had a closer look at Charlington Lane."

"Watson! My soup!"

"Finish up, then. Finish up."

Considering how many people lived in and around Farnham, it was surprising how little used Charlington Lane was. We passed a few farmer's carts and a few young people out for a stroll, but no others. Indeed, there was little of interest until we at last came to Charlington Hall. Its grounds had once been separated from Charlington Lane by a hedge maze. Once, I say, because the maze was now riddled with holes, making it less of a barrier and more of an ideal staging point from which to sneak onto or off the lane. Peeking my head into a few of these holes, I could see that Lord Charlington's fascination with the tricycle was no recent phenomenon, nor was it reasonable in its scope. Several of the machines were stored within the maze—some in fine condition, some little more than three-wheeled rust sculptures. The man must have been a fanatic.

Just past Charlington Hall, the lane turned a corner. About a third of a mile past was a little hill on the far side of the road, with a dirt path running up it and a few squat little yew trees. Apart from the hedge maze, it seemed the only reasonable concealment in the area. From the hill, up to Mr. Carruthers' house—Chiltern Grange—the lane was unsheltered on either side.

As we walked, Holmes's mood worsened. "I want to go home, Watson. Or at least back to that tavern. You made me leave half my toast. Do you think they still have it?"

"No, Holmes."

"But they'll have more, if we ask?"

"Holmes, this is important work."

"No it isn't. We're just out for a walk in the country, looking at hedges, hills and trees. There's no demons and no soup… I want to go home."

"Soon, Holmes. Look, the last time we came here to find Miss Smith's pursuers we made a hash of it. Next time we must be better prepared."

Holmes huffed his displeasure. "I am almost starting to miss Mrs. Hudson."

"Look, just a little farther to Chiltern Grange, then we can go, all right?"

Oh, how glad I am that we went on all the way. Robert Carruthers' rented home was surrounded by a low wall, overhung with ivy. Skirting the shadow of this wall made it an easy task to creep all the way around the house, unobserved. The thick ivy even gave us some concealment whenever we cared to peep over the top. As we neared the front of the house, we heard raised voices.

"Now, that sounds a little more exciting, Watson!" Holmes said, brightening. "Let's go see what that's about, eh?"

Three men stood arguing at the door of Chiltern Grange. Holmes and I peeked over the wall to observe them.

"That one has got to be Robert Carruthers," I whispered, indicating the man who stood inside the doorway, shouting out. He was in his fifties, paunchy and graying, but energetic. "See how his scalp has been mangled? Miss Smith said that Woodley struck him and that he required stitches."

Holmes made a face of disgust/admiration and nodded his agreement.

"And that one must be Horton Williamson," I said, pointing at one of the two fellows who stood upon the steps. "The little liar's walking around in a cassock, waving a Bible about. I'd say he's trying a bit too hard to pass himself off as a clergyman, eh, Holmes?"

"You're probably right, Watson," Holmes agreed, "but I hardly care. What I want to know is, who or what is *that*?"

The third gentleman was… well… *no gentleman*. Only a simpleton would ever describe him as gentle-looking and anyone might be forgiven for doubting he was a man. His well-muscled arms hung half a foot too long, were dotted with what looked like needle marks and ended in hands that reminded one a bit too much of claws. He had an unruly shock of red hair and a fierce red moustache. His brow jutted, his jaw looked tough enough to break a cricket bat on, and the savagery of his gaze made it seem as if he were eagerly waiting for some fool to try. Without a doubt, he was the second of the tricyclists we'd seen following Violet Smith—the competent one—and perfectly matched her description of the odorous Jack Woodley.

As we watched, Williamson shook his Bible and declared, "Bring her out, Carruthers, or by the power of the Living Jingo, we'll have her from you!"

Robert Carruthers laughed grimly and said, "I'll tell you what I told your friend 'Woodley' there: Violet Smith is not a piece of property to be demanded or sold. Now get off my land before I set my dogs on a man of the cloth!"

Williamson looked more than just a bit worried by that, but his companion was cut of sterner stuff. Jack Woodley roared with rage and shouted, "She belongs to me!"

"She does not!" Carruthers replied. "She belongs to herself. Or if any man may claim her, it's her young beau, Cyril. Or if she ever chose another, I hope it might be me. And anyway, I'm certain it isn't you, you great tyrant! I'm not afraid of you!"

"Then I will kill you," Woodley decided. He turned to Williamson and said, "Priest! Grant me benediction!"

"No! No, look here… no," Williamson spluttered, leaping between the two men with arms outspread. "I appeal for calm, gentlemen. Let's think this through. Mr. Woodley, I know you brought me into this matter to help you, but maybe there's a better way to deal with Miss Smith. And Mr. Carruthers, I appreciate your position and yet… well… had you not best tread carefully? The position you are in, sir, your life is not worth—I hope it's not too impious to say so—but it's not worth a duck's wet fart. Can we not find a way to work together? Think of what we might gain! Think of the profit!"

I rather hoped Mr. Williamson might go on to discuss exactly how he planned to make three men's fortunes off one bicycle-obsessed piano teacher, but it was not to be. As Williamson spoke, Jack Woodley began to sniff the air—first casually, but then with some vigor. Finally, his eyes went wide with anger and his head snapped in Holmes's and my direction. We dropped down behind the wall.

"I think we've seen enough, don't you?" I asked.

"I should say we have," whispered Holmes as we crawled away. "I never thought I'd see a Living Jingo!"

"What? No. Holmes, that is merely an expression."

"Are you sure, Watson? Because it *sounds* like a kind of monster. And—at the risk of being indelicate—that man *looks* like a kind of monster."

"Well, I won't argue that," I said. "Come on, Holmes. I want to get back to Baker Street and plan our next move."

Yet time was a luxury we were not to enjoy. The next day, we had a telegram:

WARLOCK HOLMES AND THE BAD-MOUSTACHE MAN,

I AM LEAVING! TOMORROW WHEN I GO TO SEE MUM I AM STAYING THERE. BECAUSE MR. CARRUTHERS KEEPS TRYING TO MARRY ME. AND HE KEEPS

SAYING HE LOVES ME. AND I THINK HE MEANS
IT. BUT THAT MAKES IT WORSE NOT BETTER. AND
NOW THERE'S AT LEAST THREE FELLOWS WITH
BEARDS OR MOUSTACHES THAT KEEP PEEPING
IN THE WINDOWS. AND LITTLE SYLVIA TURNS
OUT TO HAVE BEEN ABLE TO PLAY BEETHOVEN'S
NINTH FROM MEMORY THIS ENTIRE TIME. SO THE
WHOLE THING WAS ALWAYS JUST A LIE. AND
CYRIL SAYS WE CAN DO WITHOUT THE MONEY. SO
IT'S ALL RIGHT IF I COME HOME. THANK YOU
FOR YOUR HELP. BUT I DON'T THINK I NEED
YOU ANYMORE. AFTER TOMORROW I'LL BE SAFE.

"Maybe *after* tomorrow," Holmes chuckled, "but things might get a bit hot, first. What do you think, Watson?"

I pursed my lips, took a deep breath and said, "She doesn't like my moustache?"

"Of course she doesn't, but that is not the issue."

"What's wrong with it?"

"Oh… Shape. Color. Placement. The concept. The execution. Really, the whole essence of the thing is corrupt to its dark, hairy core. But look here, Watson: there are other things to worry about. I can't think it would even bother you at all, if you weren't so smitten with her."

I wished to protest that Violet Smith was peculiar in the extreme. Gangly! Clueless! Those goggles? Those *trousers*? Yet, when I thought of the beauty of her features, her accidental honesty, the unalloyed goodness that showed through her crooked smile... All I could think to say was, "I know. What's wrong with me?"

"Well whatever it is, it seems to be catching," laughed Holmes. "You, Cyril, Carruthers, Grogsson and even the Living Jingo seem to be of the same mind. Poor girl. I'd say this gaggle of suitors needs to thin itself out a bit."

"Right you are, Holmes. There can be only one."

I must have paused a bit too long, for Holmes cleared his throat and mentioned, "Er... yes... specifically *Cyril*, don't you think?"

I turned my face to the wall and grumbled something.

"I'm glad we agree," said Holmes. "Get some rest, Watson. Tomorrow we must be at our best."

Though he was much improved, Holmes's facial features still caused enough discomfort in the casual observer to ensure we had plenty of room to ourselves on the train. Or maybe it was my moustache. No sooner had he set his foot on the platform at Farnham station, Holmes made a beeline to the tricycle vendor, shouting, "Can we, Watson? Oh, can we?"

"I forbid it."

"But consider, John: what better way to catch a tricycle-mounted villain? Set a tricycle to catch a tricycle, I always say!"

"No. We shall hire a coach."

But the rental fellow gave me a sideways smirk and said, "You could do, I suppose. There is one, here in Farnham."

He turned to a well-soiled groom who stood near the end of the train platform and shouted, "Oi! Charlie! How's the coach for today?"

"Engaged, as you well know!"

The vendor shrugged.

"A bicycle, then," I decided. "I believe their superiority has been conclusively proved by our very client, has it not?"

The vendor smiled, savagely. "Illegal, I'm afraid."

"What? Illegal?"

"Lord Charlington never much cared for 'em, see? Then again, he always did have a fondness for backing local ordinances. Took every ounce of his influence to criminalize those two-wheeled health hazards but he managed it. And sure, the constables might turn a blind eye to Miss Smith, but you ain't half so pretty, is ya?"

"Damn! But then, I... We could always... er..." I sputtered for a few moments, but in the end there was nothing to do but swallow my pride, reach for my wallet and groan, "Two, please."

"Just one," said Holmes. "I'm still not at my best, Watson. I couldn't possibly. I'll just ride on the back of yours."

"Argh! One then! One and I hate the world!"

Seizing the ill-rented conveyance, I turned back to Holmes only to discover that he had gone. I found him just six steps away, waiting near the next stand over, gesturing hopefully to a huge false moustache.

"No."

"But, Watsooooooooooon!"

"I said no."

"Ah! Ah! But did you not *also* say that victory can hide in the smallest advantage? Perhaps it might be felicitous to conceal our identities from our client or even our friend Grogsson! I think you once told me that, in matters of crime-solving, only a fool fails to employ every advantage presented to him!"

"I don't remember ever saying that."

"But can you *prove* you didn't? I think you must concede, Watson, it sounds exactly like the sort of thing you yell at me all the time."

"…"

"…"

"It does, actually."

"Ha!"

Two moments later and two shillings lighter, I was fastening an enormous false moustache over my own while Holmes fussed delightedly with his new beard. I was certain mine was made of horsehair and equally sure it had not been washed during its brief transition between some unknown pair of equine buttocks and my own face. None of this seemed to bother Holmes, who turned to me, clasped both my shoulders and declared, "Ah! A grand improvement!"

Six miles of pedaling down Charlington Lane gave me ample time to regret both of the morning's purchases, as well as the three-year chain of poor life decisions that had led up to them. I'd soaked all my clothes and my new moustache with sweat. Oh, and if I thought it had smelled poorly when I first got it, I had since learned that unwashed, sweat-soaked horsehair baking in the sun has a quality all its own.

Holmes had a delightful time. He stood behind me on the little deck between the two rear wheels the whole way, humming snippets of marching tunes and enjoying the summer air. From time to time, when we got to the uphill bits, he'd lean one leg off the back of the tricycle and give a few assistance pushes, which would have been appreciated better if... I don't know... They seemed condescending, somehow.

I pedaled us to the little hill beyond Charlington Hall, pushed the tricycle behind one of the yew trees, and collapsed into the grass to wait for Violet Smith. I'd taken no more than three or four breaths before Holmes said, "Up you get, Watson. Here she comes."

Rising to my post with some reluctance, I could just make out the black dot of Violet Smith as she pedaled down Charlington Lane. Hardly had she left the grounds of Chiltern Grange than one tricyclist burst from the hedge of that very house and another from a stand of gorse just beside it. The pair bent to their pedals and made all haste after Miss Smith, though what hope they had of overtaking her must have been slight. She looked back at them with some misgiving, I think, but did not increase her pace. Even so, the pair did not gain on her.

"Come on!" I told Holmes. "We'd best get underway ourselves, lest we get too far behind."

I leapt into the saddle, laid my foot to the pedal with renewed spirit and...

Snapped the damned thing right off.

"What? Oh! Blast! Is there no such thing as craftsmanship any longer?"

I leapt from my perch and began scooping tricycle parts from the dust. The wooden pedal had snapped in half and shorn away from the metal crank of the front wheel.

"They're getting away," Holmes noted.

"I know, but I can't..."

"There's no time. Climb on, Watson."

"But... But..."

"Miss Smith is in danger! She's almost to Charlington Hall! Climb on."

I obeyed. As I climbed back to my post, I told Holmes, "All right, but let's try to accomplish this without resorting to magic, shall we?"

"And how do you propose we do that, Watson?"

"The first portion is slightly downhill; that plays to our favor. You can push, Holmes, and I can put my feet on the ground and shuffle us—"

But Holmes thrust one hand out behind us and shouted, "Forzza!" There came a sudden boom and the flash of hellfire as our tricycle heaved its front wheel skyward and shot down the hill.

"No magiiiiiiiiiiiiiiiiiiiiiiiiiiiiiiiiic!"

"Steady on, Watson. You steer."

"How? The wheel's not even touching!"

The tiniest reduction in our speed brought the front

wheel back to earth, whereupon the remaining pedal assembly spun up to speed and began battering my foot bones to dust.

"Ow! Ow! Ow!"

"Steer, I said!"

"Ow! Ow!"

"Well then… hold your feet out to the sides and steer. We're coming up on the first fellow now, don't hit him!"

The rearmost tricyclist's progress was so pathetic that not only had Violet hopelessly outdistanced him, we were quickly overtaking him, as well.

"Who is he?" Holmes yelled to me, over the roar of the rocket-like plume of hellfire he was sending out behind us.

"I think it must be Cyril Morton! He's young, with the pale complexion and weak wind of an indoor worker."

"But why would he be here, Watson, hunting his own fiancée?"

"He may be here to protect her. Recall that more and more riders have been showing up as the weeks go past. He likely came only after Violet's letters let him know she was in danger."

"So, we can learn nothing from him?"

"Unlikely. I think we will not know the true nature of these odd occurrences until we find the original stalker. That first, solitary tricyclist: he is the man who can tell us all."

"Maybe this is him," Holmes volunteered as we neared the second rider.

"It very well may be," I agreed. "That's Robert Carruthers."

"How can you tell? He's got a gigantic black beard!"

"Yes," I said, as we rocketed past, "but his clumsily re-sewn scalp is coming loose in the breeze."

"Egads! So it is!" Holmes noted.

"From which, we learn…?"

"Erm… don't let the Living Jingo punch you in the head?"

"Correct! Well done, Holmes!"

"Watson, look! What's that?"

I followed his outstretched finger and squinted down the lane. Far ahead of us—far ahead of even Violet Smith—a dark speck had just come into view from the direction of Farnham. I could make out a pedaling figure amidst a wild and swirling cloud of dust. At first it looked like a child, for the size of the rider matched the size of his machine. Yet, when one compared the height of the rider to the total width of the road…

"Is that… Grogsson?" Holmes asked.

"Grogsson," I nodded.

"What's he riding?"

"Recall that he absconded with several hundred pounds of steel tubing and one of Scotland Yard's engineers," I said. "My guess is he's built himself a battle-trike."

"It does sound like him," Holmes admitted. "By the twelve gods, look at him go!"

Yet my mind was on more pressing matters. We were still a good way behind Violet Smith, but quickly gaining. For a moment I hoped that with Holmes and me by her side and Grogsson holding the road ahead, all would be well. But no. The ill-kept hedge maze of Charlington Hall grew so close to the lane in places as to nearly overhang its edge, and as Violet neared one such spot, a monstrous arm shot out and grasped the front wheel of her bicycle. The cycle halted instantly, pitching Miss Smith over the bars. She never hit the ground. With preternatural speed, Jack Woodley burst from the foliage, caught her by the waist with one claw-like hand and dragged her into the hedge maze, bicycle and all. Holmes and I barely had time to shout our dismay before he appeared again. He was wearing a devil's grin and holding one of the more time-ravaged specimens from Lord Charlington's tricycle collection. This, he flung at us with such power and accuracy that I could not help but admire the deed, even though it held rather dire portents for my future health.

"Every man for himself!" Holmes declared, then jumped off our speeding tricycle.

What could I do? The much-abused pedal assembly was still spinning fast enough to liquefy my feet if I were so foolish as to try and stop myself. I could try to turn out of the way, but at this speed… My deliberations were cut short as Woodley's tricycle crashed into the front of my own, upended me, and sent me bouncing down Charlington Lane. As I tumbled to a halt, Holmes hovered gracefully back to earth beside me.

"Holmes! Did you just magic yourself to safety and allow me to crash?"

"I did say 'every man for himself'," he huffed.

I tried to stand up to berate him, but lost my balance

and toppled down again. Was I injured? Exactly how many times had I bounced before I'd come to rest? As I gave myself a quick roadside triage, Robert Carruthers pedaled up behind us, leapt off his machine and yelled, "Don't just sit there, checking yourself for broken bones! We've got to save her!"

"Ah," said Holmes pleasantly. "So you wish no harm upon Violet Smith?"

"No, by God! I may not have entered into this thing with the purest of intentions, but she's a good girl—a wonderful girl—and I'll leave my carcass in Charlington Wood before I let that beast have his way!"

"We call him the Living Jingo," said Holmes.

"No we don't," I protested. "We do know his actual name, after all."

"Hm. Yes. But Living Jingo's better."

Carruthers stamped and shouted, "We have to save her! Now, are you with me?"

"I don't see why not," said Holmes. "Oh, except that it's a bit unseemly to team up with creepy old men who constantly propose marriage to the young women in their employ."

Carruthers colored with that special combination of rage and embarrassment. I laughed and said, "You know, Holmes, I wouldn't be surprised if that was the plan all along."

"What do you mean, Watson?"

"It occurred to me yesterday, when you pointed out the unusual quantity of suitors Violet Smith had suddenly accumulated. It all seems to have begun when some occurrence in South Africa caused half the Englishmen who reside there to speed home with the goal of marrying her. Now, do you remember the uncle she mentioned—the one who was supposed to have renewed the family fortune in the diamond mines of South Africa? Carruthers here came and reported that he died poor. But what if that is only half the truth? What if he died rich and childless with Violet as his heir? Might that not explain why everyone is suddenly so keen to wed her?"

"That is not why *all* of us wish to wed her," said Cyril Morton, as he coasted up to join us. His tone was as haughty as a sweat-soaked, choking, gasping mechanical engineering student could manage. "Though I do admit it doesn't... *hurt* matters."

Now that our little group was met, we plunged into the maze in pursuit of Violet Smith. Our progress was ponderous. We knew not which of the overgrown paths to take, the whole mess was strewn with disused tricycles, I was shaken from my fall and Cyril was just a wheezy and out-of-breath sort of fellow. Our delay frustrated Carruthers, who shouted, "Come on! Violet is in danger!"

"Not really," I said. "I'll confess I didn't realize how a defrocked clergyman came into the story, but now I think I've deduced it. Woodley has enlisted Williamson to legally wed him to Miss Smith, against her will. A pathetic plan— almost pitiable. One cannot ambush-marry an unwilling girl. That's simply not how marriage works."

Carruthers gave me a sideways glance and muttered, "That's not his plan. You've got it wrong."

"What do you mean?" I asked.

He paused his maze-running and gazed at Holmes and me appraisingly. "Are you gentlemen with the police?" he asked.

"I am often called upon to supply their deficiencies," said Holmes, "but happily Watson and I operate outside the law. *Quite* outside. Watson, for example, frequently kills people."

"What? No I don't!"

"You killed Grimesby Roylott."

"By accident!"

"Killed me once."

"Yet here you stand."

"Shut up! Both of you!" Carruthers howled. "Look, there's every chance I don't make it through this alive and—so long as you're not coppers—I'm happy for someone to know the whole story. To start with, that thing in there is not Jack Woodley; *I* am Jack Woodley!"

"Eh?" said Holmes.

"Used to be a bit rough, in my youth. They called me Roaring Jack and it wasn't long before I got myself sentenced to transportation for life. But I was one of the last and Australia's not the prison it once was—wasn't hard to adopt the name Robert Carruthers and slip onto a steamer to South Africa with the hope of making my fortune. Which I did not. But I did meet Ralph Smith who seemed to have found just about every diamond in South Africa the De Beer brothers missed. Worked for him. Became friends. Rather thought he might remember me in his will. Imagine how I felt when I learned everything went to a niece he barely knew! So yes, Watson, you guessed that part right. I risked discovery and death to come try to marry the fortune that slipped through my fingers."

The part I'd guessed made perfect sense to me, yet other details seemed incongruous. "What I don't understand, Mr. Carruthers—or rather, Mr. Woodley—is why another man would wish to steal your name? Why would anybody want to adopt the persona of a transported criminal under sentence of death if he returned to England?"

"To unsettle me!" Woodley grunted. "You've seen that beast in there! Can you imagine anybody who knew me in my youth looking at him and mistaking it for me? No. He's safe. But I'm not. He took the name just so word would spread through town that Jack Woodley was back—to make it harder for me to operate here. And it has! I hardly dare show my face outside my home without a false beard on. He lied about his name and his history. He's never been to South Africa. Oh, and he didn't bring the clergyman just to marry Violet Smith!"

"But then, who is he and why would—"

My words were arrested by a monstrous voice, which bellowed, "Priest! Grant me benediction!"

"Here," replied the nervous voice of Horton Williamson. "Do it yourself!"

We must have been very near the exit to the maze, for the voices to be so clear. There was the sound of shuffling feet, followed by a beastly roar of pain and triumph and the voice of not-actually-Jack-Woodley (and yes, I purposely refuse to call him the Living Jingo) calling, "There! Done! Say your words, priest!"

"I keep telling you: I'm not a pr—"

"Say the words!"

"Very well. On your marks..."

"*On your marks?*" I wondered aloud, but as we turned the final corner of the maze, the scene that revealed itself to my eyes answered all my questions. There stood Horton Williamson, with a revolver and a nervous expression. Behind him, mounted on a tricycle, was the grotesque form of (oh, very well) the Living Jingo. He was removing Williamson's "benediction"—which took the form of a brass syringe—from his chest. It seems he'd just finished injecting the contents directly into his heart. He crushed the syringe in his fist and threw it to the ground as Williamson reluctantly called, "Get set..."

The grounds behind Charlington Hall had been built into a large, oval obstacle course. On the close side, the Living Jingo sat ready on his tricycle. On the far side, with half a lap's head start, sat Violet Smith, with her hands and feet tied to her beloved bicycle. She was leaning, motionless, against a tree, with only thirty feet of clear track ahead of her before she got to the earthen-bumps challenge, followed by the sand pit, the mud-slicked corner, a brief straight, the bricks-all-over-it corner and a quick run to the finish line. As soon as I saw it, I realized, "Wait! So the Living Jingo is... *Lord Charlington?*"

Woodley gave a grim nod. "Bent on revenge against the woman who nearly killed him and on achieving the final victory of the tricycle over the bicycle."

Horton Williamson leveled his pistol at us and demanded, "Stay back! The race is about to begin!"

I paid him little mind. I turned the new facts over and over in my mind and muttered, "So then... the clergyman..."

"From what I gather, Lord Charlington's heart gave out on him, following his showdown with Violet," said Woodley. "Halfway to his country retreat, they were forced to halt and call for a clergyman to perform final rites. What they got was an ex-clergyman who was certain he'd discovered a formula that could turn a man into an angel. Since Lord Charlington was dying, they agreed to let him administer it, as a last resort."

"So, that's supposed to be an angel, is it?" I asked.

"It's a Living Jingo," said Holmes, affectionately.

Horton Williamson's eyes filled with tears and he whispered to us, "I'd meant it to be an angel, but... with every dose... he's stronger, but he's less human, less reasonable, more... red-headed."

Lord Charlington gave a roar of impatience and Williamson spluttered, "Oh! Yes! What I'd meant to say was: *go!*"

He then discharged his pistol, right through Woodley's left leg.

"Oh!" Williamson cried. "I'm sorry! I didn't... I'm sorry!"

As he crumpled to the ground, Roaring Jack Woodley gave Williamson the kind of look that is intended to convey that any recent apologies the bearer has received have not been accepted as adequate. At the instant of discharge, both Lord Charlington and Violet Smith sprang to action. As we'd seen on our last visit, Lord Charlington was a right terror with a tricycle. His angel-juice-enhanced legs pumped away with grand effect. He was the picture of strength and grace, his reflexes perfect. But Violet... she was...

Wonderful.

I'd deemed her athletic the moment I'd met her and I'd read of her accomplishments in the contest that won her that bike, but I just hadn't realized the extent of her talent. She shot down the straight and onto the bumps, holding herself up off the seat as the cycle bucked beneath her until she ploughed into the power-sapping sand. When she got to the mud, she just let the rear wheel slide where it would, powering through with all her weight on the front wheel and her steely eyes already locked on the corner. She pushed her cycle to its very limits, flirting with the ragged edge of possibility.

Also to her advantage was that Lord Charlington's obstacle course was—like all forms of terrain—much easier for a bicycle than a tricycle. When she came to the bricks-all-over-it corner, Violet needed a clear path only one wheel's width across. When Lord Charlington got there his front wheel was easy to guide through, but his right wheel might catch a brick and jerk his machine off course. Or if not that, then the left. He roared at his own lack of cleverness. Only when he got to the straights or the sandpit did his enormous advantage in strength come to the fore, overwhelming the deficiencies of his machine.

"Ah, I love a good race," said Holmes, stepping over the fallen form of Jack Woodley. "Tell me, Williamson, what am I looking at?"

As Holmes approached, Williamson gave the pistol a feeble wave of warning. Holmes disregarded it and threw a jovial arm about Williamson's shoulder. The ex-clergyman stared at him in shock and muttered, "Well… it's a four-lap race. Miss Smith gets a half-lap head start. But if Lord Charlington catches her… um…" Here Williamson paused to look miserable and apologetic. "He's allowed to kill her."

"Hang on!" said Holmes. "That's a bit outside the realm of fair sport, don't you think? No, no, no. I can't allow it. I'm stopping the race."

"You can't! I have a gun!"

"I see that, and it's very scary," said Holmes, giving Williamson's shoulder a reassuring pat, "but in just one moment, I'm about to have a Grogsson."

He was right. Above the clamor of Charlington's death-race, a new sound arose. *Screek, screek, screek. Smash! Screek, screek, screek. Smash!* From the sound of things, Grogsson had elected to take the direct route through Charlington's maze.

"Aaaaaaaaaaaah! Everybody get clear!" I screamed. I ran to Woodley and grabbed his jacket, thinking to drag him to safety. But where might safety be found?

"What's a Grogsson?" Williamson wondered and

no sooner had the words come out of his mouth than he found out.

Oh God…

That tricycle…

It must have weighed three hundred pounds. It was constructed entirely of welded steel and looked capable of withstanding three or four direct artillery hits. He must have gone through all the metal he'd taken from Scotland Yard, for the cycle included one park bench and a municipal street lamp. It was gigantic—ample for even Grogsson's frame. Where had he found tires to fit tricycle rims of such size? He hadn't. The wheels were just hoops of steel, clad in jagged bits of scrap-metal that had been welded on at all angles. These rings of rolling shrapnel clawed the ground with such effectiveness that even Grogsson's mighty pedal-pumps did not cause them to slide or skid. The hedge walls didn't slow him; he smashed through with perfect impunity.

He wore his familiar bowler, jacket and tie, but had matched them (poorly) to the most immense pair of schoolboy shorts I had ever seen and a pair of gigantic hobnail boots. Oh, and he had a little pair of brass goggles, just like Violet Smith's. Other than that, the only thing he wore was the grim visage of somebody who knows he's about to enter into a fight to the death, but that's all right because he's rather good at that sort of thing. He tore through the final hedge less than a dozen feet from me. Five feet closer and he'd have sawed Jack Woodley's legs right off.

As soon as he cleared the maze, Grogsson made straight for the racecourse, howling his battle cry. He entered just ahead of Charlington and tried to ram him. But Charlington was nimbler. *Far* nimbler. He easily swerved away and kept after Violet Smith. Despite her efforts, Charlington was gaining. Grogsson set off after them, but what could he do? It was clear he didn't have the speed to catch Charlington.

So, he simply turned his machine around and set off the other way. He met them head-on as they cleared the boulders-swinging-about-on-the-end-of-ropes section and entered the angry-dogs-on-short-leads hazard. Again, Grogsson tried to ram Charlington. Again, Charlington dodged him easily. He even gave a laugh of triumph as he pedaled past.

Grogsson howled in frustration, but nevertheless adapted admirably. He pedaled straight across to the other side of the oval, dismounted and waited. As Smith and Charlington cleared the corner and sped towards him, Grogsson reached down and scooped up a few of the jagged rocks that had been strewn about as obstacles. He flung one at Charlington. Violet gave a squeal of terror as it whizzed past her, but Charlington merely swerved to one side. Grogsson loosed the second stone; Charlington dodged again.

Now, I know I may have spoken archly of Grogsson's intelligence, but I will grant him this: in battle, his creative impulses are absolutely inspired. When he next reached for a projectile, Grogsson chose not a stone, but

"Again, Charlington dodged him easily."

a magnificent log, twenty-five feet long and as thick as a man's torso. He waited for Violet to come past him, then whipped it lengthwise, across the track and hurled it forward. The thing was longer than the track was wide; Charlington had nowhere to go. He leapt clear of his saddle, just as the log smashed his beloved tricycle to scrap. He landed behind Grogsson, who turned to face him with a gloating smile.

Perhaps he should not have been so smug. True, Charlington could not equal Grogsson for strength or toughness, because... honestly... what can? Yet Charlington possessed such an abundance of agility as to render those advantages moot. As the two set at one another, it grew rapidly apparent that Grogsson was overmatched. Though his punches would have cracked brick walls and his kicks could have felled rhinoceri, they struck nothing but empty air. Charlington gleefully dodged them all, ducking in from time to time to slash at Grogsson with his claws. Most of Charlington's attacks glanced off Grogsson's hairy hide, but a few found purchase. Twenty seconds into the fight, Grogsson was amassing an impressive collection of little wounds.

Violet was coming round towards us, so I left Woodley to the clumsy, mechanical ministrations of Cyril Morton and ran to the edge of the track, shouting, "Miss Smith! This way! We'll save you!"

Though I'm sure she had better uses for her breath, she spared me just enough to yell, "There's two laps left!"

"But... What?" I spluttered. "The race doesn't matter!

Or look: there's a monster fight on the track. Surely that cancels the race, doesn't it?"

Yet Horton Williamson approached, waving his pistol imperiously and shouting, "No! This man has no say in the matter! He is not a race official!"

As Violet Smith tore past, she gave me a little shrug that said, "What can I do? You're not a race official."

She continued round to where Grogsson and Charlington battled. Grogsson scooped up his opponent's wrecked tricycle and tried to smash him with it, but Charlington danced away, then back in, slashing at Torg's eyes. Grogsson recoiled, howling. Charlington could not help but laugh at his stricken foe, which was just the opportunity Violet Smith needed to dart her bicycle between them, neatly clearing the most hazardous hazard of the day.

Charlington seemed rather surprised to see her flash past. Yet this was sufficient to remind him that—regardless of any monster duels he might be engaged in—he was losing the race. He took a page from Grogsson's book and charged straight across the track to intercept Violet near the start/finish line. Grogsson stayed on his heels, which would have been comforting if it didn't mean there was a monster battle planned for where Holmes, Williamson and I were standing.

As I scrambled to safety, Charlington stopped in the middle of the track and Grogsson nearly ploughed into him. Again, Charlington leapt aside, but you could see he was rather tired of Grogsson's interference. He'd inflicted significant damage while suffering none himself, yet if Charlington were ever going to have some nice, uninterrupted time to murder Violet Smith, it was clear Grogsson must be dealt with first. Stepping under a mighty left-handed swing, Charlington came up behind Grogsson's flailing fist and struck. He buried the claws of his right hand wrist-deep in Grogsson's side.

Grogsson smiled.

Charlington twisted his fingers in Grogsson's guts, staring up at the big detective, no doubt hoping to see him cry out. Grogsson did not. With practiced calm he reached his left hand down, grabbed Charlington's wrist and plucked the talons out of his side. Then...

And this is the key bit...

He didn't let go.

There would be no more dodging about for Lord Charlington. From that point on, it was no longer a fight, simply... well... how to put it? Ah!

Fist-murder.

Holmes, Woodley, Williamson, Morton and I watched with varying expressions of wonder and horror.

"Way to go, old chap!" Holmes cheered, as the blows rained down. "That will show him!"

"Er... yes... um... quite right," I agreed, glad for the victory but more than a bit put off by the treatment Charlington was receiving. He was a lord, after all. Woodley and Williamson stared, mouths agape. Cyril Morton began to cry.

"Get him again!" Holmes shouted. "Again! One more!

Oh look, Watson: Grogsson's pulled the Jingo's false moustache off! I suppose we might remove ours as well."

"You seem to be half-right, Holmes," I said.

"Eh?"

"It appears Lord Charlington was the only one present whose grandiose facial hair was genuine. Yes, Grogsson has removed it, but note that the upper lip has come away as well."

Woodley, who had regained his feet with Cyril's help, went positively green and declared, "By God! I don't think I shall ever be able to eat again."

"You'd have an easier time of it than Lord Charlington, I'll bet," Holmes noted.

Grogsson whipped what was left of Charlington up over his head and smashed him down onto the ground. Then up again and down on the other side. Then back to the first side again. Then he flung the pulpy mess away into the trees.

"No! My angel!" Williamson cried. "What have you done?" With tears in his eyes, he pointed his pistol at Grogsson's back and pulled back the hammer. This proved to be a deadly mistake. The click alerted Grogsson, who spun around and smote Williamson with the only weapon he had to hand: the disembodied leg of the until-so-recently-Living Jingo. The blow was so savage that two of the Jingo's talon-like toes poked through Williamson's temple and into his brain. He fell, twitching and writhing.

"Well," I said, gazing from Williamson, to the leg-shot

Woodley, to the well-lacerated Grogsson. "Looks like I've got a bit of work to do, eh?"

Having at last negotiated the slower section of the track, Violet Smith rattled up to us.

Aaaaand right on past, causing me to stammer, "What is she...? Oh... No, of course... One more lap."

Grogsson stalked up, wiping his nose with the back of his blood-soaked forearm. As he neared, Holmes and I at last divested ourselves of our false facial hair—an act that caused Grogsson to jump back and cry, "Warlock? Watson? What you doing here?"

"Oh, Lestrade thought you might like a little help," Holmes chirped. "Not that you needed it, eh?"

Grogsson nodded and moved past us, towards our two companions, approaching Woodley first. Towering over the fifty-something transportee, Grogsson demanded, "Who you? Good man? Or *bad* man?"

"Um... well... I suppose I entered into this adventure as a bad man," Woodley stammered, "but I repented of it, you see, and I tried to do my best by Violet and I never harmed anybody, so... please don't hurt me?"

Grogsson stared down at him for a few moments, clenching and unclenching his blood-soaked fists, before he at last decided, "M'kay."

Woodley sighed his relief, soiled his britches, and fainted dead away. Grogsson next moved to Morton, poked him in the chest with one finger (leaving a pretty impressive smear of Jingo-juice) and asked, "Who you?"

I leapt to pull Cyril back and shouted, "He is Cyril

Morton, Miss Smith's fiancé, and you are not—under any circumstances—to murder him in hopes of courting her!"

Grogsson stared down at me as if he could not fathom *what* I was talking about. I harrumphed and told him, "I think it's perfectly clear to everybody that you're smitten with her. Why else would you spend two weeks following her about, construct a battle-trike and fight a monster on her behalf?"

He let my question roll about in his head for a few moments, before giving me one of the best two-word answers I've ever had. "She asked."

I recoiled, shocked. "You're not in love with Violet Smith?"

Grogsson, suddenly sheepish, cleared his throat and confided, "Real nice lady, sure. But… um… kinda weird."

Even as he said it, the non-object of his affections cleared the start/finish line for the final time and coasted over to us, exhausted and triumphant.

"Yaaaaaaaaaay!" cried Holmes. "The winner!"

That is about all there was of the matter, save cleanup. Chiltern Grange served as our infirmary. Roaring Jack Woodley was quickly put to rights. Grogsson took a bit more effort. As I worked, Holmes hovered, his mood becoming ever more glum. Finally I asked him, "What's the matter, Warlock?"

"Oh, I suppose everything turned out all right, but… we never solved the mystery!"

"Didn't we?"

"No! Who was the solitary tricyclist?"

"Oh," said Woodley, from his sickbed. "I was. I couldn't let Violet go all the way to Farnham alone, could I? Not with Charlington after her."

"Well enough, but who was the second?" Holmes pressed, determined to maintain his disappointment.

"Torg!" said Grogsson, from the next bed over.

"All right," said Holmes, "but the identity of the third tricyclist shall ever remain—"

"That was me!" Cyril piped up. "When I got Violet's letters, I had to come."

"And the fourth, we all know, was Charlington," I interjected, before Holmes could start.

"Yes, yes, yes!" tutted Holmes. "But who could it have been upon that mysterious fifth tricycle?"

"Well, that was… you and me, Holmes."

"Ah… so it was."

Horton Williamson, regrettably, could not be saved. The brain swelling was too severe and he languished in delirium. He died three days later, delivering half-sensible, fever-bred monologues on the subject of angels and how— if you place all your hopes and faith in them—they always let you down. With his passing, the formula for his angel-making serum was forever lost.

Or so I foolishly assumed.

THE HELL-HOUND OF THE BASKERVILLES

PART I

FROM THE JOURNAL OF DR. JOHN WATSON

1

MUCH AS I LONGED TO SAY SUMMER WAS SLOWLY giving way to the coming autumn, the truth was it had gone already. September is still a summer month in London, but this was the start of October, when each sunny day is an act of denial. The sky, more often gray than blue, had begun to offer its offensive autumn rains. Yet even those sudden deluges had not been enough to allow the leaves to keep their green. Orange and yellow death crept at their edges and a few of London's trees lay already bare.

As I stood divesting myself of hat, coat, gloves and cane after my morning constitutional, Holmes asked me, "How was the walk, Watson?"

I could tell he cared not a whit for my answer. He was in a proper sulk and sat wreathed in smoke, puffing at that pipe of his—a comfort to which he often turned when he had nothing else to occupy his mind.

"I wish you would join me, Holmes. The air might do you good."

"It might," he replied, evasively. Not only did he look

irritated, he also spoke numbly, as one who has a terrible head cold.

"Is something the matter, Holmes?"

"I have been tyrannized by a sneeze all morning. Do you know the feeling? You need to sneeze, but no matter how long you sit and wait, it never comes. I tell you, my head is pounding with it! I can feel it in there, Watson! It is solid as a brick and long as a man's leg."

Being a doctor, I not only knew the feeling, but also a cure. I opened the spice drawer, from which I withdrew a bit of pepper and mixed it in my palm with a pinch of chili powder. I stepped behind Holmes and waited for him to draw his next heavy, melancholic breath. As soon as he began it, I flicked my little cloud of irritant into the air in front of him. He grasped the table in surprise, but before he could protest at the treatment, he shattered the very air with a thunderous sneeze. A three-foot-long black rod flew from his nose and clattered to the table.

"By God!" I cried.

"Owwwwwwwwwwwwww!"

"What is it, Holmes?"

"Ah! Ah! My nose!"

"No—the thing that came *out* of your nose! What the deuce is it?"

"I can't look," he protested, clutching his bleeding proboscis. "You tell me."

I leaned in over the unusual projectile. "It seems to be a walking stick."

"Odd," said Holmes, who had a talent for understatements at moments such as these. "What do you think it means, Watson?"

"Well, Holmes, here is what I make of it," I began, examining it as I spoke. "It is owned by a country doctor who trained in London. He likes animals, but he has little care for impressing his fellow man."

"How do you know?"

"Well, it helps that there's an inscription: 'For James Mortimer, M.R.C.S. From his friends at C.C.H.—1876.' So we know he is a doctor, who spent time at Charing Cross Hospital, but I will promise you he no longer resides in London."

"Er… how…?"

"From the wear. Observe that it is badly worn where he grips it—and also here, in the middle—but that the steel walking cap is practically untouched. Thus, he uses it a great deal, but not on London's paved streets or the stones would have taken their toll on the tip. Equally certain is that he does not carry it in the presence of London doctors. They would mock him for allowing the badge of his gentility to look so battered."

"Did you say he managed to wear away the *middle* of his cane?" Holmes wondered. "How did he do that?"

"*He* hasn't. He relies on another to fetch and carry it for him. He has chosen his help in the typical country style—or shall I say, with the lack of style, typical in the country. In the course of serving his master, this particular aide has left tooth marks all across the middle."

"Tooth marks?" Warlock wondered.

"He keeps a dog."

"Bravo, Watson!" Warlock cheered. "But what do you suppose this could mean—sneezing out a walking stick?"

"That, I cannot say. Observation serves to illuminate *what* you have disgorged, but it fails when it comes to the concern of *why*. Surely this is your purview, Holmes. What does it usually mean when this sort of thing happens?"

"Dashed if I know," Holmes shrugged. "This is the first time I have sneezed out another man's personal effects. I don't mind telling you that it is an experience I hope not to repeat! Unless it is something smaller, like cufflinks or some such."

"Then I suggest we put it in the elephant foot, beside my own." Walking to the door, I slid it into the umbrella stand and stated, "All we can do is wait and hope for clarity to…" I did not finish my sentence, as the bell rang.

"Hey!" yelled Mrs. Hudson from outside, giving our door a kick. "Gent'man to see Mr. Holmes!"

Holmes favored me with that look of self-satisfaction he generated whenever he knew he was about to do something impressive, and loudly called out, "By all means, Dr. Mortimer, do come in and join us!"

"By Jove! However did you know me?" cried our visitor, pushing open the door. He was a man in his late thirties, with a young, eager face and an air of earnestness. His uneven whiskers and careless dress indicated he had little regard for his appearance.

Warlock, who often treated wonderment as if it were praise, smiled generously and replied, "My dear Dr.

Mortimer, there are a thousand telling traits we carry on our person at all times. Observed by the trained eye, these seemingly innocuous clues can reveal all."

"Well, yes," said Mortimer, "but you hadn't observed me yet. I was outside."

"Oh… damn…"

"And I feel I should mention: I am only a practitioner. He with his MRCS has not earned the right to the title 'doctor'."

"Tosh!" I scoffed. "I'm a doctor myself and can tell you: that is a useless distinction. Why a man who has spent eight years studying paintings should be called doctor, while a man who has helped hundreds keep their health may not, I will never know."

Mortimer seemed much pleased by this and gave me a nod of thanks. I reached out to shake his hand and declared myself, "Dr. John Watson, at your service. Waste no time in wondering how Warlock Holmes comes by his deductions, Dr. Mortimer, but take heart. What does it prove except that he is without peer at the very skills you doubtlessly came to engage him for?"

Mortimer appeared ready to agree, but paused. It seemed he was one of those rare men on whom the burden of truth rests heavily, for he said, "Well, except Alphonse Bertillon, of course. I mean, if we are to discuss the number of subjects apprehended, or contributions to the field…"

"Hey!" protested Holmes.

Yet, Mortimer had a point I could not deny. I confess that I bore—and still do—a great respect for the French savant. "Always excepting Monsieur Bertillon," I conceded.

"Hey!" said Holmes, again.

"In most matters, I mean! Most matters," Mortimer said, to placate Holmes. "I'm sure for the question of the day, you are the only man."

"How unfortunate for you," Holmes groused.

Yet Mortimer seemed already lost in his own confusion; he said, "I confess, I am quite out of my depth. I come to you with a great question—a mystery I cannot fathom. And also, this very morning, I have experienced a second mystery. I am sure it is of little importance, yet it confounds my understanding. Mr. Holmes, I need your help."

"Only with the small matter, I assume," said Holmes. "The large one is probably better left to the *impressive* Monsieur Bertillon…"

"Holmes, stop it," I said.

"Both matters may be solved by you, I hope," said Mortimer, still oblivious to Holmes's sarcasm.

"Let us begin with the lesser matter," I suggested.

"Oh… well… it's of no import, I think, but much strangeness. I am waiting for a gentleman who is to arrive by train today, as we shall discuss in a moment. This morning, I went to the station to check the schedule and what do you think happened? My walking stick! It disappeared!"

I began to formulate an explanation, but Holmes's eyes twinkled with mischief and he held up a hand to silence me. When I say that, I do not refer to the widely understood social convention of indicating with a hand or finger that you wish for somebody to remain silent.

No. Holmes waved a hand at me and I suddenly found myself gripped by a terrible, invisible force. My chest was constricted so violently, I thought my ribs would break. I could neither inhale, nor exhale and certainly not speak. I struggled against it, in vain, hardly able to move my body at all.

"Whatever can you mean, Mortimer?" asked Holmes. "Has something convinced you that you misplaced your walking stick?"

"Not misplaced," Mortimer insisted. "It disappeared! As I was leaning on it! I almost fell in front of the train."

"Poppycock!" Holmes declared. "You walked in with it in your hand, just a moment ago."

"I did no such thing."

"Excuse me, you did. You walked in, greeted us and placed it in that elephant-foot umbrella stand by the door."

"What are you talking about?" Mortimer wondered. "If that were true then it would be… right…" his words trailed off as he turned to behold his familiar walking stick, jutting its handle helpfully towards him. All the breath rushed out of him and he stood agape, helpless, trusting nevermore in his own powers of reason.

"Oh dear…" said Holmes. "Doctor, what does it indicate when somebody perceives things which are not actual? Does it not suggest insanity?"

Mortimer gave a pained look and admitted, "Yes… I suppose it does."

"Excuse me, but I was addressing Watson," Holmes said. "He is, after all, an *actual* doctor."

Warlock turned to smile at me and suddenly I felt the hellish grip fall away. My breath returned in a sudden gasp, which I used to form the words, "Holmes! Really! That was offside!"

"And yet we find the smaller matter solved." He smiled and, as I had come to know him well, I could tell his petty vengeance had run its course. "Perhaps we ought to turn our attentions to the larger concern?"

"No, no. We mustn't. Not yet," said Mortimer. "The gentleman it regards has agreed to meet me here. He is in grave danger, Mr. Holmes, and he knows nothing of it. I did not know how to tell him without seeming a fool. I thought, perhaps, if you could hear it as well and offer your opinion… He should be along at any moment."

"As you wish," said Holmes, shrugging and turning back to reclaim his still-smoking pipe.

"Dr. Mortimer, would you care for a cup of tea while you wait? I find it has a great power to soothe the nerves."

"Thank you, I would."

I settled him in a chair by the fire, wrapped his shaking shoulders in a blanket and set about making the tea. The water had scarce reached a boil when the bell rang once more.

"Another gentleman—a real gentleman—to see Mr. Holmes," Mrs. Hudson announced. From her tone, I presumed Mrs. Hudson preferred this new visitor to the last. Sure enough, as I opened the door, I found her leaning upon his arm, staring up at him with wide dewy eyes which declared, "Hello, I am a little lost puppy dog. Wouldn't you like to take me home?"

Yet such behaviors were expected from our remarkably sub-standard landlady. No, it was not she that drew my shocked gasp, but the man who accompanied her. He was short—he could not have stood more than five foot three. He was stocky, muscular and—though his youth would almost disqualify the description—grizzled. His dark hair swept up into two points just above either ear and his unkempt sideburns made a second set, just below. He wore a flannel shirt, dungarees, boots and braces: absolutely no single article of clothing fit for civilized company. The stumpy cigar he clenched in his teeth gave forth an aromatic bouquet, which declared that it was of a lordly quality and no small cost. This did little to dispel the impression that a wayward lumberjack had just been dumped upon my threshold and that I was expected to allow the filthy fellow into my house.

"By God!" I cried, staggering back. "A Canadian!"

True, my adventures with Holmes had brought me into contact with more than a few Americans, but this was my first Canadian. They may seem similar, but I assure you, they are an entirely different breed. The Americans had at least possessed the decency to rebel—to meet us upon the field of blood and fire and to assert their right to self-govern with honor. The fact that they beat us indicates that they are not without their merits.

The Canadians can make no such claim. They remain within our empire and, as such, have a closer claim to our love. Yet, it seems to me, nothing ever comes from that place but beaver pelts and disreputable behavior.

"No, no, no, Dr. Watson," Mortimer cried, flinging himself between us. "This gentleman has spent many years abroad, to be sure, but he is a British baronet, by right of birth. This is Sir Henry Baskerville."

A Canadian with hereditary rank? My worst nightmare!

Our guest extended his hand towards me and said, "You c'n just call me Hank."

"The devil I will, sir! I would sooner nail both my feet to a charging rhinoceros than call a member of the British aristocracy 'Hank'!"

The impropriety of the situation was entirely lost on Holmes, who chose that moment to breeze past me, shake the outstretched hand and say, "It is an honor to meet you, Hank. Won't you step inside?"

"Thanks, Mr…?"

"My name is Warlock Holmes. This is my friend, Dr. John Watson. James Mortimer I think you know already."

"Just by correspondence," the gruff baronet said, then shook Mortimer's hand. "Good to meet you in person, Jim."

"No," I protested. "You must address him as James. Or better still, as Mortimer."

Sir Henry slowly turned back to me and grunted, "You seem to have some kind of problem with me, eh, Doc?"

"Well… no, sir… I…" I had to take a moment to collect my thoughts. "I think I have a problem with our system of governance and social order."

"Well, why are you takin' it out on me?"

"Because you have wounded us, sir! You have hit us

right in one of our ancient injuries—one of those chinks in the venerable armor every true Englishman loves so well."

He stared at me, waiting for me to make some sense, I suppose.

"Look, we British have allowed some of our positions of authority to be inherited—your baronetcy is one such honor. Now, we would not have done this if we did not trust in English blood. We know—*we know*—that the excellence of lords is passed to their scions. The stiff upper-lippedness. The quick mind and willing courage. The fashion sense! To see someone who does not seem English advancing to such a position threatens everything we think we know about the world."

He gave me an angry look, but I could see in his eyes that he was digesting the wisdom of my words. Finally, he sighed. "Yeah. All right. I guess I gotta work on that."

"Thank you, Sir Henry."

"You'll let me know if I take a wrong step?"

"I'm not sure I could stop myself."

"Now that that is all settled," Mortimer said, "I wonder if we might address the matter of the day. I'm sure Mr. Holmes and Dr. Watson wouldn't mind if you joined us for a spot of tea…"

Sir Henry nodded, but asked, "Got any coffee?"

"Tea!" I cried, louder than I meant to.

"But… coffee's better."

"Not in your public opinion, it isn't! The day we find an English aristocrat who does not positively worship a cup of tea is the day the empire crumbles!"

"Argh… fine… tea. But with lots o' milk and sugar. That's okay, isn't it?"

"Of course it is. Don't be silly."

Mortimer handed him his cup of milky tea, which he accepted dutifully. As we all began to settle ourselves in the sitting-room chairs, Sir Henry wondered aloud, "So, is that why you had me meet you here, Mortimer? For this little tea intervention?"

"Oh no, Sir Henry, for a different reason entirely."

"Which is?"

"Um… Well, how should I say it? How does one approach the subject of…" Mortimer stammered and sputtered for a few moments, but finally gave up. He shrugged, withdrew from his pocket a document that had to be at least one hundred years old, slapped it on the table and said, "Sir Henry, you are going to be killed by a demon."

2

From the pen of Landron Baskerville
Baskerville Hall, Dartmoor, 18 August 1747

My dear boys, you are nearing that age where you must set out from this, our family seat, into the larger world. The other schoolboys will be cruel. Expect pranks, do not shy from the occasional use of fisticuffs, and be prepared to hear wicked things said. I do not doubt that the other boys will call you "cursed" and say you are "descended from blackguards and cads" and insist that you are destined to be "hunted to your death by a demonic dog".

You are not to assume that this is merely something boys say to each other. It is particular to the two of you and, I am sorry to say, it is true.

It all begins with your great-grandfather, Sir Hugo Baskerville, who was a right bastard, and no denying. Safe in this Hall, he abused the folk all about with abandon and impunity. It is rumored he used Baskerville Hall as a center for the study of dark magic. Whatever the purpose of Sir Hugo's midnight congregations, we must pause to consider the happenings at one such gathering on Michaelmas, the year of our lord 1643.

On that night, Sir Hugo was met here by several of his confederates, whose identities are lost to us. He was a widower—his wife Olivia having perished in a fall from the East Tower window—and was engaged in the search for a suitable replacement. One particular local woman had been the recipient of most of his attentions. We know little of her, save that she was sweet of appearance and disposition and wished nothing to do with the blackguard, Hugo. For months he courted her, but always she resisted. So, of course, he kidnapped her and locked her in the East Tower.

This dark deed was perpetrated only three days before Michaelmas. Sir Hugo was already planning to host an event of some sort on that night, and appears to have decided to "save" her for the festivities. Just after sundown, Michaelmas night, his confederates began to arrive. In short order, they were deep in their cups and arguing loudly. A topic of some merriment was the fate of the poor woman who waited in the tower. Doubtless, she could hear them in their revels. Driven by the horror of what approached, she risked the fate of Hugo's wife, but managed what the late Lady Baskerville could not. She climbed down the ivy and safely reached the bottom of the tower, then set off across the moor, towards her family abode.

At the witching hour, Sir Hugo arrived to take her down to the party, but found the room empty. This apparently caused no end of fun at Sir Hugo's expense amongst the assembled rabble. Hugo called for horse and hound, climbed into his saddle and set his dogs upon her.

It is not clear how the maiden met her end. I blush to say, it is likely she was run down by Sir Hugo's dogs, which he valued for their ferocity. Most probably, she was mauled by his pack and lost her life upon the moor. In any case, she never returned to her family or was seen by the eyes of men. Sir Hugo is universally blamed for her demise.

Yet, the more interesting occurrence that night (at least to you, my poor sons) must be the death of Sir Hugo. His guests followed him onto the moor. After a few minutes' gallop, they came across a strange sight: one of Sir Hugo's hounds, with all his limbs torn off, struggling to drag himself back to Baskerville Hall. In a moment more, they found themselves riding through the charnel remains of Hugo's whole pack, each of them rent and torn, such that their innards traced the path to Sir Hugo's fallen stallion and finally to the man himself.

You must know, my sons, that the moor has a certain reputation. It has long been assumed to be a realm where man is a guest and not the master. Dartmoor is home to many of England's greater ley-lines and is considered more the domain of fairies than men. Here, upon the moor, wicked deeds can walk, can breathe, can kill. The local peasants say that Hugo's evil acts, culminating with the release of the hounds upon his poor hostage, were given form by the moor and set loose to visit back upon him and his family the cruelty he had shown to others.

When Sir Hugo's guests at last found him, he lay upon his back, on blood-soaked ground. Over him stood a creature of hell, a hound of such stature as had never been seen before—burning hackle, tooth and mane, with unholy fires. In its teeth it held the front part of Sir Hugo's throat, which it had torn free, leaving him to scream the last of his wicked breath out in ever-lessening gurgles. Several of the guests are said to have harried the beast with blade and musket, but to no avail. As soon as Sir Hugo's soul had fled, the beast turned and charged them, breaking through the line of terrified steeds and disappearing upon the moor.

Since that day, the members of our family have been unhappy in their demises. Well... probably most men are, I suppose. But we are less happy than most.

My father, as you know, went out alone upon the moor one night, and never returned. If you doubt the ferocity of the beast, visit the dressing room of the second bedroom from the end, third floor, west wing. It was here your grandfather Winthrop installed his mistress, according to the Baskerville tradition (wives in the east wing, mistresses in the west). Arriving early one evening to find her still at dinner, the old lecher thought to have a bath whilst he awaited her. Woe that the dressing-room window—which we believe he left open—looks out upon the moor. The beast left us very little of him, but it did have the courtesy to leave most of the corpse in the bathtub, which aided us in cleanup. The mark of the beast's nails can still be seen upon the floorboards. The smaller ones on the walls are Sir Winthrop's; he must have clawed awfully during that final struggle.

My sons, you may be asking yourselves: what motivation have I to tread the narrow path, to be a man of virtue, if despite all my pains, I am to be slain and dragged to hell by a demon hound? The answer, of course is: none. None at all. If you are to be punished as a blackguard, it falls to you to deserve your fate and thus keep heaven's justice intact. You need not be overt murderers; in fact the legacy of our family is in subtle oppression. I therefore enjoin you to focus your school studies on topics that facilitate personal gain by socially accepted misuse of your fellow man. Politics and law are promising, but I tell you this: the future lies in banking.

Your doting father,
Sir Landron Baskerville

We all read the letter over, a few times. Dr. Mortimer fretted—afraid, I suppose, that we should laugh at him for thinking such a thing possible. Sir Henry's broad shoulders sagged, as if this were not an unexpected development but a fate long dreaded. Still, the fellow who most surprised me was Holmes. The joviality he'd gained upon the arrival of a fresh adventure fled from him. He returned to his sulk, huddled on one side of the sofa. Every one of the dark emotions crossed his brow. Anger. Guilt. Sadness. Resentment. Something in the tale of this blackguard and his hound seemed to shake Holmes to his very core.

I knew Holmes too well to seek the truth of it from him—he could be quite inscrutable when he tried. Instead, I turned to Sir Henry and said, "You look distraught, sir, and I do not blame you. Yet I cannot help but notice: you do not seem surprised."

"I ain't," he sighed. "My dad and Uncle Charlie… they took it pretty serious. I learned to shoot, firing at hound-shaped targets. They never let me have a dog. When they were drinkin' they'd take bets on which of them the hound would get first. It was good fun, but you could tell there was a hint of fear in it."

Mortimer leaned in and told Holmes and me, "Sir Henry's father never inherited the title or the Hall, for Sir Charles was the elder. Now that he is gone, all the estate passes to Sir Henry and I could not bear to let him go there—not before consulting Mr. Holmes. He is an expert in such matters, Sir Henry, the only one I could find. Please, Mr. Holmes, won't you tell us what to do?"

But Holmes did not. He was in a sulk—sunk in sullen silence. Thus, it fell to me to ask, "Sir Charles's death was recent, I take it?" Mortimer and Sir Henry nodded. "And you believe he was slain by this demon hound?"

Sir Henry gave a snort and said, "Naw. Bum ticker. Poor Uncle Charlie had a weak heart—finally gave out on him."

"Well! There you have it!" snapped Holmes, from the corner of the sofa. "If a man's heart should choose to neglect its duty and cease to beat, that is its own business, isn't it? It's not my fault! Not anyone's! A more time-honored and traditional mode of dying does not exist. Happens to lots of people. No hell-hound required. Case closed. Good day, sirs; Watson can show you out and if—"

But Mortimer cut him off, pleading, "Yes, but... don't you see... Why should Sir Charles's heart have chosen that particular moment to fail him? The situation is mystifying! Sir Charles had gone to the yew alley—alone, exposed to the moor he feared—and he must have done so in the dead of night. I've no idea what circumstance could drive him there, but I can well understand why his heart gave out."

"Nonsense! One time is as good as another for a heart attack, don't you think? You ought to think a little more, sir, before you speak!" said Holmes, who often dispensed advice when he'd do better to follow it.

"Not necessarily, Warlock," said I. "Though it is true that the human heart can fail at any time, such episodes are more common in moments of exertion, surprise, fear or excitement. I think what Dr. Mortimer is implying is that Sir Charles saw the hound he'd feared since youth and that the strain was too much for his heart to bear."

"Just so! Just so!" Mortimer agreed. "Dr. Watson, you have seen men who died of heart attacks, I suppose?"

"Of course."

"So you know that they often clutch at their arm or chest?"

"As is only natural. They feel the thing going wrong inside them."

Mortimer leaned in excitedly and whispered, "Sir Charles did not grasp his chest. He clawed the *ground*! I think he was trying to drag himself away from the thing he saw! Even in those final moments—even as he felt his own heart bursting within him—he did not fear death as much as he feared the beast upon the moor!"

"You had occasion to examine his body, then?" I asked.

"Of course. I am the only medical practitioner in the parish. As soon as Sir Charles's body was discovered, the local constable and I were immediately sent for. I was amongst the first upon the scene."

"Then I think you must tell us everything. When was he discovered? By whom? Tell us all you can remember of the location and situation."

Mortimer took a breath and began. "Sir Charles kept very little staff at Baskerville Hall—just a groom, a gardener, a scullery maid, the butler Mr. Barrymore, and his wife who serves as housekeeper and cook. On the morning of 27 July, the Barrymores missed Sir Charles at breakfast. They went to look in on him and found his bed unslept in. Frantically, the staff searched the house, then the grounds; that's where they found him. Behind Baskerville Hall, there is a yew alley which stretches out across the moor, to the guesthouse. Sir Charles had gone out for a walk, quite late at night—we know because Barrymore looked in at nine-thirty the previous evening to see if his master wanted anything before he retired. Sir Charles must have dressed himself and gone out sometime after that."

"Which, you say, was quite out of the ordinary for him?" I said.

"Unaccountable! His fear of the hound was palpable, Dr. Watson. He did not like to go alone upon the moor, even in daylight. Why he should brave it at night, alone, unbeknownst to his staff is quite beyond my wit."

"Hmmm… Mysterious already…"

"And it only gets more so," Mortimer said. "For most of the length of the yew alley, the moor is obscured by hedges. Yet Sir Charles stood at the one spot where the moor he feared was most visible and where he was most exposed: at the single gate that leads out from the alley upon the moor."

"And how do you know this?"

"From his footprints, Dr. Watson. The gravel near the gate shows that he must have waited there, pacing, for quite some time. The butts of two of Sir Charles's cigars were there, with corresponding piles of ash upon the stone wall near the gate."

I recoiled slightly. Holmes had formidable mystic powers. Some of our friends were monsters in their own right. Myself, I only had the powers of deduction and logic I'd learned for medicine and repurposed for crime. Now here was another doctor, demonstrating to me he'd already been over the scene and produced deductions that were at least the equal of any I might have made. I blushed and the feeling that I might not have much to offer began to creep into my mind.

Mortimer continued, "And here is another peculiar fact: just before he expired, Sir Charles was running. One can easily tell, for the footprints were deeper, more widely spaced and made with only the toes of his feet. To run for help might be expected, whether he were fleeing a thing that frightened him, or if he felt the onset of a heart attack. Yet, his footsteps led not back towards Baskerville Hall, but away down the yew alley! How do you account for it, Dr. Watson?"

"Only two possibilities suggest themselves," I said. "Either something prevented his flight back to the Hall, or else he was scared beyond the capacity to make a sound decision."

"Yes! Yes, I thought so too! And of course, the heart attack would seem to be the most likely cause of his fright, but there is evidence of another! I cannot prove that the hound was present that night, but I can show you where it came through the wall, if it were."

"The gate, one presumes."

"No, sir, the wall just next to the gate."

"It jumped over?"

"Ha! It melted through! Beside the gate is a blackened gap in the wall. The stone is quite melted, yet there is no trace of damage upon the gravel path, or on the moor beyond the wall."

"But such a quantity of heat must have left some mark," I insisted. "It must have come from a potent source. Surely the vegetation of the moor and the wood of the gate must have succumbed long before the stone wall, eh?"

"One would think," Mortimer shrugged. "I cannot explain the thing, merely recount what I saw. You can see it yourself, if you please."

I could not fathom the source of these phenomena and Holmes still had not offered any help. I therefore elected the most direct course and asked, "What do you make of this case, Holmes?"

"What do I make of it? Only that this story is not credible! It is *in*credible! Incongruous! Ludicrous! Risible!"

I stared at my friend with growing suspicion. Those who were not well acquainted with Holmes might have let the tirade pass, but I knew of one verbal peculiarity that most men did not: when Holmes lied, he had the tendency to sound like a thesaurus. It was as if, in running through all available synonyms for his lie, he might stumble upon one that was somehow more believable than the rest. What his reasons for discrediting Mortimer's story might be, I could not guess, but I grew evermore certain that Holmes knew more about the matter than he was letting on.

Mortimer, of course, sprung to the defense of his theory. "Now I do not say that it is the Hound of the Baskervilles who has done this thing—not with certainty. But what else could it be? The legend is pernicious, Mr. Holmes. And over the last three years, it has only grown. Ask any of the local shepherds! Most all of them claim to have heard the baying of the hound by night, and a few of them claim to have seen it! Once this legend had faded to near obscurity, but nowadays the taverns are buzzing with talk of it."

"And so, what began as a centuries-old myth has devolved into a tavern tale," Holmes scoffed. "Your story is ridiculous, sir! Preposterous! Absurd! Unbelievable! Far-fetched! Outlandish! Er… have I tried 'risible' yet?"

"You have," I said. "Yet, there are elements to Mortimer's account that are most perplexing, don't you think? I should say this bears looking into."

Holmes gave me an angry glance and I could just detect a whiff of smoke escaping from under his collar. No sooner had it slipped out than Sir Henry screwed up his nose and asked, "What's that smell?"

Brimstone. I knew it in an instant. Holmes's self-control had been strained to the breaking point. I knew that Mortimer and Sir Henry must be removed from 221B immediately, or they were likely to witness something *most* irregular. Springing from my seat, I declared, "Well, gentlemen, you have given us much to ponder. Holmes and I must consult. Alone. Yes. I presume the two of you have accommodation somewhere in London?"

"The Northumberland Hotel," Mortimer replied.

"Capital. Why don't you gentlemen return there and settle in? I'll call on you later and let you know what Holmes and I come up with, shall I? Wonderful. I'll show you out. Good day!"

"That's all?" said Mortimer, disappointment showing on his face. "You have no recommendations for us? No course of action?"

"None as yet, except this: be on your guard. Keep your eyes open for anything unusual or out of place, no matter how small!"

"Anything?" Sir Henry asked.

"Yes, anything at all," I replied, bustling him towards the door.

"Well, there was one thing," Sir Henry said. "As I was gettin' off the train, one of my boots disappeared! Right off my foot! I had to get a spare set outta my luggage. You got any idea what happened?"

I had no idea. Holmes, on the other hand, did. All the color drained from his face, replaced by a look of sorrow and hatred that seemed to declare that this was one of the least pleasant days he had ever endured and that it was about to get five times worse. His eyes came to rest on Mortimer's walking stick, jutting from our elephant's foot umbrella stand. When Holmes spoke, his tone was dolorous.

"Watson," he said, "I fear I feel a *sneeze* coming on…"

3

I DID NOT STAY TO CONSULT WITH HOLMES, AS I HAD promised our guests. No sooner had they gone than Holmes begged some time alone to re-gather his emotions and rid himself of the unwanted boot he was sure had come to rest within his nasal cavity. I heartily assented. Cafés, libraries, parks, shops: all fine places to spend the day, compared to the grim confines of our rooms. Indeed, the daylight had already begun to fail by the time I returned home. I opened the door of 221B and...

Found a wall of thick, stinking smoke. Even this miasma seemed to be eager to flee Holmes, for as soon as it had a path the smoke began to roll in sick, slimy waves, up onto the ceiling of the entryway. It spread slowly in both directions as if gravity had been reversed and someone were pouring pea soup into our rooms.

"Holmes!" I shouted. "What has happened?"

No answer came. I thrust the sleeve of my jacket over my nose and mouth, and plunged into the tenebrous haze. Two steps in, my foot came down on an unexpected pile of books and I nearly toppled. Cursing and coughing, I stumbled to first one of our windows then the other, and threw them wide. The thick, soupy smoke was now free to join the eternal haze of coal smoke, chemical vapors and body odor that is the atmosphere of this, the greatest of cities. Still, foul as the London air can be, it was a magnificent relief. I hung out our window for a few moments, wheezing and gasping until I had enough "clean" air in my lungs to turn back and survey our rooms.

There was Holmes, sitting stiffly in one of our chairs, staring at the far wall. The bookcase had been pulled away, leaving a slew of books across our entryway and a vast expanse of unadorned wall. Well, I say unadorned, but its entire surface had been covered in a latticework of scorch marks, which formed a detailed mural.

"Holmes! What is this?"

"Dartmoor," he replied, audibly hurt that I hadn't recognized it. "I've drawn out a map of Baskerville Hall, see?"

He pointed his finger at his work and a little dot of red light appeared on a scorch-drawn manor house at the center of his map. There must have been heat as well, for a fresh whiff of smoke wafted up from where the light hovered.

"Holmes! Look what you have done!"

"Do not speak to me as if I were a child, Watson."

"Well then, do not be childish! Look at the mess you've made! Look at all this magic you have used!"

"Not so very much, I should think."

"Oh? Do you have a book in front of you? Do you have a map? Did you draw this all from memory?"

"Of course not. I have allowed my mind to wander free of my body, observing Dartmoor and recording it here, in splendid detail. All for your benefit, by the way, and see how you treat me? You can be a most ungrateful wretch sometimes, I must say."

"Well that is magic, Holmes, don't you see? It is not the kind of thing a normal man could do. You know it hurts the world every time you use your powers! You've told me so yourself!"

"Pish, tosh…"

"And look at the state of our wall, Warlock! Why would you… Why on earth… I did buy you a pencil and paper, if you recall."

"I've no art with them, Watson," he said, waving the thought away as if it were a buzzing gnat, "and I feel entirely justified in today's expenditure of eldritch force. This is important, don't you see? Dartmoor is a dangerous place. We dare not tread there lightly."

"What, because of the hound?"

"Ha! One hell-hound? We should be so lucky, John. No. Look at this place. Here's overgrown plains-land. Here's a stand of trees. Rolling hills. Rocky tors. Oh, here's a deadly peat bog called the Great Grimpen Mire!"

As he spoke, his little red pointer-light lit each of the areas he described, sending puffs of fresh smoke up from the much-abused wall. At last he turned to me and demanded, "And what is the name we use for all these diverse features, eh?"

"It's the moor. Just… the moor."

"Exactly! And have you ever paused, oh master of deduction, to wonder why such a wide array of terrain should share a single name? What is the common factor, Watson?"

I was taken somewhat aback. I'd never paused to think on it, but the question was a fair one.

"Er... it's kind of pretty?"

"Bah!"

"There's not much there?"

"Now you are closer to the mark," Holmes declared, waving a finger at me. "It is still wild. In this, the most developed, most populous of countries, the moor remains unused. Why? Because it is not the domain of man, Watson, and man knows it."

"Now, Holmes, it can't be all that bad. People do live there, after all."

"Not very sane ones," he protested. "Look, see all these little circles, out among the hills; do you know what those are?"

"I cannot claim to."

"Stone huts. These are where the ancient Britons made their homes, in prehistoric times. But where are they now? What became of them?"

"I have no idea. Perhaps—"

"They moved to London!" Holmes cried. "They were ancient, not stupid! And I haven't even told you the worst bit, yet! Watson, have you ever heard of a ley-line? Do you know what that is?"

"Well... 'yes' and 'no' in that order."

"Think of a wagon wheel upon a muddy dirt road,"

said Holmes. "As it passes, it leaves a depression. The next wheel deepens it. With each subsequent passing it is worn further and further into the ground, such that all other wagons passing by are likely to fall in. They may easily travel one way along the rut of the other, but they may not extricate themselves without great difficulty."

"I've driven in the country before, Holmes."

"But have you driven in another world? That is what a ley-line is, Watson. Outside entities can hardly extend themselves here. When they do, their influences are feeble—nearly blind. The easiest thing for them to do is grope this way and that along the paths worn by the outsiders who have come before them. Thus, if a mortal man is interested to have congress with these demons, his best bet is to find a ley-line and wait until one of the little blighters stumbles along."

"And there is one such line at Baskerville Hall, one supposes?"

"No," said Holmes and pointed at his impromptu map. Five red dots appeared at the edges and streaked together, converging at Baskerville Hall. Two of them stopped there, the other three ran out the other side and kept going.

"Five," said Holmes, with dread severity. "Five of them. Three of them continue through, but two take their genesis at the Hall and radiate away. At no other place in England—at no other place in this world, that I am aware of—do five lines come together."

"It sounds like exactly the sort of place that would capture your interest."

But Holmes shook his head. "Do you remember that exhibition we went to, Watson? Those four tradesmen who placed an anvil on the center of a pane of glass? When they each lifted up a corner, the glass did not break. The anvil rose. It stayed, suspended on a translucent plane, as if it hovered on nothing!"

"Yes, but… what is your point, Holmes?"

"If there had been a crack in the glass, straight across the middle from side to side, just under the anvil, do you think it would still have held?"

"Well no, I shouldn't think so."

"What if there were five?"

"Well then definitely—"

"Yes! Precisely! I dare not go to Baskerville Hall, Watson! I dare not! To place an anvil such as myself at so vulnerable a juncture would court disaster. I cannot promise that the step of my foot across the threshold of that house would not shatter the barriers that keep this world whole."

"Oh," I said, pursing my lips and reflecting on this new information. "So, Sir Henry…"

"Sir Henry can have no help from us."

"Well, Holmes, he can have no help from *you*."

At this, Holmes went pale. His face took on a pleading aspect. "Watson… No…"

"I see no reason why a non-anvil-like fellow such as myself may not aid him."

"Failure, that's a good reason," Holmes volunteered. "Obliteration… murder at the hands of a hell-hound…

There are so many when you stop to think about it. Oh, you know what: bad weather."

"Yes, but I could act as your agent, Holmes. Don't you see? I could accompany Sir Henry, try to keep him safe, and offer such reports as I may until our shared talents reveal the true form of the threat that has slain Sir Charles and now menaces his heir."

"But... no..."

"I think you cannot deny the arcane nature of these circumstances, Holmes. The brimstone thread, which you make your special business, seems to show clearly within this patch of cloth, would you not say?"

"If something were to happen to you there, Watson, I could be of no aid."

"Then I must take special care to avoid misfortune," said I, yet I must admit that separation from Holmes's protection did unease me. "Yes... er... just how much protection do we assume I might need? Might this be the work of an actual hell-hound?"

"Oh, how pleased everyone seems to be to blame the hound!"

His anger surprised me. I had thought the question to be perfectly fair. After further reflection, Holmes seemed to come to that conclusion as well. His features softened and he mumbled, "Surgery with a claymore, Watson."

"Eh?"

"If you had to excise a tumor, would you choose your trusty scalpel or a whacking great broadsword? Someone wanted Sir Charles slain, we believe, and yes, he was slain. But *only* he. If a true hell-hound were loosed upon Dartmoor, I promise you the carnage would be tremendous. If a hound did this murder, it certainly did not do it alone. It must have been directed by a greater intelligence—one that could hold it to only one target and even overrule the beast's normal inclination to eat the body of his fallen foe."

"Is that possible, Holmes? Could such a hound-master exist?"

"I know of nothing that is truly impossible, Watson, but I can tell you this: if a hell-hound did kill Sir Charles Baskerville, only a fool would fear the hound more than the hand that mastered it!

"Well," he added, after some consideration, "unless the hound was in the same room. Then… obviously…"

The notion of going upon the moor without Holmes's protection was beginning to lose some of its allure. Nevertheless, my mind was made up. I therefore diverted Holmes to another topic. "I say, did you manage to recover Sir Henry's missing boot?"

"Ugh. Yes, I did."

"And was it lodged in your nose, as you feared?"

"Er… not quite the nose, but it was in my possession," Holmes blushed.

"Oh? But then where was—"

"I shall not say, Watson, for to recount it would be to rekindle a most unpleasant memory. Suffice to say that Sir Henry's boot may currently be found in our bathroom, just next to our bathtub, and that he might be pleased if it were given a very thorough scrubbing before it is returned to him."

With that, Holmes stalked off to his bedroom and slammed the door. I suppose it had been a rather unpleasant day for my poor friend.

4

THOUGH HOLMES HAD NOT FAVORED IT, MY PLAN WAS met with great relief by Dr. Mortimer and Sir Henry. Of course, I did not share Holmes's tales of ley-lines or the demonic hordes they might unleash if he came too close to one. Instead, I told our clients that Holmes was involved in other cases and found himself inextricably entangled in London. I promised that I should be in constant contact with "the great detective" and that his expertise should not be wanted, despite his absence. This was deemed acceptable and train tickets were purchased for that very afternoon.

Holmes accompanied us to the train station and, if his zeal to see me undertake Sir Henry's protection was meager before, it was even less as he watched me depart. "Are you sure, Watson?" he hissed.

"Yes. Stop asking."

He didn't. "This is folly, Watson. Utter folly."

"Holmes, calm down. This whole affair may be nothing, you know? Look, we've got the old legend of the hound. We've got the death of Sir Charles. We've got motive— Mortimer says the Baskerville fortune is vast and has no apparent heir, after Sir Henry. Yet have we any proof that there is a direct plot against him? It may be nothing more than a ghost story and Mortimer's over-caution. Perhaps I shall go there, scout for danger, find nothing and return."

"What?" cried Holmes. "Are you mad? There is something horrible hunting that man—something powerful and awful and otherworldly. I'm surprised you can't feel it."

"I don't have your ability to sense doom, Holmes. Few men do, I should think."

"Yes, but do you need it? Look at him! By the gods, he's practically got doom all over his shoes! You couldn't doom a man any more than that without dooming him in half. You may do your utmost, Watson, but I'd say your chances of saving him are slim indeed."

"Hmmm… What are my chances, do you think?"

"Er… I don't know… I'd say, even with your help… probably eight chances out of ten, he's dead in a month."

"And if I do not go?"

"Oh, then he will die," laughed Holmes. "Certainly, he must die."

"Then my hand is forced," I said. "I have to go."

"Oh really? To save that man? That very *Canadian*-seeming one, right over there, with the *hereditary British title*?"

"By Jove!" I cried. "That hadn't occurred to me."

"Think of the realm, Watson."

"But… no. That's no excuse. I am going, Holmes, and that's final."

Holmes kept up appearances until we departed, but

whenever Sir Henry and Mortimer's backs were turned, his true feelings showed. Once, he snuck up behind Sir Henry and gave me a little mime show. Holmes pointed at me, then down at the ground, then at Sir Henry, made a little shoo-shoo motion, then slashed one finger across his throat and shrugged. As I knew Holmes quite well by that point I could clearly understand his message: *Watson, you stay. Let Sir Henry go. He'll most likely be killed, but so what?*

I followed Sir Henry onto the train and waved to Holmes as we pulled away, trying to look cheerful. His face was dolorous.

As the train chugged westwards the day wore swiftly on into twilight. By the time the train reached Grimpen station, the world was descending into burnt-orange shadows. Trees stretched black, leafless fingers against the clouds and the moon hung fiercely bright in the eastern sky. The doors of our train car opened and the last of London's cheer disappeared as the cold blast came in upon us. Strange to think of London as cheery, but in comparison to Dartmoor, it is.

The open doors revealed another surprise: at both ends of the platform was a soldier. They stood, silent as statues, gazing out across the moor with knit brows and rifles slung ready across their waists.

"What is all this?" I wondered.

The conductor, who was helping us ready our bags said, "Oh, they'll be lookin' for Selden. It's thought that he can't make it far off the moor, lest he hops a train, so the station is always guarded."

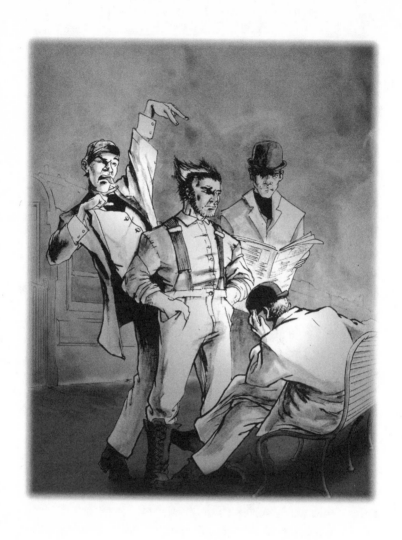

"He'll most likely be killed, but so what?"

"Selden?" I asked.

"Aye. The Notting Hill murderer. Them fools let him escape the gallows as they said he weren't of right mind— as if anybody who done what he done could ever be sane, eh? Well, weren't long afore he escaped Princetown prison as well and now he's on the moor. Or was. Ain't been seen these three weeks past, so there's many think the bogs've had him. Still, there's plenty in these parts who lock their doors every night and pray he passes 'em by."

I remembered hearing of the case. Few could forget it. The savagery of the murders had commanded headlines all over the world, but the real sensation had been the bizarre array of murder weapons. Two years previously, few Englishmen would have thought a hatbox was a deadly instrument, but Frederick Selden had proved us wrong. We had similarly learned to fear tea strainers, towel racks and bags of flour. Oh, I did not envy those men, standing all night in the autumn cold, just waiting for the Notting Hill Murderer to come up behind them and end their life with... I don't know... an oven glove, or something.

The carriage that came to take us to Baskerville Hall needed to be condemned. Any questions I had about what had caused its supreme state of decay were answered as soon as we cleared Grimpen station. At once, the paved road was gone and we were left to the scant mercies of a true English country lane. Rutted. Pitted. Obstructed by overgrowing hedgerows and dotted with mud pits beyond counting. Despite the constant battering and the cold gusts that came in at every crack, Sir Henry's mood remained steadfast. We could see a fair portion of the moor, for the moonlight was generous. Sir Henry would wonder aloud if this stream or that hill was familiar to him, or if it was only his mind playing tricks. Whenever a feature of interest presented itself, he would press Mortimer to explain it, which he happily did.

"Oh, those are the lights of Lafter Hall. Nice old place; used to be one of the greater houses of the moor. It still is, I suppose, but old Mr. Frankland has been negligent in its upkeep. All he cares about is suing people. Go nowhere near him, gentlemen, or you will find yourself slapped with a subpoena before you can say John Bull. Oh, and just over there is the Serpent's Maw—the old hollow where your ancestor, Hugo Baskerville, is said to have met his fate."

"I remember it!" Sir Henry cried. "With the two standing stones? I used to play there, when I was a child."

A few moments later, Mortimer said, "We're coming up to Merripit House, now. They and I are your closest neighbors. The Stapletons live there. Oh, you'll love them. Jack is a naturalist and his sister Beryl is… well… just wonderful."

But any further fawning upon the graces of Beryl Stapleton was arrested as our carriage lurched to the right, nearly hurling us all out the left window. Mortimer was first to recover and took the opportunity to apologize, on behalf of Dartmoor. "Ah, fairly rough bend just there. Sorry, gentlemen, yet it is imperative we turn northeast, for to continue forward would drive us into the Great Grimpen Mire. Very dangerous there. Easy to get lost in the mists, you know. Easy to stumble into a peat bog and those that do… it's the last we see of them."

I looked out the window and beheld the Grimpen Mire—the corroded soul of Dartmoor. Thick mists grew in slow, creeping tendrils across its surface. There were a few trees, but they were stunted and sometimes leaned at precarious angles as the stagnant water overtook the soil beneath them. Reeds like broken fingers jutted from the low-hanging fog. Oh, and that mist! So thick that little tentacles of it seemed to seep into our carriage, through every crack.

That is when I began to fear. I remembered Holmes's words: how this was not the domain of man and man knew it. It was true. Above it all, gathering all its disparate, distasteful physical features into a cohesive whole was…

Malevolence. Dartmoor hated us; nothing could be plainer.

It was then I saw the first light, hovering in the mist. Do you know that soft, inconstant glow around a burning candle? Not the flame itself, but the halo that surrounds it? It was as if one of those simply forgot the formality of needing a source and showed up on its own. Even as I gaped at the first light, a second appeared, just off to the left and behind it.

"What are those?" I asked.

"Ah!" said Mortimer. "One of our most famous local phenomena. They are called will-o'-the-wisps, I believe."

"Yes," I said. "Very nice. But what are they?"

"Stapleton says they are luminous methane, escaping

from the peat. The locals have a different story. They say the wisps mark where some unfortunate fellow has drowned in the mire. They say the lonely dead are signaling to us, hoping to lure the living to join in their doom."

And that was it. I could take no more. Dartmoor had taken it a step too far. I harrumphed my displeasure and said, "No. This will *not do*. Driver, stop the carriage!"

"What?" said Sir Henry. "No, do not stop this carriage. Watson, what are you on about?"

"Someone needs to get out there and teach Dartmoor it can't just go about impersonating Halloween all the time!"

"The modern festival of Halloween actually takes its roots here, so the similarities should not be surprising," helpful-tour-guide-Mortimer informed us, then shuddered a bit and added, "It's probably no coincidence they picked October, either."

"I don't care," I told him. "I promise you that somewhere on this vehicle is a shovel, kept handy for when a wheel gets stuck in a rut. We must stop the carriage and find it, so I may restore sanity to Dartmoor."

"You're gonna restore sanity?" Sir Henry asked.

"I shall."

"With a *shovel?*"

Yet it was not to him that I directed my answer. Outside our window, more wisps had gathered, bobbing along with us capriciously. Merrily. Mockingly. I pointed my finger at the nearest one and declared, "I'm going to dig you up, you little bastard!"

"Dr. Watson! Language!" cried Mortimer.

"The hell you are," Henry growled.

"Sir Henry! Language!"

"I must!" said I. "Ghosts… Ha! An easily broken hypothesis! All I need to do is dig up the peat beneath one of those wisps and, if I do not find human bones, we'll know this local poppycock for what it is!"

"You can't dig in a bog," Sir Henry said. "It's like digging in lamb stew—the stuff closes in as fast as you scoop it out."

"I don't care! I need to get out there and… er… *not* find a skeleton!"

I lunged for the door, but Sir Henry pushed me bodily back into my seat, saying, "You couldn't find one even if you were digging right over it! Any fool who goes stumbling around Grimpen Mire in the dark ain't fixin' to find a skeleton, he's fixin' to become one! Now, sit down!"

He was right, of course. I threw my arms across my chest and frowned out the window at the misty strangeness of the mire. The carriage bumped along. Soon we were clear of the peat bogs and the wisps began to fade from view. Before they were gone entirely, I promised myself, "I shall find you out. I'll know what you are, before I leave this place."

But I don't think they heard me.

In another five minutes or so, the carriage lurched to a halt. Through the right window, we could see a cozy little cottage, some distance away, with a candle burning in its front window.

"Well, this is me, gentlemen," Mortimer announced. "May I call on you tomorrow, Sir Henry?"

"Sure," he replied.

The walk to Mortimer's door was no more than twenty yards. Still, I think he, Sir Henry, the driver and myself all held our breaths. Would Mortimer reach the safety of his hearth? Or would the Notting Hill Murderer, the hell-hound, or a gang of rogue wisps drag him screaming, into the darkness? Presently, a little sliver of light glowed forth as he opened his door and stepped inside.

Lucky.

"We are not doing that," I told Sir Henry. "We are driving right up to the Hall—so close I can jump out of this carriage and through the front door."

Sir Henry chuckled at the sentiment, but he didn't disagree with it. The carriage lurched forward. About a mile further on, we finally reached Baskerville Hall.

And things got worse.

The coachman did pull up as close as he could, but there was a granite walk stretching down from the front of the house. For the occasion of Sir Henry's arrival, the Barrymores had lit the walk with a line of torches on either side. Or… they'd tried to. The poor torches, abused by the October wind, guttered and flickered. They did cast a feeble light down on the walk, but the granite of which the walkway and the house had been constructed was so dark as to defy all attempts at illumination. About the only thing that did light up were the reflective golden eyes of the hundred or so owls who had taken up residence in the eaves of Baskerville Hall. They gazed hatefully down at us, resenting the intrusion.

Yes. Angry owls. Because… why not?

Despite our misgivings and the air of avian disapproval, Sir Henry and I marched to the great doors of Baskerville Hall and knocked.

And things got worse.

I mean, they seemed better for a moment. We were greeted by the butler, John Barrymore—a strikingly handsome fellow with an easy charm. He welcomed Sir Henry and me inside and gave every outward sign that he was glad we'd come. All this was fine, except for the painting behind him.

He was in it.

It was clearly from the era of the First Civil War—some 240 years previous. But never mind; John Barrymore was in it. If the embossed frame was to be believed, it was a portrait of the hall's founder, Sir Hugo Baskerville. And yes—he was the main subject of the piece. He wore a cavalier hat and one of those ridiculous moustaches that were popular in those days. His expression was that of an insufferable ass—a sneer designed to say, "I am a very rich and powerful fellow. You are not. Let us both strive to keep it just so, shall we?" Behind him, with her hand on his shoulder, stood his long-suffering wife, Olivia Baskerville. Her blonde hair was piled high, held with a gold and pearl comb. Yet none of this was as interesting to me as the figure of their servant, who lurked in the shadows behind them. It was Barrymore. *Exactly* him. The man himself—

in flesh and blood—stood in front of me. Yet the very same face stared out from a picture that must have been over two centuries old. Such was my shock that it took me a moment to realize that the actual John Barrymore was smiling and reaching out towards me.

"Dr. Watson? Your coat… may I take it?" he repeated.

"Oh! Er… yes, thank you."

"My wife has prepared a late supper, if you will follow me."

But Sir Henry drew a deep sigh and said, "You know, Barrymore, I just can't. It's been a long trip and—if Dr. Watson doesn't mind—I think I need some shut-eye."

"I agree entirely," I said.

"Very good, sirs," said Barrymore with a nod. "I'll bring a plate up to your rooms in case you are hungry in the night. Your chambers have been prepared for you, Sir Henry…" here he paused to gesture towards the east wing, "…and a comfortable guest chamber for Dr. Watson."

He gestured to the west wing. The exact opposite side of the big, empty house.

"No, no, no! I must be close to Sir Henry! My job is to protect him."

"Ah… Well the guest quarters are traditionally in the west—"

"Well change it!" I insisted, which was a damned impropriety, in a baronet's house, with the baronet standing next to me.

Luckily, the baronet agreed. "There's gotta be a closer room, Barrymore. The other Baskervilles must have had families, right? Watson can have one of their rooms."

Barrymore tapped his fingertips together guiltily and said, "Well yes, of course, but none of those rooms have been prepared. It's just Eliza and myself tonight, sirs, but if you give me... say... an hour and a half..."

"No, no. That's all right, Barrymore," Sir Henry sighed, then turned to me and, with an exhausted shrug, said, "It's only for tonight, Watson. It'll be fine."

"Will it?" I genuinely wondered.

The matter decided, Barrymore rang for his wife, Eliza. She wasted no time in appearing and introducing herself to Sir Henry. Have you ever seen someone so fat that they seem almost spherical? Well, Eliza Barrymore was like that, only... cubic. She was short and so stoutly built that she seemed equal in all dimensions.

I allowed Eliza Barrymore to lead me to the west wing, while John Barrymore disappeared with his new master towards the east. The house was cavernous, and smelled of dust and disuse. A few hallways and staircases later, we arrived at the room where I might, at last, be allowed to slumber.

And things got worse.

Again, they seemed better at first. I began undressing myself and puttered into the dressing room that adjoined my chamber. As I filled a glass from the jug that had been left for me, my stockinged foot came down on a deep scratch in the floorboards. A moment later, I found another, just beside it. Parallel fissures, much like... claw marks? With horror, I realized where I was: the dressing room of the second bedroom from the end, third floor, west wing. The room from the letter. The room where the hound had slain lecherous old Winthrop Baskerville. My gaze flew to the wall. There they were—the crisscrossing scrapes, where Winthrop had torn at the wall in his fright. The marks were numerous and deep; I winced to think of the damage he must have done to his fingers. But he'd had other concerns, I supposed.

A sudden horror overtook me. This was not a room; it was a trap! The Barrymores! It was they who planned to take the life of Sir Henry, but first they would remove his protector! It was they who had sent me here—here, to the murder room to feed the hound! I reeled back, searching for a way to save myself. The plan I concocted was… well, I am sure it was more a product of my exhaustion than any great feat of reasoning. I rushed back to the bedroom and lit all four candles, arranging them in a line in front of the dressing-room door. I somehow hoped that this barrier—not so much of flame, but of light—would protect me. After that, there was naught to do but huddle on the bed, with the blankets pulled up around my chin. There I stayed for quite some time, eyes glued to the door, ears straining at every sound, waiting for signs of danger. I heard the wind against the stone walls. The creak of ancient floorboards. Somewhere in those labyrinthine halls, I was sure I heard a woman weeping.

I think I slept very little that night.

5

DESPITE MY UNINSPIRED ANTI-HELL-HOUND COUNTER-measures, I survived my first night at Baskerville Hall. I found Sir Henry taking breakfast in the great hall—a lone man at a preposterously large table in a preposterously large room. The effect of isolation was only worsened by an array of white stripes on the dark marble floor, which met just beneath Sir Henry's chair. It was as if they were all pointing at him, laughing, "Look! There's only one person in this empty hall! One!"

I could not fathom the reason behind this strange décor and was about to chuckle out loud at it, when something that Holmes had said occurred to me and made me pause. I counted the lines. There were three that carried straight through and two that started at the confluence and ran outwards. So… either this was just a strange coincidence of interior decoration, or the five great ley-lines of Dartmoor intersected directly beneath the master's seat in the feasting room of Baskerville Hall. Probably the latter.

Yes, the pessimist in me decided. *Definitely the latter.*

It was at that moment that Sir Henry caught sight of

me and cried, "Watson! Good! C'mere and join me."

Sir Henry gestured me towards my plate. I sighed and rolled my eyes. As was proper, I had been situated at the foot of the table, with Sir Henry at the head. I wouldn't have minded—in fact, I would have insisted on this arrangement—if it were not for the tremendous size of the table: it was forty feet long. It looked as if it were as old as the house and stout enough to serve as fine armor for any of the battleships of its age. No wonder Barrymore was in such fine physical condition. Anybody forced to buttle milk between the lord's teacup and his guest's would rival Pheidippides. I scooped up my place setting, piled everything onto the plate and walked the lot of it all the way down the vast wooden expanse, to sit next to Sir Henry.

"Looks like you survived your first night at Baskerville Hall," Sir Henry beamed.

"Well yes, but it was you we were worried about, if I recall."

"Yeah, but here I sit: hale and hardy. So, any ideas for keeping me that way?"

"A few," I said. "I must begin by scouting our surroundings. I shall go to Grimpen, I think. I'll send a quick letter to Holmes, then survey the other great houses hereabouts."

"All right. I'll tell the groom that he and the cart are at your disposal."

"That is kind of you, Sir Henry, but I think I'd rather walk."

"Eh?"

"I let my fears get the best of me last night," I told him. "I must cultivate a familiarity with Dartmoor. It's harder to fear a known thing than a mystery."

"What should I do?" Sir Henry asked.

"Keep your head down. We still do not know who it is that wishes you ill. It may be the Barrymores or any of the other servants here."

"But why would they?"

"You are the last heir to the Baskerville fortune. If you were to die, it would be up for grabs. I do not wish to be indelicate but I suspect that, between cash reserves, bank accounts, investments and the value of this house, it is a significant sum."

Sir Henry paused, then said, "You know, I think it's kinda Canadian of me to want to say, 'Hell yeah, it is.' What would a proper baronet say?"

"He would say he was quite comfortable."

"Well then, I am *quite comfortable*. But do you think it's safe to leave me here? I mean, if we suspect the Barrymores—"

I tutted this concern away. "I have no reason to suspect them, apart from their proximity to Sir Charles," I said. "Besides, anybody who sought your fortune would need to be sure they were not blamed for the murders. They are in luck, in that the local populace has a ready scapegoat to blame in the demise of any Baskerville."

"The hound."

"Precisely. But you are in luck, in that nobody is going to believe the hound ran into your bedchamber and shot you in the chest."

"So, as long as I'm in my room…"

"You are safe. Do not go outside. If somebody so much as invites you into your own garden to smell the roses, you must go with me and go armed."

Sir Henry practically growled, "You know, I ain't—"

But he caught himself just in time and amended his statement to, "I am not accustomed to such cowardice."

"Well said!" I cheered. "Both for bravery and for Britishness. Don't worry, Sir Henry, I'm sure you'll get your chance for courage. Until then, just spend some time getting accustomed to your new home."

"It's a strange place," said Sir Henry. "You know, last night I thought I heard a woman crying."

"That's odd. I thought I heard it, too."

"Odd? Well, if I could hear it, why shouldn't you?"

"Because we were in opposite wings of the Hall," I said. "For us both to have heard her, the lady must have either been walking about the whole house, weeping…"

"Or else she must have been standing right here, howling at the top of her lungs," Sir Henry chuckled.

"There can't be too many ladies in residence. I think Dr. Mortimer said—"

I did not finish, for at that moment the doors opened to admit Barrymore, bringing my breakfast. I elected to ask him directly. "Barrymore, how many people live at the Hall?"

"Well there's only Sir Henry, yourself, the missus and me. Oh, and Molly, the scullery maid. Perkins, the groom, sleeps in his shack out near the stables. Then there's the gardener, Gunther; he's in the groundskeeper's house.

Oh, and I forgot the baby. In February, Eliza and I were blessed with Jonathan Barrymore the Tenth."

"Oh? Congratulations," I said, carefully noting the other adults' names for later investigation. I might have saved myself the trouble. All three were of decidedly working-class character—honest and simple, with no guile to them at all. Molly's only concerns were her scullery and her appearance (which was more than a little... pleasant). Gunther's and Perkins's entire worlds seemed to revolve around their own duties and Molly's appearance. "Now, your wife and this scullery maid... are they quite all right? We thought we heard someone crying last night."

"Oh... well... perhaps the baby?" Barrymore volunteered. "Or if not him, then the wind I should think. Oh, it can sound quite queer when it gets to wailing around in the turrets at night."

Why is it that city folk are better at lying than their country brethren? True liars seem to be rare in England's heartland and Barrymore certainly could not count himself amongst their number. Atop his silver tray, every dish was rattling—that's how bad his tremble was.

"Yes," I agreed. "Most likely the baby or the wind. Thank you, Barrymore."

I finished my breakfast, enjoined Sir Henry to be safe and went back upstairs to dress for my country expedition. On my way to my room, I passed Mrs. Barrymore in the hall. Her eyes were red and puffy. Two things were certain. She was indeed our midnight weeper. And her husband was lying to us.

But why? What had upset her? What was he concealing?

I pondered this as I set out, down the lane towards Grimpen. Oh, it was a devil of a walk. The road, neither straight nor smooth, presented me a thousand unnecessary diversions and ten thousand bumps and ankle-twisting pits before I reached my destination.

And then, all I got for my efforts was Grimpen. The place was just as dour as its name implied. It consisted of two rival inns, a marketplace, a train station, a grocer's and a post office. Little else. Yes, I was able to hear much local gossip concerning the Hound of the Baskervilles, but little of note and nothing of use. I rattled about for a few hours, but gained no insight into the plot against Sir Henry or its potential mastermind. In the end there was nothing to do but take lunch, scribble Holmes a quick note and leave.

As I trudged back towards the Hall, lost in thought, I suddenly heard footsteps rushing towards me, across the moor, and heard a voice call out, "Hi-ho! You must be Watson!"

Turning, I beheld a khaki phantom bounding towards me. He wore a pith helmet with a sort of white gauze that hung all around the brim and obscured his face on all sides. His trousers were tucked into his boots and his sleeves were pulled down all the way to his wrists and buttoned tight over tan gloves. The butterfly net he had thrown over his shoulder bobbed comically behind him as he approached. Uncertain as my new surroundings were and despite the danger of my situation, I could not bring myself to believe I would end my days beaten to death by a butterfly-net-wielding country fop, so I called back, "I am Dr. John Watson. And who might you be?"

"Stapleton," he chirped. "Jack Stapleton, at your service."

He drew back the gauze surrounding his face. He had a little shock of black hair, which escaped from under his hat, over his ears and down his forehead. I would have placed him in his early forties, but he had a youthful and energetic quality, like a child. Or a spaniel. His wide-eyed earnestness led me to suspect that, so far as he was concerned, I was the most exciting thing to come upon the moor in a dog's age.

"Ah yes, the naturalist. I believe Dr. Mortimer mentioned you," I said. "Yet, that does not explain how you know me."

"Quite the same way," said he. "James and I are friends and he made much of his decision to go to London to find you and Warlock Holmes. I say, is he here? I should very much like to meet him!"

"Warlock, sadly, is detained in London," I told him.

"Dashed shame. We could use a man like him. Why, there's mystery everywhere and nobody seems willing to address it. Nobody pays any attention to the moor at all. I'm here collecting rare and unknown species—and I am the only one. People go to Peru to find new flora and fauna, but they won't come here! Isn't it strange?"

"Passing strange."

"But then, you aren't afraid of strange things! You adventure with Warlock Holmes! Mortimer showed me clips of your exploits from the London papers. Oh, the things you've seen, I imagine… Oh, you must let me help you! I can be of so much use to you, Dr. Watson! The moor is alien to you, yes? But I—I have studied it! I'm sure I must have a thousand facts you might want to know. Such as… well… ah! Look over there, to the northeast, do you see those purple patches on the ground?"

Squinting, I could just make out what he was talking about. Through the hectic tangle of gorse and heather, I thought I could make out areas of the ground that were slightly more purple than the others. "Yes… I think so… What is that?"

"Death," he said. "That is the Great Grimpen Mire. It doesn't look like much, because weeds will grow on the surface of the peat, but if you should step upon one of those seemingly solid pools of loose earth, we would not be hearing from you again. I don't mean to boast, Dr. Watson, but do you see that hill just there?"

"Of course."

"It lies almost in the center of the marsh. There is a mine built into the side of it. It is abandoned, not because it was unprofitable but because too many miners were lost on their way there or back. I think I am the only living man who can now navigate there safely."

All of a sudden, a terrible baying broke out across the moor. The still air erupted with vengeful howling, which curled from horizon to horizon for a moment, before fading into nothingness. I jumped, then crouched into a ready stance and grabbed for my pistol (which was, at that moment, safe in my room at Baskerville Hall).

"What the hell was that?" I cried.

Stapleton—who looked fairly shaken himself—suggested, "A bird?"

"A bird?" I exclaimed. "Certainly not! No it sounded just like a hound, but... more..."

"Well yes, of course, that's what the locals say," Stapleton scoffed. "The hound. Yet, to those of a more scientific mind we must consider other options."

"But a bird?"

"Some birds are very loud. Or very large. The California condor has a wingspan of—"

"Look! There!" I interrupted him. "The hound!"

He spun to follow my outstretched finger. A gigantic quadruped hove into view over one of the many bluffs. It was hard to judge exactly at that distance, but based on the bushes near its feet, it must have been four or five feet tall. It charged across the moor much faster than a man could run. I gave a sharp gasp, but Stapleton began to laugh and grasped my shoulder.

"Ah, Dr. Watson! You gave me such a fright! The hound, indeed! That is a pony, sir."

"A pony?"

"A wild pony; the moor is home to several herds. Look, here come two more."

Sure enough, two more of the creatures appeared over the rise. Yes, now that he pointed it out, the size of their heads and their gait was certainly more equine than canine. I had just a moment of relief, before Stapleton muttered, "Oh dear. Turn, little ponies."

"What was that?" I asked, but before he could answer, another horrible cry echoed over the moor. The lead pony had run headlong into the Great Grimpen Mire and was now thrashing in a peat bog, already chest deep. The two other animals had managed to pull up short. They bucked and kicked in circles, their eyes wide and rolling. As disconcerting as the trapped pony's screams were to Stapleton and I, I'm sure it must have been worse for them.

"Poor devil," Stapleton said, then added, "I say, Watson, come to tea."

"Tea?" I cried. "At a moment like this? Shouldn't we…"

I had no ideas. Stapleton gave a hangman's smile and said, "Shouldn't we… what? There is nothing we can do, Dr. Watson. If we had a rifle we could shoot it, which would be a mercy, but beyond that…"

"Can we not help him get out?" I asked.

"Dr. Watson, it is dangerous enough to go into a peat bog alone. With a thrashing, kicking pony present, the outcome is even more certain than usual. That said, if a human—with his broad, paddle-like feet and opposable thumbs—cannot usually extricate himself from such a bog… well… how would it go if you only had hooves? No; in an hour or so, that pony will be gone."

"An hour? By God, is he going to scream like that the whole time?"

"Wouldn't you?" Stapleton shrugged. "Do come to tea. It must be more pleasant than walking all the way back to Baskerville Hall, listening to the pony. We'll close the windows. We have a piano; perhaps we could persuade my sister Beryl to play for us. Oh, you must come; she'll be ever so pleased to meet you. We get so few visitors here upon the moor. I have my butterflies and my studies of flora and fauna, but I fear she gets bored. Say you'll come!"

Torn between returning to Sir Henry and reconnoitering the locals, I let the pony be the tie-breaker. I agreed to tea and the two of us set off. Stapleton was in high spirits; he stopped from time to time to point out unique flowers or particular butterflies, but I had little regard for them. I could not force myself to ignore the screams of that poor, trapped pony, dying behind us.

Merripit House came into view. It was a charming little structure, unusual for the area in that it had two floors. It was the perfect country cottage, pastoral and charming. I turned to relate my compliments to Stapleton only to find that he was gone. I could just make out his butterfly net bobbing over the nearest hill. It seemed that the merest glance of a grizzled skipper fluttering over a heather bloom was enough to send him charging into the bush, without so much as a fare-you-well.

I shook my head and turned back to resume my way, but immediately stopped. In the path stood a woman. I had no idea where she had come from, but I didn't care. I have no power to lay upon this page a description of Beryl Stapleton's beauty, or even enough of one to justify the immediate and total mastery that I allowed her to practice over me. I could tell you of her raven hair. I could tell you of her eyes—dark and almost unbelievably large—which seemed to every man on whom they gazed to be interested only in him. No. Allow me only this: that as a doctor, who has studied anatomy, I have often beheld the human form in a totally nude state and felt nothing. Beryl, even as she appeared then, conservatively clothed from neck to toe was… lurid.

My breath escaped. She ran to me. She laid a hand upon my sleeve and leaned her face close to my ear. I could not speak. If she had slid a knife between my ribs, I could only have watched her do it in worshipful fascination. Instead she whispered, "Go! Leave this place! You are in terrible danger! You cannot stay upon the moor!"

I nodded, dumbly. The earnestness of her touch upon my arm… the scent of her… I need to stop writing about this, right now.

In any case, we were suddenly interrupted by a sharp voice, calling, "Beryl! What are you doing out here?"

"Oh, Jack," she said, turning to Stapleton, who was coming towards us over the heath. "You look as if you've had quite the chase."

He gazed at her severely for a moment then grumbled, "I see you have already introduced yourself."

"Oh, yes," she said. "I was just telling Sir Henry he has come too late to see the full beauty of the moor."

"Sir Henry? This is not Sir Henry!" Stapleton sneered, as if only the greatest fool could think I was. "This is his friend, Dr. Watson."

"Oh?" said Beryl. "Oh… well then, welcome to Merripit House, Dr. Watson. Though you are not the new lord, still I am sorry that you have not seen the moor in her full bloom. It is… enchanting."

If my mind had been its usual self, I'm sure I could not have failed to notice Stapleton's sudden transformation. How—in the presence of his sister—the foppish amateur scientist faded away, replaced by a disquieting, paternalistic bully. Yet, in that moment, I was incapable of deduction, insight, or even rational speech. All I could do was stare at Beryl.

"Watson's going to join us for tea."

"Oh how delightful!" Beryl declared, clasping her hands together. "We have so little company, all the way out here."

She took my arm and led me inside. We had tea, I presume. I fear I am a poor narrator, when it comes to relating my first adventure in Merripit House. I can remember almost nothing of it, except Beryl leaning across a tray for a lump of sugar. Or Beryl laughing—at what I cannot say. Or Beryl touching a napkin to her lips to brush away a crumb. These images are as clear to me now as they were the day they occurred—indeed, I think they shall be on the day I die. But as to what actually transpired that day in Merripit House, I have forgotten it all.

I remember stepping back out. I remember tipping my hat to Stapleton and starting back up the lane to the main road. The pony was quiet by then. As I turned onto the main lane and began my stumbling progress past the rear of Merripit House, I found one of my arms arrested; I turned to see if I had caught it on something.

There stood Beryl Stapleton, holding the crook of my right arm. She smiled at me and said, "Dr. Watson, I'm glad I caught you. I just wanted to apologize for what I said."

"What you said?"

"Yes, when I told you there was great danger and you must leave. You must forget all that."

"You thought I was Sir Henry," I reflected. My thoughts came like peas, rolling through gravy—slow and clumsy.

"It doesn't matter who I thought you to be," she insisted. "It was a foolish fancy. So easy for a woman alone to be disconcerted by the moor—by a foolish, dying pony. But don't forget to tell Sir Henry: my brother will be calling on him."

"Oh? Shall I?"

"Yes. You said you would be our messenger. You said he wouldn't mind if Jack came round to meet him."

"Oh. No. He won't mind."

"Thank you, Dr. Watson. I suppose I'll see you again, soon."

She smiled. She leaned in and gave me a little kiss on the cheek. It was nothing more than friendly. Even sisterly. There was no harm in it, no great impropriety. Yet, I could not have been more stunned if someone had cracked my skull with an iron maul.

She left. I stood there. I've no idea how long. I don't know what I was thinking, or what I was looking at. Eventually, it grew dark and the wind began to rise. With a start, I realized how cold I had become. I realized there was nothing else for it but to shamble off in the direction of Baskerville Hall. Thank God there was a clear road for my feet to follow. If I had been forced to rely upon my wits, I am sure I would have wandered into the mire.

6

From the third letter to Warlock Holmes, 13 October 1882

To the esteemed consulting detective,
Mr. Warlock Holmes,

Where the hell are you? Why have you not answered my previous letters? Yes, I know, there's not much in them. Precious little has been accomplished in these days at Baskerville Hall, but that means I am all the more eager for your help, Holmes.

I am lost at sea.

I've checked out all the neighbors and detected no plots. Dr. Mortimer claims to have seen the hound one night. He describes it as a huge dog with luminous eyes, smoldering all over its skin. To me, it sounds suspiciously like one of the moor ponies who has just been rained on, water steaming off its back while moonlight reflects from its eyes. Time will tell, I suppose.

The Mortimers regularly join us for dinner. The Stapletons come even more often. Jack is so soft and foppish you would sometimes think he was playing a part, simply to discredit the entire race of country scientists. Though he certainly enjoys torturing butterflies, he seems incapable of anger towards a human. Well, he does snap at Beryl a great deal more than he ought. Oh, and his sense of dress, Holmes... He wears these ridiculous high-necked jackets with ruffs. The age of Elizabeth may have ended nearly three hundred years hence, but it seems nobody has informed the Dartmoor tailors. Between those coats and his beekeeper's garb, I've never seen anything of the man but his head and hands. The rest of his body may be a complete myth, for all I know.

As for Beryl, oh it pains me to write this, Holmes, but she and Sir Henry seem to be forming quite the attachment. I should be happy for him, I know, but I find Beryl to be such a charming girl... It brings the very worst aspects of my character to the surface, to see the way they look at each other. I shall not write of it.

Mr. Frankland, the owner of Lafter Hall, has visited. Once. We realized it might be seen as a slight—a censure from the local baronet—not to invite him to dine. Unfortunately, he came on the same night Mortimer proudly displayed a skull that he had found on one of his amateur archeological digs. The very next morning, Frankland brought a suit against Mortimer for disinterring human remains without permission from the deceased's next of kin. Despite the impossibility of tracking a Stone Age skull's family to his current relatives, the letter of the law is on Frankland's side. It is expected he will win his suit.

Sir Henry has not seen fit to extend a second invitation.

Speaking of Sir Henry, you'd like him, Holmes. He's a brave soul and a good man, too. His anti-Canada lessons are proceeding admirably. Of course now, if I fail to protect him, I will have the death of a friend upon my conscience. I have moved to new quarters—just two rooms down from Sir Henry—the better to guard him.

Some nights, I go to the window and look out over the moor. The wisps are practically epidemic. They come particularly on foggy nights, seeming to exult in obfuscation. They never show themselves plainly, fading and flickering with a frustrating lack of constancy. Sir Henry leaves a hunting rifle by the window in case the hound or the Notting Hill Murderer is espied. If I claimed never to have snatched up that rifle and blazed away at some wisp that had suddenly come to look like a pair of luminous canine eyes or a torch in the hand of a creeping man, I would be guilty of a falsehood.

I wish you would come to Dartmoor, Holmes. Or at least write and give me some direction. No plot has manifested against Sir Henry. Still, an overwhelming sense of evil pervades this place. When I think of your warning to me that Sir Henry is almost certainly doomed, I am overcome by a feeling of helplessness. Why can I not find the root of it, Holmes? Why can I not spy it out?

Yours in frustration and abject failure,
John H. Watson

7

ON THURSDAY MORNING, JOHN BARRYMORE DEVELOPED a limp. He tried to hide it—tried to continue his duties as if nothing were amiss—but he was pale and weak. By Friday evening, he had a fever. As Sir Henry prepared for sleep, he was surprised to find that it was Eliza Barrymore who arrived with his traditional nightcap. She said her husband was indisposed. Sir Henry well believed it.

Well enough, in fact, to step two doors over and enlist my aid. Despite Eliza Barrymore's repeated protests, Sir Henry and I went to the Barrymores' quarters and knocked. John Barrymore was surprised to see us and more than a little afraid. He tried to shoo us away, claiming, "Oh, it is nothing, sirs. Just a small injury. I shall be better presently, I know it."

"Nonsense, Barrymore," I said. "You've got an underemployed doctor, right here in the house. I'm surprised you didn't have the sense to come to me right away."

Barrymore had clumsily wrapped his leg with strips torn from an old nightshirt. Scarcely had I uncovered the wound before its exact nature occurred to me.

"Barrymore… this is a graze from a bullet. You've been shot!"

"What? No, sir. No. It is a scratch. Down near the stables, there is an old nail, protruding from the fence. I caught myself on it; that is all."

I could not help but wonder what an indoor worker such as a butler might be doing, charging up and down along the stable fence with enough vigor for a simple nail to cause a wound like this. I almost confronted him, but held my tongue. What would be the point? I knew he would lie to me. Yet, an army doctor knows a bullet wound when he sees one. I cleaned, stitched and bound it, gave him a belt of Sir Henry's brandy and sent him to bed.

Over breakfast the next morning, I told Sir Henry exactly what I thought of Barrymore's wound and his corresponding level of truthfulness.

"That's not all, Watson," Sir Henry said. "Did you know he was sneaking around outside our rooms last night?"

"He was *what*?"

"Yeah. I've suspected it for some time. I can hear someone in the corridor outside my room some nights. I've peeked out to see who it is a few times, but never caught the man. But now Barrymore's got that limp, hasn't he? Heh. The way that fellow was bumpin' around out there, last night… had to be Barrymore."

"Sir Henry, you… you *ninnymuffin*! I am here to protect you, Sir Henry. This is exactly the sort of thing you are to bring to my attention, don't you see?"

"Well, yeah, I guess," he mumbled. "But I wasn't

certain of anything until last night. Could have just been my mind playin' tricks, you know?"

"Or it could have been your murderer."

"Okay, but it wasn't. I don't know what he's doing out there, but I don't think he's trying to kill me."

"Oh, after tonight we'll know," I told him. "Have a nap today, Sir Henry, and be ready for a late night. You and I are going butler hunting, I think."

That night was… just… fun.

Sir Henry let himself be put to bed by Barrymore as usual, then dismissed him for the night. I heard Barrymore scuffle by in the hallway and smiled. Not two minutes later, the grinning Sir Henry burst into my room.

"Hush!" I told him, in a harsh whisper. "You were supposed to wait half an hour! What if Barrymore had seen you?"

"Calm down," said Sir Henry. "You worry too much. It's done. He's downstairs and I'm here, safe and sound."

"And what of our decoy?"

"I stuck all the pillows under my covers and pulled the blankets up. I put the candle on the far bedpost, so if anybody peeps in at the keyhole or cracks open the door, it'll look like I'm sleepin', with my back to 'em. It's pretty clever. Go and see."

"I will not!" I scolded him. "We must stay here and keep as quiet as we can, lest we alert Barrymore to our plan."

"Come on! He's nearly deaf," Sir Henry laughed.

"Nevertheless, it is unwise to invite more risk than is

necessary. You must trust me, Sir Henry, this is the sort of business I get wrapped up in all the time."

"Well, it's a hell of a thrill," Sir Henry said.

"Of course, but it is also… well… yes it is. It's a great job."

Though I continually urged caution, Sir Henry paid my words no mind and, I must admit, neither did I. Shortly before midnight, we crept into the hallway and mounted a covert raid on Sir Henry's vacant room. We returned laden with brandy, cigars, and pride in our successful mission. Now we were properly outfitted for the evening's work and we began it in earnest. My room filled with smoke, laughter, the clink of glasses and the most shocking tales Sir Henry and I could relate to one another.

If Barrymore had not tripped on the second-floor steps, landed with a loud thump and cursed his injury, we would have been discovered. Even so, it was well for us that this mistake came during one of the lulls in our laughter, or we should not have heard it. I have been present at struggles where two impossibly powerful forces collide to determine which is stronger, but that night the contest was to see which party was slightly less inept.

Sir Henry and I fell silent and listened for Barrymore's step. As soon as I was sure our target had turned the corner at the end of the corridor, I ushered Sir Henry out and we began our pursuit.

Barrymore's capacity for stealth did, indeed, seem to have been hampered by his leg injury. We had no trouble tracking him as he passed Sir Henry's room, turned the corner and made up the stairway to the next floor. He went all the way down the upstairs corridor until, at last, he selected one of the many doors and slipped inside. His mistake was to leave it slightly ajar. Sir Henry and I had no great challenge creeping up behind him and pushing it open a few inches more, so we might spy him. He'd stopped in front of one of the windows and lit a candle. He squinted out through the glass for a moment, then waved the candle slowly back and forth in front of it.

"What's he doing?" Sir Henry whispered.

"I have no idea."

"How do we find out?"

I shrugged—the wrong thing to do, I now realize—for when Sir Henry found himself in the absence of a plan, he was the sort of gentleman who always opted for the direct route. He put his foot to the door and kicked it open with sudden violence, shouting, "Barrymore! What are you doing?"

Barrymore cried out in surprise. "What? Sir Henry? Nothing! I'm not doing anything, sir."

Sir Henry leveled his finger at his terrified butler's chest and growled, "Someone killed my uncle! Now they're prob'ly after me! And we find you sneaking around, plottin' against me?"

"Not against you, sir. Never against *you.*"

"What then? What are you at? You better spill the beans, Barrymore!"

"I… well… beans?" Barrymore stammered.

"He means he'd like you to tell us your secret now, please," I said.

Barrymore's tremble increased. "But, it isn't my secret to tell." His hands were shaking so badly, the candle flame was a lengthwise smear of light.

"I don't care!" Sir Henry roared. "You tell me what's goin' on or you and your wife can just get out! Tonight!"

"But, sir, the baby—"

"Is gonna have a pretty cold night, unless his father smarts up!"

Barrymore hesitated for a moment, clearly in agony, considering his position. Finally he shook his head and said, "I cannot, sir. I am sorry. But you must believe me: we never did anything to bring you harm, nor your uncle neither, God rest him."

It looked as if Barrymore were about to have a rather ungentle answer to that, but Sir Henry was interrupted by a terrible shriek from the corridor outside and the sound of rushing feet. I whirled back towards the door, cursing that I'd left my service revolver back in my room, sure that Sir Henry's hidden murderer was about to burst in upon us.

It was Eliza Barrymore, reprising the midnight weeping performance that had so surprised Sir Henry and me that first night. She charged past us and threw her arms around her husband, crying, "No! 'Tisn't John's fault, Sir Henry! 'Tis mine! You mustn't blame John, please!"

"What isn't his fault? What have you done? What is going on here?" Sir Henry demanded, but any response the Barrymores might have given would have to wait. Just behind them, through the darkened window, I saw a light—a tiny flickering flame. I might have thought it were a wisp, but it was too clear, too cohesive. It was a candle. Someone outside Baskerville Hall was answering Barrymore's signal, slowly waving a candle back and forth.

"Sir Henry! Look!" I said, pointing into the darkness.

My host gazed, steely-eyed, out the window and grunted, "I see him," then turned to Barrymore and said, "Who is that you've got out there and what are you plotting?"

"It isn't a plot, sir," Barrymore wailed. "We're just… just helping him."

Eliza gave his hand a warning squeeze and shook her head almost imperceptibly to indicate that he should say no more. But he didn't have to. My eyes fell to Eliza. She'd said it was her fault. Her secret. By the combination of good deduction and great fortune, I happened upon the solution.

"Barrymore is not your original name…" I said. "What was your maiden name?"

She shook her head and refused to answer.

"Come now, it is a matter of public record. It won't take me long to find out. Why, I'll bet I could ask Perkins and he'd tell me. But I might save myself the trouble. It's Selden, isn't it?"

She hid her eyes and I knew I'd guessed it right.

"Selden?" wondered Sir Henry. "I've heard that name before…"

"The Notting Hill Murderer," I told him. "Let us recall that he's been loose upon the moor for some weeks now. Yet none of the local houses have been burgled for food, clothing or tools. The roads and the railway station are constantly watched; it is not thought he could have escaped the moor. It therefore stands to reason, either he has died or someone has been supplying him."

Barrymore's face went white as a sheet. "Why would you… why would you think a thing like that, Dr. Watson?"

"Why? Your leg! I will confess, in moments of weakness, I have been known to let off with that old rifle at lights that I momentarily believed to be not wisps, but torches. It seems that—at least once—I was correct. I hit you, didn't I?"

Anger lit Barrymore's face, but, like the quintessential English butler he was, he mastered it in an instant and said, "I have often heard you denigrate your own skill as a marksman, Dr. Watson. I really feel you ought to extend yourself more credit in the matter."

"No, Barrymore. You don't have to compliment me. It's all right to be upset. I have, after all, shot you."

"You are too kind, Dr. Watson."

Sir Henry shook his head and said, "But why did you guys help out the Notting Hill Murderer? He's a damn monster!"

"So he is, but he's not only that. I suspect he is Eliza's brother."

Eliza Barrymore turned tearful but defiant eyes up at me and shouted, "Oh yes! To you, he's a monster! To you, he's nothing more than the things he's done! But to me? Why, he's still just Little Freddy—that tousle-headed boy what used to fill Mummy's bed up with all them knives! I couldn't turn my back on my own brother, no matter what he done!"

"Little Freddy?" I gasped. "If I recall from the papers, your *Little Freddy* murdered four families in their sleep, then killed three constables with the same butter knife before they brought him down."

"That he did, sir, and no denying," Eliza admitted.

"And they didn't hang him?" wondered Sir Henry.

"Because he said they ought to do Queen Victoria first as he had only killed about forty folk, whereas she'd got half of China hooked on opium. He said she was the only living human to cause more misery and death than he had. He said he'd turn her in if only they'd be lenient with him. Said he knew where to find her," Eliza sobbed. "That's how we knew him to be mad!"

I leapt to the defense of my realm. "But everyone knows the Chinese love that opium! It's the greatest kindness Britain ever did for them!"

"Aye," John Barrymore agreed. "But there was no doctor who could convince young Freddy of that and, in the end, they declared him insane. Said he wasn't mentally fit to hang for all those murders."

"So he knocked off forty people and they just sent him t' jail for it?" asked Sir Henry.

"Oh no," said Eliza. "Can't blame a crazy murderer for killing folks, can you? No, not any more than you can blame a bird for flyin'. He went in for treason, for that… for that… horrible stuff he said about our queen!"

Eliza once more renewed her sobs. Her husband put his arm around her shoulders and comfortingly said, "God save the Queen."

"God save the Queen," we all agreed and shared a quiet moment.

The Barrymores' actions were monstrous, of course, but to watch Eliza weep at her brother's fate would melt the stoniest heart. Sir Henry and I stood and traded glances with each other, silently wondering what must come next. Finally I spoke. "We cannot leave a man such as that free. Imagine the mischief he might do. I'm going out after him."

"No!" cried Eliza. "Please, have mercy, Dr. Watson! I know what he did was wrong, but... I still... every time I think of him, I still see that golden little boy, playin' with his cat's paw collection. Before he... before he said all them terrible things."

"Yet, he did say them," I reminded her, sternly, "and if I should stay my hand this night, why then, I will be partly to blame for all the things he might say in the future. No. For the realm, I must go."

"I'm goin' too!" Sir Henry decided.

"No," I told him. "It cannot be. You are the last Baskerville. It may be death to you to go upon the moor in the hours of darkness—even without you confronting a murderer."

"I know you don't think of me as an Englishman, Watson, and I guess there's still a bit too much of the logging camp in me. But I am one of you. I owe Her Majesty my title, so... she's my queen, too."

What could I say, against that? What could any true Englishman say against that?

We made ourselves ready as quickly as we could, pulling on our boots and coats. I thrust my Webley in my coat pocket and we set out. The moon shone down with particular luminosity that night and I prayed it would not betray us. At least we had two advantages over Selden: we had seen his position and he didn't know we were coming. Inwardly, I cursed myself that I had allowed Sir Henry's excellent brandy to dull my senses; I needed to stay sharp.

As we neared the rocky outcropping where I had seen the light, I glanced at Sir Henry. He walked close beside me, clutching his silver hound's-head walking stick. Finally, it occurred to me to ask, "Sir Henry, are you armed?"

"Sure am," he whispered and brandished the stick at me.

I almost shouted at him. Then again, the urge to consider a walking stick to be a deadly melee weapon is one of the strangest fixations of the English people. In our collective conscious, one rich white gentleman armed with such an ambulatory aid is sufficient to defeat an army of Zulu warriors. I cannot say what has caused this shared delusion. Yet, if I was eager for Sir Henry to embrace our national identity, did I not owe him a certain admiration for embracing our national cognitive deficiencies, as well? When one reflects that he would have worn dungarees and taken an axe only a few short days before, I suppose his progress was amazing.

I pulled him low to the ground and hissed, "A walking stick? You came out to face a murderer and perhaps a hell-hound, carrying only that? Why didn't you take one of the shotguns from the hall?"

"Nah," he said. "Too bulky."

"Funny you should say that because, if we do come to blows with the Notting Hill Murderer, you may find yourself wishing you had something 'bulky' to hit him with!"

"This is all I need," Sir Henry said. "If he gets near us, I'll make him wish he'd never been born!"

Sir Henry raised the stick up above his head for a fearsome brandish. Exposed in the moonlight, the little silver hound's head let loose the reflective brilliance only polished silver can provide. In response to this signal, the air was broken by the two voices I had most hoped not to hear.

First came the terrible howling I had heard on my walk with Stapleton—hollow and haunting—but closer now.

Just after, we heard a rough voice not ten feet behind us complain, "Hey! You idiots woke the hound!"

I sighed, dropped my head and uttered, "Frederick Selden, I presume?"

"Freddy!" he insisted, then pounced on Sir Henry, delivering a two-footed mule kick to the center of the chest that sent my friend sprawling.

Our attacker was shabby and haggard, almost feral. I went for my revolver and had him nearly in my sights, when I heard a strange noise—a metallic high-pitched *fiiiing*. For a moment I could not guess what might make such a sound.

Then the salad fork sunk an inch and a half into my chest.

Let me just say that—to this day—I still possess no idea how anyone could throw a two-ounce fork with such power and precision. The thing penetrated my coat, my shirt and several muscle layers, pinning my pectoralis major to my external and internal intercostals. In one instantaneous blow, I lost most of the control over my firing arm. A wave of admiration swept through me.

Followed closely by a wave of pain.

I cried out and raised my gun to shoot him, but as I said, the function of my right arm was mightily impaired. I had to lean my whole body back to bring the pistol high enough and my shot went wide. Still, this was enough to cause Selden to reflect that—not only had he made the mistake of bringing a fork to a gunfight—he was no longer in possession of said fork. He kneed the prostrate Sir Henry in the ribcage and fled back over the rocky outcropping from whence he had come. I fired again as he leapt over the rocks, then once more as he flashed between two bushes. I don't think I came too close. Sir Henry came up behind me, gasping for breath and asked, "Hit the bastard?"

"I can't aim," I told him, through gritted teeth. "Pull the fork out!"

"What fork?" he asked, but then saw for himself and gasped, "Oh! How'd he do that?"

"Pull it out!"

"Why me? You're the doctor."

"Well, yes, but it's your fork."

"*Mine?*"

"Note its weight and the unmistakable gleam of good silver. Combine these observations with the knowledge that Barrymore is Selden's main source of supply. Or, if that is too much work, have a look at the handle, which is embossed with the Baskerville family crest."

"Damn it, Barrymore," Sir Henry growled. "This is too much!"

"Pull it out!"

Sir Henry marched over to me and expressed his frustration with John Barrymore by reclaiming his lost cutlery with one quick yank. I gave a grunt of pain and sank to my knees. Inwardly I congratulated myself that I had let Sir Henry's excellent brandy dull my senses; I was rather pleased not to be feeling the full extent of the pain that must have been occurring in my chest. As I reflected on this happy chance, I became conscious of a sound behind me.

It sounded like laughter.

I turned to examine the moor behind me, but the moon was in my eyes so everything was in silhouette. Luckily, my quarry was careless. There on the top of one of the tors stood the distinct silhouette of a man. I could not see much of him due to the light in my eyes (and, if I am honest, a few tears). I did not know him to be tall or short, young or old. All I could say was that he was on the skinnier side and that he had seen me spy him. His laughter immediately died and he dropped down on the other side of the tor and disappeared.

Sir Henry just caught a glimpse of him as he fled. "Who's that?" he wondered.

"We must go," I said, struggling to my feet. "If the hound has a mortal master, it may well be that man we have just seen. He might have gone to set the hound on you and—by the sound of that last howl—the beast is close. We haven't much time."

Even Sir Henry—brave as he was—could not receive such news with impunity. "So… you think that howl was really it, then? The Hound of the Baskervilles?"

"Well… Stapleton thought it was a bird…"

"What? And the man is supposed to be a naturalist?"

I laughed (though perhaps a bit grimly) and said, "We must hurry. If the hound is anything like the locals say, we are badly overmatched. I have only three shots left and my aim is compromised."

"You came out to hunt a murderer on a haunted moor with only six shots?" asked Sir Henry.

"Well," I reminded him, "you brought a stick."

8

GIVEN THAT I HAD ONLY THREE BULLETS LEFT IN MY
gun and roughly the same number of brandies left in my
bloodstream, it was lucky for Sir Henry and me that we did
not encounter the hound on the way home. We mounted
the steps wordlessly and retreated to our rooms. I paused
long enough to do a cursory dressing on my fork-wound,
then fell into bed to sleep.

Dawn did not wake me, nor did the other members of
the household as they began their day. I think it was the
pain in my chest or the hollow gnawing of my belly that
finally did it. Only time would cure the former, but I knew
a fitting treatment for the latter. I threw on my dressing
gown and stepped out into the hall, in search of breakfast.
There I surprised Sir Henry, who was just leaving his
own room, walking stick in hand, dressed in his Savile
Row finest.

"Oh, hello," I said. "Are you going out?"

"Oh. Er... yes," he replied.

I knew from his tone that he had meant to sneak out
without my knowing. "Not out upon the moor! Without

me? After last night's encounters?"

"Yeah, without you. *Definitely* without you."

Being fresh from slumber, it took me a moment to realize what was happening. "Beryl Stapleton," I cried. "You're going out to meet Beryl Stapleton!"

I cannot convey the fury that rose in me as I realized this. The emotion was ridiculous and my better self tried to find some rational reason for my anger. Here is the best I could find: that for Sir Henry to endanger his person was tantamount to him disrespecting the labor I had spent trying to save him.

Ah, what a wonderful rationale it was…

It would have been even better if it had not been a complete lie. Which it was. I know, because I remember the idea that followed it.

Good, I thought (and almost said), *Go out upon the moor. Give yourself to the hound, or whatever man wishes you ill. When you are dead, I shall take Beryl's hand and we will laugh at what a fool you were.*

As unkind as my thoughts were towards Sir Henry in that moment, his were just as hostile to me. He positively shouted, "Of course I'm going to see her! She's hands-down the best thing about this whole damned moor! Don'tcha see? I'm risking my neck, being out here. And what do I get for it? *Her!* I've got this house and all this money, sure, but what I need is a wife! I can't believe my luck, finding a girl like that out in the middle of nowhere. And if you think I'm gonna waste my chance because I'm scared of some dog, you've got another thing comin'!"

At these words, my world flooded with white-hot rage. My thoughts immediately flew to the pistol I had in my room, just behind me. I could shoot him.

No, that was offside. Bit of a social blunder, shooting one's host. Well… I could do it for his own good—wound him in the leg, to keep him from going out and getting himself killed. It would be easy. I was good at wounding legs; just ask Barrymore.

But what would that accomplish? Beryl might feel sorry for him. She would coo and fuss over the wound and I should seem the villain. I! Ridiculous!

Sir Henry brushed past me and made for the exit as I fumed, helplessly. The gentleman in me made a brief appearance to say that, of course, I ought to let him go. He was quite right. A great house requires a lord and a lady and a line of succession. The Baskervilles—now dwindled to Sir Henry alone—must be replenished.

Then again, what if he *were* killed? What if my momentary lapse was all the opportunity our hidden antagonist needed to bring his wicked plans to fruition? Did it matter that I, personally, did not want to leave Sir Henry alone with Beryl? No, that was not the point. My job was to protect him, wasn't it? How could I *not* follow him? I must. I went for my gun. I wanted my gun.

Only to protect Sir Henry, of course.

Only to protect him.

My hands were fumbling and uncertain as I loaded and checked the Webley, but I knew I must hurry if I wished to prevent disaster. All my progress was arrested, however, when I passed my mirror. Wait! I couldn't let Beryl see me in a dressing gown! She could never love a fellow who looked like that. Could she?

I think I wasted twenty minutes dressing and preening, before I burst forth onto the moor. All my efforts at grooming were soon undone as I charged down the lane after Sir Henry. Yet I made it all the way to Merripit House without any sign of him. At first I howled that he had given me the slip. Then the horrible notion occurred to me that he was in there with her, alone. I don't know what made me think I had the license to burst in upon them, but that is what I did. I tore open the door and rushed in, screaming for Sir Henry to show himself.

But he was not there.

Nobody was.

I ran throughout the house, checking every door lest they were hiding from me, but the cottage was empty. Where had they gone? My head reeled and I realized I was near to fainting. Had I just... had I *run* from Baskerville Hall to Merripit House? The walk was enough to wind me. Had I just...

It didn't matter. I had more running left to do. I hadn't found them yet. Where else could they be? There was no other path to the house. No! There was! The day Beryl intercepted me (ah... Beryl, most perfect of creatures) she'd caught me as I'd passed the back garden. Was there a garden path?

Half a circuit outside Merripit House revealed a lovely little rose garden, bordered by short hedges and featuring a tiny gazebo with a rocking bench, just big enough for two. But it was empty, all empty. For an instant I despaired, but then came the sound of voices drifting across the moor. I raced along the path between the garden and the main road. I went as silently as I could, but swiftly, pistol in my hand.

I heard them before I saw them. Or rather, I heard Sir Henry. He was professing his love, I realized. He was saying how painful it was to be parted from her. At the moment, he sounded more like a bad poet than a lumberjack. To my ear he was mewling, whining, practically crying like a baby. How unseemly! How unlike a man!

I could do much better.

Grinning, I threw myself down behind a low row of rocks to watch her reject him. To my everlasting joy, she was not professing love back. Instead, she took his hands in hers and said, "Sir Henry, please listen. We haven't much time. I wanted to tell you: you must leave this place. You can never be safe here."

"I don't care, Beryl! Come on and marry me, eh? I'll make you so happy—you'll see. Come and live in that big ol' house with me and make it a place worth livin' in."

"Hank… you're the most wonderful man I've met and I would wed you if I could…"

Something about the way she said it led me to realize that I could absolutely hit Sir Henry from here, if I steadied my pistol on the rock.

Luckily for Sir Henry, she continued, "…but it cannot be. You must go. That is why I… sent for you this morning: to tell you to forget me. Forget this place. Forget

Baskerville Hall. Take your inheritance; go be happy some place in this wide world, far from here."

"It's too late for that! Don't you get it? I'm not gonna be happy here—I'm not gonna be happy anywhere—unless I got you with me! Come on, Beryl. Marry me."

I had the little bastard in my sights. I had become sure that the only way to save Sir Henry from the repercussions of this folly was to shoot him right in the face.

Twice.

At least.

But fortune was ever the friend of that man. As I pulled back the hammer, I was distracted by the sight of a shapeless blob of green mesh, bobbing towards the pair through the gorse: Jack Stapleton's butterfly net. In a moment he cleared the scrub and the man himself came into view, red as a beet and clad in his ridiculous beekeeper's garb. Why a man needed to have every inch of skin covered from top to toe in order to hunt harmless butterflies was beyond me, but I was delighted to see him charge the two lovers, demanding, "Beryl! What is this? What are you doing? Have you been carrying on with this… this cad, without my knowledge? I had thought you a man of honor, Sir Henry, but now I see you for what you are!"

Beryl began to protest that it was an innocent encounter, that Sir Henry had been out for a walk and she had seen him. Stapleton was having none of it. "Get back in the house! Back to the house now, harlot!"

Beryl turned and ran, tears in her eyes—whether from shame, from sadness or from rage, I could not tell.

Sir Henry turned on Stapleton and berated him for his terrible treatment of his sister. The two of them locked horns and began to shout each other down for some three or four minutes.

I sat in my rocky hiding place, utterly stunned. I am a creature of reason, usually. What had been wrong with me? Probably the same thing that was wrong with Stapleton and Sir Henry; the two of them were behaving like absolute schoolboys. I struggled to understand what motivated such heights of passion in the three of us. Ever since hearing that Sir Henry was meeting Beryl Stapleton, I had been... someone else entirely. With a horrified gasp, I reached up to lower the hammer of my Webley, which I had cocked and leveled at the very man I was here to save. Whatever could have made me do such a thing? Turning from the two arguing figures, I began retracing my thoughts since waking.

The fatigue of my long, irrational run from Baskerville Hall swept over me. I had reopened my fork-wound, so I rubbed at it as I waited for my breath to return. I did not even hear Sir Henry's footsteps until he stormed past my hiding place, on his way back to the road. I gave a gasp of surprise and he turned towards me. Alarm, then rage, then regret, then curiosity swept across his face in an avalanche of expression which gave me to realize: he was just as confused as I. Eventually, he settled on stammering, "Oh... hullo, Watson. What are you doing here?"

"Well I... I came to make sure you were safe, didn't I? That is my job, after all."

"Oh," he muttered, then, "Thanks," then, "I suppose you saw… all that mess, eh?"

"I did," I confessed.

"Not my finest hour, I guess. Or Stapleton's. Did you hear the way he treated Beryl? I swear, I coulda killed him!"

"It was a most unseemly display," I agreed. "I must say, all three of us seem to be quite out of our senses this morning."

"What came over us?" Sir Henry asked.

I shook my head in wonder, and opined, "Who can say? I tell you, I am beginning to believe the moor has an effect on the intellect. What else could explain such strange passions? Why are you and I and Stapleton so overwrought? Whatever could make old Sir Charles wander out to the moor gate, alone, at night?"

Sometimes framing the question in the correct fashion will provide the answer. What temptation could draw Sir Charles out alone upon the moor? Why not the same one that had just led Sir Henry to do the same—and the same one that had almost made me shoot him in spite of my better sense? I knew of only one thing that could cause such madness in us all.

Beryl Stapleton.

I did not voice this discovery, but pondered it to myself. We both sat in silence for a bit, then Sir Henry began to pace. His mood grew visibly worse for a few moments, until at last he savagely kicked a nearby log and complained, "I was such a damned fool!"

"Sir Henry! Your foot!"

"I don't care." He sank back down upon the rock and complained, "What happened, Watson? She seemed to like me before. Now I've spilled my guts and she doesn't care at all."

A wave of jealousy began to grow in me, but my better reason shoved it back down. I deflected to another topic. "I think I had better take a look at that foot, Sir Henry."

"Why bother? Here, I'll spoil the surprise: it's busted."

I felt a wave of pity for him.

"All right," I said, "let's get you to the main road. I'll head back to Baskerville Hall and return with the trap. We'll get you home."

"Too much bother," he said. "Mortimer's cottage ain't far off; we might as well head there."

He tried to stand up, but as soon as he placed his weight on the damaged foot, he gave a grunt of pain and sank down again. I shook my head and told him, "If we are to go that way, Sir Henry, there is one unpleasantry we must first address."

I knelt down before him, grasped the boot in both hands, and pulled it off as quickly as I could. He gave a howl of pain. It didn't take a doctor to see that his foot was not its proper shape.

"Come on," I said, "let's get you up. Put your arm over my shoulder."

I helped him hobble through the scrubby hills towards Mortimer's cottage. Mortimer himself was just finishing lunch when we arrived. "Watson? Sir Henry? What brings you to— Oh… I see. Best come inside."

We made Sir Henry as comfortable as we could in Mortimer's little office, while I told him, "I have not yet palpated the foot, but I suspect we have multiple dislocations of the phalanges and perhaps fractures there or in the metatarsals. I have no bandages with me, have you any on hand?"

"I do," Mortimer said, "and something better, besides. I know the London way is to wait until four o'clock, but here on the moor it is never too early for tea and morphine."

He put the kettle on and disappeared into his workshop. In a moment he reappeared with a generous dose of morphine in an ancient brass syringe. The needle was badly worn, as if it had been re-sharpened again and again—never successfully. Sir Henry made a horrible face when it jabbed him, but by the time the tea was brewed he was slumped on the sofa, smiling.

James Mortimer proved to be as apt a physician as any I have ever met, or else he had a particular aptitude for bones. Sir Henry had dislocated his three small toes and we suspected a fracture to his smallest metatarsal, but this was not as bad as I had feared. We soon had the toes set back in place and gingerly wrapped the whole foot in plaster. Plastering is not such difficult work as setting bones, but instead of relaxing to the lighter task, Mortimer grew visibly more anxious. As we worked, he kept glancing over at me and whetting his lips as if to speak, but he never did.

It made me nervous.

I found myself trying to recall any reason other than his meekness that made me assume he was not the man who sought Henry's life. Casually as I could, I asked, "Is there something on your mind, Mortimer?"

He stopped his work and stared at me with a strange urgency, then whispered, "I am not... I am not regarded as a brave man."

"Because you aren't," I reminded him.

"Well yes... but... but I would still like to be *regarded* as one. I think my wife would like it more if she were married to a man of reputation."

"Ah, but you *are* a man of reputation," I countered. "Before you came, these poor cottagers may have died of infection if they happened to break their leg. And you know how often they do it! Gads, it might almost be considered the local pastime. Now you are here to put them right, their lives are much improved. Do you think they are ungrateful?"

"They all look at me as if I were a medical book, Watson! If I could only prove I were brave... If I could only..." He dropped his voice to a conspiratorial whisper. "If I could only capture the Notting Hill Murderer."

"Oh no! I don't think much of that idea," I told him, stroking the bandaged fork-wound hidden beneath my shirt. "I am familiar with the man and I don't think you'd care for him."

"But I could catch him. I could do it."

"Mortimer, he'd kill you in an instant."

"I could take him unawares."

"I very much doubt that."

"I could! I... I have a secret, Dr. Watson. Look, it

stands to reason: if he were still out upon the moor—after all this time, with no plunder from local farmhouses, without the theft of any food or material, wouldn't that mean... someone was supplying him?"

"Ah," I said, and my heart fell. I prepared to begin the conversation that would land the Barrymores in jail. Possibly, even Sir Henry and I might be in some trouble. Had we hunted the Notting Hill Murderer? Yes. Then again, had we gone to the authorities with what we had learned? Well... not yet.

"Someone has been!" Mortimer insisted. "Someone has been bringing him food every day! I've seen him."

"Ah. Yes. Well... before we jump to any hasty conclusions..."

"Not hasty! I have watched him now, for days."

Mortimer gestured towards the old brass telescope that occupied pride of place at his front window. My brow knit. How could he possibly see Baskerville Hall from here? Were there not several large hills between? What had Barrymore been doing, to be seen at night from such a distance?

"He comes every day, about this time," Mortimer continued, now gazing hungrily at the clock upon his wall.

What? Impossible. I tried to remember any conspicuous absences of either John or Eliza Barrymore at this time of day. They always seemed to be on hand when we needed them. And why would they come so far from Baskerville Hall?

"I'm sure you must be mistaken," I said.

"I am not! Look, I shall show you. Let us spy for him!" Mortimer flicked some plaster from his fingers and scurried to his telescope. As he fumbled with the focus, he told me, "We may be too late. Or too early—the lad is not regular."

"Lad?" I wondered aloud. John Barrymore was a little old to be called a *lad*.

"Yes, yes," Mortimer said. "A young boy—looks like an urchin—dressed more like a London pauper than one of the country-folk. He always goes just along that rise over there, with pots and boxes. I tell you: he is feeding the Notting Hill Murderer! Oh! Watson, look! Here he is!"

I rushed to the telescope and put my eye to the piece just in time to see a tousle-headed lad of nine or ten disappearing over one of the nearby hills. I could make out little of him, for he appeared to me in silhouette and only for a moment, but one thing was clear: it certainly wasn't Barrymore. So who was he? What was he doing? I scanned the moor. We were not close to Baskerville Hall, and though Selden's hiding spot was closer, still it was none too near. And the boy was heading in the wrong direction. He was headed more towards…

The tor. The man on the tor who had laughed at me during Selden's attack. He was an unknown quantity—I had no guess as to his identity or his purpose, but it was possible he was master to the hound. Perhaps this boy could help me find him. But first, I figured, I had better save Mortimer's life.

"Oh no," I laughed. "That will be young William. His father is a shepherd. The boy must be bringing him lunch."

"A shepherd?" Mortimer said, deflating down into one

of his chairs. "Not the murderer? A shepherd? Am I to remain a coward, then?"

"I think it would be best. Cowards are the wisest, longest-lived fellows I know. Take heart, James, and continue as you are. Yours is a noble life."

He did not like my answer, but in the end I convinced him of it. We hitched his nag to his creaky cart, to carry poor Sir Henry home. Before I went I scanned the hills and committed them to memory as best I could. Mortimer was not suited to the business of chasing dangerous men across the moor. That was my job.

Tomorrow… I thought to myself. *I don't know who you are, Man on the Tor, but by the time the sun goes down tomorrow, I shall have you.*

I STAYED UP LATE THAT NIGHT, SURVEYING THE MOOR from the top of the East Tower and committing it to memory. I stayed longer than I should, fretting over each valley and hill, until the moonlight failed me and there was naught to do but go to bed.

I slept late the next morning then went to Sir Henry's room to tell him my plans for the day. He lay upon his bed in a magnificent array of pillows that Barrymore had arranged to support his injured leg, his arms, his breakfast, his book and any passing wildebeest that felt like it might fancy a lie-down. Barrymore buzzed about the room, arranging Sir Henry's old, new, formal and casual clothes into different piles. Sir Henry brightened as I entered and called, "Morning, Watson! You've missed a couple of good dust-ups."

"Uh-oh. Have I?"

"Yep. Two fights. Two reconciliations. Two agreements—one of 'em enough to get me smiling—and now we're organizing the old wardrobe."

"Two fights?" I asked.

"Hm. First, Barrymore here—he thinks we shouldn't have gone after Selden."

"The man is an escaped murderer!" I cried.

"He is family," Barrymore said, "and Eliza told you his secret in confidence."

"She told us because you got caught," Sir Henry reminded him. "But anyway, it's a moot point. The Barrymores have a plan to make sure Selden never harms another Englishman."

"Oh?" I asked, "What is that?"

"We have arranged for him to be transported, in secret, to America," Barrymore said.

I was rather taken aback by this and said, "Look, I have some experience with these matters, both as an investigator and a medical doctor, so I think I can tell you: a psychotic multi-murderer does not stop killing simply because he's had a change of scenery. All you are proposing is the export of our problem, not a solution. Frankly, Sir Henry, I am surprised that you would consider endangering your friends abroad."

"Oh! No, no, no," Sir Henry laughed. "*South* America."

"Oh. South America… well that does change things…"

"What d'you think of the plan then, Watson?" Sir Henry asked.

"Well, it is highly irregular," I replied. "Usually, we use Australia for that sort of thing… But, if it will restore the local peace and it is *South* America… I suppose we could overlook it, just this once."

"That's good," Sir Henry said, "'cause I've already

told Barrymore I'd help. So me and Barrymore are square now. Oh, and I've given him some of my old clothes. We're going through 'em now and Barrymore has his choice of all the stuff I'm getting rid of."

It did my heart good to see that magnificent pile of foreign work clothes leaving the baronet's possession. Perhaps my joy loosened my tongue more than it ought. "You should give him that one you're wearing," I said. He wore a ridiculous powder-blue suit.

"Hey! This is my best Toronto suit!" Sir Henry protested and I only just managed to choke back the observation that this was an oxymoronic statement, before he added, "Only you and Mortimer seem to dislike it. Stapleton thinks it looks mighty fair. He said I ought to wear it for Beryl."

"Jack Stapleton, you mean? When has he ever seen you in it?"

"Oh, he was the second fight of the morning," said Sir Henry. "I thought we were gonna have a punch-up for a minute, there. But it ended well enough."

I kicked myself for sleeping so late. I wasn't sure I trusted Jack Stapleton and I was becoming more and more certain I trusted his sister not at all. What if Stapleton sought Sir Henry's life? Had I let him alone with his would-be murderer while I slumbered, two doors down?

"What did Stapleton want?" I asked.

"He said he felt bad about yelling at me yesterday," Sir Henry said. "He came round to apologize. That didn't stop him getting pretty out of shape when I asked if I could call on Beryl. And it didn't stop me from shouting that he's her brother, not her governess. And it didn't stop a bunch of other things being said that nearly set us at each other. But it came out all right in the end. He says he's alone out here, with only his sister for company. They've been together their whole lives and he's got nobody else to speak with about his... bugs and things. So, the idea of losing her fell hard on him. I told him it wasn't right for him to prevent her from marrying and he agreed. He only asked me for three months. This time next January, I can start courting her; until then, I'm supposed to just be civil."

"That will be difficult," I said. It is hard to describe the slew of emotion that had poured through me as he spoke. Unspeakable jealousy and anger were my first reactions, but I firmly reminded myself that these were not my true emotions, but something I was being *made* to feel. In those moments where I successfully convinced myself of this, I worried for Sir Henry. Nothing good could come from courting such a temptress, of that I was certain.

"It's gonna be hard to wait," he said, "but I gave my word, so... You really don't like this suit?"

"Forgive me, Sir Henry, I do not."

"Why?"

"Allow me just to say that if Jack Stapleton encouraged you to appear in it in front of Beryl Stapleton, it was an attempt to sabotage your hopes with her."

His eyebrows went up, as if he were having trouble deciding if I were being helpful or trying to start the morning's third argument. Finally, and with studied Britishness, he said, "I will take that under advisement. I had planned to wear it when I saw them tonight. Stapleton invited me round to play cards with him. I told him I'd see whether or not my foot was fit for it. I'm sure it won't be, but... I don't know... I kinda like the idea of going anyway. I thought Beryl might make a fuss and... what a strangely happy thought that was... But anyway, what are you up to today, Watson?"

"You remember the man we saw upon the tor, when we were fighting Selden?"

"Sure."

"Today, I am hunting that man."

"Careful, Watson," Sir Henry said. "If he can control a demon hound, he's prob'ly not the nicest guy."

"One way to find out, I suppose," I said. "I confess, I am against you playing cards tonight. Not without me to protect you. Perhaps I shall make it back in time to ride with you to Merripit House. Don't make a face, I need not go in; the Stapletons needn't even know I have come. I shall sit in the trap and read a book, perhaps. I just don't want you risking your neck without me there to guard it. I shall hurry about my business and see you this evening."

Yet, it proved to be a difficult business to hurry. I hadn't made it far from Baskerville Hall when I spotted a suspicious cave, across a ravine. It took me nearly half an hour to make it down one side of the defile and up the other, only to find the cave was deep enough to shelter, perhaps, two squirrels.

If they hugged each other.

Moreover, I'd spotted six or seven other points of

interest on the journey. I had no time to check them all and was beginning to realize I was still too close to the Hall. I hadn't fathomed the enormity of my task. A thousand Watsons couldn't search the moor in a day. Perhaps it would be folly for them to try. As the day wore on I came to a second dreadful realization: I was actually going *too fast*. I'd been employing no stealth at all. My quarry could easily have spotted me and shot me dead from the safety of his hiding place. Or set the hound on me. Then there was Selden. He'd promised to stop killing, but if he'd found the perfect little eggcup to end somebody with, did I expect him to be able to control himself?

Seven hours and several miles out onto the empty moor, I began to despair that this was one of the worst ideas I'd ever had. Then, in an instant, my luck reversed itself. I smelled fire. Not still-burning fire but that sad, sour smell of last night's campfire, gone to burnt black memory. I was wandering past a little hollow in one of the tors, when I scented it. I'd been on the very point of turning back, for I knew the daylight must soon fail me.

The tor curved around, forming a natural sort of harbor. Inside were five of those little Stone Age huts Holmes had told me of. They were in better condition than any I'd seen so far. One was still full height, but lacked a roof. One was intact. I crept to the best-preserved hut and peeped inside.

It was most certainly inhabited. Though nobody was present at that moment, there was a rudimentary bedroll on one side and a tiny firepit on the other. In the center, the round cross section of an old stump had been upended to make a sort of table, with a chair of the same just beside it. On that makeshift table lay a pile of burnt breadcrumbs, a knife, a spoon, a bowl and a note—handwritten by someone who seemed barely literate—which read: *Beware. Watson searching the moor today.* So if it were my Man on the Tor, it seemed his supply boy had done a better job spotting me than I had of spying him. This was the only deduction I could form, except…

My eyes went to the silverware. Spoon. Knife. *No fork.* My left hand flew protectively to my chest. Selden! Less than two days previous, I had oh-so-cleverly divested him of that fork and had now wandered, alone, into the beast's lair! I had to…

But before I could begin truly hyperventilating, reason mastered my fear. The heirloom Baskerville silver was well worthy of its title and clearly marked with the family crest. This set was cheap and tinny. Different silverware, so… different fellow? Yet how had it come to pass that this gentleman should also have lost his fork? The coincidence was too much; there had to be some explanation…

And I had it. Oh, it is hard to explain the rage I felt in that moment—I threw the little table over, kicked the burnt wood out of the firepit, and flung my pistol at the bedroll. Before it hit, I was already cringing low, with my hands over my face. Sometimes, when one does such things with a loaded pistol, one gets exactly what one deserves. Standing near the center of a small, round chamber with walls of stone on every side might have proved to be interesting if that pistol had discharged. But luck was with me. There was nothing to do but set my jaw, cross my arms and sit grumpily on the stump to wait.

An hour passed.

So did daylight.

Finally, as twilight filled the little hollow, there came the sound of footsteps. As they neared, I raised my voice and called, "Welcome back, Holmes. Care to step inside and explain yourself?"

I suppose it would have been wiser to have kept the pistol handy, in case my deduction had proved false. Yet the strangled little scream that drifted in through the stone doorway was strikingly familiar. A moment later it was followed by Holmes's head—shaggy and disheveled—which bent in to wonder, "Watson? How did you find me? How did you even know it *was* me?"

"Simple deduction, Holmes. A pot. A spoon. A knife. Burnt breadcrumbs. No fork. The gentleman who resides here has not only been living on toast and soup, he is ill equipped to eat anything else. That is only you, Holmes. Only you."

"Bravo, Watson! Yes, well done indeed," he said, then cleared his throat with some apprehension and added, "I suppose I owe you an explanation."

"I suppose you do."

"You probably want to know what I've been doing since we parted company," said Holmes. "But if you really wish to know the full account we must go back farther. In fact, I think we'd best start at Baskerville Hall, Michaelmas 1643."

PART II

FROM SOME NEBULOUS, UNDEFINED SOURCE

10

Michaelmas 1643

IT IS THE DAY OF DUES, AND SO THEY COME. EVERY creditor knows the day and every debtor. Michaelmas: the day of expectation; the day of payment. For those who work by day, the accounts will be settled by the exchange of pounds or goods. For those who labor in secret, attending the otherworldly mumbles of darker powers, this is the day their supplications and exhortations may be repaid by direct congress with the demons and devils to whom they attach all hope.

Hugo Baskerville is there, of course, for it is in his hall where the worlds may most easily be brought together. Sheng Xia, the Lady of Secrets, has journeyed from the East. Talog To-Tek, last practitioner of the Aztec sacrifices has come, wearing the skin of his last slave. Pope Urban VIII is not well, but he will have to do without the magics of his favored doctor, for Sanzetti the Sarcomancer would never miss this day—not for all the cardinal's begging. Fasoul the Turk is here as well, though it is hard to say if he was invited as a kindness to him, or merely as entertainment for the others. Yes, his powers are impressive, but they are as much an affliction as a gift. Fasoul sees the hidden world, but not the presented one. When he beholds a man, he sees the man's intentions, his hopes, his fears, his triumphs and his failings, but he cannot see the face, the flesh or the form. Like a normal blind man, he survives on charity. He sees his benefactors' pity for him, as well as their disdain, yet he cannot taste the bread they bring. In the crowded streets of Istanbul, the showmen play their Karagöz, but he cannot see the puppets. He beholds the strings.

These five chairs are claimed and one more is expected to be filled. Today, for the first time anybody can remember, the best of them is coming. Moriarty has accepted the Michaelmas invitation.

Sir Hugo grows impatient. It is not right that he is made to wait, that he is made to sit in his hall listening to his guests dote and fawn upon the powers of Moriarty. Hardly a soul in this room does not disdain Sir Hugo and nobody bothers to hide it. They think him unworthy to sit in his own coven, welcome only because he is the steward of this sacred place: the meeting of four lines. Nowhere else in this wide world do four lines converge. Nowhere else are the powers felt so strongly, for they are never closer than here, at Baskerville Hall.

Sanzetti and Talog have already called on Sir Hugo for wine. He told them Barrymore was here to attend their needs, but when they bellow for drink, it is Baskerville's name they call. They think he is only here to serve, to bring the wine and the sacrifice. He has made all those preparations, but he has made a few more they do not know about. They will. Soon. Before the sun rises tomorrow, this brood will have a new master. Moriarty will be screaming in hell and these proud mages will bend their knees to Sir Hugo, he knows it.

But for now, they drink and trade tales of how well they don't really know Moriarty. That silly little ape of a man, Sanzetti, is gesturing wildly with his left hand and slopping wine out of the goblet in his right. Before he met Sanzetti, Sir Hugo had known physicians to use a variety of lancets. He just didn't realize they wore so many of them. The blood-crusted collection of surgical knives clinks and rattles as Sanzetti energetically recites a tale that will—everyone assumes—eventually work its way to James Moriarty.

"A man loses too much blood: he dies. Everybody knows this. So we learn that blood has a power—the power to sustain life. If too much of this power is drained, the life is lost. This much, of course, I have known. Only when I get this book do I see! Only when I read the word of Moriarty do I think: where does this power go? Can it be caught? Reclaimed? Used to a new purpose? I was nothing before I read this—a simple physician, only. Now, I plumb the secrets of life itself! Moriarty—a man I have never met—has taught me my art."

Sir Hugo glances at the heavy tome Sanzetti has placed upon the table and grunts, "It says it's by someone named Carceau."

"The writer is immaterial," Sanzetti scoffs. "I found this in a second-hand bookseller's in Orleans. But the previous owner! Ah! Moriarty had the book before. He made notes in the margins, whenever Carceau was foolish. Light in darkness! Food for the starving mind!"

"So you are in possession of Moriarty's secrets and he doesn't know you've got them?" asks Sir Hugo, who is feeling none too charitable tonight.

"What? No! Well… yes, but I brought the book, see? I will give it back to him, tonight. I will thank him for making me all that I am."

"And perhaps he won't kill you for it," says Sir Hugo, raising his glass.

Sheng applauds the story and feigns an apologetic tone as she begins to best it. "I have been honored to have *three* letters from Mr. Moriarty. In the first, he asked if I might prepare for him an unenclosing egg. With trembling hand, I wrote that I did not know how and sat back to await my doom. Instead, he wrote me instructions. One of the finest magical inventions of my own country, lost to me and all my kind, but Moriarty knows the secret. I steal a hundred-year-old egg, destined to be soup for the emperor. I make the unenclosing egg. I put it in a box of jade. I put this box in a box of wood. That one in a box of wicker. That one in a box of straw. I send five of our finest warriors to bring it over the long trade road, to Vienna. Four are slain; one returns but he has been driven mad and cannot tell me what has occurred. Yet I know Moriarty has the egg, for the madman bears a final letter. It says I have earned his thanks—this is my most prized possession."

They speak like this for over an hour. The first cask

of wine is empty; the second is unsealed. Talog is terrified and hiding it poorly. Sir Hugo is near frantic, too, but the fear does not show on his face. It invigorates him. Still, he curses his missing guest. What if Moriarty does not come? What if he has guessed Hugo's purpose and will not chance a confrontation?

Sir Hugo almost jumps from his seat when he hears the tapping. Nobody heard the hooves, or the rattle of the black carriage. Nobody felt the attentions of the demons move across the room, straining towards the front door, eager to greet their favorite. But they hear the gentle tap, tap, tap of the silver hound's-head cane on the massive oak door. Hugo curses. Barrymore goes to answer the door. He is trembling.

When the hall door sweeps open, none of the assembled mages know what to expect, but one look at Moriarty is enough to teach them that he is exactly what they should have expected. He is a large man, yet thin. His stride displays a vigor that belies his age. He is dressed all in black, but not as an affectation or a sign of forbidden strength—only as a mark of austerity. He looks just like what he is: a scholar. His small black eyes seem to take in everything, but if they come to judgment on any of it, they choose not to make it known. Compared to the others assembled here, his appearance is so normal that he might go unremarked, were it not for his companion.

The boy is naked but for a tattered loincloth. He is bent and tousle-haired and adorned with a magnificent collection of bruises. He keeps his eyes on the floor, as if all resistance and sense has been beaten from him. It very nearly has. Moriarty spares the room no greeting until he has swept off his long black cloak and flung it at Barrymore. He straightens his cuffs and without looking up, says, "Lady, gentlemen, I am James Moriarty. I am pleased to make your acquaintances."

There is silence until Moriarty and his boy cross the threshold into the great hall. With a sudden shriek Fasoul falls from his seat, crying, "Tatters and ashes! Tatters and ash! Look who comes with all the secrets! The promises... See how they dote on him? See how they fawn? Black Prince! Black Prince, we hail you!"

Nobody else has found their voice yet, so Moriarty addresses them, one by one. "Sheng Xia, so good to meet you at last. I owe you my thanks and shall express it thus: whatever happens tonight, you are spared. You shall not suffer by my hand, or any other. Let your mind be at ease. Sanzetti, keep the book. It is right and fitting you should have that knowledge; enjoy it with my regards. Talog To-Tek, you are a fool. If there is one thing I may salute in you, it is this: that you have had the audacity to put yourself in the way of your betters. Go cautiously tonight and you may learn much. If you are rash, you shall perish."

Moriarty's eyes fall on Fasoul, but he makes no greeting. What would be the point?

When he comes to Sir Hugo, he smiles. "Ah, our host. None of you lot know it, but this is the best of you."

Sheng Xia and Sanzetti laugh. Sanzetti because he has no fear of Baskerville, Xia because she thinks Moriarty is joking. Moriarty is never joking. He turns to the room and barks, "Are you all so blind? Do you measure your power in corpses? In gold? In the number of men who fear you? Who else among you has had the wit to marry their fate to a place such as this? To spend all their earthly effort commanding the spot where four lines converge? To build—not so much a house—but a stone cistern for those outside powers we all study? Yet still, *still*, his finest achievement is yet to come. It happens tonight."

Moriarty looks about the room, studying each mage's eyes. He is looking for a sign of recognition, a flicker of guilt that will betray its owner as a confederate of Hugo's, or at least somebody who expected his plot.

"None of you know?" Moriarty asks, almost dumbfounded. "None of you know why you are here? None of you understand why—tonight of all nights—I have agreed to come?" He laughs. "Tell them, Hugo."

Hugo is sweating. He is shaking and his palms are slick. This is the moment upon which all else hangs. He steps forward, points one finger in the face of his honored guest and declares, "Moriarty, you are in my power!"

"Oh, Sir Hugo, I assure you I am not," Moriarty says. "Sheng Xia, you are well versed in the ways of magic; what do you know of the Sothothian Knot?"

Everybody turns to Sheng, who mumbles, "I have not heard of such a thing."

"You may know it as The Confounding Assurance of the Fullness of Tang."

"Ah! A protective ward. Dangerous to any who attempt to dispel it."

"Correct," Moriarty says, "because there is only one thread of binding magic in it and... how many glamours?"

"Nine?" Sheng hazards.

"Sixteen. Pluck at the real thread and the spell is undone. Select one of the glamours and you invite its trap into the center of your soul. You will be bound to the will of the caster more surely than by any other spell. It takes a high degree of arrogance or desperation to dare to attempt dispelling a Sothothian Knot. Or a high degree of skill. Sir Hugo here has a particularly rudimentary version of it, woven around this very hall. Three threads that would dispel, only four to trap."

"Five!" protests Hugo.

"Four. Did you not examine the final glamour? It was so clumsily added that a tug on it would dislodge the second binding thread, long before triggering its feeble curse. Though it was a glamour, it was as good as a true thread, to a thief. Three to dispel; four to trap. Did none of you notice this ward?" Moriarty asks the room. "You all walked in unawares? Always I except Fasoul, of course, who could not have failed to notice but is incapable of fearing it. Envy him, for he will never be fooled by a thread of glamour. None of us—not even I—will ever bind Fasoul."

The assembly is shocked. Sheng, in particular, cannot believe she was fooled.

"Forgive yourselves," Moriarty decides. "It was better concealed than it was constructed. Yet, this is only one example of the many traps our host has laid to make sure that each of us—myself most of all—are at his mercy. Isn't that right, Hugo?"

"Every sorcerer has his precautions," Hugo says, his mind reeling. How many of his plots can Moriarty have discovered? How skilled is he?

"You are no sorcerer, Sir Hugo, and you certainly are not cautious. You are daring—as a true wizard should be! If you were cautious, I would have killed you already. You have the audacity to try and shed my blood—mine!—to fulfill your plan. And what a plan! Or do I miss my guess? Are there no other traps you have laid? Is this my place at the table? It must be, eh? Why then, this would be my wine. I think I shall try it. Ah, a fine vintage, though I do note it tastes just a bit like Parthian granite. Yes, I think I shall drink it all. Please, give me a moment… Yes, an excellent wine. Oh wait, one drop is left. Ah! Delicious. Now, I think I shall carelessly hold this chalice in my good right hand for a few moments, before putting it down. Is there nothing you wish to say to me, Sir Hugo?"

"…"

"No? Do you not wish to note, perhaps, that by the strength of earth, I am bound to your will?"

"…"

"Are you sure, Sir Hugo? Look, I am putting down the cup. If you believe in your spell more than you believe in me, you must say those words. Say those words and forego my mercy, or admit that you are bested!"

"…"

"Well. The moment is past. I am done with my cup. I

am pleased that you did not attempt to bind me, Sir Hugo.
There are so few geniuses left in the world, it is always a
waste to slay one."

Sir Hugo staggers, then collapses into his chair. His
world is coming down. Yet the great gears of his plan are
still grinding forward. The spell he's been weaving for
months is unstoppable, yet incomplete. If the sacrifices are
not made by midnight...

"He is a genius, you know," Moriarty says. "Did none
of you notice the floor?"

Moriarty whisks his hand and the great oak table slides
aside. A second brush and Sir Hugo's concealing layer of
granite powder is blown away, revealing the white lines
that run beneath.

"What do you suppose that white marble represents?"
Moriarty asks.

"Lines of power. Here is where the dark ones' attention
runs, back and forth," Sanzetti says.

"Correct. Two of them, you will note, are irregular
and do not continue through. They end right here, in this
hall. The others pass through the nexus and continue on.
This great hall was constructed so the lines all converge
under the chair at the head of this table. A clever touch,
but here is where it becomes masterful: how many lines
are represented?"

"Four," says Sheng. "Baskerville Hall is unique in that
it sits atop the convergence of four lines of—"

But Talog, staring at the floor, interrupts. "Five."

"Yes," Moriarty beams. "*Five*. Now do you understand

your host? No mortal has ever attempted to direct the opening of a new ley-line, or to determine its course. To endeavor it is daring; to succeed at it is wondrous. Yet that is what Sir Hugo stands to do, this very night. How could you have come to this hall for all these years and never recognized the genius of the man who built her? For shame."

Talog To-Tek is first to respond, with a cry of, "Ho! Ha-Ho!" He jumps from his chair. He bites his right thumb. He raises his fist. Six drops of blood fall to the floor in salute of Hugo Baskerville. Sheng begins a polite applause. Sanzetti joins; he had not seen it—any of it. Fasoul says nothing, but gives a little whimper. His head lolls north, south, north, east. He can see a storm, when one is coming.

"I admit I have not worked out your entire plan," Moriarty tells Hugo, "but I think I understand the basics. Have you a sacrifice of virtue prepared?"

"She is in the East Tower," Hugo says.

"Excellent," says Moriarty, and pours a cup of wine. "These grapes are not from Carpathia, I trust?"

Hugo shrugs and looks to Barrymore, who says, "No, sir. From France. Burgundy, I believe."

"Very good. It is best to be cautious. Boy!"

Moriarty's boy hastens forward and his master holds forth two cups—one of wine, one of water—saying, "Go to the prisoner in the East Tower. Give her these. She must drink them both. Tonight she dies—if she is fortunate."

The boy takes the cups and shuffles from the hall.

Barrymore goes too, at least so far as to show him the path to the East Tower. The boy drags his feet and sheds tears. He hates his master. He hates his own actions. Whether the tears are for his own lot or the girl in the tower, he cannot say. The stairs are steep; his legs are weak. Five flights up, to the top of the tower—his own heavy breaths almost hide the other sound. Crying. He comes to a door with a hatch, through which food can be passed.

"Pardon," says the boy, without looking up. "Pardon, but my master says you are to drink this."

He has surprised the occupant, who did not hear his steps. She rushes to the door. Hands clasp the bars. She pushes her face to the hatch.

"Who is it?" she asks.

"Please, you must drink this. My master says."

"Why? Who are you? Who is your master? Sir Hugo?"

"This one is water. This one is wine. You must drink."

"Why? What is happening?"

He looks up at her. He doesn't mean to. She has such a sweet face; it reminds him of his sister. Imagine, if they could escape together. If they could go far away. She would be so grateful and so would he and any time either of them cried, the other could kiss their brow and remind them: all is well, now. She is so pretty. He wishes he hadn't looked. "I... You must drink this... I'm so sorry..."

"Who are you? What are they going to do to me?"

"Please drink."

"What are they going to do?"

"My master says... he says you will die tonight."

Silence for a moment, then the boy begins to cry. He is always crying. He hates himself. She has reason to weep, not he. Yet she is strong. Coward!

"They're going to kill me?" she asks.

He only cries.

"What is your name, boy?"

He only cries.

"Please. My name is Bhehr-Lylegnag. What is your name?"

"That is a pretty name," says the boy.

It isn't. It is the worst name she can imagine, but she smiles at him. What a sad little boy. Well, he is almost her age—almost a man—but he seems so young. Funny, she feared this news would come; yet even in the face of it, she feels sorry for the boy. Maybe she is relieved it is only her life they seek.

"What is your name?" she asks again.

The boy sniffs. He wipes away his tears, but they are instantly replaced.

"Warlock Holmes."

11

DEEP UNDERGROUND, THE WORMS OF THE EARTH ARE turning. They are moaning. Realness is parting and unrealness rushes into the void. The outer truth is spilling in, to nobody's benefit. The fifth line is opening.

In the East Tower the boy can feel it. Possibility is flooding into him. He is sweating. He can feel the tiny parts—the tiny parts that make up everything. He feels it in the gold; he feels it in the lead; he feels it in the iron. The tiny parts that pull. The tiny parts that push. The tiny parts that do nothing, but contribute weight. All of them are waiting to respond to him. What is his wish? They are so bored of being trapped in their current state. Would he like to change them? Would he like to change the bars in the window? The chains upon this girl's wrists? His fists are clenched with effort. His green eyes are burning; they light the cell.

The girl is holding back her screams, terrified that she will cry out and alert the men below. What is wrong with this boy—this messenger? Is he an angel? Iron bars are become as glass, transparent and brittle. Now they are as water, running down the cold black stone. Now they are gone. Her chains have vanished. The air smells hot and strange. She cannot know it, but she is breathing in the remnants of her manacles.

Downstairs, the festive atmosphere has returned. It had been strained. Now the guests are convinced. Now they marvel at the mastery of James Moriarty. They know that this Michaelmas is special. If they are faithful to Moriarty they will survive it and bear witness to the greatest magical event of the generation, perhaps of the millennium.

"Of course, Sir Hugo here needs two sacrifices, to stabilize the line," Moriarty says. "He has a sacrifice of virtue: the girl in the tower. Yet, he also needs a sacrifice of art: a practitioner of magic. Now that I am escaped from his little trap, whom do you suppose he will choose?"

Talog To-Tek cries with alarm and leaps from his chair. Moriarty laughs, "Sit down, fool. Fasoul is the obvious choice. The man cannot secure his own food, much less defend himself from the five of us. Not to worry. I have brought an alternative. I had hoped to spend him better than this, but... well... it is an occasion, is it not?"

"What?" asks Sir Hugo. "The boy?"

"Hmm. He may not seem it, but he has accomplished more than anybody else in this room—myself excepted— and though his gifts are limited, he can do that which I still cannot. Behold." Moriarty reaches into his pocket and draws forth a heavy bar of gold. He throws it to the table. It is closely followed by a second. "That one used to be lead," Moriarty tells his fellows. "That one was iron."

"Here is a secret worth knowing," whispers Sheng.

Moriarty frowns. "I had hoped to have it out of him by now, but I am convinced he does not understand how he did it. Lucky imbecile. Well… and unlucky… What do you say, friends, shall we give him to the demons?"

There is a roar of approbation and a clinking of cups. Only Sir Hugo is uncomfortable with the offer. He has lost. He has dared to contrive against the greatest wizard in history and underestimated his foe. He knew the risk. He did not expect victory, but the possibility was there and he could not pass it by. Yet, what surprises Sir Hugo most is this… joviality. Not just mercy—an unthinkable boon, to any who know Moriarty's reputation—but the sudden transformation of this group of betrayers and murderers into laughing comrades. What is happening?

Almost in answer to his thought, Moriarty's hand claps him on the shoulder. "Of course, I'm taking your house."

"What?"

"Your house. It is mine now. And it shall be me, not you, who sits atop those white lines when the clock strikes twelve. When the fifth line opens and all the demons and devils and gods rush to the center to meet their chosen mortal vessel, I shall be waiting to dictate terms to them. This is only fair."

Sir Hugo can barely bring himself to speak. But he cannot bring himself not to. He should be silent. He should escape with his life, yet he cannot help but growl, "Fair? *Fair?*"

"Generous," Moriarty declares. "I think we all realize

that I could slay you, if I choose. Sober calculation dictates that I must. Or, as a better display of my power, I should force one of the other guests to do it. Are there any here who would not kill this man to curry my favor?"

The room is silent. Moriarty smiles. "Of course not. Yet be of good cheer, Sir Hugo: I have reason to spare you. It is time for tonight's lesson. Talog To-Tek, stand up."

He does. Moriarty faces the burly Aztec and asks, "Do you know why your powers are so weak?"

"My powers are…"

But he stops. In the jungle one always professes strength, even now, after the empire has fallen. Yet, if he proclaims himself powerful, Moriarty will demonstrate that he is not.

"Why?" Talog To-Tek asks.

"Because you rely on blood sacrifice. A man is killed in the name of a god, therefore that god is present. But only slightly. These gods—these spirits—are remote. They can hardly extend themselves, hardly be felt in our world, even when they are honored with blood. They are unable to give much power away, when their hold is so tenuous. So what are you chasing? Tiny shreds of your spirit are all that come through—of that small portion, you can barely hope that you will be given the tenth share. You have spent your whole life chasing after scraps of scraps, and you think greatness is achievable? You have not honestly evaluated your art. Baskerville has. He has had the vision to seek the greatest advantage he can derive and settle for nothing less. That is why he shall live. That is why he shall stay here, under the roof that was once his, to attend me and learn my secrets. He will be my apprentice. He will serve me and, in so doing, will become the second greatest mage on earth. Why? To teach all you other dabblers this lesson: reason is the greatest gift of man." He slaps the table to make his point, then sits, saying, "So, take heart, Hugo. You may live. It is not such a defeat, after all, is it?"

He waves his empty cup at Barrymore. He should not, for he does not normally drink and he is unused to it. But this is an occasion. Besides that, there is a part of him that hates himself for not killing Hugo. Reason is only half the cause of his success; the other half is cold-blooded unwillingness to brook the merest hint of defiance. Yet magic will never be a significant tool for mankind unless Moriarty's lesson is learned and the full vivacity of man's intellect is turned to the outer mystery. As a scholar, it irks him to see that this is not being done. He's easily vexed tonight, for he knows his victory will be tainted. It will be such a gain, when he sits atop five open lines. Yet, to see Hugo alive when that moment comes, will feel as a defeat.

"Where is that boy?" Moriarty grumbles. "He should have been back by now." He raps his knuckles on the table and shouts, "Warlock?"

"Master?" answers a meek voice, from just outside the hall door.

Hiding? He is *hiding*? He did not hasten back to report? Something is wrong. "What has happened, boy? Did she drink?"

"No…"

"Why did she not drink?"

"She is gone."

Consternation and clamor run through the assembled mages. They know enough to understand that this is not good, yet only Moriarty and his host know why, or just how dire the situation is. Baskerville goes white.

"Gone?" Moriarty bellows. "*Gone?* What has happened? Come here, you wretch! Come here and tell me all!"

Sheepish and tear-stained, the boy slinks back over the threshold.

"Aaaaaaaaiiieeah!" Fasoul shrieks. "Tears and wreck and rack and ruin! The black one has returned! Prince of tatters! Prince of ash!"

12

THE WIND HAS PICKED UP, MOANING ITS COMPLAINT AS it breaks over the East Tower. It gusts through the open window as Moriarty leans out. Below, in the courtyard, his companions' torches sputter and flicker; the light they cast is changing and uncertain, but it is enough. There is no body at the base of the tower. She is down and away.

Moriarty turns wrathful eyes down upon his host, standing five stories below. "How has this happened, Sir Hugo?"

"I cannot say! The window was barred!"

"There are no bars!"

"What has happened to them?" Sir Hugo shouts. It is hard to make himself heard over the gathering wind.

Moriarty doesn't answer. He is glad the other mages went outside. The only person with him is his boy. He should seize that boy by the hair, drag him to the window and hurl him out. Except now he is afraid to. The residue of magic is immense. To make bars disappear from a window is a simple trick. It takes a bit of art, but almost no true power. Here, the very stones of the walls reverberate with magic. Whatever occurred in this room was done with a complete lack of wit or subtlety, but with more magic than those cretins down below have gathered in all their lives.

"What have you done?" Moriarty asks the boy.

"Nothing, master."

Moriarty reaches for his cane to strike the boy, but it is downstairs; he left it with Barrymore. He could hit the lad, but his gloves are with his cane and he does not wish to have skin to skin contact with the boy. Not so soon after a spell of this magnitude.

"Come," he tells the boy.

By the time they reach the courtyard, the air is filled with the baying of hounds. The hunt will be a difficult one. The wind is high; the dogs will not scent well. And if one should happen to find her, how far will his baying carry over the noise of the storm? A few drops of rain slant down, threatening more. Sir Hugo is in his saddle and his grooms are seeing to the guests' horses.

"This could be most unfortunate, Baskerville," says Moriarty.

"I know… master," Sir Hugo says. It is good he has come to accept his place.

"Your months of ritual cannot be undone; your work cannot be recanted. The fifth line *will* open tonight. Yet without the blood of an innocent and the blood of a practitioner, it will be dangerously unstable."

"What do you think will happen?"

"I do not know, Sir Hugo. It is possible the fifth line

will simply close. Then again, it might break wide open. If it does, the other four will surely go as well and this world will become the battleground of all the demon realms that have access to those lines. They want this place, you know. After they are done fighting over it, I wonder if the victor will still be pleased with the scraps."

Baskerville nods. This is his assessment, too. To think: he could be the man who breaks the world. Worlds are not fragile things, unless you can find a spot where they are already cracked.

"Where would the girl go?" Moriarty asks.

"Her family's farm," Sir Hugo answers, "almost certainly."

"You know where this farm is?" Moriarty asks. Sir Hugo nods. "I want you to picture in your mind exactly where it lies," Moriarty commands. "Have you got it?" Hugo nods again and Moriarty pulls Hugo down in the saddle and places a palm to his forehead. Hugo feels a sudden sharp pain. His nose begins to bleed. He cannot remember where that farm is.

"I shall go in my carriage," Moriarty says. "Send Sanzetti and Sheng back to the town, in case she tries to flee to the safety of the townsfolk instead of her family. You must hunt her by horse and hound. You have no memory of her home now, so you will follow her scent. We must recapture the sacrifice of innocence! You and I shall take her—one man at her heels and one at her house."

Baskerville shakes his head. "No good. There is no road. Your carriage cannot…"

"How many grooms have you here?" Moriarty asks, "How many stable boys?"

"Only two grooms, one stable boy."

"Ah. My horses will leave one of the grooms; he will have to prepare the rest of our mounts alone."

"What about the other two?"

"If my horses are to bring a carriage where there is no road, they must eat. Two men are scanty fare, but enough to get us there, I think. They'll have to eat her family to get us back."

Moriarty turns from his host-turned-vassal and calls, "Barrymore, get Fasoul into my carriage."

"Fasoul?" Baskerville asks.

"If he has any insight as to how the evening is playing out, I want to hear it."

Baskerville nods. "And what of To-Tek?"

"I have different employment for him. Now go. I will see you at the girl's house, or close thereby."

Sir Hugo shouts for his kennel master to loose the hounds. Then wheels his horse and sets off across the moor.

Checking to make sure the boy is still lingering near the door, Moriarty goes to Talog To-Tek and says, "I have need of your skills."

Talog chafes at this. "You say I have no skills."

"It is not magic I need," says Moriarty, "but steel. Have you your knife?"

"Yes, but it is not steel. Flint. Stone."

"That will do," Moriarty says. "The life of a mage must be lost through the fifth line, before midnight. Take my boy, over there, and see that it is done."

"But how will I know where the line is?" asks Talog.

Moriarty sighs. "Spill his blood in the great hall where the five lines meet and you cannot miss it. Can you do this?"

Talog looks over at the boy and asks, "He does not look fit to outrun me; I can go fast as the jaguar, far as the whale. Can he fight?"

"No."

"Then he will die."

"Good," says Moriarty, then shouts, "Boy!"

The boy is not listening. He is staring up at the wall of the East Tower. Moriarty grabs him by his hair. "Boy! Go with Talog! Do as he says!"

Warlock Holmes nods dumbly. Moriarty hastens away to the stables. As Barrymore drags Fasoul past, the blind Turk and Warlock lock eyes. For an instant, Warlock sees Fasoul as Fasoul sees the world. There is no skin, no clothes, only hard bits inside the man, stringy bits holding him together. There are two burning green balls of gas— his eyes. They are full of fear. *Everything* is full of fear. The earth is afraid of what is happening; Warlock can feel it. He can see where Bhehr-Lylegnag climbed down the wall. She was so frightened, especially near the top; her fingers left traces of fear on the stones. So many powerful things are present tonight, but fear is the best of them. Everyone feels it. If anything is to take shape tonight—to grow legs and walk and breathe—it is fear.

The Roman and the Chinawoman ride past. From the direction of the stables, the screaming starts. The last groom and the kennel master come running by, just before Moriarty's black carriage. There is blood on the flagstones, where the horses' hooves have struck. The big Aztec is walking towards Warlock.

"Even you are afraid," Warlock tells him.

The big man nods and suddenly strikes the boy just below the ribs. All the air leaves Warlock and he begins to gasp and cough. The Aztec winds the fingers of his left hand into Warlock's long, unkempt hair and begins dragging him towards the hall. In his other hand is a blade of jagged stone.

He's going to kill me, Warlock realizes.

Well… that is foolish. That is wrong. It won't help anybody. Yes, Warlock's death could help stop the cracking of the earth, but it cannot heal it, only work to keep the wound forever open. The earth is not served by this. Baskerville and Moriarty will not be helped; they want to be wanted by the outside powers, but those demons do not wish to treat with such men. The demons will not be served by Warlock's death. They will be furious. They have chosen him. Can't Talog see that? Can't he hear them, chattering in Warlock's head? Promising him favors? Giving him gifts?

"I am the sacred smoke," says one, "and I grant you sway. No smoke shall choke you, or stop your sight. I ask nothing in return. Only remember me. I am your friend."

"No, no," says another. "Foolish. Now, if they burn you at the stake, you will burn—you cannot choke. He is no friend. Take me. I am the goddess of the hearth. I am the mother. I give you the gifts of the hearth: warm bread and soothing broth. When all those you love have passed from this earth, when all good things have been lost to the flow of time, my food shall bring you comfort. Hestia! Hestia!"

"Ash shall be thy ally," says another. "Whatever secrets it may hold shall be shared with thee—the burned thing known by its wreck. Remember me and praise my name: Sxaah."

"No. Blast and ruin. Purple flame and red, red blood. Hit! Smite! I am Azazel!"

These and a hundred more. He can barely hear them all. Can't Talog tell? Why would the demons wish to deal with a man such as Moriarty—a man who will bargain with them and control them, bend them to his will? Why not a boy with no will? Why not a beaten dog?

But Warlock cannot tell these things to Talog. He's got no breath and he's got no time; they're nearly at the hall. This man is going to murder him. Is he afraid? He can't tell. He doesn't feel the grip of fear in his heart, but he can feel it all around him, pressing in, begging to have form and breath and pulsing blood. Only, Warlock doesn't know the shape of it.

Talog kicks the door open. No, the shape of fear is not a door. It is not a stone knife, or five white lines on a black floor. It is not sweat on the palm or tears in the eye. What is it? Fear wants to know. Horror wants to know. It wants Warlock to tell it.

What is my shape?

Oh! He knows! It is leaning in towards the portal in the

door, to kiss Bhehr-Lylegnag. It is the moment before lips touch, when she still might refuse. That is the shape!

No! That is not the same fear! There is too much hope in it! What is the shape of fear, bereft of hope? Without love, without happiness, without shame or loss. What is the shape of the world, when only fear is in it?

The boy cannot think of it.

But he sees it. Near the door: his master's cane. The silver hound.

As soon as he spies it, he feels the lash of it on his back. Memories, like a solid wall, hit him in the chest. The bruises on his chest and face and arms and legs and back are not old. Yet with all these lashes, he feels the hundreds of marks that have faded. All those blows are struck anew. The hound, whose growl looks like a smile. Moriarty and the hound, smiling at him.

"Your father sold you too cheap, boy," Moriarty had said, that first day in the carriage. He was running his gloved fingers over the silver hound's head, pausing to feel its cleverly wrought little teeth.

Warlock remembers a night he spent on the floor, having once again failed to explain the movements of the tiny elements within the lead. He is bleeding. He can taste his teeth and his tears and the cold stone tiles. But he will not die. Again tonight, he will not die. Moriarty is too careful to strike a mortal blow without meaning to. The hound will be finished with Warlock only when Moriarty knows the secrets in the metal. Then, he promises, the hound will strike one last time.

"Strike your throat out, boy."

Warlock is screaming now and struggling. Talog feels better; he always hates it when his victims show no fear. It makes him worry they know something he does not. He strikes Warlock's head twice against the floor to quiet him, and drags him to the focal point. Talog does not know if he should call upon his gods before he cuts, but habit is stronger than sense, so he begins. He calls upon the snake that flies and slithers, and bids him not to watch. He calls to Smoke Jaguar and tells him to wet his fangs. The first cut goes deep down the boy's leg, from hip to knee. *Drink, Jaguar.*

There is a noise by the door. Talog looks up. An interloper? Rescuer? No. Professor Moriarty's silver cane has fallen, tipped past the edge of the door. Talog laughs. The tiny silver dog has peeped around the door to watch. *Very well, little dog, we will make an extra cut before we take the heart—on the foot, perhaps. The jaguar must drink, then the sky and the gourd and the stone step. Then you may have some, too.*

Something is wrong. The room is green. The boy! His eyes are fire—green fire! He gives one last scream, then he stiffens and is still. Has he died at the first cut? Talog does not know what god or spirit he is servicing here, but he hopes this will do. In his own country his gods would be very angry if the offering died before everyone could drink.

Talog cannot sense much of the hidden world. He does not feel the movement of magic, nor can he tell when the attention of an outside being is on him. So he does not feel the great rush of force as all the fear and horror of this momentous evening speeds into one spot, just outside the door of the great hall. Suddenly, there is fire—an explosion of flame that shakes Baskerville Hall to its deep stone roots. Fire, smoke and shadow coalesce into a shape—a magnificent hound. It smiles at the Aztec—a human expression laden with malice and intent—then comes at him. Talog cries out and rises to face it, but the knife is slick with blood and he drops it. He fumbles for his blade, screaming to have to face the beast unarmed.

There is something on Warlock's cheek—that is what wakes him. Something is nuzzling him. It is hot—in fact, it's burning—but the fire does not scorch Warlock. He opens his eyes. A flaming black wolf the size of a stag is standing over him. It is hard to tell where the dog begins and ends; it seems as if it is made of shadow, wreathed and interspersed by flame. He can hear it thinking, *Master. Maker. I love you. You found my shape.*

The boy feels a swell of love, too. It may just be the gratitude of one whose life has been saved, but the truth is—growing up poor and lonely—Warlock Holmes always wanted a dog. And however evil this beast may be, it has no malice for Warlock. He can feel its feelings. It loves him without limit or condition. Warlock sits up and looks around. The hall is large—it could easily seat sixty, maybe eighty men—but there is no wall of it that is not decked in scraps of Talog To-Tek. Holmes is not in much better shape, himself. His head is pounding; mortal frames are simply not meant to be the focus of as much power as has passed through him tonight. His body is beaten and stiff.

His thoughts are confused. His leg! The cut is so deep, he may die of it. Look how much blood is on the floor.

Yet, this fear is instantly quelled. There are so many blood gods whispering promises to him. He will never want for blood. The exercise of his art shall be marked by it. Walls will bleed. Rocks will bleed. The crimson flood shall attend him, always.

The hell-hound puts its muzzle just behind his ear. "Master, what would you have me do?"

Nothing? Get out of here? Make the voices stop? Get me back to my family? Keep me safe from Moriarty? No! Warlock knows exactly what the hound must do.

"Bhehr-Lylegnag! They're going to sacrifice her! Hound, you must get her somewhere safe—somewhere Sir Hugo and my master can't kill her!"

The hound turns and begins to run, battering open the massive oak doors. Scenting the outside air, it pauses to bay its hunting howl, then is gone out onto the moor. Running to the door as best as his injured leg will allow, Warlock can see the hound glowing in the night like a fleck of fire.

Holmes sets out after the beast. He cannot travel fast. He is tired and disoriented; his leg is lame. But what is there for him here? He sees a light and wanders towards it, but suddenly it is gone. It reappears over his shoulder, so he goes that way, but this light disappears as well. There are two more, in front of him now. Another appears on his right. Three more behind. The wisps close in on him, from all sides, flickering, fading, laughing at him.

Where can he go? He wanders in an otherworldly realm

of wisp-light. The wind brings him fragmentary reports of battle. He hears Sir Hugo's hounds baying, for they are close to Bhehr-Lylegnag. Then suddenly they're yelping and squealing with mortal terror. Snatches of speech: Moriarty demanding to know where the farmer's daughter is. The farmer screaming. Horses chewing. One of Hugo's hounds drags itself past Holmes. It has only one leg remaining. Sir Hugo's cry of triumph: he has found Bhehr-Lylegnag. His horse, screaming as the hound strikes. A shot. Sir Hugo, gurgling terribly. The wisps all blink out.

And there they are.

There is Holmes, looking at his dog. There is Hugo, with his throat torn out, grabbing at the hound's fur, as if holding on to his murderer might staunch the flowing blood. There is Bhehr-Lylegnag, cowering before the advancing hound, grasping at her chest. There is blood between her fingers. The hound looks at Holmes and lowers its nose to the ground in apology. There has been a mistake. Sir Hugo's shot has missed the hound and hit the girl. Bhehr-Lylegnag is gasping for breath. Air wheezes out through her wound.

"I am sorry, master."

"No!"

"Don't worry, I know a safe place."

There is a flash and a horrible cracking noise. Holmes is flung back. His hound is gone. Bhehr-Lylegnag is gone. Sir Hugo is gone. Where the humans were, two pointed pillars of stone rise into the sky.

From his coach, Moriarty sees the hound disappear.

Where, he cannot tell, but he can feel the tumult in the earth subside as the pointed pillars rise. The line is stable now. The sacrifice is made. An innocent and a magician have been lost from this world, through the new line, into one of the thousand realms beyond. At least the convulsing lines will not break open tonight; there will be no demon invasion. Moriarty will have to take comfort in that. The rest of the evening has been disappointing in the extreme.

Look at them all. He can see the flood of demon promises hovering around Warlock Holmes. He should have guessed it. There is a cursed providence that attends the boy. Moriarty wants to kill him. Perhaps it would be easy; Holmes's mortal form is exhausted and injured. But look at all the help he has! What makes that damned boy so special?

Moriarty reluctantly settles back into his seat and calls to his driver, "Home, Grimesby."

"Home?" the man asks. "What about the Turk?"

"I'm keeping him," Moriarty says. "I must have something to show for all this effort, mustn't I?"

"And the boy?"

"Leave him. If there is such a thing as luck or justice, the wretch will starve."

WATSON'S NOTE

AT THIS POINT, I PAUSE TO ADDRESS A CONCERN THAT may have been growing in many of my readers' minds.

It is possible that some of you may have encountered the term "warlock" before. Though my own magical studies are superficial, still it did not take long for me to come across this word. I assumed my friend Holmes had been named after this particular type of magical practitioner, but could never draw him to discuss it. He had a reason for his silence, I knew, but I'd always failed to guess what it was. So funny in retrospect, for the reason was as simple a one as could be conceived.

The term is named for him.

Yes, it's been in usage for over 200 years, but we are now at the point where the reader knows that Holmes himself has been around for over 250, so this is not unaccountable.

What then, is a warlock?

There are many types of magician. Shamans practice ancestral magic, calling upon the spirits of their dead and their elemental surroundings. Witches tend to focus on the subtly supernatural effects that can be coaxed from brewing various herbs. Glamourists twist the ephemeral threads of perception, weaving it against the even more elusive threads of truth. Wizards spend great deals of time in study, pursuing knowledge of the most powerful magics they can find. Sages practice very little—not at all, sometimes—but are the keepers of that magical knowledge wizards so earnestly crave. A warlock may be any of these, or any of the vast number of other types of magic-users, which I have not herein named. It is not a type of magical practice, in and of itself; it is something you are in addition to the main avenue of study.

A warlock is a magician of any type who has something fundamentally, terribly *wrong* with him.

I would cite the case of the mad sage, Fh'tagn, who is often referred to as a warlock. It is said that his mind failed suddenly, upon his discovery of a certain secret. On that day, he changed from a hoarder of magical knowledge to a teacher of it—willing to speak arcane truths to any who would listen. He referred to the secret that had broken his mind as "The Song of All Ending," and spoke of it as if it were a consciousness. Despite his hatred of it, he feverishly spent the remainder of his life seeking to spread his knowledge—and with it, his madness—devoting the remainder of his days to the service of his tormentor. Indeed, he may have spread this thought contagion to us all and doomed the race of man if it were not for one important fact: nobody wanted to listen to him. He was, after all, just *barking mad*.

Though his story is older than the term, the wizard

Souk'seth is retroactively (and almost universally) called the Warlock of Katesh. He was a uniquely powerful fellow, but not an overly kind one. He used his magic for his own gain, crushing all opposition with spells so powerful and so terrible, modern sages are still unsure of how he accomplished them. One thing is certain: he could do no magic without chewing off one of his own fingers. This, of course, limited the extent of his practice. At last, when he had only the index finger and thumb of his right hand remaining, a coalition of forty-two magicians rose against him, thinking to hold him accountable for his crimes. They supposed he would be unwilling to sacrifice either of these last two digits—a thumb is of little use without at least one finger and he who has neither is barred from many of the privileges of humanity. They should have known better. Though he could easily have accomplished it with only the loss of one finger, Souk'seth chose to eat both. The demise of the forty-two was particularly ghastly. Only one survived and this, it is thought, was a conscious choice on Souk'seth's part so there might be one witness to speak of his might. Of course by that time, his power was spent. He could do no more magic, nor did he possess fingers to work even simple tools. He was slain some time later, by a cow-herd he had wronged in his youth.

To these and many others, the title "warlock" has been applied. Still, as the remainder of my stories will show, none of them were as potent, as dangerous, or as afflicted as the man for whom the term was named.

PART III

ONCE AGAIN, FROM THE JOURNALS
OF DR. JOHN WATSON

13

WE SAT IN SILENCE FOR SOME TIME. HOLMES HUNCHED forward, staring at me much in the way I imagined the hell-hound must have looked at him all those years ago— sheepishly, afraid of judgment.

"So," I began, as softly as I could, "you are over two hundred and fifty years old, then?"

Holmes nodded.

"And that is how you came by your... peculiar abilities?"

"Most of them," he said.

"And your love of toast and soup."

"Yes, though I have since come to suspect Hestia tricked me. After all, who *isn't* comforted by toast and soup?"

"Why didn't you tell me any of this before?"

Holmes threw up his hands. "Well... it's embarrassing! I'm running around in a loincloth. I summon a hell-hound. I don't stop the ley-line from opening. I don't stop Baskerville. I don't stop Moriarty. I don't save Bhehr-Lylegnag. In fact, I wind up dooming her to a hell dimension, beyond even the salvation of death. So... you know... not my finest hour, Watson."

"Still, you didn't think I might need to know some of this, before setting off to investigate the hound-related murder of a Baskerville?"

"Honestly," Warlock shrugged, "I wanted you here only to protect Sir Henry. I rather hoped to solve it on my own, before you discovered anything about this humiliating fiasco. That is why I came in secret. Wiggles was kind enough to come down, as well, to keep an eye on you and bring me food."

"And how much did you know, when you sent me off to my potential doom?"

"Hey! You wished to go! If you recall, I urged you to stay in Lo—"

"Did you know who was hunting Sir Henry?"

"No. Sadly, I did not."

"Did you know who killed Sir Charles?"

"I feared I did," Holmes said. "Yet all my guesses stemmed from my original adventure here and that is a shaky base for rational thought. Dartmoor was in an uproar. It didn't take people long to discover that Baskerville's groom and stable boy and Bhehr-Lylegnag's entire family had been horse-murdered, which—it turns out—is somewhat upsetting to most folk. Plus there were bits of hunting dog spread all across the moor, two new standing stones to explain, and all the usual strangeness surrounding a major change in the earth's magical field."

"The earth has a magical field?"

"Yes, for want of a better term."

"And what 'usually' occurs when this is disturbed?"

"In what is now Grimpen, it rained cows for two hours," Holmes said.

"My God!"

"Not a building left standing. Folks were quite put out—well... those that survived. On top of all that, Hugo Baskerville seemed to be gone, yet without a body, the succession issue was rather clouded. Half the moor was crying out for justice and the other half was manufacturing claims on Baskerville Hall and the attendant fortune. Plus there was beef, just everywhere..."

"And what were you doing, Holmes?"

"I? Wandering, I suppose. Listening to counsel from the thousand demons in my head, trying to figure out what was real and what was not. I worked out that Bhehr-Lylegnag, Hugo and my hound had gone through to another world. I tried to think of a way to find them and bring them back. Well... two of them, anyway. But I had no luck. I decided to try and close off the ley-lines as best I could. Again, I met with no success. I had no help but a multitude of demons, each of whom wanted the lines to stay open wide. I returned in the 1670s to try and put things in better stead, but again I failed."

I began to feel vastly sorry for Holmes. We sat a while longer until at last, I asked, "So... was it your dog that killed Sir Charles?"

"No," he said, brightening. "I feared it might be. When Mortimer told us what had chanced, I immediately thought Foofy—I call him Foofy; oh, it makes him mad—I thought Foofy had slipped back into our world, alone and uncommanded, and begun killing. Imagine how I felt."

"But that is not what happened? This Foofy of yours did not come back?"

"He did, but not alone. Oh, you should meet him! Do you want to meet him, Watson?"

"A hell-hound? Not likely!"

"He is a perfectly agreeable dog!"

"Er… an agreeable *hell-hound*, you mean?"

"You cannot assume an animal's behavior based entirely on its breed."

"He dragged two people to a torture dimension!"

"Well, he didn't know what else to do. It wasn't mean-spirited," Holmes insisted.

"He is made of pure fear. He is terror, given shape."

"He does have that effect on people," said Holmes with a defeated sigh, "but he really did try his best to help me and Bhehr-Lylegnag. He's a very kind, obedient dog. Come on, Watson, come meet him. As long as you are with me, you are perfectly safe, I assure you."

Holmes was tugging my arm as if he wanted me to meet his hellish pet that very instant.

"Is he… is he nearby?"

"Oh yes! The next hut over."

"The next hut?"

"Indeed."

"Just… twenty feet that way, or so?"

"As you say."

I suddenly felt queasy and had the overwhelming desire for a snifter of brandy and a good sit down. "So,"

I reflected, "quite a good thing I tried this hut first, eh?"

"What? Oh! Oh… yes; probably a good thing. For all of us. I would have felt awful. Foofy would have been yelled at…"

"And I would have been torn to pieces, I assume," I said.

Holmes shrugged. "Judge for yourself."

At his continued insistence, I dragged my unwilling feet over to the next hut and peered in the door.

"Hullo, boy, it's me," Holmes called. "I've brought a friend! This is Watson. I've told you about him, remember?"

Curled up on the floor of the little stone hut was a… well… a very ancient hell-hound. As a breed they are just as promised: gigantic black dogs, composed of smoke and shadow, wreathed in flame. Yet, for all that, it was hard to fear Foofy. Hard not to pity, in fact.

"Keep in mind," Holmes said, "it has been almost seventeen hundred dog years."

The poor animal tried to stand, but its back legs no longer functioned as they ought. He feebly wagged his tail, brushing soot around in the old stone hut. Foofy resembled nothing so much as a moose skeleton, wrapped in wrinkled butcher's paper and painted black. His muzzle was gray, his eyes milky and blind. The years had cooled his hellish flame; he smoldered, weakly.

"Hell-hounds usually live for an hour or two, I surmise," Holmes said. "They are more suited to a bloody blaze of glory than to old age. Yet here he is. As soon as I arrived I heard him calling to me. I found him at the center of the Great Grimpen Mire. There's an old mine shaft in the hill at the center; he was chained up there."

I reached out my palm to the monster, who sniffed it and gave one feeble lick. His tongue was sizzling hot, but not enough to burn, only to pink the skin. Against my better judgment, I gave his head a little pat, musing, "Tied up in the mine, you say? On the day I met him, Stapleton said he was the only man who could navigate there."

"Well, I managed it too," said Holmes, "but you've put your finger on it, I think."

"He is our enemy?"

"He is. I am preparing to face him—I have been for several days. To my great regret, some of this preparation must be done at Baskerville Hall. I think we should go there now. When we arrive, I shall show you things that will make the whole matter more clear."

We set off. I'd have liked to interview Holmes further as we walked, but the sun had gone down and my entire attention was spent trying to keep from tripping over bushes. The darkness didn't bother Holmes, but when he saw me stumbling about he said, "Perhaps we'd better get a little light, eh?"

"I think it is best if we avoid the use of magic, don't you?"

"I heartily agree, Watson, but there is no need for sorcery," Holmes said, then raised one arm above his head and commanded, "Dead of the Dartmoor bogs, attend me!"

A milky light grew from the darkness just between us, then another and two more. Soon, Holmes was surrounded by a quartet of wisps.

"They *are* ghosts?" I said, aghast.

"Well, most of them are just luminous methane," Holmes said, "but yes, some are spirits. Have no fear, Watson, they mean us no harm. They are victims of fortune and in their tragic tales, the diverse history of the people of Dartmoor may be read."

"Really?"

"Without a doubt. See here…" Holmes selected the wisp hovering nearest to me and announced, "This is Horrace Dunne. He was a farmer in the fifteenth century. One night he got drunk, wandered into the bogs and drowned. This one is Guinnwilfe—an ancient druid. He got drunk one night, wandered into a bog and drowned."

"Hm… What about that little one?"

"Saddest story of them all, Watson. His name was William. Just a babe when he died. He woke one night and could not find his mother. In searching, poor Willy wandered into the bogs and drowned."

"The history of the Dartmoor people may not be quite so 'diverse' as you promised, Holmes. How about the last one?"

"Oh, that's Willy's mum. She got drunk one night, wandered into a bog and—"

"Yes, yes. I know."

Despite their unhappy state (and their penchant, while living, for alcoholism) the wisps did an admirable job. They bobbed merrily beside us, lighting our way until we reached the main road. Once there, I encouraged Holmes to dismiss them. I didn't relish the notion of local farmers spotting Holmes and me, using four of the area's ancient dead as torches.

It is fortunate we went without them. We'd gone less than a half mile and were just nearing Merripit House when the distant sound of screaming came to our ears. At first I saw nothing, but a moment later a figure broke over the rise of a hill. He was running at full tilt, his hands clawing at his face and chest. His eyes burned as if made of flame and, when he opened his mouth to scream, I saw that it seemed full of fire too. The man—who likely had more present concerns than where he was headed—was running directly towards the steep, rocky slope of the hill, where it fell away next to the road. I was about to warn that he was running towards a cliff, but as his whole body crested the rise, the moonlight caught him and I saw what he was wearing: a horrid blue Canadian suit.

"Sir Henry!" I cried. I sprinted towards him as fast as I could go. I had no chance of reaching him before he came to the precipitous drop and plummeted down to the road, but I ran nonetheless. Only a few steps before the drop-off, his face and hands suddenly burst into flame. I gasped. There was no external source of ignition visible; rather it seemed as if the heat came from within his body. This was borne out by the fact that only the man burst into flame; his clothes did not (more's the pity). Screaming and flailing, he fell from the top of the cliff and landed with a thud, just a few feet from the road. I was at his side less than a minute later, but what could I do? Every inch of the man was burnt to bloody cinders.

I cursed myself for leaving him. I balled my fists and struck the earth and my own breast, but what help was that to poor Sir Henry? Suddenly, Warlock was with me, shaking me.

"Watson! Watson, damn you! Get off the road! Stapleton is coming!"

Warlock grabbed me by the collar and hauled me away from Sir Henry, towards the face of the cliff, and clapped a hand across my mouth. I tried to wiggle free, but he pressed us into a little hollow in the cliff and whispered, "Quiet, Watson, please. Too much noise and you might earn us the same treatment Sir Henry got. Hush. Our enemy is coming."

At first I heard nothing. Yet a sound gradually grew, over the soft hiss of wind. Footsteps. Someone was running towards us. Presently, I could hear his gulping breaths. As he neared the top of the bluff, he slowed. He came to the very edge and began pacing back and forth, above us. Though we were hidden in our depression in the rock, I could see his shadow upon the road. He leaned out over the drop–off and clapped his hands. There was a strange rustling noise, then a woman's voice asked, "What should we do with him?"

A second shadow appeared next to Stapleton's and I nearly cried out in surprise. I was sure I'd heard only one person run up. Where had she come from? It's as if she'd just dropped out of the sky. Yet, if her arrival was mysterious, her identity was clear. It was Beryl Stapleton, without a doubt. She sounded glum.

"Do?" Her brother's voice rang with triumph. "We

shall do nothing, idiot! Do you think we want to bring attention to ourselves by being the ones to discover the body? He's right in the road. And look at the state of him. It's perfect! The first local to drive this road in the morning cannot help but see him. When they find out who it is, will there be any question that it's the hound that did him in? The only thing left for us to do is head home and wait for some neighbor to bring us the 'terrible' news."

He laughed. Beryl sighed. "Good-bye, Sir Henry," she said.

I heard them move away, over the moor. Holmes and I waited, motionless and quiet, long after they were gone.

"Let's go," said Holmes. "I don't fancy being caught out here in the open by Stapleton."

"Wait," I said. "There's one more thing we need to do."

"Eh?"

"If Stapleton wants that body discovered, I say we had better take pains to see that it isn't."

"We haven't got time to bury him, Watson."

"No. I know."

I took off my belt and looped it under Sir Henry's shoulders, to pull him off the road. I drew him around the hill, to a little ravine, and left him there. He deserved better, but I hadn't the time or the energy. I'm sure Holmes and I left enough footprints and signs of our passing that a competent detective could have linked us to the body.

How fortunate that Dartmoor had no competent detectives.

We made our way back to the road. I had many

questions, but Holmes insisted we hurry along. Only after we cleared the turnoff between Grimpen and Baskerville Hall did Holmes grumble, "How did the villain manage it, do you think?"

"I have no idea," I puffed, quite out of breath. "Some form of accelerant in the victim's blood, I suppose. But how did he ignite it?"

"Not the burning part!" Holmes said. "I understand the *burning part*. It was a curse, Watson, and not the work of an amateur. No, what confuses me is how he knew where Sir Henry would be. How did he know where to attack?"

"He invited Sir Henry over, to play cards."

"Dashed clever of him," Holmes grunted. "I must say, the simplest ways are best, eh?"

"I should say so," I grumbled. "Look how well he has carried it off. He's right: the folk around here will only blame the hound. I wonder what claim Stapleton has concocted to the Baskerville fortune."

"It's not the fortune he's after," Holmes said, "but the house itself."

Even as he said it, the house came into view and, in a few moments more, we were there. I pushed open the heavy front door only to surprise Perkins, the groom, who happened to be passing at that moment.

"Dr. Watson!" he cried. "You're back! Where have you been? And who is this with you?"

"This is my colleague, Warlock Holmes," I told him. "I have been out investigating all day and I have some heavy news: Sir Henry is dead."

"What?" stammered Perkins. "That isn't possible!"

"It is true, I'm afraid. Burned to death. Warlock and I saw it happen."

Perkins stared at me as if he did not understand, or thought I was making an off-color joke. I heard the shuffling of feet and the tapping of a cane behind him.

"Well, you can count me among the fellows who are pretty surprised to hear it," said Sir Henry, limping into view behind his groom.

"Sir Henry!" I cried and rushed to clasp his hand. "By Jove, I am glad to see you!"

"Hullo, Watson. And good to see you again, Mr. Holmes," he grinned. "Funny thing: you were so late coming back, Watson, that we were starting to worry something had happened to *you*. We were just about to start the search."

"No!" I shouted. "You must not go out there, Sir Henry! Things have come to a head. We must hide you. He thinks you dead; we must use that to our advantage."

"He? He who? And why is everyone so sure I'm all burnt up? What's going on?"

I held my answer until Perkins was dismissed, then Warlock and I filled Sir Henry in on the events of the evening. When we got to the part about the burning man, Sir Henry stopped me to say, "Well that's amazing. And unfortunate. But why'd you think it was me?"

"Well he… he had a suit, just like your blue one and I… I didn't suppose there could be two. Not here, in a civilized country."

Sir Henry bristled a bit, ready to fight for the honor

of his once-beloved suit, but finally muttered, "Well probably there ain't. But I don't have that suit any more. I gave it to Barrymore."

"Barrymore?" I said. "No, it couldn't have been him. He's almost a foot taller than you. So… Wait a moment… Why would he even *want* a suit of yours? It would never fit him. And why would he be out upon the moor?"

My poor, cluttered head reeled with the strangeness of it. My hunt, Holmes's sudden appearance, the story of his youth, the murder and then recovery of Sir Henry—all these contrived to numb my senses. I had to take a moment to breathe deeply. To concentrate. To focus my thoughts. As soon as I did, I muttered, "Oh…"

"Oh? What do you mean, 'oh'?" Sir Henry asked.

"I think our little problem with the Notting Hill Murderer may be at an end. I suppose we had best tell Eliza."

"I don't follow," said Sir Henry.

"Barrymore is taller than you," I explained, "but Selden isn't. Well… wasn't. I think Barrymore was happy to have your old clothes, so he could send Selden to South America in something other than prison rags. He must have handed your suit off, earlier today. Stapleton, having seen you in it only this morning, would have assumed Selden to be you. After all, he expected to see you on that road. He invited you to cards, didn't he? He'd even hinted how much Beryl would enjoy seeing you in that very suit. In the moonlight, Stapleton would not have been able to distinguish his victim's face, but the suit must have stood out a mile off."

"That all makes sense," Sir Henry agreed, "except the

part where Stapleton can make men burst into flames. Are you sure you saw what you think you saw?"

"He did," Warlock interjected. "There is much we have not told you, Sir Henry, not to keep you in the dark or abuse your trust, but because it is the kind of thing most men would be unwilling to believe."

Warlock then gave an account so full and so shockingly honest about his and Stapleton's abilities that I found myself wincing. Never before had he been this forthcoming with the secrets of magic.

"Strange stuff," Sir Henry said, shaking his head. "It's all a bit much… Even if Stapleton can roast a fellow alive, why would he come after my uncle and me?"

"Well, Warlock hasn't got so far as explaining all that yet," I told him, "but there is apparently a good exp…"

I trailed off, for my eyes had come to rest upon the picture of Sir Hugo—that same one I had remarked on the night we first arrived at Baskerville Hall. My mouth hung open. What a fool I had been.

What an *utter fool*.

Warlock had said things would be made clear to me once I reached the Hall…

Holmes began to laugh. He clapped me on the back and said, "Don't blame yourself, Watson; how could you have guessed?"

"Guessed what? I don't understand!" Sir Henry complained.

I grasped him by the shoulders and turned him to the painting of the foppish cavalier.

"Who is that?" I asked him.

"Sir Hugo Baskerville. The frame says."

"Yes," I said, running to the picture. I threw my arms up on either side of the face to cover the long black ringlets. "But if I cover his hair and ask you to imagine him without that silly moustache, who is it?"

"Well, I don't know, it's… Hey! It's Stapleton!" Sir Henry cried. "How come Stapleton is the spittin' image of Sir Hugo?"

Holmes gave a wry laugh. "Because Stapleton *is* Sir Hugo."

14

THAT NIGHT, IN SIR HENRY'S ROOM, WE HELD OUR WAR council.

"Here is the story, as I figure it," said Holmes. "Three years ago, Sir Hugo found a way to break back into our world, bringing with him Bhehr-Lylegnag and Foofy. Foofy was either spotted, or his baying re-stoked the local legend of the hound. Sir Hugo either earned or conjured enough funds to take Merripit House and adopt the persona of Jack Stapleton. He passed Bhehr-Lylegnag off as his sister and began laying designs to reclaim Baskerville Hall."

"Why does he want it so badly?" I asked.

Holmes gave a grim laugh. "Because he's 285 years old and he's had his throat torn out! He needs the magic of the ley-lines to keep himself alive. Yes, there's one that runs under Merripit House, but how long can just one line maintain him? Therein lies the great threat of Hugo Baskerville: he's unsustainable. If he gets this house, in only a few years' time he'll be spending every night down in that great hall, begging favors from all five lines just to keep himself alive. It won't be long until the outsiders crack through and the world of man is overrun."

"Holmes, this is slightly off-topic…" I said.

"Yes?"

"But you seem to be growing horns."

Sir Henry was thrilled. "Get over here! I want to touch them."

Holmes looked annoyed. "Horns? Then… Oh, dash it! I thought I was sweating!"

"No. Blood, I'm afraid," I told him. "Here, take my handkerchief."

"Thank you, Watson," said Holmes. He mopped at the crimson trickles that seeped from his brow and complained, "That's not even the worst of it. Have you seen my right hand?"

"Well… you've had it in your pocket."

"Would you like to see why?"

He withdrew it. Both Sir Henry and I recoiled. I think my host very nearly vomited some of the brandies he'd been downing all night.

"Yes… erm… as a doctor, I can confidently state that your fingers have all twisted themselves around backwards. Yes, they… they seem to flex the other way, now. From a medical standpoint, most interesting. From an aesthetic standpoint, I would be most appreciative if you put that horrific mess back in your pocket, please."

"What is it doing?" Sir Henry asked.

"Can't you tell? It's getting sinister. It is trying to become a left hand. It's jealous. With all this evil magic flying about—what a poor day to be a right hand."

"So… it might be wise if your stay was brief?"

"That's what I've been trying to tell you all along, Watson. Yet I fear my presence may be a secondary concern."

"Bad enough to wreck the world, though."

"Yes, but still secondary. If Sir Hugo takes the Hall, all is lost."

I let all I'd learned that evening roll through my head. Something seemed out of place, but it took me a few moments to recognize it.

"Oh! Holmes! There is a flaw in our understanding! If Sir Hugo only returned three years ago, he cannot be our enemy! Don't you see: the Baskervilles have been hunted by the hound for generations."

"Bah," scoffed Holmes. "Local superstition and imagination."

"Hmm… Much as I would like to agree, Holmes, I know better. What about the death of Winthrop Baskerville in the dressing room?"

"What? Oh… er… can we not talk about that? It certainly wasn't the hound. Nor was it Sir Hugo."

"You cannot be sure of that, Holmes."

"Actually, I can."

"No. I have been to that room, Holmes. I have seen evidence of the attack!"

"What evidence? Trust me, Watson. You weren't there when he died! I was! And I can tell you—"

"Wait! You were there?"

"Of course I was! I… er… oh…" Holmes began to

pale. He stared nervously at his feet for a moment, then turned to Sir Henry. "I am afraid that I may have killed your great-great-great-great grandfather."

"No!" cried Sir Henry, more impressed than angered.

"Holmes! Why did you do it?" I demanded.

"Well, I didn't mean to! I told you I came back once, to try to close the lines, remember? And I told you I did not succeed. Did you ever stop to consider, Watson, that the most likely reason for my failure might be that I climbed through what I supposed to be the window of an unoccupied room, only to find some lecherous old coot waiting for his mistress?"

"But, Holmes, I saw the mark of the hound upon the floor."

"I used a grappling hook."

"And the violence of it all... Have you seen the wall where Winthrop Baskerville clawed at it?"

"No, *I* scratched the wall, Watson. And you would, too, if you had some naked old grandpa trying to strangle you in a bathtub. By the gods, the man was a terror! Honestly, if it hadn't been for a few bolts of demon-fire from my good friend Azazel, I don't think I'd be standing here today."

"Azazel," I mused. "That's why there was so little of Sir Winthrop left, I imagine."

"You don't know the half of it, Watson. I had to throw all my clothes away. Never could get all the Baskerville out of them."

"Well done!" cried Sir Henry. "That'll show 'em!"

"Er... but I killed your great-great-great-great

grandfather," Holmes reminded him.

"Well… yeah, I guess… but if you grow up a Baskerville, you get used to certain things. Whenever you hear stories about your ancestors you know you're going to end up rooting against 'em."

"I don't blame you for that," Holmes said. "You're the best Baskerville I've ever met, by a good margin. In fact, you're the first who hasn't tried to kill me. And now the worst of them has returned."

I had a sudden realization. "Oh! Holmes! Now that Hugo thinks Sir Henry is dead, it won't be long before he comes to make his claim on the Hall. What do you think, will it be a legal issue, or will he just conquer the place?"

"I cannot tell, but if he is planning to take this place by force, he's got a decent chance of pulling it off," Holmes said. "When Sir Hugo was lost out of our dimension two hundred and forty years ago, he had some magical knowledge and a sharp mind, but no significant ability. Now he can burn a man alive at a hundred yards. Oh, and he used not a whit of subtlety in doing it. The amount of power he expended was unnecessary and grotesque. In all our history, the world has known only one other sorcerer who can command that sort of raw might."

"Moriarty?" I hazarded.

"Me," Holmes replied, slightly hurt. "Yet that is of little use to us. If Sir Hugo and I do battle atop five open lines, it scarcely matters which of us wins. Such a strain… such damage…"

"Holmes," I said, "we cannot face him here. Let it be

anywhere else. Let us lure him to some more favorable field and do battle there."

"Would that I could, Watson, but he will not—I suspect he cannot—venture far from Baskerville Hall."

"Because his throat's torn out?" Sir Henry wondered, his eyes alight with enthusiasm. "Is it still gone, do you think?"

"Well, that's not the sort of thing that normally heals," Holmes replied, with a shrug, "but you two might know better than I. Have either of you ever seen his throat?"

"No," I said. "He always seems to be wearing his beekeeper's gear or his ridiculous high-collared jackets."

"Not without reason, I suspect."

"But, Holmes, this sets two of our goals together!" I realized. "To close these damned rifts would greatly benefit our world and it would also kill Sir Hugo, would it not?"

"It would, but I do not have that art," Holmes explained. "Even Moriarty did not, I am certain. No, the greatest expert on the opening, closing, and directing of ley-lines is the very man we must face. Remember, Watson: all my power comes from beings on the other side of those lines who wish nothing more than for them to remain open, unless it is for them to finally break."

"Are there no entities on the other side that could help?" I asked.

"Well… no. I mean… not so…"

My friend trailed off. His gaze became distant. I could tell he'd seen a ray of hope. After a time, he admitted, "Look, perhaps there are a few spirits that might. If someone were victimized by Sir Hugo and lost their life because of it, near one of the lines... well some shreds of them must have been pulled through. They're not likely to be a whole person—more probably echoes of their last moments, disembodied fears or hatreds who fancy themselves people. Still, they're likely to be intimately tied with the power of these lines."

"And unlikely to be well disposed towards Sir Hugo," I surmised.

"One would suppose so," said Holmes. "You know, Watson, this may be our best plan yet."

"This is all strange waters for me," Sir Henry said, "but... you think these spirits could close the ley-lines?"

"No. I don't know how the lines might ever be closed," replied Holmes. "Yet perhaps we don't need to close them... Think of cupping your hands beneath a massive hourglass, trying to stop the sand. You cannot hold back the sand forever; indeed, some would slip between your fingers, almost from the start. But if we could hold *enough* magic back, for even a few minutes... Watson, how long does it take for a man with no throat to die?"

"Hard to say, exactly. It's slower than sneezing, quicker than poaching an egg..."

"Not so bad," Holmes reflected. "We might manage it... But, there are so many lines! I'm sure I could find one or two helpful entities, but we'd need one to block each of the lines that start here and two to block each of the three lines that continue through! Where might I find six entities who—"

"Eight, Holmes."

"No, but... there are three lines to be blocked on each side..."

"Trust me, it's eight."

"And two one-sided ones, so..."

"Eight," Sir Henry assured him.

Holmes threw up his hands, drawing slight retches from Sir Henry and me at the sight of his twisted fingers. "Well, eight, then, if you're both so certain about it! That's even worse! How could I ever find so many?"

"I don't know, Holmes," I said, laying a hand upon his shoulder, "but unless a better plan should present itself, this is the clearest course to victory. Come, let us get some rest. Tomorrow we will begin our search for allies."

"You two may rest," said Holmes. "I fear I must go down to the great hall and show myself to the entities that dwell beyond the lines. Watson, you'll come down and lock the door behind me, won't you? I don't want any of the staff wandering in and being driven insane by the outer mysteries."

"No, that wouldn't do at all. Of course I'll come."

As we went downstairs, Holmes racked his memory for victims, rivals or enemies of Sir Hugo. Most of what he said was piecemeal remembrances, but one of these random ramblings proved to be of great importance.

"It needn't be only dead people, I suppose. If there were someone on this side who had been greatly affected by the magic of those lines..."

I got Holmes settled in, then headed back towards my room. I expected I'd be too fatigued to even think, but in fact, I was energetic and laughing. That last thing Holmes had said…

I knew one of our eight.

15

THE NEXT DAY, I READIED MYSELF FOR BATTLE.

Well… I mean… I spent most of it wearing a dressing gown. But still…

As soon as I awoke, I ran downstairs to check on Holmes. I hoped he'd met with some success (and that he had not accidentally melted the intellect of any of the staff). I knocked upon the door of the great hall, but had no answer. Had something happened? Was he too deep in concentration to hear me? I laid my ear against the door and listened. Nothing. Silence. Did I dare?

With trembling hand, I reached inside the pocket of my dressing gown and withdrew the key I'd placed there the night before. I opened the door but kept my eyes shut as I called out, "Holmes?"

No answer.

I opened my eyes. Nothing. An empty room. He was gone. All hope for the race of man was gone. He'd been sucked through, to the realms beyond, spinning through dark infinities, slowly digested by the immensity of horrors that lay without.

Or—as turned out to be the case—he had left through the servants' entrance at the back, badgered Mrs. Barrymore into making him toast and soup, begged use of the horse and cart, and trotted off across the moor.

So, thank heaven for small mercies.

Holmes had been busy all night it seemed, searching Baskerville Hall, and bothering everybody who slept therein. Included in the long list of social niceties Holmes was ignorant of was this: that most people do not enjoy being woken in the small hours of the morning by an intruder who leans in over one's bed and shakes one to wakefulness. If said intruder has recently grown goat horns, which have lacerated his scalp and caused a not-insignificant amount of blood to run down his face, it turns out he is likely to be even less well received. There had been a great deal of screaming, I was informed.

Despite this, Holmes's search had not been fruitless; he'd left me something. On the great table, I found a battered hatbox. I had no idea what treasure might lie within, but if I'd taken a moment to think, I might have guessed.

It was a top hat and—apart from some wear around the brim and a dent here or there—it appeared new, unremarkable and utterly mundane. There was also a ladies' comb, beautifully made of gold and pearl, nestled in beside the hat and a note that said: *Watson, guard these with your life*.

Very well, but I had plans of my own to attend to. With the help of Perkins, I selected and removed three of the ancestral Baskerville paintings. These we carried up to Sir Henry's room. He looked rather surprised by the whole endeavor and asked what was going on.

"I felt it was somewhat unsporting of me to deny you your fun last night," I told him. "And—what with that broken foot of yours—I thought I might bring the morning's entertainment to you."

"What d'you mean, Watson?"

"Just wait."

Perkins and I arranged the paintings along the far wall of Sir Henry's room. Then I dismissed Perkins and told Sir Henry to ring for Barrymore to bring his breakfast.

I took a position just beside the door, so I might be hidden by it as it swung open. In a few moments Barrymore arrived, bearing a silver tray. The smell nearly distracted me from my task, but no—I remained steadfast. Stiff upper lip, Watson! Action! Answers!

Then bacon.

I waited until Barrymore had taken six or seven steps into the room, then swung the door closed behind him, with a loud bang. Barrymore—a natural coward—leapt away with surprising dexterity and spun to see what was the matter, painting the floor of Sir Henry's bedchamber with bacon and eggs.

"What are you?" I demanded, leveling a finger at Barrymore.

"Oh! I... Dr. Watson! You gave me a fright. I... What am I? A butler, I suppose."

"Are you? I suppose something quite different," I

said, striding to the paintings I'd set against the wall. I indicated the portrait of Sir Charles, and the figure in the background—John Barrymore. Next, I stepped to an eighteenth-century portrait of a bewigged Baskerville and again, John Barrymore. Finally, I moved to the portrait of Sir Hugo, depicted with his unfortunate wife Olivia and… John Barrymore.

"What are you?" I repeated.

He looked as if he might cry. "Down at the local taverns, it's easy to hear stories of the Curse of the Baskervilles. But if you stay long enough, you might hear of another Dartmoor oddity: the Curse of the Barrymores."

"Which is?" I prompted.

"Folks say that the first John Barrymore was a bad fellow. They say that when Sir Hugo left this world, he laid a curse on Barrymore to wait for his master's return, to serve him again in his wickedness."

"Which couldn't have gone as planned, since Hugo Baskerville didn't come back for 240 years," I surmised.

"Right. So John Barrymore aged and died, just like decent folks do. But here's what he did different: his son was just… him again. His looks, the way he spoke, the way he thought, even the things he remembered—John Junior *was* John Senior."

"Ha!" Sir Henry laughed. "So, John Barrymore the Third was…"

"Rather similar to John Barrymore the Second," Barrymore confirmed. "And not so far off from the fourth, fifth, or sixth. I myself am John Barrymore the Ninth and

Little John, downstairs, looks an awful lot like I did at his age."

"And you actually believe that story?" asked Sir Henry, who rather looked as if he believed it himself.

"I didn't want to, sir," Barrymore wailed, "but there's days when I wake up, ready to march into the master's room and apologize for burning down the old stable. Then I realize: how could I have? I'd not been born yet. In fact, I'd not been born when the new one we built on the ashes burned down, too. Then I remember that the person I was going to confess to has been dead for 150 years and I never met them and... well... yes, I do believe it. I'm sorry, Sir Henry. I didn't mean to be anything unnatural."

"Oh, well, hey... not your fault, Barrymore. Right? Sins of the father, and so on," Sir Henry replied.

"Thank you, sir."

"So you see, Sir Henry?" I asked, raising a conspiratorial eyebrow at my host. "It would seem that—though he is yet living—John Barrymore the Ninth here has a strong, mystical link to those ley-lines downstairs."

"So he might be able to help close them, eh?"

"That is my hope," I said, then turned to Barrymore and asked, "What do you say, Barrymore? Do you think you would be willing to help us end all this mystic nonsense? Perhaps break the Curse of the Barrymores?"

"I might," he muttered, beginning simultaneously to sweat and to edge towards the door. "Yes. But, er... I don't know anything about breaking curses, sir. Not sure I'd be much use. I'd just be in the way, I would think. I'll bring

Sir Henry another breakfast. Shall I bring you one, Dr. Watson? Yes, I think I better had."

And with one final lunge, John Barrymore IX cleared Sir Henry's bedchamber and escaped down the hall.

"We can't let him out of it," I said, taking the wastepaper basket from near Sir Henry's desk and scooping the scattered remains of his first breakfast from the floor into it.

"You're right," Sir Henry agreed. "We've got too little going for us to let him weasel out now. Really though, the only thing I want right now is breakfast."

"Me too."

"Can you smell that bacon? I keep reminding myself I'm a lord and I got dignity and all, but my belly keeps sayin' that ain't true—that I'm nothing but a hungry Canadian. Oh, and I'd be lying if I said that was the dirtiest food I've ever eaten. Why, in the lumber camp—"

"Stop! Sir Henry, I absolutely forbid it!" I put the wastepaper basket in the farthest corner. It was my duty to the realm to dispose of this temptation, before Sir Henry regressed once more to that primal state his misspent youth had taught him: half-man, half-Canadian. Not that there weren't moments when I considered sneaking a bite. If Sir Henry hadn't been watching me with hungry, resentful eyes, I think I might have.

To make matters worse, Barrymore did not hurry back with a replacement. We were just beginning to grumble about what might be keeping the man—trying not to stare at the wastebasket full of slowly cooling eggs and bacon—when we heard footsteps in the hall. Not one person's footsteps, either, but two.

When John Barrymore at last pushed open Sir Henry's door, his expression was even more terrified than when he'd left. But at least he had breakfast with him. He was followed by his wife who, to my lasting delight, was similarly laden with food. She barged past her husband and unceremoniously deposited her tray on Sir Henry's dressing table, then turned to us with a vengeful eye. It seemed that, between the death of her brother, Holmes's late-night searches and our interrogation of her husband, Eliza Barrymore had just about had it with Sir Henry and me.

"John here says you've had the story out of him, about the Curse of the Barrymores?" she demanded of Sir Henry.

It was hardly a fitting way to address a baronet, especially one's employer, but there was enough of the displeased school matron about her that neither Sir Henry nor I thought to protest at the treatment.

"Er... um... yes," he replied.

"And you think you've got a way to break it?" she demanded, turning on me.

"Yes," I said, sheepish beneath her terrible gaze. "We thought, if we found eight individuals who had been affected by the magic that seeps up through the lines on the floor of the great hall, they could stand on those lines and block off the magic. Might be enough to break the curse."

"And lots of other problems, too," Sir Henry volunteered. "There's all sorts of bad stuff Sir Hugo Baskerville did, with those lines."

"Sir Hugo?" said Eliza. "Sir Hugo from 240 years ago, who everyone says is back and burned up my little Freddy?"

"Well, yeah. I know it sounds—"

But he was interrupted by Eliza Barrymore's fist, which she slammed down upon the dressing table, rattling the much anticipated breakfast and nearly sending a second iteration of that meal to the floor.

"We'll help!" she shouted.

"You'll… what was that?" said Sir Henry. I think it took us a moment to realize we'd just won. Neither of us was used to being offered help so combatively.

"Thank you for volunteering your husband," I told her, "but I think your own services may not be needed. My colleague, Holmes, seems to think that only people or spirits who are directly affected by the magic of those lines may participate in the—"

"You think I'm not *directly affected*?" she demanded.

"Er… no?"

Eliza Barrymore marched up to me, stuck her face an inch or so from mine and said, through gritted teeth, "I had to give birth to my husband! The Greeks wrote plays about that!"

"Well yes, but not in that context, madam."

"Tell me, Mr. Big-City-Doctor-Man, have you ever had to suckle the tiny baby version of your husband, with the grown-up version looking on? Huh? *Not affected?*"

"I… I stand corrected," I said.

She turned on her heel, headed back for the door and said, "We'll do your ritual, Sir Henry. You let us know when. This one might try to run…" here she paused, to jerk a thumb at her husband, "but I won't let him."

I well believed her.

With a defeated sigh, John Barrymore placed the second breakfast tray upon Sir Henry's lap, turned, and was gone.

Breakfast was all the better that morning, for it was seasoned with victory. Sir Henry and I resolved to race Warlock. If we could get four allies, we would consider it a tie. If we got five or more, we would never let Holmes live it down.

So bored had Sir Henry become with the confines of his chamber, that he demanded to be moved down to the great hall for the day. Once installed, his disregard for secrecy was so profound that the entire staff soon knew nearly every particular of our predicament. Strange to say, but this created a somewhat carnival atmosphere. Duties were ignored, chores overlooked. The day was spent trading dark tales and daring ideas. Gunther asked to see my Webley, which I brought down only to discover he was planning on dipping my live rounds into molten silver. This would not have resulted in the anti-demon weapon he hoped for. In fact, it would have resulted in a bullet too wide to fit through the Webley's barrel, if it didn't heat the bullet to the point of accidental discharge. Still, it was hardly the worst plan of the day.

Holmes returned just after noon. I was pleased to see he'd divested himself of horns, though whether he'd employed magic or one of the kitchen knives, I could not tell. He'd been to Grimpen, he said, and had gathered information on where next to look for aid.

"There can't be too many farms about where people were eaten by horses, eh, Watson?" he said. "Sir Henry has agreed to let me use the trap. I'm going to send Wiggles back to London and do a bit of snooping about. Look for me by nightfall. If I am not back by midnight, I might not be coming. Probably best to flee Dartmoor at that point. Or England, to be safer. Then just try to spend all your money and have a generally good time until... well... you know."

Holmes left and the congenial air of arcane creativity resumed. We had little luck thinking of people or spirits who might have been wronged by Sir Hugo. We almost held a séance, but felt so ridiculous pacing up and down the great hall with lit candles that fits of laughter always stopped us from undertaking it in earnest. By five o'clock, biscuit crumbs and unfinished cups of tea littered the table. Darkness gathered. Holmes failed to return. Ten o'clock had come and gone and bedtime had been mentioned several times when, at last, I heard hoof beats in the drive. The doors to the great hall were open and the main door of Baskerville Hall lay just across the foyer, clearly visible. Presently, this door opened a crack and admitted Holmes, red-faced and sniffing. He closed the door as quietly as he could and crept to the great hall before returning any greeting.

"How'd it go, Holmes?" Sir Henry asked. "Any luck?"

"Quite a lot. Some good, some bad. I found a few objects that might help us," Holmes said, patting his knapsack. "Unfortunately, my return trip took me closer than I would have liked to Merripit House and I half suspect I may have been seen."

This, at least, is what *I think* he said. It is hard to be sure, as the last few words were drowned out by a terrific explosion, which tore the doors from Baskerville Hall.

16

THE THING ONE DOES NOT EXPECT ABOUT EXPLOSIONS is the confusion they engender. I found myself off my feet before I knew what was happening. I realized I had been thrown, but not in which direction. The room was full of dust. The amount of force that had been applied to the front of Baskerville Hall had been sufficient to vaporize the aged mortar from between its stones. This, along with centuries of accumulated house dust, took to the air and went swirling into the unprepared lungs of everybody present.

I couldn't think or feel, only cough. I could not even discern up from down. I heard nothing but a desperate ringing in my ears. Luckily, I felt the floor beneath my hands. This not only steadied me but came with the bonus knowledge of where "down" was. As soon as my powers of cognition recovered enough to grasp the concept of antonyms, I realized I must therefore know where "up" was. I pushed myself to my feet and began to look around. I reeled—disoriented and unsteady. I nearly tripped over Perkins, which would have been bad for him, since he had a most magnificently shattered leg. The clouds of dust limited my vision, but the ringing in my ears began to resolve into the shouts and coughing fits of my stricken companions. The only thing I could hear clearly was the sound of Warlock's voice saying, "*Watson, I need you.*"

A second later something huge and flat scythed through the dust towards me. It seems Sir Hugo had wrenched both of the magnificent oak doors right off their hinges and then—exhibiting the changeability that evil sorcerers are known for—reversed his decision and sent them both flying into the body of the Hall. The first of these doors now approached and would, I think, have crushed a number of us to paste, had Warlock not stood to bar its way. He held one hand out before him, like a constable ordering traffic to stop. The first door hit his outstretched palm and exploded into a few hundred pounds of flying oak splinters. I'm sure anybody standing next to Holmes would have been shredded by the shrapnel, but the door had been shattered so completely that the tiny projectiles quickly lost all their force. In only a few feet, the deadly spray was reduced to nothing more than a suffusion of toothpicks, clattering across the stone tiles. Holmes shook no more than he would if a gentle spring breeze had broken across his palm and seemed exactly as unconcerned.

The second door didn't even make it to us. As it rocketed in to spell our doom, Holmes fixed it with a look of intense displeasure. It ceased its advance and hovered in the air. Loath as I am to attribute emotional processes to wood, there seemed to be a touch of reluctance in its bearing. Repentant of its earlier rashness, it reversed its course and spun off into the night to crash down on some unsuspecting patch of moor or other. Glad as I was that the door would not be joining our gathering, I was forced to admit that the next attendees to arrive were even more dangerous.

The Stapletons were dressed for dinner.

Jack—well… *Sir Hugo*—cut quite the figure in a black dinner suit, so excellent it could not be spoiled even by the ridiculous collar he'd fitted to it. Beryl wore a blue evening gown that suited her perfectly. Oh, she was radiant.

"I told you," she said, indicating Holmes. "It's him. It's the boy."

"You may be right, darling," Sir Hugo said, stepping over the rubble in the doorway. "It's been a very long time, Warlock Holmes. I must say, I didn't expect to see you about."

"*Me?*" said Holmes. "I admit I've lasted a bit longer than most fellows do, but at least I've still got my throat. *You* are the one who ought not to be here, Sir Hugo. On a lighter note: welcome back, Bhehr-Lylegnag."

"It's Beryl now," she said.

"You see?" said Holmes. "I told you it was a pretty name."

"*Watson, I need you!*" Holmes said again, but this time it came in the middle of his conversation with Beryl. I was certain his lips had not moved. I scratched my ear. Had I perhaps suffered a concussion?

On the off chance, I said, "You need me?"

His eyes flashed in my direction for just a moment and

I distinctly heard, "*Don't talk to me, Watson; think to me! I am sending you instructions as best I can. If you wish to tell me something, you must* think *it at me. I know it is strange, but it's the only way we can talk without them knowing what we're up to. Have you the hatbox?*"

"It's on the table… or it was," I replied.

"*Find it, Watson. Oh, and you're still talking out loud—just think.*"

I began casting about in the rubble for the hatbox Holmes had left me that morning. I was vaguely aware that Holmes and Sir Hugo were negotiating for my life.

"I have no quarrel with you," Sir Hugo said, "and I suppose you must have some art, or you would not have lived this long. Let us avoid unnecessary conflict. I offer you Watson; take him and go."

"A generous offer, Sir Hugo, but I cannot accept."

I could not find that damned box! The force of the first explosion had sent chairs, plates and portraits bouncing all over the great hall. At last, I spotted a chair leaning at a suspicious angle. When I looked to see what was propping it up, there was the hatbox.

"*Got it!*" I thought to Holmes.

"*Ah! Good. Take the hat and comb and put them on one of the ley-lines. They've got to go on opposite ends of the same line.*"

With horror, I realized my situation. I think part of me had been hoping just to sit back and cheer on my favorite sorcerer, with no personal say in the outcome of the evening's conflict. But no. Clearly, Holmes was only stalling Sir Hugo while I did the actual work. I prayed I'd be able to finish it before Hugo became suspicious and burned me alive.

Holmes had adopted a new tack, and was speaking to Beryl. "I just wanted to say that I am very sorry for what happened to you, Bhehr-Lylegnag. I can't imagine what you've suffered all these years. I only told Foofy to take you somewhere safe, where Sir Hugo couldn't kill you. Once you were shot, the only place he could think of was… well…"

"Foofy?" Beryl asked.

"The *hound*?" asked Sir Hugo, wide-eyed.

"Yes. I made him and told him to go save Bhehr-Lylegnag, but—"

"You *made* the hound?" she asked, incredulous.

"Well… not on purpose. But yes, I did."

"It took me to hell!" Beryl screamed. "It took me to a burning plane of sadness, with only it and Sir Hugo to keep me safe!"

I reached the west side of the room and dropped the comb onto one of the lines with feigned nonchalance. I glanced up nervously to see if I'd been noticed, then popped the top hat on my head and set off across the room, for the other end of the line.

Near the ruined entry, Beryl was screaming, "For forty years I hoped you'd come and rescue me! I didn't know how, but you were the only one who'd ever tried so… I just hoped it would be you! You never came! What did you eat for breakfast those forty years? I had burning maggots that bit the inside of my throat! That's what I had! What did you have? Crumpets?"

"I've never been partial to crumpets, really," said Holmes, which turned out not to be a very good answer.

"Forty years, I held out against him! Forty years I did not give in! I didn't change myself! But you didn't come! I had to give myself to him! I had to!"

Suddenly, inky black bat wings erupted from Beryl's back. Well, I shouldn't say that, as if they burst through her skin, or appeared from nowhere. It was a much more natural thing than that. She merely unfolded them and I realized they had always been there. We'd all just been ignoring them, so we could convince ourselves she was perfect. How long had I known?

"That is why I am so sorry, Beryl," Holmes said. "I only meant to help. You know that, don't you? I only meant to rescue you."

"Worst! Rescue! Ever!" Beryl raged. She had claws now, and the burning eyes that typified highly magical individuals. Fire ringed her dark brown irises. Somehow, it made them even prettier.

On the pretense of tripping over a chunk of stone, I "dropped" my hat onto the far end of the ley-line and thought, "*Done! Now what?*"

"*Get John Barrymore onto one end of a line and Eliza on the end opposite him.*"

John Barrymore had moved to a point not far from me and was crouched over a huddled figure, which I soon realized was Sir Henry. He lay unconscious with a remarkable lump forming on one side of his brow. Still, his breathing was regular and I knew from past experience that the man could take a beating better than most.

I bolted over to Barrymore and hissed, "Leave him. He'll be fine. Go stand on that line over there and do not abandon it! Even if something kills you, make sure your corpse falls *on that line* or we are all done for!"

John looked as if he wanted to cry, but he shuffled off to the nearest line. I left him and began casually sidling over to Eliza. I passed Gunther on the way, huddled behind a table doing his best to comfort Molly. True, she was neither as terrified nor as injured as many of the others, but she was pretty, damn it, and he was going to comfort her.

At the entrance, Holmes was stammering, "So, I don't mean to be rude... but... er... ah... it seems you've transformed into a succubus. Is that right?"

Let it never be said that Warlock Holmes had a way with the ladies.

"That's what he wanted!" Beryl protested. "That's what he made me!"

"Now, this is just a guess, but—I imagine it was your... enhanced wiles that lured Sir Charles out so Hugo could scare him to death, yes?" Holmes wondered.

"I am bound to my master's will," she said, evasively. I thought I saw her blush just a bit.

Holmes gave a sad smile and said, "No longer. Tonight, I will unmake you. But I just wanted you to know I was sorry."

Sir Hugo grunted out a wry laugh. "I wondered if

it was really you. When Mortimer said he was going to consult the famous detective Warlock Holmes I thought, 'Perhaps it is a common name. It can't be the same, stupid child, can it?' Your little Watson-pet gave up no clue."

"Good old Watson," said Holmes.

"I'm glad it's you," Sir Hugo snarled. "Now that I know it was *your* hound that killed me and doomed me to hell, I am pleased to have the chance to thank you as you deserve."

Sir Hugo lunged into the air and hung there. All five lines on the floor of Baskerville Hall gave a collective creak and began to emit a faint light. Sir Hugo uttered a few words in some hideous, foreign tongue and streaks of purple fire shot from him towards Holmes. Much to my wonderment, Warlock seemed pleased by this. The first fireball he simply sidestepped. The second two he blocked by raising chunks of rubble into their paths. The fourth was disabled when Holmes said, "Azazel. Stop it."

From beneath the earth, a great and powerful creature could be heard, saying, "Awwwwwwwwwwww!" and the fireball winked out, just a few feet from Holmes.

I made good use of the time, dodging across the room to Eliza Barrymore who, I must say, was cooler under fire than many of my army comrades had been at Maiwand. I told her the same thing I had told John. This, she took in her stride, saying, "You have no worry of me. I will stay my ground."

"*They are in place*," I thought at Holmes.

"*Good. Get my knapsack. Use the items in it to block another line.*"

That required more boldness than I cared for. The

knapsack lay at Holmes's very feet and he was the subject of quite a bit of negative attention.

Sir Hugo hissed, "Vetches-Res-Hroth," and a number of translucent arms rose from the ground to clutch at Holmes's feet. I'm fairly certain it was an accident, but one of them grabbed the knapsack as it groped blindly about. I had to kick and kick at it, but it finally let go.

Holmes was doing his best to keep Sir Hugo engaged in conversation, rather than battle. "A pity you weren't Moriarty's slave longer," Holmes shouted. "He could have taught you some art. Look at this: so much power! No subtlety. No restraint."

I scooped up the knapsack and ran. When I reached inside to draw out the objects, my hand came down on a slippery, wet, flesh-like gob. I almost yelped, but mastered my disgust and drew out a mildew-covered leather feedbag. The second item was not as bad: an old wooden spindle from some long-forgotten spinning wheel. That was all.

"A proposal, Sir Hugo," said Holmes. "Let us take turns hitting each other with the softest killing spell we know, until one of us is dead. I wish you to know how little it takes to destroy you. You may go first. Muster your wit. Hit me with your softest shot."

Sir Hugo did take a turn, but not the one Holmes had asked for. He smiled back, raised his hands and shouted, "Mulciber!"

Even I could feel the magic gathering. The white lines on the floor pulsed with energy. For an instant, fire burst from Holmes's mouth and eyes, just as it had from Selden's the night before. I thought all was lost, until Holmes said, "I think not," and raised his hand skyward. All the candles in the hall's many dusty candelabra burst into flame at once. Holmes shook his head. "All force. No art."

All around me I could feel the suffusion of magic coming to life. On the far side of the room, the top hat I had placed began to shake and bump, and I swear I heard it harrumph. Nearer to me I heard a lady's voice say, "Oh look! Look what I have found!" The jeweled comb clinked and slid an inch further away from me.

I plopped the disgusting leather feedbag down onto the last two-way line and began my headlong run for the other side of the room. I no longer cared for subtlety, hoping my enemy was too embattled to notice. Sir Hugo was, but as I plunged past the table Beryl yelled, "What is that one up to?"

"Shut up," Sir Hugo yelled back. "Holmes! Grab Holmes!"

"Er... please don't?" Holmes suggested, but Beryl spread her wings and flew straight at him. I saw her claws cut his arm and shoulder as she dragged him backwards. When he hit the table, Sir Hugo smiled and uttered a few more words in his guttural, demon tongue. The dining table sprouted two six-foot splinters, right through Holmes's legs. He cried out in pain. I don't know if it was a legitimate accident, or if Sir Hugo really had so little care for Beryl, but one of the splinters pierced her through her abdomen, just above the left hip. She screamed. For an instant, she and Holmes were pegged together by the great table of Baskerville Hall. But only for an instant; no sooner had the splinters pierced Holmes than his eyes lit up their fiercest green and the great table liquefied and splashed down onto the floor. It was amongst the strangest things I had ever seen. It is not that it turned to water, oil or any known liquid. It was *still wood*. It flowed like water. It splashed as I ran through it. Yet, even in its strange new state, it kept its grain.

Oh, and it gave me a devil of a time, finding the other side of the third ley-line. Throwing myself to the floor in what I judged to be basically the right area, I feverishly swiped wood-sauce this way and that, until I caught a glimpse of the lighter marble. With a relieved sigh, I dropped the spindle into place.

"*Done! What now?*"

In response, my mind flooded with agony and I fell, grasping at my legs. I slapped at them, trying to understand what had injured me. But there was nothing, only the projection of what Holmes was feeling. It came through with the rest of his thought. It was hard to tell which was more terrible.

"*Nothing, Watson*," Holmes thought. "*That was all I found.*"

The pain subsided, yet the horror of that statement remained. We had not addressed the two short lines at all and I hadn't seen any effect from my work on the other three. If only we'd had time to find more allies, or time to form a better plan... but no.

Our time was up.

Sir Hugo hovered farther into the room, sighing, "Ahhhhhh, it feels so good to be home. Do you know how hard it was, restraining myself at all Sir Charles's damned parties, with the lines just right here?"

As he neared, the glow from the ley-lines increased. From across the room, I heard a man's voice. It was distorted, as if from deep under water. The accent was rural and strange. "Morag? Morag? Where are ye? Run! The horses! They bite! Me legs! Oh, me legs… Run, Morag!"

Warlock tried to stand, but crumpled with a cry. Having just felt what I presumed to be his pain, I understood that the fight was not going our way. Until a moment before I had kept up hope but now it seemed to have been only a fool's dream.

Was there nothing I could do?

One solution presented: there, in the rubble to my right, I could just see the gleam of my trusty Webley.

When in doubt…

I dove upon it, yanked back the hammer, aimed and shot Sir Hugo, square in the chest.

He turned to me and muttered, "Watson, don't be ridiculous."

"It's not!" I protested, and shot him again. "It has two beneficial effects…" I shot him again. "First: it makes me feel better!" And again. "Second: victory may be yours; you may end the race of man…" My fifth shot landed low, just above the hip. "But you won't be keeping that jacket!"

My last bullet tore through his shoulder. The Webley's hammer clicked against an empty casing. I was done. Sir

Hugo did not appear best pleased by my behavior. He snarled and flicked one hand at me, shouting, "Vres Jech!"

I felt all my bones begin pulling out through my skin. I can hardly describe my agony as my skeleton began to bend and shift. I'm not sure I even managed to scream, but I promise you I tried. To my lasting joy, Holmes saved me. He shouted in protest and flung both his arms upwards. As he did, the torturous feeling in my bones rocketed up out of me. The chandelier creaked, squealed and tore itself into a hundred pieces. I rolled on the floor coughing, trying to regain my breath. Candles rained down around me, into the wood-water. I expected they would extinguish, but the few that landed on their sides set pools of the strange wood alight.

From below me came a cracking noise. I could feel the ley-lines heave and shift. Holmes had used magic to save me, but to use much more might doom us all. From outside, I heard a terrible baying—otherworldly, distorted by wind and pain. The Hound of the Baskervilles must be coming, I realized. To whose benefit, I could not say.

As I drew myself to my knees, Sir Hugo again turned his rage on me. He summoned a dark ray of unlight, which streaked from his finger towards my heart. Holmes reached out his hand as if to grab it and the ray suddenly bent, striking one of the stones of the fireplace. The unlucky stone burst into two dozen live bats, which flew about for a few seconds, before expiring and plummeting to the floor, their fuzzy corpses splashing into the liquid wood.

Holmes made it to his feet—quite the achievement,

considering the state of his legs. He turned to face Sir Hugo. A wiser man might have looked behind, first. Beryl took him utterly by surprise, slamming into his back. Though she looked to be in poor shape—pale from blood loss—she nevertheless spread her wings and dragged Holmes up into the air. I think she meant to haul him up into the high rafters and drop him, but I will never know for sure. Holmes interrupted her plan with one of the least gentlemanly things I have ever seen: he elbowed her, right in the abdominal wound. Beryl cried out and the two of them tumbled out of the air. Holmes took the brunt of the crash landing and Sir Hugo laughed with delight as he watched them struggle on the floor. Even in the midst of battle, I found his mistreatment of his sister abhorrent.

Or, rather, his mistreatment of the enslaved temptation demon he'd been passing off as his sister.

But still…

A stirring in the rubble beside me indicated that Sir Henry was awake. I scuttled over to him and whispered, "Are you injured?"

"I ain't at my best, but I guess I've been worse. What's going on, Watson?"

"You should have stayed unconscious, Sir Henry. You seem to have woken up just in time for the end of this fight and I'm afraid you won't like it."

"We're fightin' Sir Hugo?"

"Yes. Well spotted."

"And losin'?"

"I'm afraid we are," I said. "We must turn the tide

quickly or all is lost. Holmes is faltering."

"Damn. Can we help? Have you spotted any weakness?"

"There is one thing," I reflected. "Unlike Holmes, Sir Hugo speaks whenever he casts a spell. If we could stop his voice, we may gain a great advantage."

"Well, he's had his throat torn out, ain't he?" Sir Henry asked.

"What are you proposing? That we should bum-rush the hovering hell-wizard?"

Sir Henry shrugged.

"I wish I had a better idea," I said. "I don't suppose you're armed?"

"I am!" declared Sir Henry. From the rubble beside him, he produced the hound's-head walking stick and brandished it.

"What?" I cried. "No! Why does everybody assume…? That is *not* a weapon! Have you ever gone to a museum and seen a painting of armored knights, laying about each other with walking sticks? Honestly!"

"It's the best we got, Watson."

"Oh, very well. I'll try to get his legs and bring him down a bit. You get his throat."

Our plan was delayed somewhat by a shift in the fight. John Barrymore pointed out through the shattered entryway and gave a scream of terror. In a moment, Eliza and Perkins joined him. The Hound of the Baskervilles had come to join the fray.

Or anyway, he attempted to.

Though I'm sure he was trying with all his might,

Foofy's charge was somewhat... leisurely. Like many older dogs with bad hips, his front half stayed focused on his target, but his back half kept drifting off to one side. He cleared the entry rubble with a feeble leap, then trundled into the great hall. Poor fellow—dry ground was enough of a challenge for him, but when he made it into the puddle of liquefied table, he was quite overmatched. His back legs slipped and gave out. He tumbled sidelong into the oaken slop, his haunches passing his head as he slid in a slow semi-circle and skidded to a halt. He made some show of trying to move again, dragging himself forward a few feet, but then gave a grand, tired snort and let his head collapse down on his forepaws, utterly bested.

I suppose I was less than charitable. "Oh *well done*, Mankind's-Terror-Given-Shape. Thanks for all your help!"

"You think he was here to help us?" Sir Henry asked.

"I'm not sure," I said. "The point seems somewhat academic now."

Sir Hugo drifted closer to Holmes, his voice rising in a litany of demon-speak. Ghostly black chains materialized from the corners of the room and snaked about Holmes's limbs, pulling each of his damaged appendages in a different direction. Holmes cried out and his green eyes blazed. One by one, the chains burst into smoke, but were replaced by Sir Hugo as quickly as Holmes could dispel them. Attempting to regain the offensive, Holmes levitated several chunks of rubble and flung them at Sir Hugo. Now it was Hugo's turn to brush aside wayward chunks of Baskerville Hall. He dismissed each of them with a word and a wave, drawing ever closer to the writhing figure of Holmes.

In the entire year I'd spent in the company of Warlock Holmes, I do not think all the magical expenditures I'd ever seen him make could match the amount of power he used that one night in Baskerville Hall. Sir Hugo used even more. At that moment, it seemed, they crossed a threshold. Anyone who's ever broken a bone knows: you can feel it bending for a moment—strained but not bested—until at last it moves beyond tolerance and gives with a snap. An audible crack emitted from all five ley-lines and the floor heaved. All the lights in the room—the blaze in the great hearth, the candles, the burning pools of liquid wood—winked out. The lines went dull. For the tiniest moment, all was dark. Moonlight through the broken wall and Foofy's feeble smolder were the only illumination. In the darkness, the room filled with phantom voices. From the direction of the spindle I'd placed, I heard a woman's muffled cry: "Samuel? Samuel? Where are you?"

It was answered by a terrible wail from the other side of the line, near the moldy feedbag. It was a sound of utter terror and pain. Beneath the screaming, one could just make out hoof beats and the sound of teeth crunching bone.

It was counterpointed by the strident, non-ghostly voice of Eliza Barrymore shouting, "John Barrymore, don't you run! You stay right where you are!"

"Husband, why?" said a woman's voice. It was erudite

and educated, and came from under the gold and pearl comb. "Why did you push me?"

From behind me, another ghost spoke. "Oh! I say! Is that my hat?"

Then, with redoubled force, the five lines of white marble relit with a bright, white glow. True, much of this was hidden by wood-juice, but enough of the lines showed through that the whole room was lit in phantom splendor. From the lines, thick, luminescent white smoke began to emerge, even filtering lazily up through the liquid table. It was hypnotizing to watch—and beautiful. Sometimes it drifted, as smoke might, but in different directions as if each thin tendril was blown by its own wind. Sometimes it darted towards a thing or a person, as if it wanted them, but would then pause a few inches away. Shapes began to swim and coalesce within the mist. I swear I saw a cart carrying a huge throne, pulled by two oxen, but it dissolved before I could be sure. There was a woman dancing; her spine was supple, her arms were snakes. Or perhaps it was only my imagination. It was like watching clouds: suggested shapes seemed suddenly vital, but then—in the next folding of the billows—preposterous.

Beside me, a portly man in his mid-fifties, made all of light and smoke, came striding up to the top hat I had dropped and said, "Glad to have that back. Always wanted to be buried in this one, you know, not the ridiculous thing they stuck on me. Good God, did they think me still a schoolboy?"

"Sir Charles?" Barrymore cried.

The phantom reached up, removed the spectral straw boater it wore and replaced it with the top hat, then looked about and cried, "By Jove! What have you done to my house?"

Directly across from him, a lady's hand reached out from the floor to grasp the comb. An instant later, a matronly woman stood tucking it into her hair, saying, "Ah! Ah! Look! I had it from Hugo, the day we wed. Before things turned so sour. Before he killed me."

"Lies! She lies!" cried Sir Hugo, pointing at the ghost of his murdered wife. "She fell!"

Beryl staggered to her feet, mumbling, "I remember you—both of you. You were both so kind."

"Falling! Falling!" the phantom of Lady Olivia Baskerville called, then she fixed Hugo with suddenly vengeful eyes. "You killed me!"

"I say!" said Sir Charles's shade. "The bastard killed me, as well. But I'm not so easy to frighten now, am I, Stapleton?"

A phantom farmer was pulling himself up now, taking up the moldering feedbag I had left for him. Across the room, his spectral wife was picking up her spindle.

Our battle was momentarily forgotten. All of us mortals, mages and the demon too, were staring at the ghosts. With a start, I realized this was just the chance I needed. I grasped Sir Henry's sleeve and hissed, "Quick! Sir Hugo is distracted!"

Sir Henry gave a resolute nod and whispered, "One banana… two banana… three banana… go!"

We were up out of the rubble and at him in a flash. I suppose it's lucky he was engaged in an argument with his dead wife, or he may well have zapped us to ash before we got near him. He was hovering five feet or so above the floor. Thus, with a fairly easy leap, I got my arms about his knees and pulled him down. I reached up to his jacket and yanked downwards, exposing a hideous patch of sewn-on skin, which covered his old throat wound. Brave Sir Henry came in right behind me. He planted both feet wide and gave…

Well, I suppose the best way to say it was that he gave us all a hideous parody of the Scottish sport of golf. With a grand, two-handed sweep, he swung the silver hound's-head cane up into Sir Hugo's neck. The sound was exactly that familiar whoosh-and-swack that can be heard on any of Edinburgh's finer greens. The patch of skin tore free and took, majestically, to the sky. For about… three feet. It had no weight to it and a great deal of surface area so, in no time at all, the air caught it and it began to flutter and drift about. It finally flopped to the floor about ten feet from Sir Hugo, with a gentle *splat*.

Sir Hugo gurgled with rage and clutched at his throat. Well… where his throat *wasn't*. He gave me a kick that sent me tumbling to the ground. I landed, staring at a pair of tasteful black evening slippers. Between them, a prehensile tail brushed gently at the floor. I looked ruefully upwards, sure I would see Beryl's claws lancing towards my eyes. Luckily, the seventeenth-century farm-girl-turned-succubus had other things on her mind. She stepped away from me, towards the ghostly farmer's wife, asking, "Mama? Is it you?"

The specter ignored her and screamed, "Samuel? Where are you? They're so close! I can hear the hooves!"

As I found myself with a moment's respite, I sought Holmes, looking for direction. He sat motionless upon the floor, frozen with horror, staring at Sir Henry's walking stick. Or—as I suddenly realized—Moriarty's walking stick. The one he used to beat Holmes, as a child. If it had been left here on that fateful Michaelmas, would it not have been passed from generation to generation with all the other Baskerville heirlooms?

"Holmes!" I shouted. "Focus!"

"Eh? Oh. Yes. Quite right, Watson. Quite right."

He drew both hands together and thrust them upwards. As he did, the liquid wood of the great oak table drew itself together under Sir Hugo and splashed upwards. The instant it caught him, it re-solidified—frozen into a... well... a tree? A sort of barkless tree with an evil, throatless sorcerer trapped in it. You know the kind I mean.

"Help me to my feet, Watson!" cried Holmes.

He was in wretched shape. The doctor in me wanted to insist that he lie down. Yet, the person–who–does–not–wish–to–be–slain–by–magic in me agreed to help him up. I put my arm beneath his less–bloody shoulder and helped him stand. Even with his weight on me, he barely could.

"Well done, Watson. You too, Sir Henry," Holmes said. "I think your little attack has bought us some precious time. We must hurry though. There are other ways to do magic apart from speech and I do not think Sir Hugo will take long in discovering one."

"What must we do?" I asked.

"Beryl. I need Beryl."

Sir Henry came to help and the two of us turned Holmes towards Beryl, who still stood, talking to the phantom woman.

"Mama? Why won't you answer me?"

"She can't," Holmes said. "That's not a whole person you're talking to. Not even a whole ghost. After so long, there was very little left of your parents, just the horror of their final moments."

"What happened to them?" Beryl demanded.

"You know, I've been dreading that question," said Holmes, "because there is no delicate way to answer it. They were eaten by horses."

Beryl turned around, spread her wings and claws and roared as if she meant to kill us all. I suppose I could hardly blame her.

"Please," Holmes said. "Bhehr-Lylegnag, please, listen to me. It is all down to you. I have done what I can, but it is not enough. You will choose the victor tonight, not I or any other."

Holmes clumsily turned to the room at large and shouted, "Hear me, spirits! Each of you met your end because of the wickedness of this man—Sir Hugo Baskerville! Do you feel the energy coming to this place? Do you feel it, flowing through the lines? That is all that sustains him—all that keeps your murderer alive! If we

"A sort of barkless tree with an evil, throatless sorcerer trapped in it. You know the kind I mean."

all push together, we can stop it! Stop the flow and bring justice to the wicked!"

"But, Holmes," I said, "there are still two lines unblocked!"

"One, Watson," said Holmes, pointing at Foofy. The tired old beast had collapsed across one of the open lines. It must have been his goal all along.

"Only one line left to block," Holmes said, "and Bhehr-Lylegnag, it is yours. You are the only one left who can."

"I am not a fool!" she spat. "That would kill me!"

"I know," said Holmes.

"Then why do you think I would help you?"

"Because if you do not block that line, Sir Hugo will win. He will live here, for a time. But, look at him; look at his wounds. Each day, it will take more and more energy to sustain him, until at last he breaks the bounds and demons overrun this world. They'll kill everyone."

"Not me," Beryl laughed. "I'm not sure how it escaped your notice, Warlock Holmes, but *I* am a demon."

"No, you're not."

She stared at Holmes, incredulous. She gave a little flick with her claws, indicating her body—her wings and tail.

"I know what happened to you, Bhehr-Lylegnag. I know what he made you, but that's not *who you are*. This is your home. This world sustained you and everyone you loved. It still does. I know you fancy Sir Henry—"

"Wait! She does? Do you?" asked Sir Henry, so overcome by hope that he nearly dropped Holmes.

Beryl colored, averted her eyes to a nearby wall and insisted, "I am a demon."

"You're really not."

"I lured Sir Charles to his death!"

This charge was answered not by Holmes, but the ghost of Sir Charles himself. He grunted out a laugh and scoffed, "Oh, never mind about all that. It was Sir Hugo's fault, wasn't it? I should have known you wouldn't really want an old codger like me, but... well... I was flattered to be asked."

Beryl blinked, wonderstruck at his readiness to forgive her. Unwilling to concede her goodness, she demanded, "What about Sir Henry? I lured him; I made him want me. Watson too! I turned them against one another. I have done—"

"I know," Holmes interrupted. "I know; the demon Beryl has done wicked things. But Bhehr-Lylegnag? She never would have—not if she'd had any choice in the matter. And now you do. Walk away from Sir Hugo and what he has made you. Come back to the world you love and that loves you. Die as Bhehr-Lylegnag; it's all I can offer."

"Well, that offer is just as terrible as your rescue was!"

"Then you should decline it," said Holmes. He gave a sad smile—the look of a man at the end of a long game, with only one card left to turn. A man who knows the final card will bring him victory, but also long regret. "But what will happen to Sir Henry if you do?"

Beryl's eyes turned to Sir Henry. He stared back at her. It was easy to see the yearning they shared. Despite my jealousy, I had to admit: those two belonged to one another.

Yet, what did it matter? Whatever the strength of it, what is one human feeling against such a gulf of circumstance? This was to be either a world of demons, or a world of men. Not both.

"Come on, Holmes!" Sir Henry roared, though he did not turn his eyes from Beryl. "That ain't fair! You can't ask her to make a choice like that!"

"It is not fair," Holmes agreed, "but it is fact. I am not giving her this choice, nor do I have any power to take it away. It has fallen to her. Beryl may choose to live as a demon in a world of torment where you must certainly die, Sir Henry. Or she may give you life and restore hope to the race of men, knowing she will never join them. Whether or not she's a demon, she's got the devil's choice to make."

Beryl tore her eyes from Sir Henry and stared at Holmes with murderous rage. Yet, in only an instant, they drifted back to Sir Henry and softened.

"Hank…" she said, "I've got to go."

I have never seen a man look so aghast. "No!" Sir Henry insisted. "There has to be another way!"

"Can you think of one?"

Sir Henry gazed about in helpless desperation. The demon Beryl wiped her eyes, thrust her chin forward and stepped onto the final line. The ghoulish form of Sir Hugo stirred in his tree and made a gruesome gurgle that ended in a fairly legible, "Beryl, don't!"

"Aagh! Oh no!" cried Holmes. "I don't know how he's doing that, but I don't like it! All you spirits, beasts and people who are bound to the lines: find the flow! Do you feel it? Push it back! Push now!"

From far below us came a deep basso creak. Foofy began to whine and yip in pain. The light dimmed from the lines.

"It's working!" Holmes crowed, then looked around at the still-lit lines and added, "Well… it's working a *bit*. We haven't got all of the magic, but… maybe enough? Watson, with Sir Hugo's throat out, how long 'til he dies?"

I think I got a bit smug. I brushed some of the dust from my sleeves and said, "Well, at the risk of self-congratulation in a moment of tragedy: I did recently have the foresight to inflict *six* fresh bullet wounds on the man."

I saw Sir Hugo's eyes flip down towards his torso as he realized, with horror, that this was true.

"Push it back!" Holmes urged the spirits. "*Push!*"

Even as the ghosts' faces lined with strain, they became less real—more changeable, like old ideas, half forgotten. Beryl gave a final grunt of effort and all the specters evaporated into wisps of white smoke. Hugo gave a last, retching gurgle, shook, and fell still. Foofy's strength fled him; he sagged where he lay—no breath in that great, wide chest. Beryl swayed and fell flat on her face. Holmes did too.

"Holmes! What has happened to you?"

"You know how Sir Hugo was misappropriating the power of the lines, to keep himself alive?"

I nodded.

"I… er… *might* have been guilty of just a bit of that too, so…"

His eyes rolled back. He fell still.

17

I SHALL ENDEAVOR NOT TO BURDEN THE READER WITH the full account of the aftermath of the Battle of Baskerville Hall. Suffice to say, that joyous moment where we all realized, "Yaaaaay, we won!" was rapidly supplanted by the moment where we all realized, "Oooooh… we seem to have several wounded, arrayed around the throatless, shot-up corpse of one of the area's most prominent citizens, which is frozen in a magically crafted table/tree, right next to a dead hell-hound, a dying demon girl and a possibly dying London gentleman who is growing goat horns—all of which would be a lot easier to hide if this building *still had a front wall.*"

Dr. Mortimer was sent for with all dispatch. The wounded were shuttled into private rooms. Sir Henry insisted that Beryl be moved next door to his own chamber. Perkins and Gunther were moved to the room on the other side. Holmes had to go in the stable. Though he was unconscious, his twisted right hand continued to grope about with an unsettling level of autonomy and the bloody black horns began to once again curl forth from his scalp.

When the bones of his legs began to shift and elongate into a suspiciously goatish formation, that was the final straw. Was the stable an ideal infirmary? No, but it was vastly preferable to leaving Holmes atop the confluence of five ley-lines. I set a blanket on three bales of hay, to form a makeshift bed for him. No sooner had I left than all the horses kicked down their stall doors and ran away.

The problem of the tree-table, Sir Hugo's body and Foofy's were all solved by the application of Sir Henry's biggest saw, a laborious drag outside, two jugs of paraffin and one judiciously placed match. We'd have to wait for the ashes to cool, to hide the bones.

When Mortimer arrived, he was too horrified at Beryl's demonic form to touch her, but wasted no time attending to the others. Everyone with so much as a scratch found themselves well-stupefied by morphine, then the work began in earnest. Sir Henry was re-patched and sent to bed. Perkins kept his leg—a fact I attribute entirely to Mortimer's skill as a trauma physician. Gunther's wounds proved to be superficial, so as soon as he was bandaged he came downstairs to be helpful. Well… as helpful as a man can be, with his brain pickled by opiates.

With Mortimer overseeing our impromptu infirmary, I was free to check on Holmes. There was blood *everywhere*. I hadn't quite realized the extent of the damage Beryl's claws had done to him. I'm sure he couldn't have survived it, if he hadn't enjoyed the patronage of quite so many blood-gods. As I cut away his clothing to access his wounds, he awoke and grasped my arm.

"Watson? Is that you?"

"Holmes, you must rest. Yes, it is me."

"Is Bhehr-Lylegnag alive?"

I sighed and shook my head. "She was when I left her. But it cannot last, Holmes. There's nothing I can do."

"But try, won't you? You have to try! She's the worst mistake I ever made, Watson. If you can save her... if you can give her back that life I took from her, all those years ago... wouldn't it be great?"

I leaned back in to see to his wounds, but he pushed me feebly aside and insisted, "I'll be fine! Go help Bhehr-Lylegnag."

"Holmes... I can't."

"Go try. Here, we'll both go."

"What? No! You're not going anywhere, Holmes!"

"Sure, I am. I'll see you later."

He gave me a little smile. Then he fainted. I shook my head. Foolish Holmes... I had so much work to do on him, I hardly knew where to start. His shoulder was either broken or out of joint and he had sustained massive damage to both arms and legs.

Yet...

I kept looking at his face. I had seen him live through worse, hadn't I? I knew I could not trust my own medical knowledge when it came to Holmes. Then again, could I trust *his*? A half-delirious promise to be all right was hardly sound medical advice. So... damn it...

Hoping it was not a mistake—praying that it would not be a choice I'd regret the rest of my life—I stood up and trudged back to Baskerville Hall.

Beryl was alive, but her condition was… weird. With Sir Hugo gone and his spell broken, her demon tissues were withering. Her wings drooped; her tail was lifeless leather. Unfortunately, the rest of her was becoming more real—the 240-year-old mummified pistol wound was returning to a lifelike state. It was beginning to bleed. I could hear the wheeze of lost air. But there was little I could do except (and oh, how I hope the British Medical Association never reads this) stick a brandy cork in the wound and bandage it up. I had no idea if this would be beneficial. The only certainty was infection. Her abdominal wound took me some hours to patch up, but at least it was within my skill.

As I emerged from her room, bleary and exhausted, Sir Henry called out through his open door, "Hey! Watson, how is she?"

I went in and told him, "Unaccountably, she is still alive."

"Good. I'm glad she's doing better."

"Sir Henry… she isn't."

"Nah. She'll be fine."

I think I let my fatigue and frustration guide my tongue more than I ought. "Fine? She can never be *fine*, Sir Henry! Even if she lives, do you think she will be unchanged by this? You think she's still going to be delightful Miss Stapleton, from down the moor? That person never existed! She is the survivor of hundreds of years of torture and imprisonment, she's barely clinging to life and who can answer for the state of her sanity? You need to give up on Beryl Stapleton!"

I have no excuse for snapping at him like I did. He fixed me with a cool glare and stated, in only two words, the position that no extremity of fortune—fair or foul— could ever shake him from.

"Ain't gonna."

So I didn't either.

I ate some bacon and eggs, drank three quick cups of tea and went in to perform my first demonectomy. It went unaccountably well—the first thing that did. When I touched my scalpel to her left wing, the dried tissue broke away, fell to the floor and crumbled to so much ash. Her right went just as easily and so did her tail. At first I had no idea how I might salvage her hands, but simply rubbing them was enough to flake away the scaly talons, to reveal pink fingers underneath. Since her appearance was once again human, I went and found Mortimer (who had been dutifully attending to Holmes) and bullied him into helping me with Beryl's chest wound. We worked for hours, binding and rejoining the damaged tissues of her chest as best we could. It was one of the steepest medical challenges of my life. Mortimer and I staggered out of that room exhausted, but wiser.

Three hours later, Beryl woke up and asked for water.

And I got a nap.

Yet, as I had predicted, Beryl's wounds were not the full extent of her problems. Over the next few days, as the others improved and began their return to normalcy, Beryl's mental state worsened. She spoke of herself as Sir Henry's prisoner—a monster surrounded by the humans she'd betrayed—waiting for the constables to come and hang her or burn her alive for her misdeeds. She even mourned Sir Hugo. Yes, he'd been her captor and tormentor, but he'd also been her confidant and her only comrade during the four human lifetimes she'd spent trapped in a land of constant torture. The twisted emotional bond it formed, once broken, left her adrift and uncertain. I had no idea how to help her.

Sir Henry did. He summoned us all to his bedside and held a meeting. He spoke of financial help for the survivors and what might be done to repair the gaping hole in his ancestral home. Yet the real business of the day was a toast. He called for champagne and bid us all raise our glasses in salute to "the true hero of the Battle of Baskerville Hall: Beryl Stapleton."

This was met with some coolness. Barrymore was still terrified of her. Molly was deeply religious and fairly sure her priest wouldn't like her saluting anyone with wings and a tail.

Sir Henry launched into a vigorous campaign of convincing, cajoling and insisting that he was a lord and lords were always right. Had Beryl spent some time as a temptation demon? Sure. Had she played a part in Sir Charles's death? What of it? The important thing was this: that her first act, once freed from Sir Hugo's tyranny, was to save all humanity. This boon overshadowed and assuaged all her sins. It engendered a debt so profound, it could not be repaid by any living man—not by *all* living men. She'd given us back our world. Sir Henry did not stop his tirade until all present had loudly and publicly admitted the truth of his claim.

Due to a pre-arranged accident, which Sir Henry had asked me to see to, his door had been left open. So had Beryl's. She heard every word. I think it helped her. Of course, she still refused to admit that she should not be hung, drawn and quartered in the public square. This was not a total cure, merely the opening salvo in a battle of wills betwixt the headstrong Canadian baronet and the 262-year-old twenty-two-year-old who refused to forgive herself and embrace happiness. The war spanned a hundred dinner parties and garden gatherings and tested the wit, the fortitude and the patience of everyone involved.

By all accounts, the wedding was lovely.

Of all the survivors, the last to come around was Holmes. I took to sitting out in the stable, beside his hay bed. I always brought my medical kit, even when I knew I wouldn't use it. Often I just sat and watched him. Sometimes I told him things I thought might interest him. One night I said, "Beryl's doing much better."

Holmes drew in a sudden gasp, opened his eyes and sat halfway up. In a raspy voice, he muttered, "By the Gods, Watson... it took you long enough."

"Holmes! You're awake!"

"Of course I am."

"Wait... do you mean... you've just been waiting for me to...?"

"Where do you think I've been all this time, Watson?

I've been engaged in a somewhat spirited debate with my old friend Sepsis, trying to get him to leave us all alone."

I should have realized it. To have so many patients, with wounds so grievous, and none of them had developed an infection? None? It was nearly unaccountable. Holmes really had gone to help Beryl, that first night. I was overcome with gratitude. I might have wept, if it were not for what he said next.

"Watson, can I have some toast?"

"*Toast?* Certainly not! Are you mad?"

"Please, Watson? I really need some."

"I'll not be bringing you any *toast*. By Jingo, I'll shoot the man who tries! Toast, indeed!"

"Well… soup, though?"

"Water! You may have a few sips of water!"

"But, Waaaaaatsonnnnnn…"

"Maybe broth. Only if the water doesn't kill you. We shall see."

The news that Holmes was awake was met with celebration. Of course, it did make it that much harder to keep him in a stable. Though he might have liked to keep us as pets, Sir Henry arranged for transport for Holmes and me, back to London. Before we left he presented Holmes with the hound's-head cane, mounted in a tasteful frame, to put above our mantel.

So, I come to end this volume nearly where it began: with Holmes half-dead in his room and me overseeing his recovery, safe in our haven at 221B. There's a symmetry to that, but it is not why I chose to end here. A reader who wishes to credit my wit more than it deserves might point out that this volume starts with beryls and ends with Beryl, but that is not the reason either. Indeed, if there is a reader who can spot what this period truly was, then that person might have been wise enough to do what I could not: stop the impending calamity.

This was our respite.

When I shot Warlock Holmes, Moriarty ruled his mind and body. When Holmes recovered, he was himself once more. So great was my joy that I never paused to wonder *why that was*.

Did I suppose I'd killed Holmes's great nemesis?

Did I imagine Holmes had subsumed him, once more? I never heard Holmes speak in his voice during that time.

I think I simply forgot to pay Moriarty any mind. Gods, it sounds so foolish now. When I think of how blithely I continued on, having my little adventures and thinking everything was well... These were my last days of innocence, in a way.

The book you hold is nothing more or less than this: it is chronicle to the period of time between Moriarty's departure...

...and when he came back.

ACKNOWLEDGEMENTS

THANKS TO MY AGENT, SAM, WHOSE LIVER STILL—unaccountably—functions.

Thanks to my editor, Miranda Jewess, who is so Super English, y'all wouldn't believe it.

Thanks to Sean who continues to doodle away, underpaid but most appreciated.

Thanks to Benedict Cumberbatch, who agreed to portray Warlock Holmes on film. (Er…well, he's Dr. Strange and Sherlock, so if you turn them both on at once and sort of squint…)

And, to Sir Arthur Whatsis Stillneverheardofhim: quit trying to hog my glory.

ABOUT THE AUTHOR

GABRIEL DENNING LIVES IN LAS VEGAS WITH HIS WIFE and two daughters. Oh, and a dog. And millions of micro-organisms. He's a twenty-year veteran of Orlando Theatersports, Seattle Theatersports, Jet City Improv and has finally figured out to write some of that stuff down. His first novel, *Warlock Holmes: A Study in Brimstone*, was published in 2016, and the *Booklist* review said "Mashup fans will be eagerly awaiting more," which is why he wrote a sequel. Without any similar provocation, the third Warlock Holmes novel will be published by Titan Books in 2018.

For more fantastic fiction, author events, competitions,
limited editions and more

VISIT OUR WEBSITE
titanbooks.com

LIKE US ON FACEBOOK
facebook.com/titanbooks

FOLLOW US ON TWITTER
@TitanBooks

EMAIL US
readerfeedback@titanemail.com